RANDOM ACTS OF UNKINDNESS

THE JAN PEARCE SERIES
BOOK 1

JACQUELINE WARD

Re-published in 2023 by Bloodhound Books.

www.bloodhoundbooks.com

Print ISBN: 978-1-5040-8595-3

For my children, Michelle, Victoria and Toby.

ALSO BY JACQUELINE WARD

The Replacement

———

<u>The Jan Pearce Series</u>

Random Acts of Unkindness

What I Left Behind

CHAPTER ONE

I look a little closer and instinctively back away.

Her eyes are hollow holes where the birds have pecked away at her skull and she's covered in tiny soft feathers and greying bird shit. Fragments of silvered hair lie on her shoulders, pulled out at the roots and exposing pinprick follicles made bigger by beaks. Her mouth is set in a wry smile showing yellow teeth, as if somehow, despite the torn skin and the deeply painful twist of her body, she's having the last laugh.

The shock is so deep that it hurts more than it should, and tears threaten as I gaze at her. A human life ending in such a terrible, lonely way. It hits me with sadness so intense that I take a moment to sit with her, to tell her broken shell of a body that someone cares. Then fear oozes through the sadness, pushing it under and reminding me of why I'm here. *Where are you, Aiden? Where is my son?*

I slump onto a brown box sealed with Sellotape that's sitting next to a small blue suitcase. It looks like this old woman was going somewhere. Somewhere she never got to.

Bessy Swain, by the looks of post on the doormat. A couple

of bills and some takeaway menus. A letter from social services that arrived too late to make any difference.

As well as the boxes there are piles of newspapers and scrapbooks stacked up against ancient peeling sepia wallpaper. From the state of the house this woman has been suffering for a while. Poor Bessy.

Outside, starlings perch on the windowsill, quietly watching, judging me as I put off the inevitable phone call. Through the open kitchen door I can see a couple of blackbirds standing on the shed roof, and I can hear their song of accusation. I know I need to call this in and get Bessy some dignity, but I also need to finish what I came here to do.

The day job kicks in and I pull my scarf around my nose and mouth to protect my senses from the rancid fumes I hadn't even noticed until now. My phone starts to ring, forcing me into the here and now.

I look at Bessy's body and then at the flashing screen. Shit. It's Mike. My partner in crime. Crime solving, that is. Like me, he's a Detective Constable working on Special Operations.

'Jan. Where the hell are you?'

I pause. How am I going to explain this? I take a big breath and then pull down my scarf.

'Right, yeah. I was just . . .'

'Looking for Aiden. Come on, you're going to get us both sacked. You're supposed to be in Lytham Road, attending the Operation Prophesy briefing.'

On the worn kitchen worktop that separates the lounge from the kitchen a dead starling stares at me, its dried eyes condemning me from the pits of death.

A small metal toaster holds the remains of two slices of bread, which have been pecked right down to the toaster elements. The dead bird is lying close to the toaster, its feathers puffed from electrocution.

How many birds are there in here?

In my hurry to get inside I hadn't registered anything apart from needing to know if Aiden was here. But now, sitting here with my mobile hot against my cheek, I realise I am sitting in a house covered in bird feathers and faeces.

The back door slams shut in a gust of wind. A few stray starlings are flying about in the kitchen, but most of the birds are now outside, my entrance breaking open their jail. What I can't understand is why the windowsills are covered in them, their wings and curled up feet scratching at the dirty glass.

Then I realise they want to get back in.

'Jan? Jan? Are you there?'

I nod at my mobile phone.

'Yep. Look, I'll just finish off here. I got a tip off about there being a funny smell coming from a house and I thought . . .'

Mike sighs deeply.

'I know exactly what you thought. But this has to stop. Or you have to do it in your own time. It's not just your own life you're fucking up here. I'm your partner and I'll back you up, but there's a line. There's a fucking line. Where are you anyway?'

The secure safety net I have in Mike has started to fracture recently and it shatters a little more now with the pain in his voice. I desperately want to put it right, but I can't. Not yet. I have to deal with this.

'57 Ney Street, Ashton.'

'Connelly's rented houses, aren't they? I'm telling you, you're heading for trouble.'

I end the call there. He's right. I'm heading for trouble. But put any parent in my position and try telling me they'd do differently. I have a good reason. Mike knows that, but he also knows that everyone else's lives are moving on and he's trying to drag me on with him.

I push the phone into my bag and I pull my scarf back up against the smell. It's invaded my hair, clothes and skin, but the action gives me a bit of comfort and control.

There's a sudden noise from upstairs and my heart skips. The memory of Aiden calls me back and overpowers the sensible part of my brain urgently screaming that maybe poor Bessy wasn't alone after all. Maybe someone killed her. Maybe I shouldn't be here on my own. Maybe I shouldn't be here at all. *Maybe, maybe, maybe.*

I tread the worn stair carpet and creep up, nudging open the first door on the right. It's a boy's bedroom, all red and white, Manchester United. So she has children. Or grandchildren? But no one is in here now.

Slowly I move on to the next door and there's a flash of feathers. Two starlings fly past and circle the landing. Another flies at me as I step inside, hitting the side of my head. It's a dull thud on the temple that causes a slight flash, then turns into a sickening stinging sensation. The shock bursts the tears that have been waiting to be shed since I found Bessy and not Aiden. I slump on an old double bed and touch my forehead, feeling for the dampness of blood, but luckily there is none. I shift my weight onto a pretty pink quilt and pillows for respite.

Suddenly, sitting alone in the empty house, I feel so very small and wish someone would tell me what to do next. Tell me how to find my son.

The thought that he could be captive, suffering, or dead suffocates me, and I feel my body begin to panic. Large hands squeezing my lungs. And then there's another bird flapping, this time in a large wooden wardrobe. Sounds loosen the squeeze and I can breathe again. I need to finish this.

I open the double wardrobe door and duck out of the way this time as the bird escapes onto the landing, joining the others.

'How did you get in there, little guy?'

They fly round and round, looking for a way out, some kind of escape, and I know how that feels. This release calms me somehow and I take an enormous breath and find raw comfort from the material of my scarf as it sucks into the crevices of my mouth.

There's a chest lodged at the bottom of the wardrobe, like a forgotten treasure. It's against regulations, it's against everything I thought I stood for, but I open it anyway. I need to find out more about Bessy.

Inside, there's another box and some papers, on top of a rolled-up baby shawl. Pink. She must have a son and a daughter.

I'm not sure what I'm searching for. A way to avoid it happening to me? What not to do. How to not die alone.

I open the inner box and there are bundles of twenty-pound notes. My fingers trace the smooth paper and lines of thick rubber bands. It isn't often you see money like this, all rolled up and waiting for something important. My thoughts switch back to Aiden.

I remember his dark hair and angry teenage skin. I remember that I will do anything to get him home. And somehow, at this moment, the realisation of something happening to my son makes me stoop down and contemplate the unknown territory of stealing.

I've worked in the police force for almost two decades; I know how criminal minds work. I know that whoever has Aiden could come knocking any second, minute, hour, day now demanding money. I'm surprised they haven't already. Time I have, but money I don't and, as I realise the weight of a potential ransom, an intense panic prickles in my fingers. Before I can refuse this primal urge, I push the notes into my deep shoulder bag, along with the papers.

I know it's wrong, of course; even as I'm doing it I sense my own desperation. I'm a member of the police force. I'm the most honest person I know, committed to catching the scum who do this sort of thing. Yet I can't help myself. This is different. This is for Aiden. This could be the only way I will ever see my son again.

I've been involved in missing person cases before and I've looked at the mother, desperate and determined, and wondered how far you would go to find your child. Now I know. *All the way Aiden, I'll go all the way to find you, son.*

I unravel the pink shawl, hoping I will, for a moment, lose myself inside someone else's memories or pain instead of my own. No such luck. My hand touches fragile bone, and a tiny skeletal hand falls into mine.

I almost scream, but aren't I Detective Sergeant Janet Pearce, Surveillance Specialist? Aren't I hard? Tough? Impenetrable? I close the lid with shaking fingers and replace the box, hurrying now, fighting back tears. This is all wrong. It's all too much and I rush downstairs.

My phone rings just as I'm standing in front of poor Bessy. *Mike. Again.*

'Jan? Have you left there yet? You need to be here. We're starting the briefing in half an hour and if you don't make this one . . .'

The bag is heavy on my shoulder and pinching at the skin under my cotton T-shirt. I need to get it to my car before I ring this in, but now I have no choice. If I don't say anything to Mike someone will suspect further down the line. I check my watch. I've been here ten minutes.

'OK. I'll be there. But I need to ring in a suspicious death.'

There's a silence for a moment. I can hear him breathing. Mike knows what I'm going through. He gets it. He's probably my best friend in the whole world right now. He speaks again.

'Not...?'

'No. An old woman. Looks like natural causes, but a bit

gruesome. Anyway. That's what I found when I got here. I'll wait until someone arrives, then I'll be right with you.'

I sound composed, professional, but I'm still shaking. I hang up. He'll be pleased, because I've got a legitimate excuse to miss the briefing. I hurry through the kitchen, out the door, and through the yard. The birds scatter then regroup on the telephone wires above.

My car's in the back alleyway. I take the money and push it under the front seat. I push the letters into the elasticated pocket on the side of the door and pull my bag back onto my shoulder. Oh my God. What am I doing? I know this is so fucking wrong and I try to tell myself again that it's necessary. But away from the drama of the house, sense creeps in. If there was going to be a ransom from Connelly wouldn't it have come weeks ago?

No. I can't do it. I can't. I pull out the money and push it back into my bag and hurry back to the house. What was I thinking? This isn't me. The birds just sit there, their heads turning as they watch me rushing around. I try to shoo them away, because they are witnesses to my uncharacteristic misdemeanour, but they won't go.

I move past Bessy, running now, and toward the narrow stairs, silently apologising for disturbing her secret.

But it's too late. I see a blue flashing light against the darkness of the room and hear the back door open. Two uniformed police officers appear and someone is banging on the door.

Hugging my bag and shame to my chest, I fumble with the lock and open it. DS Jack Newsome, one of my opposite numbers in the regional police, pushes past me, followed by two uniformed officers.

'Jesus Christ. That's awful. How long's it been here?'

I don't like Jack. He hasn't got a compassionate bone in his body. I find myself moving protectively between him and Bessy.

'She, Jack, she. This is a person. A woman. She deserves a little respect.'

The word sticks on my tongue, heavy with mockery. Respectful, unlike me, who has just stolen her life savings. I've never felt guilt like this before, and I wonder how people can live with it. He smirks.

'Right, Jan. She. How long has *she* been here?'

I see Bessy with fresh eyes. As Jack does, as any policeman would. Her faded dress is sagging in odd shapes against the decomposition of her body, and brown lace-up shoes sit the wrong way round, her ankles ballooning awkwardly in the crossed position they must have rested in as she died.

'I don't know, Jack. But I arrived fifteen minutes ago. Had a tip off about a bad smell and was just passing.'

He's nodding and grinning. Yet underneath I can see his annoyance as he sighs and wipes his hand through his dark hair, then wipes tiny beads of perspiration away from his forehead. And, of course, the giveaway twitch at the corner of his eye that always tells me when Jack thinks he's onto something.

'Just passing, were you? A little bit out of town, isn't it? Away from your usual place of work? So who was the tip off from?'

I smile now and wonder if it covers up my devastation.

'Member of the public. In a public place. Just on my way to Ashton Market buying some bacon for the weekend when I heard two women talking about this property and the smell. Simple as that.'

He's shaking his head.

'OK, Jan, if that's how you want it. I suppose all's well that ends well.'

We look at Bessy. She's someone's mother. Like me.

'Not for her, though. Which is why we're here, not to find out the ins and outs of my shopping habits. No?'

Jack turns away now. He's looking toward the kitchen. As he approaches the door, I hear a flutter of wings and beaks tapping on glass.

'What the bloody hell? Get those birds out of here. And search the house. Get forensics down here, and we need a coroner's wagon for the old bird here. Cover her up, John. She's giving me the creeps.'

So the police machine swings into action. I stand there for a moment, wondering if there is a way for me to put the money back, but the two uniformed officers are upstairs now, battling with angry starlings.

I don't mention that they will need two coroner's vehicles, one for poor Bessy and one for the tiny baby. God only knows why she's got a dead baby in her wardrobe. That poor woman must have had a terrible life if the state of this place is anything to go by. Without a word I leave by the front door and walk around to the back alley.

The houses are well maintained and I feel a little easier now the neighbours are out and I have a reason for being here. I get in my car and, with the bag still over my shoulder, drive off. In my rearview mirror the birds still watch, their heads cocking.

Two streets away, I pull up outside an old peoples' home. I know this is a safe spot away from CCTV. My phone hasn't even got a signal here. I'm a surveillance expert, latterly of the Communications Department, more lately promoted to DS in Special Operations. It's my job to know these things.

Even so, guilt overwhelms me, and I remember when I first became a police detective; so full of goodwill and always on the side of the person who had been harmed. I spent hours poring over mind maps and evidence boards, midnight sessions in the operation room and endless visits to witnesses.

Sometimes when I lie awake at night thinking about Aiden, I wonder if I would have shuffled events in a different way this wouldn't have happened. That always leads to me swearing that from now on I'll do the right thing, be good, anything, as long as I get him back. Holding myself bolt upright, smiling, being polite, saying thank you; are they all little combinations to finding out what has happened?

In the clarity of daylight it all seems different. No hippy thinking will get me through the day. Action is needed. And, after all, in this game it's almost impossible to be good all the time. The deeper you get into something, the more complex the relationships, the situations. Everyone's got something on someone, and they're going to use it at some point. Until now I'd kept my fingers out of the till, been good as gold. But this is different. This is personal.

I count the money. There's forty-four thousand pounds. *Jesus.* I automatically scan the horizon for the signs I know are there, at the root of my suspicions of where my son is. Connelly. I see the scarves and shoes hanging from the telephone wires, silent messages in an unspoken world and my heart turns back to stone.

I push the money under the seat, still distraught that I took it, more distraught that I couldn't put it back, and seeing no way to return it now. I decide that, in return for it, I'll do what I can to see Bessy Swain's case resolved. I'll do what I can to find out why she had to hide a baby. Someone owes her that, at least.

CHAPTER TWO

B ack at the station I'm just in time for the briefing and Mike smiles widely when he sees me. I sit at the back and look at him. He's been my sidekick for five years now, enough time for him to get to know me well. He cheers me up. Even now, with all this going on, I can't help but smile back.

He's a regular guy, married to a woman who hates me. And who can blame her? I'm out with her husband at all hours, in all kinds of dangerous situations. He'd do anything for me, I'm sure of it.

I know she calls me Barbie because Mike has his phone volume set too loud. When I was younger this would have made me smile and a little bit proud of my average good looks, but now it really is an insult. I can't think that anyone is farther away from the image of Barbie than I am right now.

I stare down at my feet, slightly too big, made worse by flat pumps. Highly inappropriate for the late autumn weather, but I'm in such a rush every morning I never end up wearing what I have planned. Always the same black pumps, jeans, and T-shirt. My mind's always on something else. My mind's always on Aiden.

Jim Stewart steps up and begins to speak.

'OK, people. Operation Prophesy. We need to nail this once and for all. Connelly's slipped through the net too many times now. He might look like a saint on the outside but we've got hard evidence that he's keeping explosives at his HQ. We've got reliable information that he's storing drugs on the premises, but they're like Fort Knox so we have to get the evidence first then do it the right way. With a warrant. Initially, I want Keith and Jason on a fact finder locally. I've brought in Sandra and Alison to do some undercover with his girls, and Jose and Julia will concentrate on the comms and the vehicle movements. I want proper logs kept of everything. I don't want a repeat of Hurricane.'

I sigh under my breath. Operation Hurricane. Twenty-two months of work thrown out of court because of poor record keeping. Jim Stewart had tried to get Connelly on his own, but his solicitor was shit hot and got him bail. That was the first mistake. Then, it turned out, the comms team hadn't been keeping records correctly and there was a huge gap, which meant that the rest of the evidence didn't make sense.

This time, we'd all been on admin courses and the operation was bigger. Jim Stewart wasn't a man to be beaten, and Operation Prophesy would be run with a hand of steel. Which would make it much more difficult for me to do what I have to do. To search for my son.

'OK. So, Mike and Jan, I need you to be the general eyes and ears, feeding back. Bring in the usual informants, get them interviewed. We only have a small budget for this one after the big spend last time so don't go mad.'

I raise my hand and everyone turns around.

'Haven't you forgotten something? Sir?'

Jim Stewart turns slowly. He's seething and he knows exactly what's coming.

'No, DS Pearce. I don't think I have.'

I stare at him for a second.

'What about Aiden? What about the link between Connelly and Aiden? Aren't you going to include that in Operation Prophesy?'

The room is heavy with silence. No one's looking at me now. Alison, who's been drafted in from the Met, looks a little bit embarrassed. Even she's heard about me. Mike's shaking his head. Jose is texting someone, giving them the Jan Pearce update, how mad she is today, how she should be signed off sick. Jim is sweating now. He walks toward me.

'What do you think has happened to Aiden, Jan? Really? Let's get this out once and for all, eh?'

He looks around the room for nods of support, but everyone is suddenly busy. I nod though. We've been through all this before, but not publicly. Although I know he's setting me up, gathering witnesses to my mental state so he can have me suspended, I carry on.

'I think he's got Aiden, sir. I think he's kidnapped him. As a kind of revenge for Operation Hurricane.'

'OK. Look, Jan. I see what you're saying, but we've got no evidence. If we had some evidence, then we could investigate, but as it is, we don't have any. No evidence at all linking Aiden to Sean Connelly. In fact, we've got nothing on Connelly at all, not actually on him. Some of his cronies, but not a single shred of evidence on Sean Connelly. We might think things, but we have to actually prove it. And that's why we're gathered here today. So, again, there's no evidence to link Aiden and Connelly.'

I nod. On the surface he's right. But I know there's something going on. I've pieced it together. I've met Connelly twice, and he's the opposite of what you would expect someone into extortion to be. Blond and hefty, he's polite and humble.

But his eyes give him away, mocking and cruel. Of course, there's no direct evidence. That's the problem. He uses other people to do his dirty work, and we're so near to finding out just what he's up to. The problem is, proving it. Until then, it's hearsay.

But I know what he's up to. When I was in surveillance I had to do the legwork. Sitting around on the sink estates, watching what happens and feeding it back. Endless days in grubby cafés and half-stocked mini-markets mean you get to know the people, what goes on, and who's behind it.

You become ingrained in it, and it in you. I heard stories about Connelly and his boys, stories about if you crossed him, he'd hit you where it hurt. Stories about abductions and violence, so terrible that it was hardly believable. But the trouble was, and still is, that it's all contained. All kept on Northlands.

No evidence, and therefore, as far as the police is concerned, all unproven. Rumours and speculation. But I've seen and heard things about Connelly that make me sure that he's got Aiden. Things that the officers here in special operations haven't seen or heard first hand.

'I understand that, but you won't get evidence unless you investigate it. So it's a bit chicken and egg, isn't it?' I realise that I'm doing an egg shape with my hands, which makes me look more mentally disjointed. 'And now we're investigating Connelly as a whole, shouldn't we include this?'

He's shaking his head.

'No. And that's the end of it. We need all hands on deck with this. We need to get something solid, something to smash that saintly image Connelly seems to have built up for himself on Northlands. And I don't want to find out you've been wasting time with this while you're supposed to be doing your job. Understood?'

I stand up. Even though my head's telling me to sit down. It's my heart doing this.

'Wasting time?'

Most of my colleagues are looking at the floor. I sink back down and he smiles a corporate smile.

'Sorry, Jan. Wrong words. But Aiden's a separate issue. Come and have a chat with me later and we'll see what we can do. But for now, it's Operation Prophesy. And I don't want any mistakes on this one. No petty crime, no small time scams. I want to go right to the top on this one.'

Mike goes to stand up to defend me, but Jose pulls him back into his seat. There's a bustle toward the door, leaving me sitting alone in the room. I think about the money under the seat of my car, and why I took it. Because I feel so alone. I feel I have to do this on my own and I'm desperate.

I watch through the glass plates that separate the rooms as Jim Stewart goes back to his office. He's laughing now with his PA, and he's shaking hands with one of the local councillors who's come to be briefed on the battle against crime.

I wonder if I should sign off sick for a while? I've considered it before, but I'd just be sitting at home all the time then, unable to do anything. At least this way I'm hearing the latest on Connelly, on any leads that might be worth following up. Like the one this morning on Ney Street.

I'd heard about that one by sitting in the Tameside area with a police radio tuned in. Person not seen for days and bad smell coming from house. This would normally go onto the investigation log and be attended that day, but I was only around the corner and recognised it as one of the houses Connelly rents out.

I go to my desk now and start to type up the report, sticking to the story that I overheard two women talking about it. I'm not supposed to have the radio; I took it out of the operations room in case I was ever in danger in an area where there's no mobile signal. And, of course, to find Aiden. I only use it outside our area, so I won't be tracked.

I know all the backdoors. I should do. Up until five years ago, I was responsible for closing them. I was originally brought in to monitor internal wrongdoing, and I learned all the little tricks of the trade that way. I learned advanced surveillance techniques. I know this area like the back of my hand.

I know where every camera is, where the holes in the mobile networks are. And by association, I know how they can be avoided by people who don't want to be seen or heard. I've honed my skills. I never imagined in my wildest dreams I'd ever use them.

Right on cue, I get a call from Jack asking me for a report about the incident earlier, Ney Street and Bessy. I feel the tears return as I think of Bessy dying alone in that stinking mess.

'Funny how you were right there, Jan, isn't it?'

I nod. Even Jack knows my daily habits and the reason for them.

'Right place at the right time. I've filed the report already. And before you ask, the back door was unlocked. That's how I got in. Not even a break and enter without a warrant.'

'Funny that, though, who leaves their back door open in this day and age? Great. Oh, by the way. We found further human remains at the property.'

I feign amazement now.

'You're joking. Who is it?'

'A baby. Newborn, it looks like. Forensics are there looking for anything else.'

I panic for a moment, and go over me stealing the money again in my mind's eye. What if one of my eyelashes had dropped onto the shawl? What if a stray hair had dropped in the bedroom? They can even detect tiny snot globules. Shit. I'm an opportunist thief, no better than the fucking lowlife working for Connelly.

'Bloody hell. That poor woman was bad enough.'

He pauses.

'That poor woman's probably a child killer. So don't feel too sorry for her.'

I take a breath and then let it out. 'Innocent until proven guilty, Jack. Who says it's her baby? You're making big assumptions there.'

He sighs.

'Yeah. I suppose. Anyway, I might need to talk to you further about this.'

'OK. But just so you know, I've been assigned to Operation Prophesy. You know, with Special Ops, so I might not be available. All hands on deck.'

Except you, Jack. You don't work with the big boys here at HQ, do you? The silence is palpable and eventually he breathes out.

'OK, Jan. I'll be in touch.'

Aiden surfaces in my consciousness again and I make a plan. The money. The opportunity. Everything's in place now. Everything I need to find Aiden. In only six weeks everyone's forgotten him. No body, Mum and Dad divorced, area with high youth crime statistics, so everyone's assumed that he's just another teenage runaway. Everyone except me.

I've settled into a pattern of living that involves putting on a front at work, basic eating and sleeping, and an underbelly of deep grief over his disappearance. Two lives, merging into one in my nightmares about Connelly and his threats.

I feel bad about the money. I can't put it back now, no matter how much I want to. It would probably have gone to Bessy's son, the one with the Manchester United bedroom. Or would that be her grandson? Her son would be too old now to have a room like that. I don't know, but I'll keep my promise to find out what happened to her. It won't take much interfering to find out about the baby and her life. Someone's probably onto it, saving me the trouble.

For now, I've got to keep up the façade of Operation Prophesy. It's going to be difficult, because, underneath it all, every waking moment is focused on getting my son back.

CHAPTER THREE

I wake up in the middle of the night drenched in sweat. I go downstairs and get a drink of milk, because something in milk helps people to sleep. Something in mother's milk helps babies to sleep. That's what the midwife told me when Aiden was very young and screamed all night.

I look through the kitchen window and into the garden, where he used to play with Ruby, our little Jack Russell. Ruby's gone now, and so is Aiden. His cat, Percy, is sitting on the wheelie bin and jumps down when he sees me. I let him in and bury my face in his fur. He's all I've got left that's Aiden's. I pour some of my milk into a saucer and he laps it up as I stroke his head.

It's two o'clock. I check my phone and there's a message from Sal. Aiden's dad. My ex-husband. The reality trickles back into my sleepy brain as I remember what has happened. Aiden had stayed over at Sal's for the weekend while I worked overtime on a tricky case. I'd spoken to him on the Saturday morning; he'd been nagging me to get him a pair of expensive headphones. He'd told me that he was going out later, with some friends.

'What friends?'

There had been a silence.

'Just some mates.'

'Anyone I know? Maybe you could give your dad a contact number?'

I couldn't see him, but I could imagine him standing in Sal's flat, frowning.

'I doubt it. I'm not a child. I don't need you telling me what to do.'

It had been my turn to pause. I'd thought about saying that I only cared because I loved him, and I wish I had now.

'Yes, you are, Aidy. You're fifteen.'

'I'm sixteen next week.'

Sixteen. He'd reminded me that he was sixteen the next week then vanished. That was the last time I spoke to my son. Sal had called me on Sunday morning asking to speak to him, demanding to know why neither of us had bothered to let him know that Aiden was coming home that night. We still called this house home, all of us. It was home to all of us at one time. Now it's just mine.

I'd waited until Sal had finished his shouting and accusing; I know how to handle him. Then I'd quietly stated my own case.

'But he didn't come here, Sal. He's not been home.'

He went off on a tangent about teenage girls and Aiden's friends and didn't I know where my own son was. What kind of a police officer was I? What kind of a parent was I? All questions that I have continually asked myself ever since. But it's futile when he's like this to call him out now and remind him that he had Aiden that weekend. When the bickering finally stopped, Sal was silent for a full minute then spoke.

'So where is he? What do we do now?'

I remember my mouth being very dry and feeling faint.

'We should wait until teatime, give him a chance to come back. If he's not back by then, we should phone the police.'

Sal snorted.

'Yeah, great. But you *are* the police. Aren't you going to do something?'

I did do something. Even though I knew it would be fruitless, I called all of Aiden's school friends' parents. I called my family and Sal's family. At three o'clock, I heard a knock on the front door. He'd forgotten his keys. Been in a fight? Been mugged? Was he hurt? But it was Sal, all angry. I told him whom I'd phoned and we looked at each other, strangers now.

'I suppose I'd better ring it in then.'

Sal nodded.

'Yeah, you ring it in. Make a report. If anything's happened to him I'll . . .'

'What? What will you do? Eh?'

My tolerance for Sal's threats is zero. I'm used to being blamed for everything, but I don't have to take it. We couldn't even pull together with a crisis looming. He was all red and huffy now, a sure sign that any minute he was going to explode.

'You. That's the problem. You. Your fucking job. He's probably run away because of you. You drove me away and now you've done it to him. Shit, Jan, this is down to you.'

If I were a different person I might have taken this on board and felt guilty, but I'm so used to Sal's blame and shame routine by now that it bypasses me. I watched as he reached into the fridge and pulled out a bottle of wine. He went to the cupboard and got one glass and poured. I turned away and dialed the operation room number.

'Hi. It's Jan Pearce. Can I speak to Ian Douglas, please?'

The call transferred and I waited. Eventually he answered.

'Ian, it's Jan. I've got a bit of a situation.'

Ian is the missing people guy at the station, the one who coordinates the searches.

'Hi, Jan. You do know it's Sunday, yeah? Only I'm round at family.'

I suddenly stepped back into reality.

'I'm so sorry, Ian. Look, I'll get uniformed out and file a report that way, maybe you could have a look at it tomorrow?'

I heard children in the background, laughing. And music.

'Report? Why? What's happened? Are you OK?'

I'd swallowed back the tears. Someone asked if I was OK. The first time in ages anyone bothered to ask.

'No. Not really. Aiden's gone missing. He hasn't been home.'

'Right. How old is he? How long's he been gone?'

'He's been gone since yesterday teatime. He's fifteen. Sixteen next week.'

I heard Ian walk into a silent area.

'OK. And has he done this sort of thing before?'

'No. Never. He's never spent a night away from at least one of his parents. He's round at his dad's a lot. There was one time, after an argument, between me and Sal really, not him, that he stayed out at his friend's but . . .'

There was a silence as we both mentally latched onto the word 'runaway.'

'Any problems recently? Drink? Drugs? Arguments?'

I thought. I hadn't noticed any signs. I hadn't noticed anything.

'Not that I know of. What can we do?'

Sal was on his second glass of wine and I needed to get him out of there before he got drunk. Ian paused and then replied.

'Wait. Just wait and see if he comes home tonight. He might have been to a party, or got in a car and gone somewhere and can't get back easily. He might phone. Endless possibilities. But if he's still gone tomorrow, call me first thing, OK?'

Tomorrow. No, not good enough. What about tonight? What if he's not home by two, out there alone who knows where? I'm trained to stay calm, but I felt hysteria rising.

'What about tonight?'

Ian coughed.

'Let's wait and see. Stay there, see if he comes back. Let's take it from there.' I heard a voice, a small girl shouting 'Daddy.' 'Look, I have to go now. I'll speak to you first thing, OK. Don't worry. He'll probably turn up with a hangover later on. Bye, Jan.'

He was gone. Back to his family party. Sal had gulped down the second glass of wine and he was beetroot red.

'So what are they doing? Are they going to look for him?'

I shook my head.

'No. He said to wait, he'll probably come back later. If he doesn't, call it in tomorrow and they'll assess it.'

He sniggered.

'Great. Well, I'm going out to look. Drive round, see what I can see.'

I nodded.

'You're over the limit, Sal.'

'So fucking arrest me, then. Go on. Arrest me, so I can't go out and search for my own son. Fuck off, Jan. Just fuck off.'

He left and slammed the door hard. So hard the whole house shook. Just like old times. That's the thing with Sal. He can't change. He had lots of chances to curb his temper, to stop blaming me for everything, but he didn't.

I'd been in the police force when he met me, so it was no state secret that I was committed to my job. It was as if he was in direct competition with it from the moment we married, him finding increasingly more bizarre ways to make me stay off work.

When Aiden was born nine months into our marriage, I could sense Sal's delight as I took a full year off work. He thought I wouldn't go back, but I did. I couldn't not. Instead of taking it easy, I worked my way up, juggling for all I was worth, and eventually it paid off. Better job, bigger salary, nice house.

Aiden was ten when Sal finally snapped and walked out. It hit us both hard. I hadn't realized how much I depended on him to look after Aiden, and Sal tried to punish me by refusing to look after him while I went to work, or bringing him to the station at exactly the time I said I would pick him up.

He tried everything. Going for sole custody, trying to force me to work a nine-to-five. Being unreliable, so I was constantly late or absent. I'd known he would do this, but I also knew that if I weathered the storm, he would eventually do it for Aiden. And he did. He settled into one weekend every two weeks with Aiden, and half the school holidays.

I'd thought it would be a relief, some time to myself, but it was a nightmare. I'd miss Aiden and call him all the time when he was at Sal's. That's exactly why I'd called him the night he disappeared. To talk to him because I missed him.

Sal had left the bottle of wine on the kitchen side and I picked it up and smelled it. I'd bought it to cook with, and it smelled cheap and vinegary. I almost took a swig but stopped at the last minute. I needed a clear head. I sat at the table and pulled a green folder toward me.

It was full of receipts and business cards, bits of information I instinctively didn't throw away. Bits of paper with threats on them, pushed through my door or pinned on my car. All from the same person, same handwriting, block capitals to hide the style, and the same paper, a creamy Post-it–size bond.

I keep them because I work a lot on instincts. It doesn't

make sense, that gut feeling you get, a sinking doom. But it's real to me, and I felt it that Sunday. Ever since Sal had told me Aiden hadn't come home I was itching to open the folder and finger the dirty pieces of paper. I knew, deep down, that this was something to do with Connelly.

Like everything that revolved around Connelly, there was no proof it was him. He had his cronies do all the dirty work. On Northlands he was considered some kind of mysterious benefactor, funding this and setting up that, and no one would believe that he was involved in crime. Just a local boy done good, creating jobs and funding community goodness.

But I think it's him who has Aiden. It has to be. Someone had been threatening me alongside Operation Hurricane and now Aiden was missing. What else could it be?

We did as Ian said and waited until morning, me awake and Sal, who'd returned at ten o'clock, lying pissed on the sofa. I'd tried to get him to go home in case Aiden went to his flat, but he point blank refused, saying Aiden would come here if he wasn't in.

The next morning Aiden wasn't home and Sal went out to look for him again. I rang everyone and then I rang Ian.

'OK. Look, Jan, I'll report him as a missing child. Get it broadcast. When you come in today bring some photographs. And when did you last see him?'

'I haven't seen him since Friday. He was staying with his dad.'

'OK. We'll need a statement from him as well. Bring all Aiden's details.'

'He could come in with me.'

I heard Ian miss a beat. He was thinking what to say next to placate me.

'He could, yeah, but then there's all the waiting.' Roughly translated as we've got other things to think about. Things that aren't a fifteen-year-old who's gone off with some mates. Even at that point I was beginning to understand how this would be treated. 'I'll get some uniforms out to him. Might be later on today. Get a statement. I'll see you when you get in. OK? Don't worry.'

Don't worry. Easy for him to say. Don't worry. I know from years of policing that it's highly unlikely that he's dead. It's hard to conceal a dead body. Much easier to keep someone alive.

I also know that nine out of ten missing teenagers are acting out, flexing their freedom muscles. But not Aiden. And I've got my reasons. Everyone thinks he's run away from home. But I know he would never do that. He would never do this to me, his mother.

Even now, right at this moment, in the middle of the night, I can't drag my mind's eye away from the lead up to Aiden's disappearance and the aftermath. The surface of the storm was tumultuous, with Sal losing the plot and wrecking an interview room as I watched through the one-sided glass, frozen. It was like viewing my whole marriage, summed up in ten minutes of temper-fed violence.

He'd tried to blame me. He'd told the interviewers that all this was my fault for being a bad mother, for having a job I loved, for making us split up. He'd told them about the time Aiden stayed out before, how he'd slunk off in the middle of an argument between Sal and I and not come home. How we had to phone his friends, until he waltzed back in at nine o'clock in the morning to get his football gear.

At that point Stan had closed his notebook. Stan Bores, the elderly detective interviewing him, all they could spare for a 'runaway' case, as they labelled it, told him that the police force weren't social services and whatever the reasons, it was their job simply to establish Aiden's location.

Poor Sal. It seemed that no one wanted to listen to his

continual character assassination of me; every conversation wheedled around to that subject. So he reverted to type and blew. But what bothered me was that, in his anger and recrimination, he had more or less suggested that he too thought Aiden had run away. I knew he hadn't.

If the surface was choppy and rough going with sleepless nights and endless wondering, the undercurrent was more dangerous.

Sal heaved the blame for Aiden running away—he had become convinced that this was what had happened now after copious amounts of statistics and data provided by officials who just don't know where to look when nobody turns up—squarely on my shoulders. It was clearly all my fault.

This was the main current driving the investigation forward, scaled down after a week of nothing—no use of bank card, no CCTV, no evidence at all.

Yet I knew where to look. The underlying current was my doubt. Doubt that he had just upped and left. True, there had been arguments and there had been playing up, but nothing out of the ordinary. He was like Sal—quick tempered and unforgiving. At times I thought he hated me; he would just sit and stare at me. But that was no reason to run. He had two homes, always an alternative if one got too much.

And I knew where to look. In the weeks running up to Aiden's disappearance I'd received some menacing text messages. Then a couple of threatening emails. There'd been a dead rat left on my doorstep and my car door handles had been covered in anti-vandal paint.

I'd dutifully reported all these things, and they were linked to the case I'd been working on for the past two years. Operation Hurricane. I wasn't the only officer receiving threats.

Julie Winters was told that someone would shave her head. Stuart Peterson received a letter with a picture of his Jack

Russell saying that it would be decapitated. All par for the operational course, when you're dealing with a lowlife like Connelly. Even so, nothing had actually happened so far.

Connelly's henchmen concentrate on killing or maiming rival gang members, or occasionally each other. They leave us alone because, let's face it, to harm one of us would launch a major, blood-fuelled investigation.

Or so you would think. When I went to Jim Stewart and spewed out my accusation, that Connelly had kidnapped Aiden in an attempt to get revenge, he shook his head.

'Has he threatened you? Is there something you haven't told us? Because all I can see in your Hurricane report log is a couple of texts and emails and some notes telling you to be careful and so on. No mention of your family. And we don't even know all these texts and emails and associated behaviour are from Connelly's lot. Don't forget. Innocent until proven guilty. We don't have anything at all on Connelly yet. Looks like it, but all bark and no bite so far. And we've got undercover around them, as you know, and no mention of a kidnap.'

He might as well have hung a huge sign on me saying 'I am paranoid. Disregard anything I say.' He was tapping away at his keyboard, checking my file, running a search on Aiden's case. Not really listening, but I answered all the same.

'No. He hasn't threatened my family directly. But I know it's him. There's something funny going on with Connelly. It's not just the drugs and the violence, sir. It's more than that. I've put it in a detailed report. I think there's more going on here.'

He was nodding, and I could see pity in his eyes.

'Right. To be honest, Jan, I think you should take a break from it. Just for a few weeks. I'm putting together a renewed campaign against Connelly, one that'll work this time. One where we all focus just on one case, with no distraction. Focused on the most probable place that he can be operating from, based on renewed activity. Old Mill. We know that much. So until then, just everyday work. Got that? If we get any evidence about Aiden you'll be the first to know. But my opinion is that it's nothing to do with Connelly. And until we have some solid evidence, neither is anything else. Have you considered that it might not be Connelly running Old Mill? Maybe he's retired now and someone else is at the bottom of all this. What we do know is that he runs a kitchen factory and he's inherited a property business. Both of which are legal. We do know there are criminal goings on, but maybe we're on the wrong track and the girls on the game and the drugs are down to someone else. But I think that it's a hierarchy that's hiding him. Always someone else to do the dirty work while he looks clean. Until we get some evidence, no one's in the frame. We won't know until we've completed the investigation, will we?'

I wanted to believe him, I wanted to believe that I was obsessed with Connelly and on the wrong track, but as soon as Aiden disappeared the threats stopped. A week later I was back in Jim's office.

'The messages stopped. They've got him. I know it.'

My hand was shaking around my coffee cup, splashing coffee onto my jeans. He stood up and opened the door.

'Get a grip. You know we're near to Connelly. If Aiden is there, which I don't think he is, we'll find him. We're all over that place.'

Sean Connelly had a little empire. He and his own family lived on a bought up council estate on the outskirts of town. Northlands. It was semirural, on the edge of the river.

A large cotton mill hung behind the estate, until recently, used as a catalogue clothing distribution company. Connelly had bought up all the units, then the building, and branded it as a fitted kitchen outlet. It was even registered with Companies House. All nice and legal.

I'd done my homework, sitting for hours outside, hoping to catch a vibe from Aiden. *Are you in there, son?*

I discovered that Connelly had been buying up rented houses all over town. When I dug deeper, I found out that his father, dead now, had started this, and owned a good portion of the tiny mill houses in the surrounding areas. Signature two-up, two-down poverty houses for those people of a bygone age who worked in the mills.

Connelly Snr appeared to have gotten funding in the sixties to tart them up and install inside toilets. It looked like Connelly Jnr had carried this on, opening a letting agency to manage it. None of this made finding Aiden any easier.

At first I'd imagined that they had him captured in the mill, but I quickly realized that he could be anywhere, lying dead in one of Connelly's tiny box houses. Why would they though? To get at me. Us. The police. To try to blackmail us into slowing down the operation. The threats, they all point to this.

He could be lying dead anywhere, my son. No one would know. No one would suspect. It had been six weeks now, and he could have been lying dead all that time, all alone.

Which is how I came to be at 57 Ney Street. I had an Ordnance Survey map with all Connelly's houses marked in green on it. I'd listen on the radio for any suspicious reports at any of the addresses, and attend. Usually it was a fight or a burglary, nothing to concern me, but this one had been different. No one seen at the property for weeks and there was a horrible smell when someone looked through the letter box for signs of life.

And this brings me to now, standing here in my nightgown, a bundle of money in front of me. I have a surge of guilt, a moment when I realize this is probably the end of my policing career, even if I never get found out. Now I'm a criminal, aren't

I? How could I ever do my job knowing I'd stolen from a scene of crime?

Then I remember that it's potential ransom money. That's why I took it. If they have him, they're going to want paying off, aren't they? I count the money and put it in a nearly empty washing powder box under the sink. Even acting like a criminal now. Using tricks I'd seen others use. If you can't beat them, join them.

I can't sleep. It's two thirty now and I can hear the distant rumble of the M60. Twenty-four-seven travel. Percy is lying on the end of my bed, reminding me that, even though I'm in turmoil inside, I still have to get up and feed him, change his litter tray—do all the things I and he need to survive. It's comforting, though, the feeling that Percy needs me.

I search around for something to occupy me, something that isn't late-night TV or old family videos of Aiden when he was young. I remember poor Bessy in the chair, and the birds.

I stiffen with shock as I realize that I'd hardly flinched at the baby's tiny, flesh-free hand as it fell into mine, my mind on the money and a ransom and, at the end of a long train of thought, Aiden. Aiden. Aiden. Aiden. I need a break, something to distract me just for a moment.

My hand strays to the papers bundled in with the money. Some bills, a birth certificate for a Thomas Swain. Mother Bessy, father Colin. Receipts and a book of old cooperative divi stamps. Another book of Green Shield Stamps.

At the bottom, an exercise book, grey and well thumbed, with narrow, feint, ruled lines. I expect to see a child's hand, maybe English or maths, but the writing inside is fine handwriting, looped and formal. It draws my eyes and I'm gripped.

BESSY

GOING AWAY

Lucky I'm writing it all down. Because it's the only way I'm ever going to explain what's bloody well gone on here. It started on 26th August 1963. I'll never forget that day. I was in the middle of getting my life back after raising a son right after the war. Thomas was a big, strapping seventeen-year-old, in the middle of a training course to be a joiner. He'd been left school less than a year.

I'd had Thomas when I was seventeen myself in 1946, when rationing was still in force. His dad, Colin Swain, was a little bit older than me. He was eighteen when he got me into trouble. We had to get married at the local chapel and I wore a grey suit that'd cover my big belly.

No white dress for me. No bouquet. Just two witnesses and a tiny cake. My mam and dad were there, glad to get me off their hands so they could see to my younger brothers and sisters. Off he goes to do his two years National Service, so I had to birth Thomas on my own and look after him on my own for nearly two years until his daddy gets back.

Not that I'm complaining. It made us closer. We were like two kids playing together, in my little terraced house that I didn't know how to clean. I didn't know how to cook either, and I'd go to the shops and ask how to cook things before I bought them.

I fed Thomas myself until he was old enough to eat porridge, then somehow I managed to keep him alive until Colin came home and his mam took an interest in us.

Well, Colin really. She wanted to know he was looked after, and that meant teaching me to cook. It bloody annoyed me at the time, and I used to grit my teeth at her, but now I can see her reasoning. She just wanted to see her son safe. I can see that now.

So Thomas went to school and did ever so well, took his eleven plus and went to the grammar. When he was fourteen he got scarlet fever and missed a lot of school, so we transferred him to the local school. Not academic, our Thomas. No. More handy like his dad. More of a maker. Wanted to be a joiner, he did.

We bought him a bike for his seventeenth birthday and he'd ride it round like Billy-oh. Him and Phil, his friend, would ride round to a different part of town and drop in a pub for a pint. They would have been hung, drawn and quartered round these parts, drinking so young, but they were after girls and the new music; they rode everywhere together. Phil was courting a young woman from Ainsley Street, but Thomas hadn't found anyone.

On that day, he'd gone off to work on his bike. He had an apprenticeship in Hyde; a joiner took him on, training him in cabinet making. He liked it, and even though he got paid a small amount, he gave most of it to me, saving only a tiny bit for himself. Mostly for new tyres or the odd pint. I'd kissed him goodbye and given him a Billy can with tea in it, and his butties. Had corned beef on them. He'd shrugged me off.

'Geroff, Mam! I'm too big for that now!'

He'd shouted it at me as he pedalled away. I remember I laughed loud and shouted back.

'Never too big for your mammy's love. You'll always be my baby, no matter how big you get.'

Colin had come to the door in his overalls to see what the shouting was about and I remember his hand on my shoulder as we waved him off. We'd gone back in the house and had a cup of tea before Colin went to work.

I remember laughing again at one of his jokes, silly like, and patting down my hair in the mirror, little creases at the side of my eyes. Colin said they told the story of our lives—if you had the crow's feet you'd laughed enough. If not, you were a miserable sod! He'd said it that morning and I'd told him that I looked like a whole murder of crows had hopped on my face.

A murder of crows. Afterward, it was like somehow I had made it happen. Colin had set off to work, both of us grinning into the distance. My face ached with smiling and I'd gone back in and made some food for the rest of the day.

Teatime had come and Colin came back. Thomas was usually in before him, but he wasn't home yet. We waited a bit, then ate our tea. We were still laughing and joking, thinking he'd snuck off for a pint, that he'd come home later on, a bit unsteady and slurring his words.

We'd planned to sniff at him, through the beer fumes, for scent, or check his face for lipstick. We couldn't wait for him to have a girlfriend, a daughter we'd never been able to have in them happy days—not for lack of trying, I can tell you. All his friends had girlfriends and he didn't. He was a good-looking lad, and Colin said he must be a bit fussy. I'd nodded and wondered if he was shy, if I should sort out some introductions?

But he didn't come home. We sat up until midnight and he didn't come. I turned out the light under the potato hash I'd saved for him and stomped upstairs in anger. Colin sat for a while longer then came up. Neither of us slept, waiting for the door to click open.

Maybe he'd met a girl? He might have stayed at Phil's or, God forbid, had an accident. I had him off his bike in a gutter on Coal Pit Lane, then in the infirmary. We couldn't rest, and Colin got up at six and ran over to Phil's.

It turned out that Thomas had been there in the morning and left his bike. They'd planned to go to the pub later, after work, after tea, and he'd leave his bike until then. He'd taken his dinner with him. The Billy can of tea and the sandwiches.

Phil had seen him off across Hyde Road, only half a mile from the joinery. But he never got there. My Thomas never arrived for work.

Johnny Stokes, his boss, told the police later that he'd never missed a minute of work. In fact, he'd been early every day. He'd shown willing and was gifted. But he hadn't turned up that day.

He'd not turned up later on at Phil's either. Phil told Colin that he thought he must have changed his mind and gone home. That he'd come and pick his bike up later or in the morning. I knew when I saw Colin pushing his bike over the cobbles that something was badly wrong. Colin's face was grey and he looked very tired.

'He's not been at Phillip's, Bess. He's not been at work yesterday.'

'What do you mean? Where the bloody hell is he then?'

In contrast with Colin, who'd had more time to think about it, my cheeks flamed red and I felt a fire inside rise up to my mouth, where the words spat out as hot as flames. Colin went through the whole story again.

'I'll bloody kill him. He'll be somewhere drunk. Too much like my bloody father. I'll kill him when I get my hands on him.'

Again, a careless turn of phrase that would haunt me afterward, somehow beckoning what happened closer.

Colin set off for Stake's Joinery to get the full story and I sat down in the kitchen and lit a cigarette. I smoked Park Drive, unfiltered. Everyone did. My teeth were yellowed through the heavy-duty drawing in and blowing out of the acrid smoke. I fumed through five cigarettes, one after another, watching as the ash floated through the air and fell to the floor.

By the time Colin returned I was surrounded by a ring of grey fallout, my colourful dress hidden behind the smoke hanging in the air around me. I only remember because it was exactly the same as how I felt on the inside. Cloudy, slightly hazy. And partially hidden from view. I smiled weakly as Colin shook his head.

'He's not been to work yesterday.'

I could see his eye on the clock, wondering about his own job. I sucked on another Park Drive and the thought that Colin had never really cared about Thomas, due to the fact that he missed the first two years of his life, that they never really gelled, flashed through my mind. He wanted to go to work when I was so worried about our son.

'You go on, Col. I'll go out and look for him. He might be back later. He might have got himself a girl.'

I rose out of the grey haze and stepped out of the ash circle around me. The spell was broken and I pushed myself into reality as I pulled on a headscarf.

'I'll go down to the infirmary. If he's nowhere else, then he's there.'

Colin slammed the door shut behind him and I locked the back door. How would Thomas get in if I wasn't here? He didn't have a key because I was always here. I unbolted the door and called to Jenny next door.

'Ey, Jen, watch the door for me. I'm just popping out.'

'Ay, all right then.'

I didn't see her, just heard a weak voice in her kitchen. I

walked through the house and opened the front door. I half expected Thomas to be cycling down the road waving. He wasn't and I caught the bus to the hospital.

I stood outside smoking a cigarette as people rolled around in wheelchairs. There were amputees from the war, women with huge bellies, people in standard hospital dressing gowns, all smoking cigarettes and talking.

I peered past them into the entrance, where a wooden desk acted as a booking in area. The woman behind the desk looked friendly so I went in.

'Hiya. I'm looking for my son, Thomas Swain. He's not been home last night, see, and I wondered . . .'

'How old is he?'

The woman was staring at me and for the first time I felt scared.

'Seventeen. He set off for work yesterday and never got there. We wondered if he'd been in an accident?'

'Have you told the police?'

It was a perfectly reasonable question and I suddenly thought that I should have called the local bobby, Sam Mackie. Everything felt as if it had gone wrong all at once and I started to cry.

'No, no I didn't. Me and his dad, we thought he might have fell off his bike. Except he wasn't on it because it was at Phillip's. Or maybe he went under a bus? Can you check?'

'Yes, love. Go an' have a sit down over there, would you? Wipe your eyes, love. I'm sure he'll turn up. Funny at that age, aren't they?'

I sat and thought. Yes, they are funny at that age. I had a baby at his age. He was grown now and here I am sitting scricing in the infirmary about him when he's probably with a lass. I'm thinking the worst. Getting all excited over nothing. Colin had gone to work and no one else seemed overly concerned.

I tapped my foot on the floor and waited. Eventually she returned and waved me over.

'No one here by that name, love. No young men admitted in the past twenty-four hours as an emergency.'

'That's good news. Thanks.'

I hurried out of the reception and lit another cigarette. So he wasn't in the hospital. He wasn't at work. He wasn't at Philip's. He wasn't at home. Where the bloody hell was he?

I was angry again now. I caught the bus back to Philip's and walked the route he'd have to take to work. I caught the same bus, an old charabanc, walked the same pavements, and finally arrived at the joinery.

I could see Thomas's boss and the other two apprentices working away, engrossed in their labour. I'd been here before, to bring his lunch. I stood awhile, wondering if he was in there now, if he'd just gone straight from where he had been to work.

I pushed on the door, then hesitated. If he was there I would be able to see him. I turned to walk away and caught the bus home. He was probably at home. I hurried up the street, stopping at the shop too, bought twenty Park Drives, and ran into the house.

'Tom? Thomas?' Nothing. Probably asleep. Sleeping it off. Little sod. 'Tom? Wake up.'

I went into his room, but he wasn't there. His bed wasn't slept in. I stared at the candlewick tufts, at the pattern he has picked away as a child. A map of England. I looked around the room at his possessions: trophies for football, a cup for cricket, cycling proficiency certificate. His best suit hanging on the back of the door.

Nothing appeared to be missing, except the clothes he had on when he left for work. I knew his clothes by heart, the pile of his sweaters, the collars of his shirts, even his socks—items I took care of as an extension of caring for my child.

My child. Although he was a man, he was still my child. It struck me then that this must be what people mean by flying the nest. I'd heard some mothers go mad with it. I'd never really imagined that Thomas would leave home. He wasn't courting and he was happy here.

We'd had our differences, mainly about the late-night bike riding and drinking, but we all mostly got on. Had I upset him yesterday morning? Had I done something to annoy him? Had Colin said something I didn't know about?

I examined every detail of yesterday and soon found myself sitting in another ashen circle. The smoke hung in the air and I blinked into it. Where was he?

Colin came back at lunchtime with Sam Mackie. By then, I was expecting it and was a little calmer. I lit yet another cigarette and smiled.

'He'll be with some lass. He's at that age. He'll be 'fraid to come back because he's in trouble.'

Colin and Sam looked at each other. Sam sat down opposite me.

'That's as maybe, Bessy, but we're going to do a search. We're going to do the route from here to Stoke's, see if we can turn up anything. If that doesn't, we'll go further afield.'

I nodded and sucked on a Park Drive.

'I'll come with you. I might be able to give you some tips.'

Colin and Sam looked at each other.

'Might be better if you stay here, love, in case he comes back.'

I stood up and tied on my headscarf.

'I'll leave the door on the snick. I'll come with you.'

Colin sat down and took my hands in his. His legs were spread out and he pulled his chair closer.

'Look, Bess, there somat you need to know, take into account, like. There been some troubles with folk. Children.

Goin' missing. Round here over the past year. You know what I'm sayin', love?'

I stared him out.

'You're sayin' someone might have taken our Thomas? Don't be stupid. He's a man. No one could take him; he'd fight. You've seen the size of him. He's a fully grown man. Children are taken, not seventeen-year-olds.'

Again, they looked at each other. Colin looked completely grey now, like someone had tried to rub out his features with an India rubber. Sam stepped forward.

'The thing is, Mrs Swain, a fifteen-year-old was taken and . . .'

Colin grabbed his arm.

'Let them do their job, love. Let them go and find him. Chances are he'll be back before we know it. They'll have a talk to Phillip as well, to see if he knows anything.' Sam nodded. 'I'll go with 'em up to the joinery then I'll come back. It'll take most of the day. Will you be all right here?'

BESSY
THE SEARCH

I remember this part better than any. It's like it was yesterday. I've written exactly what happened to me, nothing more and nothing less. I can only tell you what I know, you'd have to ask the police the rest. I don't mind. Some of it's a bit personal like, but I've just jotted it down how it was.

So. I'd been sitting in the kitchen for four hours, well into teatime, and I'd not put anything on for Colin and Thomas's tea. I just sat there. Smoking and drinking tea until the brown teapot was drained.

The moment the door shut behind Sam and Colin I felt a strange pulling in my insides. It was like all my vital organs were shrinking, and my belly was pulled in. My head went very sharp, like, and all the colours in the room felt brighter.

I thought about sending out my thoughts to wherever Thomas was and asking him to please come home, to not do this to me. And his dad. My self, folding in on me, building a thick, invisible skin over my body, a case that I could stare out of later, one that kept me swimming in my own tears inside it.

By the time the four hours was up, I had realised Thomas wasn't coming back today. One way or another, he was missing.

I tried to think about him being kidnapped, or worse, but the thoughts couldn't crack that shell around me, holding me together.

A panda car arrived at six o'clock, with Sam and Colin in the backseat and two other men in the front. I scanned them for my son but he wasn't one of them. The curtains across the road moved and my neighbours on either side came out to see what the fuss was.

Children from up the street came to see the panda car and soon everyone was interested in the police visit. The only police activity we usually get on Ney Street is Sam Mackie having a quick ciggie up the ginnel, but everyone knew this was serious. These police were from town. Everyone knew it was serious. Everyone could see me and Colin stood outside. So everyone would know it was about our Thomas.

They all came into the house and I looked at Colin. His eyes were red rimmed and he held his cap in front of him. Sam Mackie stood beside him and the other two men pulled up chairs and sat in front of me.

'I'm Inspector Little, Mrs Swain. This is DC MacDonald. We've come to have a little word about Thomas. Just some information about him.'

I started to tell them what had happened the previous morning, the scene well-rehearsed in my head. They wrote everything down in notebooks and nodded. When I'd got to lunchtime today they stopped me.

'Look, Bessy, you said that Thomas had his lunch with him? In his Billy can and box? Corned beef sandwiches and tea?'

I nodded, watching as the other man reached into a bag, and everything goes into slow motion. I could hear the tap in the kitchen dripping and I wanted to go and twist it tight to stop it. My face crumbled into disbelief. DC MacDonald produced

Thomas's can and sandwiches, his lunch that I had put up for him. I stared at them.

'Yes. That's them. Where did you get them?'

They all looked at each other. Inspector Little spoke.

'We found them during a search of the route. They were in a front garden, just over the wall. We think someone could have just dropped them there.'

'Someone?'

'Yes. Either Thomas or someone else.'

I snigger. I can't help it.

'But why would Thomas throw his dinner over a wall?'

'Look, Bessy, we have to investigate everything. He could have gone off somewhere, made a plan, gone off with a friend. In that case he could just walk back in anytime. You know what teenagers are like.'

I stared them out.

'But Thomas isn't like that. He's not that kind of boy. He likes his bed.'

'His dad told us he likes a pint. He can pass for eighteen easy. Some lads just go off, Bessy. Only they know why. Was he worried about National Service or anything?'

We'd never discussed it. We'd known it was coming, next year, but it was just unspoken. I started to worry that I hadn't spoken to him enough about adult things. I knew Colin had told him about the birds and the bees. But I hadn't really talked to him like that. He was still my little boy.

'No. I don't think so. He just wanted to go to work, then come home and have his tea. He's never done anything like this before.'

Colin went into the kitchen to make a pot of tea. I could see his hands shaking as he picked up the teapot. I wanted to touch him, tell him I was scared, but I couldn't. Not with strangers here. Inspector Little carried on.

'Look, Bessy, the other thing we have to consider is that something has happened to Thomas. You know there's been other incidents around here of people going missing, kids and teenagers, and we can't rule out that with Thomas. It's something else we're looking at. But I don't want you to worry. We don't think it's that at the moment. We're thinking he might have just gone on an adventure.'

The casing cracked for a moment and I erupted.

'An adventure? This isn't Boy's bloody Own, you know. It's my son.' Colin rushed over and put his hands on my shoulders. A tear squeezed out of my eye and all the men looked relieved that I was upset, as if that's what should happen next. 'I just want him to come back. I just want him to come back for his tea.' I picked up the tea can that's left on the table as the police filed out of our small living room.

This house used to be my idea of heaven. A manageable little haven for me and my boys, first Colin, then Colin and Thomas. I never wanted any more than this.

The sofa was a bit threadbare, but I always joked that no one could see it with two big men to cover it up. They'd laugh and push each other and rush to sit down when I put the tea out. All shirtsleeves and razor cuts, the two of them.

Now the room looked dark and dingy. It was brown and stained with all the cigarettes we've smoked between us over the years. I didn't mind so much until today, because folk took us as they found us and if they didn't like it they could bugger off.

I'd felt a change, though, because all of a sudden all the neighbours were out and three big police were sitting in my private space, where I didn't put on a show, where my legs were white, my face un-made-up and my long hair uncurled and pinned.

Once they were gone, Colin fiddled in the kitchen for a while, then came in and sat down.

'Do you want some tea, love? You haven't eaten all day.'

I shook my head.

'What'll happen now, Colin? What will they do?'

'They'll make enquiries, love, see if anyone's seen him. I'm going to the Collier's later putting the word out. If anyone sees him local like, maybe in the pub, to tell him to get in touch.' His hand covered mine. 'You know what it's like. Once you do somat wrong, the longer you leave it the harder it is to admit to it. He probably wants to come back, but he feels stupid, or scared.'

I nodded, a fire rising inside me.

'Scared, yeah, and who can blame him. Scared of being battered.'

Colin winced.

'I wondered when you'd bring this up. So it's my fault, is it? My fault for disciplining my own son. Bloody hell, Bess, if it were up to you he'd never be told off. You're too soft with him. If it's anyone's fault, it's yours. Too soft. Lettin' him do what he wants. He's buggered off now, not tellin' us, puttin' us through all this. If you'd . . .'

'But what if he's dead, Col, what if he's been murdered? Who's fault is it then?'

Colin sat down, head in hands.

'I don't know. He's not dead. I know he's not. He's more likely playing stupid teenage games with us.'

'But he's a good lad, Col.'

'He is, but what with all that drinking and that, sounded all right to you when you let him do it, go off and go to the boozer out of town, but when I told the police earlier on they acted like he was a bloody criminal. Askin' me why he goes out of town, who he knows. What he does in his spare time. They'll go and talk to Philip and all them at Stoke's joinery. Point is, Bess, we gave in to him too easy. Scared of another argument so we just let him. To us it made an easy life. Now it makes him look like a bad 'un to the police.'

At least he'd moved on to 'we.' Thomas had told us he was off to the pub on his bike and we had begged him not to, he told us he was playing darts with Philip, that Phil had a girl up that way and they'd all go and have a few pints. We didn't want him going out of town, to Hyde, but he insisted.

We all knew that bad things had been happening round here. It was only recently that we'd had our cellars searched for that poor little girl who'd been snatched from the fairground, and a boy from Ashton Market. We'd told Thomas about them, but he'd been angry that we thought he was a child. He'd said he hated us both and he wanted to get away from us as soon as he could. But I suppose all teenagers say that at one time or another?

Colin had shouted and raised his hand and Thomas had said he was going anyway. That moment between father and son where there has to be a compromise because both are men. No doubt he'd filled the police in on the arguments. Colin likes the truth and he likes to blame.

Everything had to be someone else's fault; he found it hard to admit anything he did was wrong. Stupid pride, really, but on the other hand, he didn't do a lot wrong. His main fault was saying too much. He would have chatted to the police all the time, telling them that Thomas said he hated us, making it bigger than it was.

Making them think that this was some teenage tantrum where Thomas had drunk himself into a stupor and was lying somewhere, scared to come home, with a hangover.

Problem is, if I know Thomas, he would never throw his dinner over a wall. Teenagers do some funny things, but that can was his granddad's, and he loved his granddad more than anything.

I know it's a trivial thing, but it's things like that you cling to. All through the police search for Thomas, I held onto this thought, secretly thinking them stupid to keep telling me that he had just gone off and would soon be back.

Whoever had him had thrown his dinner over that wall. I'd sit there and listen to the almost daily at first, then weekly, police reports and know inside that Thomas would never do that to me, or his granddad. Or, I admitted grudgingly, Colin. They'd never seen us together, as a family. They could never know how close we were.

Eventually, after a few months, Inspector Little stood in my lounge and outlined the case they had put together. Me and Colin were there, and Colin's mum. A group of neighbours had gathered outside to try to hear what had happened.

'Right then. We've put together a case and here it is. This is what we've come up with and this is how we'll be directing the investigation from now on. We've spoken to Thomas's parents and they've told us that there were some arguments and unpleasantness in the weeks before Thomas left.'

He looked over my head, but I looked at his eyes.

'We've also spoken to his friend, Philip, and he told us that Thomas had been planning to get his own place when he's finished his Service. We've found no evidence of an abduction, or of any violence. We've found no evidence that Thomas has come to any harm. Therefore, we'll be focussing our attention on a missing person's enquiry from now on. The enquiry will be scaled down and I'll appoint an officer at the local station as a point of contact. Is everybody clear?'

We all nodded, but I couldn't not speak up.

'What about the can? He wouldn't do that.'

Inspector Little sighed. He looked tired, his skin worn and thin.

'Bessy, I've told you before, we don't always know what our

children are thinking. We think we do, but time after time we find that we don't.'

I nodded.

'Mmm. But what about that little girl who went missing? Ten, wasn't she? And that lad off Ashton Market? Have they left home, looking for a place of their own? What's happened to them?'

Inspector Little shifted from foot to foot.

'Well, that's a bit different, isn't it? They've just disappeared. Not the same at all, at that age they don't know their own mind. But your Thomas is older and we seriously think he's just gone and set himself up somewhere. And usually, when that happens, they reappear at some point. It's not the same, Bessy.'

I looked at the floor. I still couldn't see the difference. Thomas had disappeared just like the other children. He wouldn't just leave me and throw his can over the wall. I knew that boy inside out, and I knew he had a good heart.

Even if he had gone off, he would have come back by now because somewhere inside he would want his mum. He would care about what I felt—every time we'd rowed he'd apologised. I knew he would be feeling bad inside. Nothing would be right until he made up with me and Colin. He just wouldn't stay away so long. It'd been months now.

BESSY

THE BODIES

Now I'm up to this bit and it's not very nice. I know someone will have to read this, so I'm just warning you. It's not very nice for people to read, and I think we all know what happened, don't we, what with those books that've been written? Go into too much detail, I think.

Anyway, I'd been going about my daily business, making the beds, laying the table, making the dinner and the tea. Washing, ironing, watching the telly, waiting for Colin to come home, then waiting for him to go out so I can be on my own.

I was still making enough food for three, just in case he came back. He'd been gone a year by this time: Christmas, Mother's Day, Thomas's eighteenth birthday. I'd bought him a card for Christmas and his birthday, you know, just in case. I've still got them all here in the drawer, cards for every year. But nothing from him.

I was convinced that if he was still alive, he would have sent me a card on Mother's Day, and I got out every card he had made me over the years, as if this made me into some kind of mother whose son wouldn't disappear—a good parent.

I knew people were saying things about me, 'she must have

been a bad mother for her own son to up and go like that' and 'well, who can blame him, look at her windows.' I'd never been a very good housewife, but somehow now it seemed the dirt on my windows was in some way connected to my son being a 'missing person.'

I'd kept his room the same, his posters up, and all his football things in his drawers. The police had been through it, but I just put it back exactly the same as before. I still washed his bedclothes every week, with ours. Set him a place at the table, and I could see Colin's face tighten when he saw me put the knife and fork down carefully.

'Come on, Bess, he's not a bloody saint. You can't do this all the time. You're going to have to get used to it, you know.'

Usually I just nodded. There was no point talking to him anymore because he didn't understand what I was saying. We'd start a conversation about Thomas and I'd tell him how I was feeling. He'd get a funny look on his face and he'd sort of close down, blank over, until I'd finished talking.

It was a look of dread, sort of pain. At first I thought it was because he was feeling the same as me, but later he told me it was because he was bored with it. Bored with hearing about our son, who we didn't know if he was alive or dead. Bored.

Anyway, this particular day I'd caught the bus down to the market. I'd been sitting thinking in the morning about how happy I'd been the day Thomas went missing. How I'd been laughing really loudly.

I'd jumped up and looked in the mirror to see if the crow's feet were still there. Sure enough, they were, but slightly faded. I was aging backward! My mouth had turned upward slightly, as if, for the first time in a year I might smile.

The hard, invisible casing stopped it, tightening up around me, forcing me back into the prison of my own horrible mind, where Thomas was dead in a ditch somewhere, but no one else believed it.

I'd spoken to Florrie Taylor, who'd asked outright on the bus if we'd heard anything.

'So have the police come up with owt?'

Her ferrety face was poking toward me and I reddened.

'Not yet. No.'

I was expecting the usual 'Oh, he'll turn up when he's hungry' or 'bake him a cake, he'll be back.' The sort of cheery things people who have never lost a child say.

'Mmm. Bad business this. They say another child's gone missing as well. And a girl. They're linking it now. The four of them from round 'ere.'

It was horrific, but music to my ears as well. I stared out of the bus window at a flock of starlings swirling above the church spire, thousands of little birds, all gathering together to make a big black cloud. Thicker and thicker until it disappeared over the hill, then I saw them again over the bus station as the bus pulled in.

They were early that year; the beginning of October is very early for starlings. It was a kind of Indian Summer; the blue sky, but nippy outside, you still needed your big coat and some gloves. I waited until everyone was off the bus and watched the birds soar, a stray couple of them shooting off behind the market clock. Then they crowded together and made different shapes.

Me and Thomas used to lie in the grass at Daisy Nook, just watching them for ages. From being a small boy I'd take him paddling in the shallow brook, then we'd dry our feet and lie down staring at the autumn sky, waiting for birds. Thomas would easily see shapes in clouds, it would take me a bit longer to shake off my duty in my mind and let my imagination come through the holes, like water through a colander. I'd eventually see them and he'd shout, 'It's a rabbit, silly!' or 'Goose, goose!'

Everyone was off the bus now and I still looked at the birds. I wondered if Thomas is somewhere watching them, perhaps just beyond the market. I often stood at the back door in the dark, wearing just a nylon underslip, my hair loose and long down my back, and felt the most free I could under the circumstances.

Like a girl again, except for the lack of any emotions, or love. I'd stand at the door smoking Park Drives and staring at the sky, mine and Thomas's sky, because everywhere he goes he couldn't help but see the moon, the same moon I was seeing now, and that was our link.

Whatever had happened to him, he had to see the sky and think of his mum. Was that too much to ask? I knew him. If he was alive, he would think of his mum.

I dragged my body off the bus, my mind returning from the birds to Florrie Taylor. Four children disappeared, all linked? I desperately needed to talk to Inspector Little. Walking over to the police station took ten minutes, across the market square and through the Victorian Market Hall. Lots of people said. 'Aya, Bessy' but I was in a hurry.

I practically ran the last few hundred yards, and pushed the door dramatically. The counter bobby looked up from his paper.

'Eyup, Bessy, what can we do for you?'

'Can I talk to Ken Little?'

He folded his *Daily Mirror* in half and I sat on the wooden bench opposite. I could see PC Dodds—Lennie to me and Colin —talking and smiling.

'He's gone out on an investigation down Hattersley. Won't be back anytime soon, love. Welcome to wait if you want.'

I stared at him.

'What's happening in Hattersley? It's not Ken's part is it? I mean, doesn't he do Ashton?'

'Yep. But somat big's happened. Don't know what. They've

all trooped down there. No idea what it is. Do you want a cup of tea, Bessy, love?'

I turned and walked out. Colin's told me I've got an overactive imagination, and now I'm thinking all sorts. If there's four gone missing, maybe there's five? Or ten? Maybe Thomas is one of them? Who'd do that to kiddies? Leading onto the obvious conclusion of 'and where are they now?'

I walked back into the sunlight again, my eyes narrowing. I was kind of glad Ken Little wasn't there, otherwise I'd have had to repeat the demand I had made almost every day since Thomas went missing; that they treat this as a murder investigation. I knew I was pushing him to his limit, because he'd shouted at me more than once.

'There's no body, Bess. No body.'

I'd carried on even though I could see a huge vein in his forehead throbbing, always a danger sign when my dad was going to belt us.

'But what do you think, Ken? What do you think? Do you really think he's just gone off? Do you? Hmm?'

'It doesn't matter what I think, Bessy, love. It's the evidence. My boss won't let me go and dig next door's garden up on hearsay. Or arrest everyone who was on Ney Street that day. This isn't Cluedo, it's real life. I need some evidence. And all the evidence we have points to Thomas being a restless teenager who likes a pint and was after the lasses. I can't say why he did what he did to you and Colin, but we can't investigate a murder on the basis of that, can we?'

It was the same old story. And I had to admit I was backing my odds both ways, or else why would I bother setting the table for him every night? So I wandered out of the police station and I slipped back into my usual shopping routine.

Because that's what it's like, two lives running together, side by side. The life you have from day to day, where you have to cook and clean and wash and iron and go on the market, and the one where your son is gone, and you constantly wonder where he is and what he's doing, hoping he's not dead and if he is, that he didn't suffer. Then dying a little bit yourself because you couldn't be there with him to save him, or at the end. Was he shouting for his mum?

Then you remember that might not be the case, and he is shacked up with a girl somewhere, using another name, and you get angry because how could he do this to you?

Then there were the times I thought I'd seen him. Everywhere I went. I'd thought I'd seen him lots of times, on buses going the other way and in cars. Even in peoples' houses, I'd stared through the windows to get a better look, and people had drawn their curtains when they saw me.

I was quite used to it now, the enquiring looks from strangers, the pity. I just couldn't help it. One thing I had done was to start to look for smaller signs it might be him. He had a mole on his forehead, on the left-hand side, and a small scar on his chin. I usually tried to check for these as well as the obvious height and hair colour, but it wasn't always possible.

I bought some carrots and shin beef, and wandered back to the bus station, nodding at people I knew and, hopefully, appearing normal. Whatever that was. Ashton was a funny place back then. You'd hear the Beatles 'Help' on the radio on the market stalls, and duck beneath the swathes of net curtains that blew about in the wind.

Old men would sit on the wooden benches smoking dog ends and whistling in the sunshine. They really did wear flat caps, and some of them did have whippets. Funny now, because that's what the North is known for these days, what with Coronation Street and Andy Capp, but back then it really was like that.

Women in rain Macs and headscarves tied around their

chins would congregate outside the Town Hall and chatter, exchanging the news of the day before rushing off to spread the word. Not many of us had telephones, because we didn't need them. Our system, the Market Telegraph, was faster and more efficient than any telephone.

I saw them that day out of the corner of my eye, about ten women huddled together, listening intently to the storyteller, spellbound as they committed the details to memory. They reminded me of a group of sparrows that visited my yard to grab at the crumbs then carry them off.

I hurried over, wondering what they were chewing over today, whose life they were dissecting. The etiquette was that a newcomer to the group would touch an elbow and space would be made at the back of the group. A loud cough would tell the group that someone had more recent details than the story being told.

I approached and touched Alice Smith's elbow and she turned, her face ashen. Her blue eyes widened and she shouted loudly:

'Bessy. It's Bessy. She's here.'

Etiquette was ignored and I was hustled to the front of the group, where Ettie Groves was standing silently. The whole market became silent and I felt like a spotlight was shining on me. I hadn't felt like this since I got stage fright in the school play, and that had been stopped by an air raid warning.

I looked up at the Market Hall tower, at the huge clock. It was coming up to three and I should really be at home making Colin's tea. Ettie started to speak.

'Look, love, I don't know how to put this, but a body's been found in Hattersley. A boy, seventeen. In a house up there.'

I stared at her.

'Well, it can't be Thomas. He's eighteen. Eighteen.'

Handkerchiefs were raised to mouths and the tears began. A

woman's hand rested on my shoulder and I was guided toward a bench, where three old men moved to let me sit down.

'We thought it was best that you knew as soon as possible. I was sending Alice to tell you. Sally Jones saw the panda cars outside the house and someone said a bloke had been arrested and took away.'

I sat and tried to take the information in.

'I'd better go home and see to Colin. He'll have heard by now. I'd better go home.'

I stood up and walked to the bus stop, Alice and Ettie flanking me, and the other women looking on, their heads bowed and tears flowing. We got on the first number nine bus and sat down. I stared at the seat in front of me, my mind a funny mixture of dread and pain, stopping me thinking about any details. I wondered if Colin was in, if he'd been sent home from work.

We got off at the stop at the end of my road, and I expected to see a panda car outside my house, the kids climbing on it and the neighbours out. But the street was deserted. I opened the front door and the house was empty.

'Colin? Colin?'

I turned to Ettie and Alice.

'You can go now, I'll be all right.'

Alice shook her head.

'No. I'll wait with you till Colin gets home. I'll make a pot of tea.'

I didn't argue. What would be the point? I'd lost control over every piece of my life. And I suppose they were supporting me, in their own way. I'd no idea where my son was, whether he was dead or alive. Me and Colin hardly spoke, and he slept in the small bedroom on his own.

My parents lived away and never came to see me, and I had no brothers or sisters. Colin's mother clearly thought Thomas going away was my fault; they had convened a little blame club where they would huddle together and talk about what a bad mother I was. I had no friends, except these women who alternated between gossip and hand-holding. Thomas and Colin had been my life.

The next layer of people I knew were women like Ettie and Alice, not quite friends, and dreadful gossips. So, all in all, I had not a soul to talk to. No one at all. When you're in that position, and lots of people think they know better than you, you have no choice but to keep it inside yourself, build the shell even stronger, and just keep hoping.

We sat and had a cup of tea, Ettie and Alice trying to start a conversation and me knowing whatever I said would be on the market in the next few hours. They meant well, but I said very little. I just waited and sipped my tea. Eventually, Colin burst in.

'Is it him? Is it, Bessy? Is it? What've they said?' Alice and Ettie jumped when he shouted, but I was used to it. He often turned nasty these days and I didn't turn a hair. 'Come on, you two, out. You're like bleedin' vultures, waiting for the bloody prey so you can go and gossip it. Out!'

They scuttled away and onto the street and he slammed the door.

'Well?'

I looked at the floor.

'I don't know, Colin. I only just found out about it.'

He came closer, so close that I could feel his spittle on my cheek.

'Don't know? But I thought you knew bloody everything? More than me and me mam, eh?'

It was the usual argument, but I couldn't believe he would do this now.

'It's not the time for this, Colin. We just need to find out if that dead lad is our Thomas. Then we'll decide what to do.'

He pushed his hands in his pockets, like he did when he felt like he was going to hit me. I could see it in his face. I suppose he needed someone to blame, and I was here, completely alone, his best option.

'Do? What do you mean?'

'Let's just see if it's Thomas.'

CHAPTER FOUR

I'd fallen asleep reading the first part of Bessy's story. My imagination had gone off on a tangent that was familiar these days, one that stretched away from logic and common sense into the unknown.

What were the chances of me finding Bessy's notebook, with her son missing as well? What were the odds of that? It seems like a coincidence on the surface, something freaky that I could dwell on and wonder about. But underneath it isn't, and logic kicks in. There's a common denominator, and it's Connelly.

This is why I'm so sure that he has Aiden. I don't know what it means, but I hold it in my mind as I become more drowsy. Then, as I finally teeter on the edge of sleep, I realise that all this happened five decades ago and anyone could have found the letters. Anyone to do with Connelly because, after all, he owned this house.

I'd followed up a tentative lead and got a result. Not a coincidence at all, a link in a place where no one else was looking. Bessy must have known that someone would have found the book after she had gone. Someone who found out about the box upstairs and its contents.

But lots of people have missing relatives. Don't they? Yet I've been in the police long enough to know that somewhere in this fucked-up mess there's a link. Estranged. That was the final word as I fell into a deep sleep.

Now I'm in the car, ready to drive to Coal Pit Lane to meet Mike. I want to read more of Bessy's notebook, but I don't have time. I've been on autopilot this morning, with Percy winding through my legs as I tried to make coffee, and now I can hear him meowing. I could have sworn he was in the house on Aiden's bed. I look in the rearview mirror, but there's no sign of him so I set off.

Mike had texted to say he was going to be late, and I was glad of the leeway. Bessy's story had made me feel less alone. Harrowing though it must have been for her, at least it showed that something was eventually done about her case.

The Moors Murders. I'd policed this area long enough to know that they were what she was caught up in. Famous worldwide, any discussions always came with the qualification that cases like this were few and far between, that serial killers didn't crop up that often, and that children were relatively safe.

This is what I had believed until Aiden disappeared. Even with my privileged knowledge, that people were possibly less safe than they thought, and a keen eye for how rife crime actually was, I'd still believed my son was safe. At fifteen, wasn't it fine to let him go out with friends, travel alone across town to his father's flat?

It had been six weeks now, and Bessy's story made me realise that I had never actually checked the crime stats on missing children. Boys. Normally, that would be the first thing I'd do, to see how unusual a case was, who were the usual suspects, what it had in common with other cases.

But I hadn't done it. Not yet. I hadn't done it partly because I was still in shock and partly because, if I'm honest, even I made the assumption that the crime stats around teenage boys were correct. That stereotype of missing boys being from rough homes, running away from trouble to trouble. I hadn't bothered because I thought my son was different. But what if he was the same? A seed grows in my mind and I store it for later.

I spot Mike's car parked up on Coal Pit Lane. I lock up my car and jump into his.

'Mornin'. How's tricks?'

He looks tired.

'OK. You know. Onward and upward.'

He nods. He's not looking at me, a sure sign that he's about to tell me whatever's on his mind. I've known him long enough to be able to read his expressions.

'Yeah. Look. I need to say this before we embark on Prophesy.'

I snigger.

'Embark? Christ. Bit formal.'

'Yeah. Thing is, you've been acting a bit, erm, strange. I just want to know you're up to it. You know I've got your back one hundred percent. Problem is, this could get heavy and I need you to be on the ball. Otherwise . . .'

'What? Otherwise what? And I can't see that I've been any stranger than anyone else who's kid has gone missing. I'm fucking worried. Just think if it was one of yours.'

I see him flinch and I know this isn't fair. He's my best friend and I've hit below the belt.

'It isn't though, is it? D'you think you should have some time off? You know, to think and get over it.'

'You're acting like he's dead.'

Silence. Then he shakes his head.

'Truth is, I don't know if he is or not. Neither do you. But try looking at it from the point of view of someone on the outside. Fifteen-year-old boy, hormones, broken home, mum at work, dad, well, you'd be the first one to admit Sal's not the calmest person. Wouldn't your first thought be that he'd ran? Honestly, wouldn't it? I know it's not easy, but all this stuff about Connelly, you've got no proof.'

I nod.

'Yes. But two things. One, he wouldn't run. He doesn't know anyone. None of his friends are hiding him. He spends all his time with Sal when he's not with me. Two. What about the threats from Connelly? If we're looking at evidence . . .'

He shakes his head.

'Yeah. But didn't we all get them at some time? I got dog shit wiped across my windscreen. Jenny Smith got a voodoo doll. Load of others got other stuff. But only yours came true? Why you, Jan? Why you?'

I can feel the tears prick my eyes. He doesn't believe me. Mike doesn't believe me.

'Why anyone? What makes someone a victim of crime? Isn't it random and never their own fault?' I picture Bessy and Colin waiting for news on Thomas. 'What about them kiddies killed in the Moors Murders? Why them? Why their parents? Do you know that there are missing teenagers from around that time whose cases have never been solved? Why them too?'

He starts the engine. Then he turns to look at me.

'I don't know. And for the record, I can totally see your side of it and why you think fucking Connelly might have done this. I've sent my kids to my mum's on the strength of it, you know, just in case. It's not that. I've got a family, and I need my job. I need to stay alive too. So this isn't about believing you, it's about you being able to do your job and keep my back. I've got yours. Get a grip back on mine.' He takes my hand. 'I'm doing this because I love you, you know, as a mate, like. But I do know this.

One false move on this one and I'll have to think about going to Stewart. I don't want to, but I don't want either of us coppin' for it either. Sorry, but you need to be on the ball.'

I nod.

'Fine. Don't worry, I'll make sure I keep it under. After all, it's my problem, isn't it? Why should anyone else give a shit?'

'I'm not saying that. But there's a time and a place. People are starting to talk. It's like everything is centred on Aiden, like that's the most important part of the case, when we don't have any evidence at all that it's anything to do with Connelly. We do know he's importing and distributing drugs. We just don't know where he keeps them. We do know he's supplying prostitutes. We just don't know how he's doing it. We do know that he's got a string of associated businesses involved probably through a protection racket. We just don't know how. We have evidence for all those things. What we need to do now is find out more about them.'

We're stopped at traffic lights and he looks at me. 'Look. I'm not saying don't talk about it. God knows, we've worked together long enough. Like I said, you're my mate. But please drop this connection for now. Wait until we do catch whoever is running the crime on Northlands. Like Jim said, it might not be Connelly. It might be Brian Jameson from out of town. He's been seen there a couple of times. You've no proof. All the checks were carried out, all the procedures followed. Banks checked, school and friends interviewed. Maybe you should do the TV appeal now?'

The TV appeal. We hadn't done it at the beginning, as I'd point blank refused. Sal thought it would help. He wanted to get everything done as soon as possible. Even after three days, he was thinking Aiden had run away. Coming round to the idea.

I'd seen Sal's statement, that Aiden had taken his passport and bank card, but left a rucksack with some clothes in it.

Uniformed had been round and searched Sal's flat half-heartedly. They had filed a report saying that he had 'gone out prepared.'

When I queried this, they queried why a fifteen-year-old would have taken his passport, if he had just nipped round the corner to a mate's? It's not a normal thing to do, they said. And it planted a seed of doubt in my mind.

Maybe they were right. Maybe I was a complete bitch of a bad mother and he had run away. I wondered if it was the biannual foreign holidays, or the expensive trainers that had done it? Or maybe the entertainment system he demanded for his room? Sal dutifully reminded me that 'stuff' couldn't make up for a mother's love, and wondered out loud if I had maybe loved my job a little too much.

But even then I knew that Aiden hadn't run away. He'd never make himself suffer like that. He couldn't live on the streets or in a squat. He couldn't last five minutes. Also, he loved me. Underneath the bravado, the toughness, the black looks, and tantrums, he still loved his mum.

His goodnight hug was firm, and he sometimes slipped his arm around my shoulder. Taller than me at five-ten, he would tilt his head until his cheek rested on my hair. Only when no one was around, in the queue for the chip shop, or sometimes at the cinema. I could hear his heart beating. I knew that deep down he was a caring boy who wouldn't hurt me. Or Sal. He wouldn't.

A tear trickles down my cheek and I wipe it away before Mike can see it. Maybe the TV appeal would work. If he was out there, and he saw it, maybe it would melt his heart. I text Sal, who will be pleased that I'm giving in to his constant nagging.

Mike was driving toward Old Mill, where we would spend the morning on observations. Photographing people coming in and out, registrations of goods wagons, cars, that sort of thing. This afternoon we'd go back to the ops room and report the information and pull out the best leads for ourselves.

I had to do it. I still needed to survive. It's a catch-22. You feel like you're dying inside yet you have to appear normal outside. I thought it was bad when my mother died, shortly followed by my father. I felt like I was going mad and took two weeks off, which made it worse as I had to sit at home under Sal's daytime television regime.

It was school holidays, and he insisted that Aiden shouldn't go to the childminder because I was home. I explained that I was sick, needed time alone and he told me I was selfish. All three of us spent a full two weeks curled up on a sofa, watching *Midsummer Murders* and *Catch Phrase*, and a cacophony of children's cartoons.

Sal and Aiden loved it, but I swung between worrying about work and wanting to scream and cry for my dead parents. When I returned to work, I was in worse shape than before my time off, but managed to hide it and gradually recover. Not this time.

My anger is seeping out of every pore, and as we park up at the end of Nelson Lane, where the Old Mill stands, I'm shaking.

Mike gets out the camera and the iPad. I usually take the notes, verify times and registrations. There's an embarrassing silence between us and it makes things much harder than usual because I know Mike really does care about me. Sometimes I catch him looking sideways at me, making sure I am all right.

Container vehicles are queued up outside Connelly's mill by eleven thirty, a backlog of unloading clearly holding them up. Several drivers have gotten out of their cabs and are drinking tea and coffee at a nearby portable food cabin.

With no words needed, we get out and sit on rickety white

plastic chairs. We're often undercover together and it just comes naturally now. Mike gets the drinks. I set up the conversation. I quickly get into role. I should have been an actress.

'Is it that one over there, love?'

Mike nods and stirs his tea.

'I think so.' He turns to the driver nearest to him. 'Is that the kitchen place, mate? We're from Manchester. Don't know the area.'

He turns around and smiles. His colleague also takes an interest.

'Yep. That's it. Connelly's Kitchens. Good stuff too. But you usually order online. Not sure they have a shop here. Mainly supply trade, I think.'

I sigh.

'Wasted journey then. Bloody hell. Might as well finish my tea.'

Mike goes in for the kill.

'Where you from then? Local or . . .'

The driver nods.

'Liverpool. Bringing this stuff straight from the dock. I'm freelance, pick up consignments that have been delivered. Easy money.'

His friend obliges.

'Me too. Thing is, if you work for someone you have a wage. In this game, you can charge what you want as long as you get the stuff to them quick.'

Mike frowns.

'Right. I might be interested in that myself. Need a license, do you, or what, a special driving permit?'

The second man leans forward.

'What you doing now, mate?'

'Just been laid off.' I follow their gaze to our VW Golf. 'Proper in the shit, I am, debts everywhere. On top of that, our kitchen's had it. Had to have a damp ceiling ripped out along with all the fittings and we're managing with a camping stove. Using all our savings on the car and the kitchen.'

The driver taps his chin.

'I might be able to help you out, pal. I might need some help unloading and loading at the dock. Can you get there early? Start in a couple of days? Temp, like, but it might help?'

Mike's nodding enthusiastically. 'That'd be great. How can I get in touch with you?'

They both produce business cards. Mike pockets them and we get up.

'I'll ring you then, tomorrow. That'd be brilliant, mate.'

I move closer to them.

'I can't thank you enough. He's been out of his mind with worry. And boredom. There's only so much Jeremy Kyle you can watch.'

We walk away and get back in the car. Mike's happy again now.

'Result. I'll get clearance for that and you can carry on with this obs on your own. OK?'

I nod.

'Good work. You should get something from that.'

He's more serious now.

'Although I don't think you should do the TV thing now. They've just clocked you and they'd recognize you.'

I sigh.

'Shit. I've texted Sal now and he's probably arranged it. He'll just have to do it on his own.'

He shrugs.

'Or you could dye your hair and wear glasses or something. Might help with Hurricane, anyway. If you're right about the threats, a change of appearance wouldn't hurt would it, not with you on obs?'

He drops me off at my car and speeds off into the distance. He's going back to the station to get the OK on taking the job. I can imagine him, all excited and enthusiastic. That's what we live for in this job, a productive lead that can get you right into the centre of the action. In this case, not too close, because all Connelly's cronies know us from last time.

I tap my fingers on the steering wheel. It would have been much better if Stewart had replaced us all. He's brought in some new people, mostly the girls who would infiltrate the prostitute ring and some men who would go undercover on the drugs. But we were still here, the old faithful, on the observation jobs. It's probably just as well really.

I wonder if Mike's right and I should be off sick. But if I sign off I'm out of touch with Connelly and I'm still sure that it's him who's taken Aiden. I look at Old Mill, a dark monster in the distance, and wonder if Aiden's in there somewhere, whether they're keeping him tied up. Is he cold? Has he got enough to eat? Does he miss me?

It's happening again. It's like something is punching through everyday life to remind me that I have serious problems underneath. I wipe my eyes and look in my rearview mirror.

Just as I pull off I see it. A small bundle of fur, tied with blue garden string to my back bumper. I jump out and run around to the back of my car. I know before I get there that it's Percy.

He's mangled and his back legs are twisted, and covered in dust and blood. I pick him up hoping that he's still alive, but, of course, he's cold and dead. Oh my God. My poor cat. My little friend. All I really have left. I wrap him in an old fleece I have in the boot and lodge him behind the spare wheel. I get back in the car and turn the key, checking myself for the panic or fear that I felt at Bessy's. There is none. Only a droning determination and a deep anger.

It's happening again. Just like last time, and on the first day of the operation. Someone is out to get me. Us. Probably already got Aiden. Is that what this is about? Take Aiden to get at me? So it is my fault? I'm always like this when I feel guilty. Always working the blame round to myself. That way I can reconcile the hurt and the emptiness.

I turn right and see the black BMW pull up behind me, bumper to bumper. Probably one of Connelly's men. I take the registration number and commit it to memory. Just in case. I drive back to the station, slowly, intentionally trying to catch the driver's eye in my mirror. That's the sort of woman I am. Straightforward. I don't hold with secrecy or beating around the bush. When I'm pissed off everyone knows it.

As I cross the security gate and the BMW slopes slowly by, I stare at the man behind the wheel. Then I take Percy out of the boot of my car, cradling him gently, and carry him into the operations room. I march into Jim Stewart's office.

'Exhibit A in this operation's payback. My dead cat. It was tied to the back bumper of my car when I was on obs with Mike.'

The operations room is perfectly quiet. Jim nods.

'Sorry, Jan. That's awful. Let's log it.' It wasn't the response I was expecting. He fetches an incident report form from his filing cabinet and writes the detail at the top. 'So the cat was alive and well when you left this morning?' I get a mental picture of Aiden, age eight, opening the box containing baby Percy. The delight on his face.

'Yes. Alive this morning. Fed him just before I went to work.'

Jim looks up.

'Did you let the cat out?'

I sigh.

'No. We don't have a cat flap. He was in the house last time I saw him. On Aiden's bed.'

I feel a lump in my throat. Percy. Didn't I hear him just before I left? But how could I have? He had definitely been in the house last time I saw him. Jim continues.

'Have you been home?'

I shake my head.

'No.'

'OK. Come on then. I'll come with you, and a couple of uniformed. It'll give me a chance to have a chat with you.'

He picks up the phone and arranges for the dog handlers to come and get Percy. We walk through the car park to my car.

'They'll have him cremated and you can decide if you want the ashes or anything.'

I nod. 'Mmm. Yes. You seem like quite an expert.'

He laughs. 'Long service record. Two dogs and three cats gone. No children as yet.' He stops dead. 'That's what I wanted to talk to you about. And why I'm coming with you. A body's been found, up at the Clough. Yesterday. A young man.'

I turn to look at him.

'Is it . . .'

'We don't know. He had no ID on him. He was naked when he was found.'

I nod slowly.

'OK. Let's go. But you'd better drive.'

CHAPTER FIVE

I can't breathe. I've seen dead people before, but none of them are potentially my son. Jim Stewart's talking to a uniformed officer I don't recognise up the corridor.

I know what happens here. It's one of the few things that scares me. I'm fairly used to seeing dead bodies in morgues. Desensitized, maybe. But post-mortems, autopsies, somehow they're so final.

The body dissected, organs removed, clinically weighted, all the bits counted, then put back in the container, inside the skin and muscle, disconnected. I've looked at bodies after autopsy. I looked at my mother and wondered where the person has gone. Where the soul is. Was. Jim comes back and sits down.

'We've tried to get hold of your husband, but he's not answering.'

'Ex-husband.'

Let's get that straight at least. Ex-husband.

'Yes, of course.'

Jim's reverted to the corpse-side manner we reserve for relatives. He's lowered his eyes and he's sighing.

'You don't have to do that with me. You know. The stance.'

He smiles a little.

'Ah, but I do. I like to do things by the book, me. Straightforward. And you'd be wise to do that too. You're not doing yourself any favours.'

I don't look at him.

'I wasn't trying to do myself any favours. I was trying to find my son. Following up leads. Like I do every day.'

The door opposite opens and John Stafford, the guy who runs the mortuary, shakes our hands.

'OK. We're ready. So. Where's the family member? You know, for the ID?'

We all look at each other for a few seconds. No one wants to say it. It's suddenly unspeakable. Eventually Jim manages it.

'Jan here is going to ID. Jan's son has been reported missing. So if we can just get on with it.'

I've been in the room before, many times, with other people who need to have some closure. I'd like to think that these incidents, where people die in solitary circumstances and need identifying, are few and far between. I'm thinking just now that, in fact, they are quite frequent. More than you would expect.

Mums, dads, sisters, brothers, all here to witness someone's disappearance from the world. Never to be seen again. This is the last place before the post-mortem or autopsy. The last farewell.

John's touching the white sheet. I can see the outline of a face, nose sticking out. Further down, shoulder blades before the sheet becomes thicker and turns into a thick shroud. I realise that John is staring at me and I nod.

I can't tell at first. I can't see properly. Maybe it's the shock. I have to move forward and look closely. Brown hair, white skin, more pallid than death, long eyelashes. Eyes closed.

I remember the day Aiden was born, the day I counted his amazing fingers and toes, checked his body for completeness.

He had a small red birthmark just under his earlobe. Funny. I didn't mention that in any of the reports I gave. I check the earlobes. It's not him.

I start laughing loudly. I bend over double and rest my hands on my knees.

'It's not him. No. It's not Aiden.'

John covers the boy up again and we leave. Jim waits until we get to the car before he speaks.

'You shouldn't have started laughing. It's disrespectful.'

I lean on my car. I stopped smoking a long time ago, but now I really need a cigarette.

'You know, that's the second dead body I've seen in two days. I don't wish anyone else dead, or this feeling on anyone else. But believe me, I'm celebrating.' I breathe in deeply. 'But then again, I'm not. Because if he's not dead, he's out there somewhere, being kept prisoner against his will, isn't he?'

Jim shakes his head.

'Or tripping the light fantastic with a glow stick in each hand. You don't know where he is. For all you know he could have skipped the country and is working in Ibiza. You think you know these kids, but you never do. Not entirely. You know the drill. My boy would never do that, my daughter would never do that. Parent's natural instinct to protect their offspring. But most of the time they're thinking with their hormones and they turn up months later pregnant or skint.'

I nod.

'Yeah. I did think about that. The only flaw in your argument is that corpse in there. He's someone's son. Have there been any missing reports recently? Or have you just written them off as runaways? He's not pregnant or skint, Jim. He's dead.'

I drive him back to the station, then go home. Uniformed are there, waiting in a car for me. Sheila Lewis meets me.

'Must have got in through the back window. It's been forced. Fucking Connelly, I bet. This is the second today.'

I nod. At least it's not just me who thinks Connelly shouldn't be knighted in next year's honours.

'Oh. Right. And the other one?'

'Didn't you hear? Jim Stewart's car was covered in human shit. Covered. His wife must have run him to work, then she left it in the drive. When she went out to get it, it was dark and she even leaned against it. She's hysterical. Not as bad as your cat though. Sorry, Jan, that's horrible.'

I stare at her. She's sorry about my cat. What about my son?

'Thanks, Sheila.'

She shifts from one foot to the other.

'Erm, we've been posted outside here tonight. Can we make some hot chocolate? We're bloody freezing.'

I smile at her. I used to do her job.

'Course. Look, why don't you come in and stay in the lounge. I'll only be upstairs. Better than sitting in a cramped car all night, yes?'

She nods and signals to her colleague. They settle in the lounge, sipping hot chocolate and watching Sky Movies. I go to bed and sleep for twelve hours solid.

When I come downstairs in the morning the two women are asleep on the sofa. They stir and then sit bolt upright.

'It's OK, ladies, I'm still alive. No thanks to you two.'

Sheila picks up a stray biscuit.

'We must have dropped off. The *Matrix* trilogy was on back to back and it was just too good to resist.'

I make tea and toast. It's good to cook for someone again and I overdo it slightly. Then a joiner arrives to fix the window and I offer him some.

Mike calls to tell me that he's been cleared for the job and that he'll keep me updated and feed-back any info for me to record. I tell him I'm doing the TV appeal and he just sighs and tells me to be careful.

I guess he's heard about Percy. I look at Percy's dish. This house doesn't feel like mine anymore.

'Look, you stay as long as you like, until your shift finishes. I've got to be somewhere.'

Sheila takes another piece of toast.

'Oh. You sure? To be fair, we'll probably be more of a deterrent from in here.'

I text Sal to tell him that I'll pick him up. So I drive over to his flat. Unlike most people, who listen to music when they're driving, or sing along, or even learn a language, I'm still working.

I was trained at the start of my career to keep my eyes and ears open for everything. Early on, I thought that 'everything' meant the ever more intrusive CCTV cameras and mobile phone masts. The shop CCTV and the people who stand on street corners every day and know the area intimately; newspaper stands, prostitutes, paperboys, milkmen. That sort of thing.

I thought I had it sussed. But then, when it became a little bit boring and predictable, just when I thought there was nothing left to learn, I realised that the world was full of silent messages and signs. The kind of thing that was shared between a group of people, a kind of code.

They're everywhere. In graffiti, in music, even unintentionally, the clothes people wear and how they decorate their houses. Everywhere. So, when I first saw the various items hanging on the telephone wires—the shoes, the scarves, the sweaters, and hats—I thought they were just some kind of tribal decoration. Little did I know, back then.

I see them now, hanging in the backstreets, a pair of high heels marking off the working girls' territory. Stray beyond that boundary and you're strung up. Silent messages, an entry point to an unknown world. Usually a criminal world. You have to be in it to read it.

Reading the messages passes the time on the short drive to Sal's. He hasn't replied by the time I've got to his flat about two miles away, so I park and skip up the steps at the front. Someone's conveniently coming out so I slip in through the half-closed door and take the lift to the second floor. I knock and he doesn't answer. It's an open fronted building with the doors set back and I look over the balcony. I bend down and shout through the letter box.

'Sal? Sal.'

No reply. I try his phone, but he doesn't answer. It's only then I remember about the disguise. I need a hat, or a scarf to tie around my hair, and some sunglasses. I look around, thinking where Sal would hide a key.

Some things never change. It's exactly where I thought it would be, wedged between two bricks on the balcony. I let myself in and see that nothing has actually changed.

The place is absolutely pristine; completely spotless. None of my household laxness spoiling Sal's vision of beauty. I go into his bedroom and open the top drawer of his blond pine cabinet. His accessory drawer. When you've lived with someone, you can imagine that when they leave, they simply transplant all their little nuances onto another location. Like Sal had. Had Aiden done that too?

I take out a black lightweight scarf and fold it in half, running it around my hair like a loose headband. Then I go to the bathroom and take out my makeup bag. I apply a lot of makeup, much more than usual, and some very pink lipstick. Finally, I find a pair of amber aviator sunglasses and put those on. People will just assume I've been crying. Except my colleagues, who won't bat an eyelid because we're trained to do this. To alter our appearances temporally whilst on a case.

Then I pass Aiden's room. I haven't been here for a long time, not since we first split. I do know that this was the last place he ever was, the last time he was real and touchable.

I can't resist. I open the door and I see the bed is made and there is a neat pile of T-shirts on the white computer desk. No computer—that's been taken away for testing weeks ago. But his sports bag is still there.

I pull out his blue-and-green-striped sweatshirt and hold it up to my face. He was wearing this when he left my house. It's flat and empty and I reach further into the bag. Spare Adidas trainers, two pairs of socks, two shirts, underwear. All have been washed now, no Aiden smell about them, just Sal's sterility.

I open the side pocket of the bag. I don't know what made me do it, maybe the chance that there was an explanation, some clue that only I would recognise. His pencil case was stuffed in tightly. Inside his pencil case was his passport and bank card.

I hold them momentarily, trying to think why these hadn't been found. The search report distinctly mentioned that he must have taken his bank card and passport with him to wherever he was, as they found no trace of them in Sal's flat or my house. And they hadn't recovered them. No wonder. They were here.

I tear out of the flat, slamming the door and ramming the key between the stones. Speeding to the station, I can feel my heart thudding. I haven't drawn any conclusions, but I need to see Sal. I park up and rush through the building to the room where I know the appeal will be held. Sal's standing there with one of the producers.

'Fuck me. It's Lady Gaga.'

I grab him.

'Come with me. Just come with me.'

I open the door of an adjoining interview room and throw him inside. Door shut, I hold up the passport in one hand and the bank card in the other. I watch him very carefully, knowing that he knows exactly what I'm doing. He simply frowns.

'Where did you get them? I thought . . .'

I think for a moment. If he doesn't know they were there I've no need to tell him I was in his flat. No. Fuck it.

'Well, I went to pick you up, Sal. I was being nice, doing what you wanted, a proper little family doing a TV appeal. But I needed something to put over my hair so I went into your flat and borrowed your scarf. Which I'll fucking strangle you with if you don't tell me exactly what you know.'

He takes a used car salesman stance, palms upturned.

'You've been in my flat? Why didn't you just ask?'

'I tried to call you, but I expect you were too busy pretending to be a film star.'

He touches his newly cut hair and ridiculous makeup.

'But you still haven't answered me. Where did you get those from?'

'Aiden's sports bag. Side pocket. Pencil case.'

'Impossible. Your lot searched that room.'

I weigh up the situation. Sal knows perfectly well that the whole case has hinged on if he left prepared or not. Yet it looks like he's kept back this evidence. He's clever enough to turn it back on me, saying I had them all along. Pull the madness card, like he did when he divorced me.

'Not well enough, it seems. Haven't you even looked in that bag, Sal? You must have, because you washed his clothes.'

He sits heavily on a chair.

'Yes. Of course. I went through it with a fine-tooth comb. But I must have missed it. It couldn't have been obvious. And the police, they looked too. They searched the whole room.'

Maybe he is telling the truth. He rubs his eye and a bit of orange makeup smudges across his temple. I automatically want to go and wipe it away, but I can't touch Sal any more. He's a bastard. And he's no longer mine. There's a knock on the door and they're ready for us. Now Sal looks more realistic, the agitated father who had just been crying. I look like some middle class hippie who insists on wearing shades indoors. The journalists file in and the cameras roll. The producer sets the scene.

'OK, people. This is an appeal for a boy who has been missing for six weeks now. Concerns are growing for him. We've got a press pack that you can take on your way out.' He turns to us. 'These people are Aiden Margiotta's parents. There will be a short appeal then time for questions at the end.'

Sal has prepared and begins to read from a single, lined sheet of paper.

'Aiden. We miss you a lot, son. Please come back, or get in touch, even if it's only to let us know you are OK. We love you, son, and whatever has gone on in the past, we can put it right.' I turn my head slightly. Whatever had gone on in the past? Aiden's had a great upbringing, apart from us divorcing. Nearly half of couples divorce, but their kids don't unusually go missing. 'Me and your mum here are upset and miss you loads. Please come home, son.'

I clear my throat. The journalists are on the starting blocks.

'Aiden, I just want to say that I love you and if you are watching this, please let us know you are OK. You can ring any of the help lines, even if you don't want to come back. And to anyone who knows anything about this . . .' I pause as I see Jim Stewart's face at the back of the crowded room. 'Anyone who's taken Aiden, who might be holding him, or has harmed him, for whatever reason they might have, let him go or tell us where he is. I'll gladly put myself in his place. Please don't hurt my son.'

There's a flurry and some questions shouted out.

'Who do you think has him, Mrs Margiotta?' 'What's gone on in the past, Mr Margiotta?' 'What's so bad that a fifteen-year-old would run away and not come back?' 'Why didn't you make an appeal when he went missing?'

The producer quietens them down and Susan Smith from the family liaison department explains the case to them, and then they leave hurriedly.

'Pack of rabid dogs,' I say to no one in particular. Sal's still sitting beside me.

'Don't go in my flat again. It's my space. Get it, Janet? My. Space.'

I snigger.

'You left the key in an obvious place. Good job I'm not a burglar.'

He nods.

'You might as well be, though. In and out of my fucking life whenever you feel like it. You made it perfectly clear what your priorities were. You couldn't even be bothered to change your fucking name. Then you think you can just walk into my flat.'

I don't look at him, even now.

'You cheeky bastard. You walk into my house whenever you feel like it.'

'Yeah. Well, it's the marital home.'

'Fuck off, Sal. I bought you out. It's mine now. You stay out of mine and I'll stay out of yours. OK? Oh, and by the way, someone will be over to talk to you later on. Another crime professional, not the one you fucked over.'

He scrapes his chair back noisily.

'Pointless. I don't know anything about the passport or the bank card. I don't know how they got there. They could have been there all along. I just don't know.'

He's gone and I'm relieved. As relieved as I can be anyway, with the growing realisation that if Aiden didn't take his bank card or passport, it looked more likely that something bad had happened to him. I walk back to the operations room and knock on Jim Stewart's door. He waves me in.

'Good job in the appeal. Not too hysterical.'

I nod.

'Yeah. Difficult under the circumstances. There's been a new development.' I drop the passport and the bank card on the desk. 'I was in Sal's flat this morning and I found these. They were in a bag that had already been searched. Granted, in a fairly discreet side pocket, concealed in a pencil case. I found them immediately. How come neither Sal or uniformed found them?'

Silence. He's thinking.

'Right. So. He's out there without ID and money. Changes things a bit. I'll alert the comms people, tell them to get the word out there. And pull the appeal to prime time.'

'Mmm.'

'What?'

'Bit worried about Mike and that. Those guys he's working with got a good look at me yesterday.'

He nods again.

'I'll take a chance. We need to do this for once and for all. Oh yeah. You mentioned yesterday that you'd seen two dead people. So that would be the boy, and who else?'

I try to head him off.

'The boy. What did the report give? Anything?'

He nods.

'Looks like a typical Northlands suicide. Cause of death unestablished, probably exposure due to collapse from drugs overdose. Some recent bruising, looks like he'd been in a fight about a week ago, but not the cause of death. Traces of amphetamine and diamorphine found on his skin, awaiting toxicology, which will take a couple of days. Contents of stomach were fried chicken eaten the day before. Complexion pallid, muscle wastage, typical of Xbox generation sitting in front of the bloody telly all day drugged up and eating takeaway food while they wait for their Giro. Checked on the family. Mum divorced from Dad, who lives nearby, four younger brothers. We're not looking for anyone else. Accidental death or suicide, depending on toxicology.'

He's tapping his pen on the desk, waiting for me to say something. When I don't he asks me again.

'So who was the other body?'

'Yeah. An old woman. Heard some intelligence saying a bad smell was coming from a house and I went there to wait for uniformed.'

'So you called it in?'

'Not immediately. It could have been a blocked drain. It's all in my report.'

He takes a sip from a bottle of water on his desk and I badly need a drink.

'Was it one of Connelly's houses?'

I nod.

'Shit, Jan. Stop, will you. How did you get in?'

I think back to Bessy's home and the unlocked door. And the birds in her kitchen. And her face. The baby. The money.

'The back door was unlocked. I went in to see what the fuss was about, found her, and phoned it in. Actually, I asked Mike to phone it in because he called me to tell me about the meeting time.'

He stands up now, and it's my signal to leave.

'Look, I'm on the verge of removing you from this case. You've only got one more chance, and if you make a mess of this you're back on regular. OK? I just want you on obs. Just around Old Mill and Northlands estate. Small cog in a big engine. Important to keep it running, but don't run too fast. I'll keep the obs on your house too, just for a while. Go and do your job. I'll let you know what's decided on the appeal. Oh, and I'll be keeping a closer eye on that husband of yours. Just in case he knows anything more about the passport and the card. I'll get him in here and ask him.'

I can't tell if it's a reward or a challenge.

'Ex-husband.'

Yes. Ex-husband. If he's lying, he'll be sorry he was ever born. But why would he lie about it? He was the kind of man who, if he was innocent and really didn't know anything about it, to suspect me.

The first thing he would have normally said was that I did it, it was my fault. That's Sal's favourite, turning the tables. But the police had searched his place and found nothing, no trace of Aiden, so why would he pretend not to have Aiden's ID?

CHAPTER SIX

So I go home. When I get there I see a police car parked outside, a different one from last night and facing the other way. There's no one in it and I pause at the gate. I can see the outline of someone standing in my lounge, and two heads popping up above the sofa. I sigh and open the door. Three policewomen turn to stare at me.

'No homes to go to, ladies?'

Sheila's still here and she jumps up.

'Oh, sorry, I thought . . .'

I wave my hand in the air.

'It's fine. Just don't eat all my chocolate biscuits.'

She looks at the others.

'Oh. Right. The thing is, we did and we noticed that you didn't have much food in really. So Sharon went to Asda. Before her shift, of course. I radioed it through. I thought I'd stick around as I managed to get a kip last night.'

I look at the TV. They're watching Sky Movies.

'Fine. Like I said, fine.'

She carries on regardless.

'Only we know you have a lot on your plate, what with IDing that lad and your son. We saw the appeal by the way.'

I nod.

'Yeah. Did they find out who the dead boy was?'

Sharon drags herself away from *Sleepless in Seattle* to answer.

'Darren Lewis. Local boy. Cause of death uncertain, so far. But he was found by a stream near the Clough. Near the train lines.'

They've even got popcorn. She shoves a handful in her mouth. The third WPC chomps on a packet of ginger nuts, breaking only to make a further announcement.

'Third one this year.'

I sit on the arm of the chair.

'Third what?'

'Third young lad. Two more. One of them a suicide, they say. Found underneath a motorway bridge, impaled on railings. Nasty wound to the chest. Others seemed to have fallen asleep on some grass. Full of drugs. Family liaison put it down to depression in young men and the high suicide rate. But Don Worral pointed something out. They were all found within Northlands.'

All found within Northlands. Northlands being Connelly's gang area.

'I fucking knew it. I knew it.'

I suddenly feel weak. The third WPC shakes her head.

'Don't read too much into it. Don Worral also said that they could well be suicides. But funny, isn't it? I mean, after Sam Fulton?'

Fulton is Connelly's nephew. Nine months ago he was found badly beaten in a car park. He'd been scarred for life, a huge V carved into his cheek. Rumour had it that it was something to do with Operation Hurricane, that the whole business had got to some of the duty cops and they had taught him a lesson.

I'd half believed it, because when no one found anything at the warehouse, nothing incriminating, the frustration was palpable. Plenty of petty crime around Connelly's estate, breaking and entering, violence, but no sign of any drugs going in and out. No sign of anything at all.

Yet Connelly appeared to be getting wealthier. He'd bought up more houses and was now driving around in a top of the range Audi. So was Mrs Connelly. Moira. Someone had been tailing her and watched as she bought twenty grand's worth of designer clothes in one shop and fifteen grand's worth of shoes.

She'd taken them back to their knocked-through Council house and left them in her car for three days, finally remembering them only when she opened the boot to push in a bag full of diamond jewellery bought in cash at Manchester's most expensive designer jewellers.

There wasn't that much money in kitchens. Or protection racket, which we also knew he was into. It had to be something bigger. All the signs were there; we'd scrutinized his bank account. It had to be something around the importing Connelly was doing. I pull out my phone and go into the back garden to ring Mike while Sheila makes everyone a cup of tea.

'Mike. How's it going?'

I hear him breathe and say the password for him being able to talk.

'Dapper.'

'Right. So?'

'Fucking hell. It's fucking impossible. These guys have got the most open and transparent system I have ever seen. There's a bloke overseeing all the work done for Connelly by these freelancers. He's got every single import, every single container, marked down here. All the customs notes, everything. Nothing's locked away. Nothing's passworded on the PC. A freight came in today and they even let me get inside and check it out with them.'

I almost laugh out loud.

'Oh my God. So what was in it?'

'Kitchens. Fucking kitchens. Seriously. He's importing loads of kitchens.'

Unbelievable. It just can't be right.

'Did you try to get under their skin?'

'Yeah. Course. I implied that I'd be up for anything and they seriously didn't know what I was on about. Just the fucking kitchens. They're making a load of money, fetching them from the docks to the factory. That's all.'

It can't be. He must have it wrong.

'So did you look at the dockets? What was the worth, was it about right?'

'For a kitchen, yes.'

'And did you check everything for anything hidden? Seems like there might be a lot of places to hide stuff in fucking kitchens.'

He laughs.

'Course. You won't believe it. They unlocked the container, told me to check off the delivery note while they went for a brew. Not just round the corner, over the road to a caff. They left me on my own with the fucking kitchens for more than an hour. Believe me, there was nothing funny in that or any of the other consignments. I even went most of the way to Connelly's with my guy. Right up to the gates, before I made my excuses and fucked off home. I'll go again tomorrow but . . .'

'Right. Might be a dead end. But if it's not the containers, what is it?'

'Search me. I'm out of ideas now. You'll have to think of something. Sane. Something we can take back to Stewart and not get sacked.' I laugh and he laughs. We're OK again. 'By the way, you know that woman you found yesterday in Connelly's house, I heard there was a young baby's skeleton upstairs. Turned into a murder enquiry. You've uncovered a right can of worms there.'

I look up at the sky. It's late afternoon now and I see a scourge of starlings. Scourge. I wonder for a moment where that came from, where in my memory I had filed that one, but then I realise it was Aiden's English homework. The starlings swirl round and round, hypnotizing me, pulling my attention from the phone call, from Sheila tapping on the window with my cup of tea, even from Aiden, just for a second.

'They'd pecked out her eyes.'

Mike tuts.

'What? What did you say?'

'The birds. They'd pecked out her eyes. That woman yesterday.'

Bessy, I think. But I don't say her name, it feels like a betrayal.

'Bloody hell. No wonder you were acting a bit strange. What else?'

'Nothing. She was just in the chair, dead. With a load of birds in her house. And the back door open.'

He tuts again.

'That'll be why they're treating it as a suspicious death. They're doing full forensics.'

My stomach lurches and I feel like I'm going to be sick. The money. It's hidden under the sink and there have been three policewomen in the house all day.

'I'd better go, Mike. Ta for the update, see you tomorrow.'

I rush inside and all three of them are sitting on the settee with hot beverages, watching *P.S. I Love You*. None of their eyes leave the screen, and I wonder what would really happen if one of Connelly's henchmen tried to break in or fired a shot outside.

I pull the money out and go upstairs. What had I been thinking? I'd taken it to pay a ransom that hadn't been demanded. For a son who could have just walked away. Although that was looking less likely now, and the undercurrent of my soul tells me that it isn't the case.

I push Aiden's passport and bank card behind the fitted cupboard in the corner of my room. I couldn't put the money back even if I wanted to, as Ney Street is now a crime scene. Too risky. Shit. I hide it in the ceiling space, behind some laminated tiles.

I go back downstairs and make small talk with Sheila, Sharon and, it turns out, Caroline. I can tell that they resent me sitting there, a distraction from the movies, but I need to find out what they will be doing tonight. I need to know who will be here when.

'So when do you clock off?'

Sheila appears to be the ringleader and chief tea maker and she answers.

'These two reprobates are off at seven and I clock on then with Sue. We'll be here until morning. If that's OK? We bought quite a lot of provisions to see us through. It's that or sit outside in the car.'

I nod. I've already looked in the cupboards. Looks like they could be here awhile.

'Fine. I can't thank you enough. You girls make me feel safe. Very safe.'

There's smiling and synchronized dipping of chocolate biscuits in tepid tea.

I go up to my room and get ready. Black trousers, black top. Black hat. Black pumps. Tonight's the night. I need to see what's going on in Old Mill, find out once and for all exactly what

Connelly's doing there. If it is flogging kitchens, at least I'll know it's a dead end. Dead end.

I think about those three boys now. The coincidence is almost too much to bear, and I wonder if Aiden is OK. I wonder if someone is torturing him, making him do things he doesn't want to do. I fall asleep sobbing and my phone alarm wakes me up at 2:00 a.m.

I jump out of bed and pad across the room. I've done this dozens of times when I've started a night shift, gone to bed dressed, padded across the floor so as not to wake Aiden or Sal. It became an art form during my marriage, because if I woke Sal up he'd turn nasty. Very nasty.

No one knows him like I do, but who knows anyone? Who knows what goes on behind closed doors, between two people? I've interviewed dozens of people who've almost collapsed with shock when we've told them that their friend or family member has killed someone.

'But he's so gentle, so kind.' And 'But she's so softly spoken, so calm.'

We just never know.

I pad down the stairs and behind Sue and Sheila, who are asleep leaning against each other like a pair of bookends, with a set of cushions wedged between them. Sue stirs a little and I freeze and duck, but she's fast asleep.

I pull the vestibule door open without a sound. I used to go around the house daily and oil all the doors so the minutest squeak wouldn't wake Sal. I've never lost the habit. The front door opens likewise, and I'm outside. I go into the garage through the side door and pull the cover off my motorbike.

I only use it in the direst of circumstances when I want to get somewhere fast and undetected. It just about fits through the doorframe and I push it up the drive and out onto the road. I look back at the house. No one will even miss me.

I keep to the left-hand side of the road as I push the bike out of hearing range, because I know that on the right-hand side of the junction there is a CCTV camera. I've checked, and I know there's a small area to the left that isn't covered.

Most areas are covered by some kind of surveillance equipment these days, with small pockets that escape detection. I'm so used to it that I can tell by the angle of the cameras what area they cover. I've tested myself.

When I've been on obs with Mike I've been so bored that I've mapped the cameras and then, back at the station, looked them up to see if I'm right. Nine times out of ten I am. I've been doing it for years, and as I enter this particular black spot, I'm careful to ride at an angle that looks like I've ridden out of someone's drive. I've put black mesh on the number plate so it's not easily read, but not obscured.

I hope I've thought of everything, because if anyone finds out what I'm about to do, I'll lose my job and possibly a lot more.

I speed along the streets, avoiding the main roads as much as possible and weaving in and out of black spots. That way, there will never be any consecutive evidence of my route.

I'm used to looking upward, searching for the cameras that are fixed to the high lampposts and telegraph poles, to the tops of buildings. Looking up toward mobile phone masts—I know where every single one is in my area.

The thing is, when you're looking up so often you see a whole new world. One where words aren't necessary, a world of signals and barriers and boundaries that ordinary people cross without even thinking. Unless you know what to look for, they will mean nothing. And I know.

About three years ago a woman walked into the station and asked to see me. She was heavily pregnant and she told me that she wanted protection for her and her baby. Lisa.

She was the girlfriend of one of Connelly's nephews, deeply

involved in their world. I told her that we needed information in return, and she told me something that's been invaluable. She told me that the boundaries of Connelly's territory are marked skyward.

A pair of trainers slung over a telegraph wire marks the edges. Football scarves carry messages, as well as babies' bonnets. I see all these messages, a language that's specific to a small group of hardened criminals, one of the few methods of communication that is never going to be offered as evidence in court, or even understood by most people, including the police.

There are continuous rumours that it's all a conspiracy theory, that Connelly's gang does it just to wind us up, but I know different. I know because I saw the fear on the girl's face when she told me there are things going on that she can't live with. That she'd rather leave her family and take her baby somewhere she could never be found.

Something, she said, that was completely unacceptable. She held her stomach as she said it. Then she flung a pink baby bonnet on the desk.

'There you are. There's the proof. We know she's going to be a girl, and they made me promise that she'd be named a Connelly. That she'd be promised to them. They're all about family, they are. But there are bad things. Bad things. That's just the way it is and they all seem to accept it. But how could they?'

'Accept what? What is it they have to accept?'

She shook her head.

'No. I've told you enough. No one knows, outside the family. But there's no smoke without fire. No smoke. Without fire.'

She was shaking now. Her eyes were dark and she was nodding slightly as she spoke. But I had to press her further.

'What do you mean? Does that mean something?'

'Like I said, not many people know outside the family. So if I told you they'd have to kill me.'

A play on the old SAS words. I stared at her. By the next day she was gone, magicked away by reciprocal programs. Eventually, after being threatened, her parents went too. But me, I just kept looking upward. The day she disappeared, a black scarf and a black baby bonnet appeared on a telegraph wire over the main road.

I'm almost at Old Mill now, past the hanging trainers and the footy scarves, past the cameras and into the heart of Connelly's patch. Ironically, there's less surveillance here than anywhere else, as all the cameras have been painted over or vandalized.

I park up at a side wall and push through a loose piece of fencing that I've had my eye on for weeks now. I spot a rotten mill window and put pressure on it. The wood crumbles and the safety glass feels like it will fall inward for a moment, then stabilizes.

I peer through the gap into the brightly lit warehouse and wait to see if there's any activity. Then I take the plunge. I pull on the glass with my gloved hands and it breaks halfway down into a single sheet, which I place on the ground. I climb through and look around. This appears to be the office area.

I duck behind desks and look for cameras. None that I can see, so I look around the rest of the floor, which is crammed with various parts of fitted kitchens, appliances, and a huge stock of marble worktops. Kitchens. Fucking kitchens.

I spend an hour looking around, looking inside cupboards, inside the appliance packaging, anywhere a large supply of drugs could be. It appears that there is no alarm system, no security guards, except on the main doors. Nothing.

I walk up the poorly lit stairs to the second floor and stop dead. The whole of the second floor is completely empty and painted stark white. Nothing except white walls and windows. I try each floor and they are exactly the same. It's almost beautiful, an old mill completely whitewashed and pristine.

But I'm not here to look at nothing, so I go back down to the first floor and search for access to a basement. There were no signs of a cellar or basement from the outside, no supply chutes or air bricks. And no access anywhere on the first floor. Just a lot of kitchens.

I've been here two hours now, and as a last straw I check the computers in the office. It's an open network, unpassworded, running standard off-the-shelf software. I click on the accounts software and look at sales invoices. For kitchens. At reasonable prices.

I also look at purchase invoices. Various purchase of transport. For kitchens imported from Denmark and Germany. Unbelievably, Connelly appears to be actually running a kitchen business from Old Mill. A horrible notion grows inside my brain. What if Connelly really is only selling imported kitchens? But we know he isn't. We've got intelligence that he's behind everything criminal around here, but he has everyone else doing his dirty work. We need to catch him at it. But he doesn't appear to be at it here.

I climb back through the window and collect my motorbike. I ride away quickly to a small black spot at the side of an all-night kebab shop, just outside Connelly's territory. It's open, and a lone reveller is undecided on which kebab he will have.

I sit on the pavement behind my bike. I need to think. Maybe I have got it wrong. Maybe Aiden has gone off somewhere, living in a squat with a girl he met. Maybe he'll come back soon. Maybe Connelly hasn't got him. Maybe Connelly didn't kill the three boys. Maybe they did kill themselves. Maybe I'm going mad. Or maybe I'm paranoid.

Then I remember why I'm sure that I'm not. Why Sharon's

news about the three boys came as little surprise. I'd been expecting it.

Only just before Aiden had gone, I'd been reading the sky and I saw it. A twisted back T-shirt tied around the top of a lamp post on the boundary just before the city. Black was never good, and this was placed prominently so that everyone could see. Everyone who was looking upward, anyway.

Because I knew about it, I was waiting. Some people wait for dog shit to fall through their letter box. Some people wait for a brick to rain glass through their lounge, terrorizing their family. For me, this felt like a sign. Even before Aiden went, I was expecting something to happen.

I felt like this was a sign, specifically for me, to tell me that they knew I knew. A day later, Declan Connelly was spotted holding his baby daughter and we got a call to tell us that the mother had disappeared from protection. So, I thought, the scarf was for her.

Until Aiden disappeared. Then I thought it was for me. It's only now that I remember three other black scarves, strategically placed on the edges of the territory at intervals over the past month.

I ride back home, weaving in and out of the camera space, and sneak past the sleeping policewomen. I'm too wired to sleep, so I pull out Bessy's exercise book and begin to read.

BESSY
THE REALISATION

So here's the next part. I expect this is the bit people will be interested in, because it's been in the papers.

When I tell people about all this palaver, people glaze over when I talk about our Thomas, but perk up at this bit. I suppose it's because it's all documented. I can only say it how I see it, and I don't know if you're interested in the bits about my life, anyone who's had me telling this bit before has cut that out.

The thing is, something funny happened that day when we were waiting for news. Me and Colin sat in that house, drinking tea and smoking, and we lost a day. How can you do that?

It was Monday night when we sat down to wait, and Wednesday afternoon when Little came to talk to us. So where had Tuesday gone? It wasn't as if we had talked for hours.

We'd sat in the front room, curtains drawn, ignoring anyone who knocked on the door. I didn't personally know anyone who had died then, both our parents and grandparents were still alive, old, but still kicking around.

I'd seen some of my friends lose their mum and dad, and their door had been shut for a week or so, until the funeral, and

I'd wondered what they were doing in there. Were they all crying, sleeping, praying? Until now I hadn't known.

Colin would get up every now and again and look out of the curtain. We'd seen two reporters pull up in their cars, and someone on a motorbike, all of the knocking on the door and shouting through the letter box.

'Come out, Mrs Swain, Mr Swain. We just want to talk to you.'

The neighbours had chased them off. Colin's mother had been twice, but, for once, he ignored her. We got through more than a hundred Park Drives, and when the police finally arrived and I opened the front door, a cloud of smoke wafted out into the October sunshine.

Little had walked in flanked by two other plainclothes, and sat down at the table with us. When I saw him I was shocked, he looked poorly. Again, the minute between us sitting down and him speaking seemed like an hour.

'It's not Thomas.'

We both exhaled and Colin flexed his neck.

'Bloody hell. What's happened?'

Little stared at the table.

'Can't say, Col, but believe me, it's bad. The worst thing I've ever seen. Grown men crying. A young lad, he's been . . .'

I couldn't hold it in any longer and I ran to the sink and vomited. No one helped me; they all just sat at the table, staring silently. I wiped my mouth and sat back down.

'So what happens now?'

My voice was small in the room and Ken Little stared at me.

'Well, we've told his parents and we've arrested the man who did this. There's further investigations going on.'

I shook my head.

'No, I meant about Thomas. What happens now?'

There was silence in the room and I felt the tension grow, until Colin finally snapped.

'Bloody hell, woman, there's a young lad lying in Ashton hospital mortuary, not bleeding cold yet, murdered in cold blood, and you're mithering straight away about our soft lad whose probably in the pub having a pint, or with a lass. Alive.'

I stood up and shouted back.

'I know, Colin, but it's not right. No one's looking for him. I want to know where he is.'

Ken Little stood up.

'We are looking, Bessy. Look, it's going to be hard for you both now, with this lad being a similar age to your Thomas, but if you want anything, let me know, just come down to the station. And we will keep looking for him, but at the moment we've got bigger things to look at.'

I nodded and they left. Colin was seething and pacing around.

'Why did you have to say that? You're obsessed, woman. Haven't you no respect for the dead? Some bastard's murdered a young lad and all you can think about is yourself.'

'I was worried about Thomas. If one lad's been killed, how do we know there isn't more? Ken said right at the beginning that kids had been going missing from round here. What if that bloke's had them all, and murdered them?'

Colin sat down.

'Well, I don't know about that, but you showed me up, Bessy. You need to calm down. Forget about Thomas for a bit, and think about that poor family whose son's dead. Only time will tell, won't it? Only time will tell.'

Our lives went on and we never discussed it again until the paper came a week the following Wednesday. The police had arrested a man at first, then a woman, for the murder of poor Edward Evans.

There were pictures of *them* in the paper and sickening rumours going round about what *they* had done to that poor lad. I had nightmares about Thomas being snatched off the street and subjected to a series of horrible attacks.

When we read in the paper that some of *their* stuff had been found and *they* had taken some other children, I saw Colin's mask slip for a moment, and his lip tremble. Me, well, I never once spoke either of their names. I couldn't. That would make it real.

I got my coat on and we went to the police station, but Ken Little was off sick so we saw another Inspector we didn't know. In a way it was worse, because at least we were used to Ken. This other officer sat us down and told us, in a very clinical way, what had happened.

'It's common knowledge now. We know *they* took three children, Edward Evans, Lesley Ann Downey, and John Kilbride.'

My hand went to my mouth and Colin looked satisfied that I was devastated. I thought about Mr and Mrs Kilbride, mirror images of my tortured soul, finally knowing what happened to their young son. I'd seen them often, out shopping or visiting, but in reality looking everywhere for their lost child.

Of course, I'd heard all the rumours about how the children he mentioned had been killed, and there needed to be no more words about that. None of us spoke for a while. The officer closed his file and stood.

'So it appears that we are no nearer finding your son. Or any of the other young men who've gone missing round here. I'm sorry. But I expect it's good news that he's not one of the kids tortured and murdered and buried in a shallow grave by those two monsters.'

He rushed out of the room, his face red and his eyes shining with tears. It was only then that I really realised what had happened, what had made grown men cry. The rumours were true and this was more than a straightforward murder you see in the films.

It was children, kiddies, who had been used for the depraved pleasure of a man and a woman, and then killed. My heart hardened a little bit more, if that was possible, at the thought of this, and for once, I wasn't thinking about Thomas, but what had really happened, right here in our town.

We'd got used to our cellars and dustbins being checked for missing kids, but this was horrific. I was in my late thirties but I felt a piece of my wonder at the world, my innocence about what people were capable of, snap off and splinter on the floor. Colin didn't speak for a week.

Weeks went by and Colin took to going out every night to search for Thomas. He wouldn't admit that he thought those two bastards could have taken him, mainly because his mother was adamant he was shacked up somewhere, possibly in the upstairs of a pub, with a girl.

Even so, he went off searching and often didn't come back until morning. I listened silently to the rumours about the Moors Murders, as they were now called. The murderers' names were on everyone's lips except mine, and everyone held their child's hand a little tighter. When it came out that *they'd* made a tape recording of that little girl asking for her mam, I sat and cried all day.

I wondered if Thomas would have asked for me at the end. Or, if he was alive, if he ever looked up at the clouds and remembered me. I knew it was selfish, but I couldn't stop thinking about him. I could never talk about him, because in everyone else's eyes I was disrespecting the dead children by mentioning my runaway son, but my heart was fuller than ever of Thomas.

One particular day I had the radio on and someone was

talking about how they'd dug up the moor and how the little girl's mother had been there. She wasn't there when her body was dug up, but she'd been up there, high above Oldham, at the final resting place of her daughter.

I'd wanted to go there. I passed the days thinking that if Thomas was buried up there, and no one could know if he was or not because there were more children unaccounted for than had been found, I would be nearer to him, to where he might be. It was my best bet, and more than once I had my coat and headscarf on ready to go, before I remembered that he could be anywhere, and I might be wasting my time.

I did go to Wardle Avenue, though. Colin never knew, and I never told anyone until now. I set off one day to get some cow heel for Colin's tea, and before I knew it, I was outside the 'house of horror,' as the papers called it. I'd caught two buses to Hattersley and stared out of the window in case anyone asked me what I was doing.

I was a bit of a celebrity in Ashton, on the market, mother of a missing lad, and all the stares and whispers told me that I wasn't alone in my thinking that our Thomas had been another victim. Here, though, I was just another woman is a Mac and a headscarf, going shopping for her husband's tea.

I'd walked along the street, my feet heavy, wondering if Thomas had been brought here, hoping I could feel something, something small to tell me that I was right, that his young life had ended here.

I wasn't thinking about the how; that would come if they ever found him, his body telling another story of how he died. It was more the ending to our story, to the mother and son story that, for me, was left to carry on, day after painful day, until I knew where he was.

I stood outside the house for a few minutes, willing myself to feel him, that love flooding back from when he was a toddler shouting 'Mam!' all over Ney Street. That pride when he passed his grammar exams. The tears when he gave me a homemade Mother's Day card, to me proof of our love for each other. I wonder for a moment why we have to send cards, why we have to have material proof of how much we care.

I'd loved Thomas with all my heart, and with all my soul, and I thought he loved me, which was why I was so sure he would never leave of his own accord.

I felt nothing except anger. Standing outside the house, I wondered how a woman could have been part of these horrors. Ever since I'd been a young girl I'd been keen on having a baby. I'd wanted a job as well, but my parents had other ideas. I'd met Colin early and we'd had Thomas and got married. Until that day when I went into labour, it hadn't really sunk in what my life would be like.

I still thought I'd be a pin-up, like Betty Grable and Jane Russell, I wasn't bad looking and my dad said that's all I had going for me. I was a good speaker and looked all right in makeup, I'd even applied for a job at the General Post Office as a telephonist before I caught with Thomas.

Until I actually saw him, I couldn't have ever imagined what it would be like to have a baby. Something changed inside me, I got a sort of determination that nothing would ever stop me from caring about this little thing, nothing would ever come between us.

His tiny fingers were curled round mine and I realised then what I was here for. I was here to have children and to look after them. I forgot about the GPO and my wonky writing and just looked after him. I fed him myself, and he'd look into my eyes and make gooing noises. If I thought I'd been in love before, I was now.

She'd never had that. And *she* snuffed it out for me. I felt sick and dizzy at the thought of another mother listening to her daughter dying, and my knees buckled. *They'd* tape recorded all of it, their screams and everything. It was no accident, something gone wrong. It was intentional; *they* knew what *they* were doing.

Now we all knew what *they* had done, here in this house. The mothers of the children knew, the fathers, and it became slightly diluted for those who didn't have children involved. I didn't know exactly how to feel, if the horror and anger I felt was right, but I knew one thing: I was in limbo. A mother without a child, with no idea where her child was. It wasn't natural. Didn't the world owe me that knowledge?

I knew that anyone who was part of it was equally responsible and that *they* should both go to prison; I never agreed with hanging, but now I wondered if an exception should be made for these two. It just seemed worse that a woman could do this.

Hadn't *she* any maternal feelings? Had *she* been so taken by *him* that *she'd* do anything? None of it was normal. How could *she* stand by and watch *him* bury children? Take photographs? *She'd* denied it all, but just by knowing and being there *she* was guilty, wasn't *she*?

And the sex. None of us ever spoke about sex. Not between adults and certainly not with kiddies. We all knew of someone who'd got an underage girl pregnant and she'd been whisked off and the baby adopted, or of a poor child who'd been messed about with.

We talked about it once, in hushed tones. This wasn't the content for marketplace gossip. It was serious family business, often dealt with outside the law by uncles and cousins. But a woman? I'd never heard of that before. Someone who had the natural instincts, like we all have, for children. Even the women who I knew who didn't have children had maternal instincts.

Why had *she* done it? I'd heard of women doing daft things

for their lovers, their husbands, turning to drink and dancing till dawn, but this was unexplainable. I'd even heard of some funny bedroom goings on, what some women would do because their husbands liked it, to stop them straying, they said, but this wasn't like that. The things that had happened.

They were the Devil's work, and no amount of love and romance could explain it. Infatuation my arse. *She* was a grown woman, not a besotted teenager. It didn't wash with me.

It was disgusting. My mind fought with itself over why it was more disgusting for a woman than for a man. Wasn't it equally disgusting because kiddies were involved? But somehow it seemed worse. There'd be a confession and a short trial, then jail. The rumours were that these two had tortured and sexually abused in this house flooded back and the bile rose in my throat. What the hell was I doing here?

I rushed up the street, ashamed of my lingering at a place where those children had died so recently, looking back as a couple stopped outside the house. I hadn't even brought flowers. In my keenness to grasp at my own feelings for Thomas, my hopes that I would feel him there, I'd forgotten to mourn other people. Colin's words rung in my ears.

'You're obsessed, woman.'

All the way home on the bus I worried that I was, and that it was getting worse.

BESSY

THE TRIAL

Another six months went by, a Christmas and Mother's Day. A set of carefully written cards stored in the top drawer of the sideboard.

I'd asked Colin to sign them, but he'd refused point blank. He was still out looking for Thomas, but we never talked about it. Instead, I scoured the newspapers for the object of my developing hate. I found pictures of *her* everywhere, *her* blonde beehive haircut and stern features reminding me of my Aunty Dot.

I cut out the pictures and burned them over the stove. I took the reports and glued them into a scrapbook that I would look at every night, searching for any clue that Thomas had been murdered by them.

Rumours of the trial had been rife. When we finally got the place and the date, there was much talk about turning up and throwing bricks at the van. I wasn't the only woman consumed with hate for *her*, most of the street where seething for *her* blood. I kept quiet, going to Ashton Train Station as soon as I could to book my ticket for Chester.

On the day, I waved Colin off to work and raced to the

station. I got there just before the van carrying *him* drew up. For a horrible moment I thought I had missed *her*, but soon it raced along outside the court, people chasing it and banging on the sides.

The windows were blacked out, but I still stood on tiptoes, wanting to get on a level with *her*, to try to catch a glimpse of *her*. I willed *her* to hear me, to hear my plea. What was I pleading for? I just wanted to know if *they'd* murdered my son. If he was buried up on Saddleworth Moor.

I felt a little bit woozy and I sat down as soon as the van had gone in. Soon, the people had cleared and workers walked past me, glancing down as I sat on the kerb. A few reporters gathered to stare at me, asked me if I was the mother of a murdered child. I shook my head. I wasn't. No one knew what had happened to my son. They dispersed, over to a café and two policemen were stationed outside.

I repeated this every day the trial was held. There was no need to rush home, because Colin had stopped coming home for his tea, telling me he was looking for Thomas, but I guessed he was round at his mother's listening to her poison words about me and Thomas.

On the 6th of May *they* were both found guilty of the murders. There was an uproar in the court. It spilled out onto the street and flashbulbs exploded everywhere as the police team came out onto the street. I was standing at the side of the court door and I blinked as the explosions of light blinded me.

For two hours I was trapped behind a large crowd of people waiting around for the police, then the lawyers, then the families to come out. My train wasn't until teatime, and I could get a later one if I missed it.

I sat on the pavement outside the court, waiting for *her* to pass in the prison van, like *she* had the previous fourteen days of the trial. Waiting to make that connection with *her*, to ask *her* if *she* had seen my son.

The crowds became thinner, then the reporters left, and finally the two policemen went off duty and were no replaced. It was getting dark. As I sat alone on the pavement, staring at the courthouse, I realised that I had no control over this situation at all.

Until the day Thomas had gone missing, I'd been able to lie in bed at night and bless everyone. God bless me mam and dad, me gran and granddad, Colin and Thomas. As I blessed each one of them, I pictured them in their beds, peaceful and asleep. My family in Chadderton, all living together in a semidetached. Colin beside me and Thomas in the next room, lying on his side with one foot out of the blankets. I liked that feeling of certainty, of knowing where you are, of safety.

Now, it was gone. When I imagined Thomas, there was a blank space. Even Colin slept who knows where; I always pictured him in the single bed at his mum's. I always knew there'd be a time when Thomas left, and I might not know his exact whereabouts every moment of the day, and just before he went missing I had stopped worrying about him cutting his fingers off at the joinery.

Now I had no idea where he was. Other people would know him, but not me. I'd missed him growing up. From seventeen to twenty, out of his teens, shaving, meeting a girl, maybe having a kiddie. If truth be known, he was still a boy when he went.

He had a teenage air about him, a ruddy embarrassment if you mentioned girls, and a temper on him that was just like his dad's. Not that he ever used it against me, not really. He looked at me like I imagined I looked at him; with pure love. Somehow his eyes softened and he'd bend over me as if he were protecting me. He'd carry my bags and hug me and kiss my cheek.

His red cheeks, his turning into a man, getting a job. His

eighteenth birthday, my birthday cards that he always chose with care, and wrote that I was the best mum in the world. Mother of the groom. I'd never wear that hat I bought when he was just fifteen, the white hat I saw on the second-hand market, probably chucked out by some posh woman, made by a London hat firm.

I'd bought it with my bread money and carried it home like it was a tray of eggs. I'd thought what I could wear with it; anything would go with white. Thomas and Colin in suits, his fiancé in a white dress, silk most probably, and me standing proudly next to them in the photographs.

Then a couple of years later, at the hospital, when she had a kiddie, my grandchild. Would I be Granny or Nan? I couldn't decide. All I knew was that life looked good, like our little family would grow and thrive and I would be surrounded by love. I'd missed it. It had been taken away from me. Or maybe he was dead. He hadn't had an accident because they would have found his body by now.

I lit a cigarette and sighed. All the probabilities pointed toward him being murdered by these two and being buried. But because *they* hadn't written his name on a random piece of paper, recorded his last screams, taken photographs as *they* abused him, or got caught killing him, I wasn't allowed to say it. I wasn't allowed.

More importantly, I wasn't allowed to ask *them*. I wondered if, at any point, someone had asked either of *them*, to their faces, if *they* had taken Thomas Swain. Shown *them* a photograph. I'd asked the police, but they'd never told me the answer. Said they were too busy with the actual murders, and afterward they'd focus on Thomas's case again.

The top and bottom of it was, no one cared anymore. Unless he had been a victim, no one cared. Colin's mum headed up the 'he's buggered off with a girl' camp, while a reporter had started a rumour that he was living in Manchester. Not that any of that mattered. I loved my son no matter what.

Don't get me wrong, I often thought about the poor parents of those kiddies. I'd seen the Kilbrides since the discoveries and they looked like shadows, grey and pallid, bent over in their grief. Like the rest of us, shopping for the food we needed to survive, survive our children, in a world that shouldn't be like that. I was as bitter for their lack of grandchildren as I was for my own.

I'd started to add the reports about the families to my scrapbook, hoping for a snippet that would lead me to another line of thinking, apart from the he's dead/he's alive confusion at the forefront of every day.

In my own life, I'd been cooking breakfast, dinner, and tea for three people every day and eventually I had to stop. One night I asked Colin if he'd be home for tea.

'No, Bess. No, I won't.'

'So where are you having it, then?'

He looked up from polishing his shoes. I'd ironed all his shirts and they hung on the back of the chair. He picked one and pulled it on. When he didn't answer, I persisted.

'At your mam's?'

He smoothed Brylcream over his hair and he looked handsome. He had a good colour and his clothes were smart, his shoes gleaming. He was wearing his good watch and I felt a surge of unfamiliar affection for him. I went to straighten his collar, but he edged backward.

'Leave it, Bess.'

'But you're never here. I know you're always out looking for our Thomas, and I'm grateful for that, but can we spend some time? You know just us two.'

He looked confused and his face softened.

'All right love. On Saturday. We'll go out on Saturday night.

Make a change, won't it?' He pulled five pounds out of his pocket and gave it to me. 'Here, on top of your housekeeping. Go and get a new dress. Something that fits you. And get your hair done.'

He grabbed his jacket and he'd gone. I went upstairs and looked at myself in the full-length wardrobe mirror. I knew I'd put on weight and my clothes were tight. My roots were inches long and my hair unkempt.

I felt a little bit excited and thought about the hairdressers, but then I felt guilty about wanting to do something without our Thomas. We should all be going out now, to the singsong at the Prince of Orange, or to the pictures.

Then I realised. Saturday was Thomas's twenty-first. His special twenty-first birthday. I'd planned to cook a lovely dinner and decorate the house with bunting, just in case he came back. I'd gone into a wild panic, wondering if I should call it off with Colin, but something told me not to. Somewhere inside I knew that I still needed him, that if the worst happened at least we could share the grief.

I was equally determined to celebrate Thomas's twenty-first. I'd been collecting little bits and pieces for a long while, blue ribbons and all the ingredients for the cake, which I'd already baked months ago. It was like a Christmas cake, but for a birthday, rich fruit and brandy and best butter. It was in the pantry, sitting under a Tupperware cake cloche. I'd wanted to get it right, and it said in the recipe that the longer you leave it the better it is. That's what Colin had said about me once.

'Like a good wine, Bess, the older it gets the better it is.'

I'd still celebrate. I was determined. After all, in my optimistic moments, I knew that he could knock at the door at any time, or come striding through the back way. In my fantasies, I saw him in the kitchen making a brew, or knocking on the front door, I'd peer through the curtains and see him and his new wife with a pram. He'd tell me he couldn't keep away and he was sorry and we'd all sit around and chat.

In my fantasy scenes, there was always one person missing. Colin was never there. I was still cooking for him and Thomas, doing their washing, but in reality, neither of them were really here anymore. Somewhere in the back of my mind I knew that Saturday would be make or break for me and Colin.

I decided to tone down Thomas's birthday to a card and a cake, and concentrate on my date with Colin. I went and had my hair done, chatting about anything except the Moors Murders, as all the women in the salon knew better than to get me started. Then I picked a dress off the market and spent the rest of the money on a scrapbook and some notepaper. Finally, I picked up a lined exercise book. It was a children's exercise book, with a picture of a nursery rhyme chicken on the front, but it would do for what I wanted.

As an afterthought, I got some prawn cocktail, steak and after eights for a special tea on Saturday. Thomas wouldn't want party food now, not at twenty-one. He'd want proper, sophisticated food. Colin would think it was for our romantic evening, but it would do for if Thomas turned up.

BESSY
THE SEPARATION

Saturday came and I had butterflies in my stomach. I'd seen Colin just after tea on Friday when he came home to change his shirt. I'd put his pools coupon on the kitchen table, ready for him to fill in, and he sat down for a minute.

I watched as he put the tiny crosses in the boxes. When we'd been married for ten years, we'd had a small win on the pools and gone on holiday to Margate. We'd been to Blackpool since, but never anywhere farther. I knew Colin wanted to go to France.

'Keep fillin' 'em in, love. You never know.'

It had been a secret message between us, a way of saying we'd escape together to the country. We'd laugh and nod and Colin's eyebrows would go up and down. Now, he snorted and carried on with the crossing.

He hadn't looked at me or noticed my new haircut, a shorter bob. It was blonde and slightly wavy, a bit too young for me, I thought. The pools man arrived and Colin spent a lot of time talking to him on the doorstep. When he came back in I held out my hand for the new coupon so I could put it away safely in the sideboard. He looked at my feet.

'I won't be doing it any more. You know, the money.'

'Are we short? I could get a job.'

'No. No. It's all right, Bess. I'm just not doing it anymore.'

His voice was funny and he went out. I knew he'd been doing overtime, but I never thought we were short. Our house was on a mortgage loan from the bank and it would be ours one day, to pass on to Thomas. My insides had shuddered at the thought of not being able to pay the monthly bills, the shame, on top of everything else.

I lit another cigarette and my mind wandered to the scrapbook. Tonight, on the eve of Thomas's twenty-first, I'd sit here with it. If he came back, I'd be able to show him. I wouldn't let myself think that he would knock on the door, in case it jinxed it.

I looked through the pages and frowned at the reports, then the pictures of *her*. How could *she*? *She* had at least one answer that I needed. Even if it was a no, that would give me hope. But how could I know if *she* was telling the truth? *She* could say no and mean yes. After all, hadn't *she* lied to the police, saying *she* was never there at the murders? Besides the photographs and the tape, it was obvious *she* was there. How could *she*?

I took Thomas's birthday cake out and mixed the icing. I'd even bought marzipan, and when the cake was cool, I draped the yellow sweetness over it, a mountain of a creation that looked professional. I stiffened the royal icing with corn flour and rolled it out. I cut around the bottom and I had the perfect canvas.

I mixed blue icing and white icing, and I piped and intricate edging around the side, with elegant swirls. My hand shook as I piped the tiny dots into words: My Dearest Thomas—21 Today.

A tear dropped onto the icing and I covered the pockmark it made with a blue dot. By midnight I'd put up all the bunting. Blue and white twists, all around the room. I'd made a collage of pictures from when he was a baby until when he disappeared. I'd already considered that if he did knock on the door, he probably wouldn't stay, just visit, and he could take the collage, as some kind of history.

I had a box of family photographs upstairs, and mementos from all through my life. It struck me as strange that someone could leave all that behind, as if they had no history, nowhere they belonged. I knew I shouldn't judge. People were different.

In the morning, early on, there was a knock at the door. I rushed downstairs, but it was Connie Rodger's son, with a note from Colin. He wanted me to meet him outside the Gormont at eight, because he was working overtime. We'd go and see a film. I hadn't been to the pictures before. I wondered what I'd do with the things I got for tea, and later in the day I cooked them anyway and laid the table for three as usual.

No one knocked on the door. I sat at the table, facing the front door, for hours, willing Thomas to come home for his big birthday. No one knocked. None of the neighbours, not even Colin's mum. A fly landed on the cake and I batted it off, loosening the icing on the top edge. I repaired it and sat again.

The tension was pressing on the air, and eventually I went upstairs and put my new dress on. I brushed my hair out and crushed my feet into high heels. I'd seen women putting on modern makeup on the TV, and I carefully applied thick eyeliner and mascara. The result didn't look like me at all. I was like the cake, covered in layers, invisible.

I sat some more, waiting, then set off. It was a fifteen-minute walk, my shoes tip-tapping up the cobbled road to to the bus, where I watched couples getting on, hand in hand. I was older now, thirty-eight and I missed the days where me and Colin would link arms and walk into town, where he'd have his arm around my shoulder. It was like a dim memory now, hidden under a black cloud of pain.

I got to the Gormont dead on eight, and he was waiting. It was like stepping back in time. He paid, I followed. We used to go dancing in this building when we were courting, and I felt a stirring of excitement as we clicked through the turnstile.

Colin hadn't spoken yet, or really looked at me. The film was *To Sir with Love,* with Sidney Portiere, and when it finished and we stepped outside into the night. I touched Colin's arm. I remember him drawing it away quickly, not wanting to touch me.

'Shall we go for a drink? Do you fancy a pint?'

He looked sad and shook his head.

'No, Bess, let's go back to the house.'

I dutifully followed him and we got the bus home. It seemed like I'd made a lot of effort to sit in a dark cinema, but maybe he'd get some cans in, or we could sit and talk like we used to.

When we reached the door, I waited for him to get his bunch of keys out, but he just got the front door key and the back door key and let us in. I threw my bag on the chair and he stood looking around the room at the bunting. I went into the kitchen and heard him shout to me.

'What's this?'

'Thomas's birthday. I made him a cake. Do you want a piece?'

I brought the cake through. I'd expected him to have his shoes and coat off, sitting in his chair. He was standing near the door, reading the card I had written for Thomas from both of us. He put the card down and looked at me. I could see the man I married, the friendly face, but distanced now, wearing an expression he saved for gossips and gypsies.

'Sit down, Bess.'

'I'm all right.'

I stood in the middle of the room, still holding the cake. He took a deep breath in.

'You know how I said I was going out searching for our Thomas, in the pubs and that, all over?'

'Yes. Did you hear somat?'

'No. No, I didn't. Because I haven't been.'

I sat down and put the cake on the table between us.

'Right. Have you been stopping at your mam's then?'

He gulped and looked at his hands.

'No, Bess. I haven't been living at me mam's. I've been living with Lizzie Shufflebottom on Wood Lane.'

I felt the blow to my stomach first, the shock wave from what he said. Then it rumbled to my head, penetrating the hard shell I built up and wiping out the little part of my heart that was still alive.

'What do you mean? You live here with me. How's this happened?'

'Bessy, love, we haven't been living together for a good while now. I haven't eaten a meal here for over a year. I only come back to get changed and fill me pools in. I've been leaving for work from here to keep it decent, but I can't do it anymore. I'm taking me stuff and moving in with Lizzie.'

The tears threatened, but didn't come.

'What about me? About our marriage? Only a couple of years short of our silver wedding. Bloody hell, Colin, you've got a son here you need to keep.'

'That's just it, Bessy, I haven't got a son. He's gone. He's not been here for four years. And you're obsessed with him. There's no room for me.'

I jumped up.

'No, I'm not. I'm not. I make your tea every night and do your washing. I do everything for you.'

'You don't, Bess. We haven't, you know, for ages. Not since

he left. Your whole life is arranged around finding him, and he's not going to be found.'

I lit a cigarette.

'So you haven't been looking for him at all?'

'No. Well, I did at first. Then I met Lizzie and we started going out. If I thought you'd ever get over this, Bess, that we'd ever be like we were before, I'd call it off now, but all you think about is him. I know he's your son, but you have to let go sometime.'

'Our son, and I'll do what I want.'

'Just one word would have done, Bess, to show you still wanted me. Even now.'

I tried, but it wouldn't come.

'What about the house? Where will I go?'

He sat down again.

'We'll sell it. It's a shame, it's got a lot of happy memories. Me and you when we were first married, all that laughter and dancing, upstairs goings on.'

I heard him, but the panic was growing inside me. I ran over to him and threw my arms round his neck.

'Don't go, Col, don't leave. Don't. I can't bear it.' He kissed the top of my head and held me, relaxing now. I sobbed into his jacket, deep, hard breaths. 'I can't bear it, I just can't.'

We collapsed into the familiar huddle where our bodies merged together. Rushing upstairs, we pulled the blankets back and climbed into our bed, familiar movements and a sweet routine taking over.

When it was over I felt safe. Not because Colin's arm was around me or his breath was on my face, but because I knew I would be able to stay in the house. Eventually, after falling in and out of sleep, he spoke.

'I'll go round to Lizzie's and call it off. I'm sorry, Bess, I thought . . . Well, you know. But I'll stay here with you. We'll make a fresh start. We could go on holiday. Or better than that. We could move, out of the village, to the other side of Ashton and forget all this.'

I waited a moment.

'Forget it? I'll never be able to forget it.'

He sighed heavily.

'All I'm saying, love, is that we need a change, get away from all this. A fresh start for us two, where we can be happy.'

It was sinking in. He wanted me to leave this house. My home. Thomas's home.

'The house? Where will I go? What'll happen if he comes back, if he knocks on the door, and I'm gone? He'll think I forgot about him.'

He pushed me away.

'See? Even after all I've just said and what we've just done, it's still all about Thomas. It's not about our marriage. You've forgotten that. It's about Thomas.'

He jumped out of bed and pulled on his clothes, and I pulled my dress over my head. I ran downstairs after him,

He stared around the room and pointed at the bunting. 'Can't you see, Bess, how mad this is? I've been living with someone else for a year and you haven't noticed. I know a lot's happened, but really it's no different from the day he went, is it? We're no nearer finding him, and you're sitting here cooking his meals and washing his sheets. Do yourself a favour, love, and stop it. Have a good hard think about it, because if you don't you'll end up with nobody. I'm off now. I'll send me mam round for the rest of my things.'

The keys clattered on the table, the back door key spinning round. He stared at it until it came to a stop. I looked at him, and he looked at the table, all the years of our marriage, everything we had done together, hanging in the air between us.

I knew that even if I did what I had to and played his game,

I'd still be looking for Thomas and he'd still not. It would never be right.

'Suit yourself.'

I threw my cigarette in the ashtray and lit another. The door shut behind him and I picked a piece of icing off the cake and ate it. My heart was broken, smashed into little sharp pieces, but the hurt wasn't quite as bad as when Thomas left.

So that was that then. Except it wasn't quite. My monthlys stopped. I'd heard whispers about 'The Change' and wondered if that's what was happening to me. Just after my birthday, after I treated myself to a cream bun in the inside market, and a milkshake, I went to the library and looked up women's problems.

It certainly seemed like I was on the change. Weight gain, funny thoughts, crying, no monthlys. Except I was a bit young, but the book said you could get it early. So I carried on and it wasn't until about six or seven months after Colin went that I knew something was wrong.

I'd decided to catch the bus up to Greenfield and have a walk in the village there. It was quiet, but maybe Thomas wanted to hide? Maybe he thought that, after all the fuss, he should go somewhere remote.

I'd packed up a lunch, some butties, and a piece of cake and hurried to catch the number 9 bus. As I was running up the road I felt a cold drip on my leg and, when I looked at the ground, there was a pink puddle. Course, it stopped me dead in my tracks and I went home.

I really thought I had cancer. I'd also heard that monthlys can stop when something was wrong down there, and I just lay on the bed, hoping it would be quick.

I expect I'd dropped off for a bit, because when I wakened up I had a horrible pain in my stomach. I was ready to say goodbye to the world, I thought I was dying, I can tell you. But then, after a bit, I remembered when I'd had Thomas, and the similar pain I'd had then.

By that time I was bearing down and clutching at the bedclothes. It couldn't be, could it? Another kiddie, from when me and Colin had relations just before he went? I'd never even thought about it. We'd not taken precautions. Surely I was too old now, for God's sake.

I staggered downstairs and lit a ciggie. For once, through the sharp pain, I tried to imagine what would happen if I called an ambulance? If the midwife came? I looked around at the piles of papers everywhere, newspaper cuttings and bits of scrap all over the place. The carpet, matted with dirt—I'd not bothered to vac since Colin had gone. Why bother?

I couldn't even look after myself and now I had a kiddie on the way. The pain got worse and worse and my mind was jumbled. I thought I heard someone moaning and then I realised it was me. I was counting back, it was seven months since me and Colin had lain in this bed. Too soon for a baby. Maybe I was ill? Maybe I was dying?

But, as daylight broke through the manky curtains, my body lurched and there was a slither between my legs. There it was. She. A tiny girl. She didn't move or make any noise, and I picked her up and took her to the sink downstairs to wash her. I rubbed her and cut the cord with the bread knife, stemming the blood with an elastic band from the growing ball in the sideboard.

She still didn't move, and I wrapped her up in a tea towel, the cleanest I could find. Then I was crippled again. I fell to the greasy floor, still holding her, and felt another huge pain. Suddenly there was a loud cry, and I looked at the little girl in my arms, checking for movement there still was none.

But there, on the dirty tiles between my legs, was another one. Another girl. I almost laughed, but even I knew this was no laughing matter. She was fatter and wriggly, and I put her dead sister on the table and picked her up. I was hypnotised by her and I somehow managed to cut the cord and tie it, and automatically put her to my breast, where she latched on and started drinking.

I held her, and with my other hand, I rubbed the little girl on the table, and held her to my chest, listening for breath, there was none, and she was limp now. Lifeless. I managed to stagger upstairs, and put them both on the bed while I cleaned myself up. It felt great, buzzing around, seeing to a crying baby. Someone to look after again.

I have to admit it, for that few hours, I didn't think about Thomas. I'd been staring at the tiny girl, the one that was alive and kicking, for what seemed like hours, when I remembered the bundle of baby clothes I'd kept.

Colin's mam had kitted a lovely pink shawl, and stared at me accusingly when a boy popped out, as if it was another scheme I'd had against her. But I kept the shawl, just in case. Just in case me and Colin had another baby. Now we had.

I started to wrap the kicking little girl in the lovely shawl, but then I looked at her sister. She was blue. I couldn't bear it. It was no good. I wrapped her cold little body in the beautiful shawl. Her face was peaceful, and I put her between two pillows.

I had to get someone. There was no way I could manage on my own with this. So I wrapped the live wire in a clean towel, one of Thomas's, and went downstairs. I looked at the clock—six o'clock. I thought it was later than that. Or earlier.

I didn't even know what day it was. Was it tomorrow? Had I been upstairs with my little girls a full day and night? I must have been. I looked in the cracked mirror and I was a right sight. I pulled on a long anorak over my nightie and opened the door, looking left and right.

No one about as yet, and I sneaked up to the end of the

road, then through the back ginnels to the phone box. When I got there she was crying. Probably hungry. I stood inside the red box, with my daughter on the metal shelf. I picked up the phone and dialled the first nine. Then I put the receiver down again. The crying was louder and I didn't really know what to do.

I had no nappies, no pram, no baby clothes. And the shame. No one to tell, no one to help me. I couldn't tell Colin. It'd ruin his new life and he might come back, wanting us to move, and then how would Thomas find us? So I left her there. In the phone box.

I put her on the floor and hurried back up the ginnels. I won't say ran, because I was too exhausted. But I went as fast as could, away from the loud crying. But I had to go back. I couldn't do it. As I got there I saw a few people standing around the phone box, and I hid around the corner. A woman was holding her.

'Eyare, Jack, go and get one of them bottles and put some baby milk in it out of the fridge. Warm it up in a pan, and I'll bring her.'

A small woman with beady eyes turned around, scouring the alleyways.

'Where's her mam? She must be somewhere round here.'

The other woman, the one holding my daughter, nodded.

'Yeah. Best wait here a minute till she comes back.'

I was frozen, watching them. The man brought the bottle and I watched these strangers feed her and check that she was all right. They were making baby noises and clucking as she drunk the milk. I remember thinking that she was better off with them, someone who can look after her. The man came back with a pram and the woman put her in it.

'She's not coming back, is she?'

Everyone shook their heads.

'Better call the police.'

I stumbled backward, hitting my head on a back gate. I thought they'd just take her, not call the police. The woman was in the phone box, picking up the receiver, dialling and talking. She came out, arms folded.

'They're on their way. To my house. Come on, Jack, let's bring her inside.'

She'd gone. Across the road and into their house. I didn't hang around. No doubt the police would be looking for the mother, and it was for the best they didn't catch me. Yes. For the best. For her, anyway. She'd be well looked after and happen I'd find out through the papers where she got put. With someone nice.

I walked home slowly, and when I got there I went straight upstairs. My dead daughter was on my bed, and I hardly looked at her as I lifted her up, light as a feather, and put her in an old box in my wardrobe. Pretty in pink.

I thought that would be a temporary place, that I would, at some point, take her out and bury her, maybe in the church grounds. But I never did. I couldn't because it would be like another memory slipping away, another thing that I would wake up one day and think, 'did that really happen?' I'd search the house for proof and there would be none, and those children would be forgotten.

I know now, as the years have gone on, that all this makes me look cold and unloving. I left my daughter in a phone box. And my dead baby in a cardboard box. What kind of woman would do that?

Well, I'll tell you what kind of woman. One who's desperate, that's what. One who doesn't even know what's going to happen to her, who's going to pay the mortgage, or if someone will come and take this child away as well. That's what kind. I was wondering what would happen to me, and how I would carry on after this. But I soon found out.

CHAPTER SEVEN

O h my God. It's morning and I haven't even been to sleep. I'm shocked at poor Bessy's story, but even more shocked that she was closed out by almost everyone, left to suffer on her own. And she closed everyone out.

Her friends, her husband, everyone who tried to help her. Like I seem to be doing. She suffered so badly she didn't even tell anyone she had those babies. I lie on my bed and somewhere, on a very deep level, I wonder if everyone who loses a child reacts in the same way? Do we all sink into an invisible pit of despair that lies just below the life we have to live on the surface?

I flick back through the pages to where Bessy visits the police. My eyes rest on one particular line, the only about Thomas and the other boys. Bessy hadn't mentioned the other boys up until now, only the murder victims. She must have known about them? Or maybe she was too consumed with her own grief to stay in touch with wider news?

It shakes me back into reality. Bessy was alone, no one to turn to, and she risked her own life to save Colin's shame, and to try to find Thomas. I look around my bedroom, large and roomy and empty, except for me. Me, in my black clothes purposely donned for breaking and entering. Me, with two policewomen sleeping downstairs. Even they had each other. But who did I have?

Everyone around me seemed to be suggesting that time had gone on now and Aiden was gone, one way or another. I know they mean well, and that they're trying to help me. Somehow silently urging me to stop and forget about him, like he was an object that had been stolen, and all enquiries had led to nothing.

They think I should grieve now, carry on, and recover. Maybe it's something only a parent can feel, that presence that goes on and on. The only person who still believed me was Mike, but I could tell that even he had his doubts. But I can't ever forget. Just like Bessy, I have to keep searching.

I want answers. I don't want to give up. I'm not going to. Thomas and the other boys. I have no idea how the police system worked all those years ago, but I'm pretty sure that there would be some records in the archives. We keep everything, and most of it is on microfiche.

I think about the money I took, Bessy's life savings that rightly belonged to Thomas or the baby she left on the doorstep. I need to find out about Thomas, what happened to him. And the little twin girl, what happened to her. At least then I could make part of this right. At least I could honour Bessy's memory and do the right thing.

I don't even know why I took it now, some kind of idea about a ransom that Connelly would no doubt ask for, because I was so sure he had Aiden. I ask myself the question again. Did I still believe that Aiden's disappearance was something to do with Connelly? I receive the same answer. Yes. Yes, yes, yes.

It's all to do with instinct. Good coppers have brilliant analytic skills, fantastic people skills, and a sense of duty. But a really good cop listens to their gut feeling about something.

Time and time again I've looked around the landscape of a case and found seemingly unconnected clues and signs that have eventually been drawn together by a single thread of evidence.

It's like knitting in a way. You start with a single stitch and gather the yarn together to make a complete piece. You have an idea of what it will look like when it's finished, but you need the thread to complete it.

And that's what's missing. The thread. I know it's there, somewhere, and I decide to do something different today, something unconnected to Operation Prophesy. Get a little distance. I want to read more of Bessy's notebook, find out more, but instinct tells me I need proof to link it to Sean Connelly's operation before I can take action. *One step at a time, Jan.*

I call Jim Stewart and leave a message on his phone.

'Jim. Jan. I'm going to do a bit of digging today in the archives, see if I can find anything on Connelly. You know, collating old charges, list of offences. Seeing if there are any details in the reports we've missed. I'm really getting a feel for this case now. I'll let you know what I come up with.'

I can almost feel his relief as he listens to the message. I can tell that he considers me risky, dangerous to have on the ground. He'll be pleased that I've seen sense and used my initiative. Another task from the operations board to pull a thick black line through. And one no one else wanted.

Of course, I wouldn't be doing that at all. I'd be searching the public records for any traces of Bessy's children. I'd be finding Thomas Swain's case and discovering exactly what was done about his disappearance and the other boys' cases.

I get dressed and go downstairs. There's a shift change going on in the lounge and Sheila is handing over the important details to the new team, Sally and Joanne.

'Tea and coffee in the top cupboard, I've bought milk.

Biscuits and bread for toast in the bread bin. There's some bacon in the fridge and some pop and crisps in the bottom cupboard. Help yourself to bits and bats.'

They all turn as I appear on the stairs. Sheila leads a delegation.

'We wondered if you wanted us to do anything while we were here? I mean, we have to be here, watching your house, and we feel a bit guilty, so do you want us to, for instance, wash those curtains?'

I look at the curtains. They're covered with dust and debris from my plants. Then I look back at the WPC's.

'No. Go ahead. Do what you have to do.'

Shelia nods.

'Righto. I hope you're not offended?'

I shake my head.

'Nope. I never was housewife of the year.'

I see that their raised eyebrows confirm this. Just as I leave my phone rings. It's Sal and I nearly don't answer it. At the sixth ring I relent, just in case it's about Aiden. He speaks before I do.

'There's been a sighting. A sighting. In London.'

I stare at the surrounding rooftops, heavy with starlings. Their voices are sharp and irritate me. I look at my phone. When I look up again, the starlings are in the birch tree at the end of my garden. Nearer and nearer.

'Right. Good. Where?'

'In the West End. He's been caught on face recognition video. Someone's been trying to get hold of you on your landline, but no one answered.'

I look back into the house and the WPCs were sitting on the sofa and the floor watching *Jayne Eyre*. I expect they had turned the phone down so it wouldn't interrupt the film.

'OK. I'm going in now. I'll review it and speak to Jim Stewart.

Sal clicked his tongue.

'Too late. Jim's already suspended the case. He told me. When they couldn't get hold of you at home in the night they called me. I went in and watched the film and made a positive ID.'

I pause and think. Sal's been in the station. He's there more than me at the moment.

'So you went in to see it? Couldn't you have waited for me?'

I hear him snigger.

'What, so we can present a united family front? Bit late for that, isn't it? Anyway, Jim phoned me and I went to his office.'

'In the ops room? He let you into his office?'

It's almost unheard of that the public are allowed into the ops room.

'Yeah. We had a coffee and he showed me around. Why? Shocked he trusts me, are you? Why shouldn't he? He just wanted my side of the story, for me to ID Aiden.'

'But is it him, Sal? Is it definitely him? Are you absolutely sure?'

'Well, it's a bit grainy and he's with a bunch of lads who are dodging in front of him, but it's him. He's alive. I knew he was. All that shit about Connelly and his gang, it was all in your head.' I can picture him holding his finger up to his temple. 'So, after all that, after driving your husband and son away with your fucking job, you're not that good a detective after all, are you? Eh?'

I click off the phone. I'm angry that the WPC's didn't pass the message on.

'Keep that phone on. Call me if anyone tries to contact me.'

They nod and I leave, no time for an angry exchange. I speed down to the station trying to stay calm, but end up bright red and fuming in Jim Stewart's office.

'What the hell . . .'

He sits me down with a wave and clicks on the CCTV footage. A grainy film plays in slow motion, fragmented as the camera flicks over every five seconds. Four boys appear from a bar and walk up the road laughing. Young boys, sixteen or seventeen. Underage drinking.

I focus on the third boy in the line, tall and lean and, for a second, my whole body relaxes. It certainly looks like Aiden. But he's pointing in the air and appears to be drunk.

I give him the benefit of the doubt for a few more seconds, then, as he looks up into the camera and a match is made with an old picture of him, taken at his last birthday party, where I caught him unawares, I see it. This boy has a mole on his neck. He also has genetically defective teeth. Aiden has neither. He does look like Aiden, but it's not him.

'It's not Aiden.'

Jim runs his fingers through his hair.

'Well a national computer and your husband says it is Aiden.'

'Ex-husband.'

'Yes. Ex-husband, but not ex-father.'

I'm shaking now.

'I know my own son. And that boy is not my son. You know as well as me that face rec software only has a one in ten accuracy rate, and that's when the suspect is in clear view. If the cameras at a slight angle or not straight on it distorts the image and gives a false result. This boy isn't even in clear view most of the time. Did anyone bring him in?'

'No. They'd disappeared into a bar when someone got there. And no CCTV afterward. None that could pinpoint him.'

I play it back a few times.

'It does look like him, but it's not him. Aiden's teeth are

perfectly straight. And he hasn't got a mole on his neck. It's not him. It's not.'

Aiden's teeth are perfectly straight. His perfect teeth. Jim's shaking his head.

'Look. Go home, Jan. Think about it. I've got two IDs—the computer and your husband.'

'But the computer isn't admissible.'

'No. If it were to go to court it wouldn't be. But this is all going nowhere. Your husband says Aiden is out there and has IDed the footage. That's enough for me.'

'Ex-fucking-husband. Sir.'

'Ex-husband. Anyway, I'm suspending the case pending further evidence. It's MisPer now. I know it's not what you want, but I have no choice.'

Somehow I remain calm. Underneath I feel like jumping over the desk and shaking him, telling him to find my boy, bring him home. I don't. I sit calmly, looking at the frozen image of the boy who is not my son, who would return home to his mother, or at least phone her soon.

'OK. I can see that. But I'd like to carry on with my work, if that's OK? Did you get my message?'

He smiles.

'Yes, yes. Very sensible. Until you feel better just work on the collations. We need someone to do that. Yes. Of course. But no more of this with Aiden and Connelly, OK?'

He's patronising me, but I swallow it.

'Fine. Fine.'

He clicks off the screen and the boy with a mother disappears.

'I expect he'll come home when he's ready.'

It's almost too much, and I nod, tight-lipped, and hurry down to the archive room.

I flick through the microfiche, back over the decades

through thousands of missing cases. I reach 1963 and search through for Thomas Swain's file. The beginning of it agrees with Bessy's account.

He was seventeen, and they thought he'd run away. There was a suggestion that he was a victim of the Moors Murderers, just as Bessy thought. Yet the records stop at Thomas's eighteenth birthday. Case closed.

I read the summary carefully, and it could be a précis of exactly what Jim Stewart just said to me. There had been some sightings and, despite the commitment Mrs Swain has shown to finding her son, we believe, in the absence of a body, that Thomas Swain is still alive. There are some added notes later on, mostly about Bessy's continuing visits to the police station, but these trail off around 1970.

It's frightening. Bessy believed that Thomas was dead, or at least she didn't believe that he had simply left. She had her reasons. It had clearly ruined her life and I get a feeling in the pit of my stomach that, if I pursue this line with Aiden, the persistence and the constant harassment of the police, my life will go the same way.

But I believe. I do. I still believe that my little boy is out there somewhere. It's times like this, when I call him my little boy, my baby, night night, sleep tight, mind the bed bugs don't bite, that the pain seeps through the chinks in my armour and the searing pain hits me.

Funnily enough, it's these times that make my resolve stronger. Aiden couldn't do this, not to me. We're so close. Were. Are. I don't believe in God. I don't believe in anything, not after the cruel things I've seen in my life, in my job. Indescribable acts, carried out by people who don't have empathy. Or just don't care about anyone else. But, as if to hedge my bets, I say a silent prayer, just in case there is some ultimate reason for all this pain.

I flick through the 1963 missing cases to see who the other boys in Bessy's stories are, and how many of them turned up. I count five boys between fourteen and seventeen missing in 1963, none of them returned or found. No bodies. All labelled runaways.

Shortly after I joined the police, I read a book about the Moors Murders. It made me want to get right to the top in law enforcement, if only to catch people like those two bastards. At my interview for DC I gave a presentation on policing and prolific cases, and my theories about them. I was quite young and very enthusiastic.

Afterward, Ted Scholes, the Chief Inspector at the time, sat me down and told me that murders were few and far between and serial killers even fewer. He told me that murdering someone and hiding a body was practically impossible, that the body was always found at some point. Therefore, the number of people murdered roughly equalled the number of bodies found.

Our job was to find the body and create a case against the person who had committed the crime. If there wasn't a body, there wasn't a crime. I remember asking him then, what about the people who go missing and a body's never found? What then? When you know that someone's done it, but you can't prove it. He just shrugged.

'You have to prove it one way or another. Otherwise, let it go. Chances are the body will turn up later and someone else will go back over your work and build on it. Random acts of unkindness, Janet. Random acts. Few and far between. Outside human nature.'

Random acts of unkindness. It's always stuck with me. Acts committed in the heat of the moment, in distant locations, unplanned. Few and far between.

It didn't look like that from the microfiche. I've reached the present day and the missing person files, runaways aged fourteen to seventeen, have risen and risen. By last year an average of three boys a year went missing. A couple of girls every few years. Some of them never turned up, but some of them were recorded as suicides. That's around a hundred boys and ten girls in total. How come we never hear about it? Where are the appeals, like the one me and Sal did last yesterday?

I read three sample cases, the interview notes with the parents, and the recommendation reports. Same questions, any trouble at home? Any arguments? Girlfriend trouble? Boyfriend trouble? Problems at school or college?

Of course, the answer was always the same. They were mostly teenage boys, young people finding their identity. Of course there were challenges, arguments. Some had problems at school, some had relationship problems. In each report, the particular problem that had arisen had been taken, made bigger and the focus of the investigation and eventually the reason the case is closed.

'Jason had a bad school report and the day before he went missing he had skipped a geography lesson.'

'Darren's girlfriend had ended a short relationship two months before he disappeared and he was upset.'

'Stuart's parents had divorced six months previously and this had upset him.'

I stare at the file. None of these reasons constitute evidence for the boys running away, or committing suicide, as it turned out poor Darren was thought to have done, when they found his body on a railway line in Northlands. I go to the PC and log in. I bring up Aiden's case, which would have been updated and archived by now. I find the case closure notes.

'Aiden's parents were engaged in a tug of love following their divorce and Aiden was upset about it, and this is the probable reason for him running away.'

Sal. Fucking Sal. I resolve to watch his interview, although I know by heart the reasons he would have given for Aiden's disappearance.

Bloody hell. All those boys missing. I do the obvious thing and cross check the stats with other areas. It's the highest in the country. This appears to have been spotted and blamed on high deprivation in the area.

The thread running through this, the completing rationale, isn't convincing. Someone in the report I'm reading argues that a quarter of a million people go missing each year. Someone else argues that most of those come back at some point, which brings what I'm looking at into focus. All of these missing boys have either never turned up, or are dead, presumed suicides.

It doesn't add up, not over such a long period. Even though it's been investigated, something is wrong. I can hear Ted Scholes's voice echo through my mind. 'Few and far between.' Not here. Boys are going missing all the time. And as far back as 1963, maybe even further. I really haven't got the heart to look.

I pull out the files of three of the boys who have eventually been recovered. I read the autopsy reports. All causes of death undetermined at first, then confirmed as a drug overdose. All found outside. All pallid complexions, as if they hadn't been outside for a while. All with problem family backgrounds.

On the surface of it, it seemed exactly like Jim had said, a product of a desperate generation, disadvantaged and numbing the pain with drugs until it all got too much. After all, the teenage suicide rate is at an all-time high, with the main cause reported to be depression and disadvantage.

When I look a little bit closer, I see that all these boys have traces of white paint under their fingernails. Had this been linked? It links somewhere in the background of my consciousness with an image of the empty, stark rooms at Old Mill, and this strengthens my resolve. It had been investigated in each case—household paint, standard white emulsion. But they hadn't been linked between the cases. Why would they be? As soon as they were found the assumption was made, some fucked-up junkie from a broken home. And the last two had fried chicken as their last meal, just like Darren. All of them reported no recent sexual activity, but had bruising between two weeks and a month old.

I write it all down and print out the reports I need. But as I sit with this new evidence in my lap and a firmer link forming in my mind, I wonder what I can really do about it now. And I wonder how Aiden fits into all this. Will he be found under a railway bridge, all full of drugs and pale?

Is this really a fucking social trend, a convenient line on some statistical chart that tells us poor equals desperately unhappy? Or is there much more to this, with scores of young men going missing over five decades and a few of them turning up dead in similar circumstances?

The question is, what can I do about it? If I bring it up now it will just look like I'm clutching at straws and I'll be suspended. I send some of the microfiche reports to print and push the papers into my bag. My phone rings and it's Mike.

'Good news about Aiden, eh? Bet you're chuffed?'

I pause and think. *It's not him, Mike*, I think. *I love you Mike, you're my best friend, but I can't trust even you with this. I have to do this on my own.* An idea's forming in my mind and I need to keep myself on side with everyone here.

'Yeah. Case closed, then.'

'So you'll be back on Prophesy then, will you?'

I laugh.

'Already back. Currently in the archives doing collations.'

He snorts.

'Bloody hell. How did you get lumbered with that?'

'Gives me a bit of head space. You know, think about something else.'

'So come up with anything, have you?'

I stare at my bulging bag, and the pile of papers on the table.

'Not really. Nothing much at all. It'll probably take days. What about you?'

'Not much. There was a break-in at the mill last night and we were all questioned. One of Connelly's boys looked at me and did the 'haven't we met before act,' but the guy I've been working for covered for me.'

I sigh.

'Oh. Break-in? Did they take anything?'

'No. Not really. Anyway, there's only fucking kitchens to take. Someone had accessed the computer, they reckon it's a disgruntled employee. Don't have no alarm system, either. They reckon everyone's so scared of Connelly that no one would dare to break in.'

'Mmm. Except someone with nothing to lose.'

I kind of wish I hadn't said that, and Mike passes over it.

'Yeah. OK, well, I'll see you in a couple of days when you've finished your admin. Bye.'

'Bye.'

I take the papers home, past the sky messages and past Connelly's territory. When I arrive I see an unfamiliar orange glow from my lounge window. I go inside and Sheila is there, with a new woman called Annie. Sheila smiles. She's wearing slippers. They're pink, with a bunny rabbit face on the front and big fluffy ears

'I hope you don't mind, but I nipped to Housing Units to get some dimmer bulbs. Yours were a bit harsh, you know, hard on the eyes. Much more homely, isn't it? Want a cuppa?'

I nod and throw my bag on the chair, placing the pile of papers on the table. Annie is eating a Crunchie and watching a nature programme.

'Did you know that fairy-wren chicks are taught a

'password' by their mothers while they're still in their eggs. It's a specific note that they must cheep in order to be given food after they hatch. It's thought that this is a defence against nest parasites like cuckoos.'

I focus on the TV and three fairy-wren chicks are calling to their mother. I'm tempted to take a maudlin dip into mother and child relationships, but I focus on something else. A password, is it? Like a code. Like a shared understanding, one that outsiders don't get.

There's more to this than meets the eye. I think about the black T-shirts and scarves, the yellows and the greens, and the blacks, blowing in the wind high above the traffic, a secret language. It's obvious really. I've been looking in the wrong place. We should have known at the end of Operation Hurricane that Old Mill wasn't a crime scene.

Like Mike said, there wasn't even an alarm. It's as if they want us to just walk in and see that they are doing absolutely nothing wrong in there. But where is it? Where is the fucking crime scene? Something must be pointing to it.

All I have is three missing boys with a pattern in their crime reports that could be coincidence or could be crucial, four with Aiden, silent sky messages, and an invisible crime scene in an unseen world that I know nothing about, hidden somewhere between the kitchens, a makeshift protection racket, and the dead boys.

The mother bird comes back and feed the babies and I feel a stab of pain in my soul. Where is my son?

CHAPTER EIGHT

After two nights of broken sleep, I sleep for ten hours. When I wake up I can smell bacon. I shower and go downstairs and Sheila is just dishing out a full breakfast for four.

'Mornin'. Do you want some?'

It does look good. And I need to pick their brains.

'Oh, yeah. Sausages, and a few beans. And some toast, please.'

She's dishing up and holding the hot pan with a new set of tea towels with robins on the edge.

'There you go.'

I sit at the table and pour myself some tea from the big earthenware teapot that has magically appeared. It's lovely and warm and I almost feel at home. In my own home. Almost. I look around and see that they've moved Percy's dish and his tray. Thinking about it, I hadn't even had the heating on since Aiden disappeared. Most of my life had been centred around caring for him and Sal, then just him. Now it had stopped and the elephant in the room was me. Even the WPCs looked more at home than me, with their fluffy slippers under their regulation trews.

'Thanks. That's lovely. I haven't had breakfast with anyone since, well, you know.'

They collectively tilt their heads to one side. Sheila represents their expressions.

'It must be so hard for you. Losing a child like that. Not that he's . . .'

I wave my handful of toast.

'It's OK. It's fine. I'm gradually getting used to it, that he's not coming back. I just feel like I need some support.'

Annie smiles and touches my arm.

'You've got us. Just think of us as sisters.'

I nod. And I was becoming fond of them, in a strange way. You don't have many friends in this job, but at least they were backing me up.

'That's very kind, and I will. But I was thinking some kind of support group. There's so many boys go missing from round here, there must be some kind of group that deals with it. You know, like victim support, only for mums of the missing boys.'

Sheila's chewing her sausage, thinking deeply.

'Yeah. I've heard there's one at the community centre on Northlands. Mothers for the Missing. It's been going awhile now, funded by that lovely Mr Connelly.'

I stare at her.

'Lovely Mr Connelly? You do know that he's a criminal, don't you, Sheila? You were slagging him off the other day.'

She nods.

'Oh yes, so everyone says, but you know, there's something that makes me think that he's not all bad. Us lot think he's a bloody menace, but how many people have actually seen him do anything? I mean, he lets people rent those cheap houses he's done up and he provides things like Mothers for the Missing. And he's always speaking up against crime. If anything happens, you can guarantee he's there in the front of the

Herald. Here's last week's. You know, when that house was raided and all that heroin and coke was found, he was on the front of the paper, and inside it, waging a war against drugs. I know everyone thinks it's him and he does run the estate, but I sometimes wonder if we're on the wrong track and it's not him at all. He seems so nice.'

She pushes the paper toward me. I look at Sean Connelly's face, his eyes bulging with anger, staring from the front page. Inside there's a double page spread of him handing over an oversized cheque to the local councillor. I flick through the pages. Darren's death is reported on page twenty-three. I turn back to them.

'So. Mothers for the Missing. Who runs it? And what do they do?'

'It's a woman called Pat Haywood. Her son Steven went missing twelve years ago, around the time of all that Shipman business, and he's never been found. Oh. Sorry.'

I smile at her.

'No. Go on.'

'Some of them are mums of them lads who killed themselves. That's the hardest of the lot, isn't it?'

Sheila intervenes.

'I don't reckon. It's the mums who never know. And the dads. It's harder for them. Anyway, Pat's there every day for a drop in. Never met her. Us pigs not allowed up there, are we?'

I smile around the table.

'Thanks, ladies. And thanks for the breakfast.'

I get up and walk past the new cushions, big and fluffy, past the film channel—it's *Pretty Woman* this time—past a new hedgehog boot scraper. I notice that they've cleared all the autumn leaves out of my garden and cut the last of the grass. It looks very neat. They've even spray cleaned my driveway and the back patio.

I look back at them and they're sipping tea and watching Julia Roberts arrange herself across a piano. I wonder if they have any kids, any family. I wonder if they actually know what I'm going through. I suppose I did give them free range of the house, but I didn't expect them to be here all night and day.

On the other hand, nothing had happened since they were here. No break-ins, no damage to my car. Not that I had any pets left to kill or maim. Or any children. Just me.

I drive over to the station and make a show of parking my car in the ops car park. Then I walk through the operations room and use my pass to go out the back and down the stairs to the archive rooms.

I take a file from the desk and stand on the chair under the CCTV, twisting it to the left so that it's facing the door, but not facing the research area. Then I open the window and climb out, leaving it open a fraction for later. I pull up my black hoodie and walk across the grass at the side of the station and toward the tram, making sure I keep looking at the ground. I jump on the first tram that arrives and get off in the city centre.

I walk around the back streets as much as I can and, when I reach my destination, I take off the jacket and sling it over my bag, revealing a cream Fair Isle jumper. I head for reception in the social services building and flash my police card. The receptionist barely looks up and I keep looking forward. This isn't my territory at all, but I need to know what happened to Bessy's baby. The twin that I haven't already seen.

Like the police archive centre, there are microfiche records. I quickly skim through them to find the right year. These records are filed by chronological cases, and I soon locate a baby that's been abandoned on a doorstep.

There's even a newspaper cutting attached, appealing for the mother to come forward. Of course, she never did. I follow the trails, a tiny baby turns into a toddler, fostered by someone in Duckinfield. Then adopted by a couple in Mossley. Went to junior school in Mossley, then to Ashton Grammar, then disappears from the social services records aged fourteen. Pauline Green. I wonder if she was ever told she was adopted? She'd be around fifty now, probably settled down with a family of her own.

I walk out of social services, pulling on the hoodie again. Over to the registry office, to find out if she married.

'Pauline Green. No, sorry, I don't have her date of birth, but she'd be late forties.'

The man behind the desk stares at me.

'Any relation?'

I don't know if it has to be for me to look, probably not, but I lie anyway.

'Cousin. Thing is, I need to find her.'

He smiles.

'Ah. Doing your family tree, are you?'

I nod.

'Yeah. You got me there. I am.'

He flicks through several books and eventually comes to a wedding in 1973 between John Lewes and Pauline Green. He turns around and taps this into a computer.

'You might be in luck. This woman's been married for twenty-nine years. Still is. They live on Mossley Road.' He looks at me, trying to see if I am for real. 'Number ninety-six.'

I smile.

'Thank you so much. I've got a big surprise for her.'

It would be a big surprise when I turn up with forty thousand pounds. I get a bus to Northlands and walk up Acre Road toward the community centre. All the cameras are sprayed here and I wonder what would happen if I was spotted. It's not likely, though.

They're looking for a flash copper in a nice car, someone

who looks like authority. Not some woman in Adidas trainers and a black hoodie. I could be anyone. I trudge along with my eyes on the floor, shoulders hunched, the trademark of downtrodden life on Northlands.

No one here has a spring in their step, and everyone owes Connelly something. He's got protection down to a fine art; cause trouble then charge people to protect them from it. There are some people who work, mostly at Old Mill. Making kitchens, it seems. Or arranging for kitchens to be made. The rest of them are on the dole with a sideline. Selling drugs, ringing cars, protection.

But that's only the men. Equality hasn't quite reached Northlands, and the women sit in their pristine homes while their children are at school and the men are out doing whatever racket they are into. Or in the pub.

You won't find Northlands women in the pub except for Saturday nights. There are barmaids obviously, but they are invisible women, there only for decorative purposes. Wives and girlfriends stay indoors. The last time I was here was to investigate a woman who had apparently killed her own children.

When Mike and I got to the house, she was sitting in the lounge in a forensics suit with blood still on her hands. The bodies of her two children, aged seven and five, were still upstairs. She had wounds to her lower arms, which she refused to have treated. She was just staring in front, straight ahead, but when I walked in she looked at me for a second.

When I'd been upstairs and seen the boy and girl, throats slit neatly as they lay in bed, no sign of a struggle, which later turned out to be due to an earlier dosage of Mogodon, I sat down on a buffet in front of her.

'Why? Why have you done this?'

Mike tried to read a caution, but I held my hand up. She shook her head slightly.

'I couldn't let them live through this.'

'What?'

I watched as her eyes covered the room.

'This.'

She was taken to the station, but hanged herself in her cell. Later I found out that her husband had abused her two elder daughters from a previous marriage and had raped one of them, getting her pregnant, then passed the baby off as their youngest child, the little girl she had killed.

None of the girls or women in that scenario had reported any of it to the police, fearing for their lives if they did. In her case, it was damned if you do, damned if you don't. Either way you end up dead. Women in Northlands didn't report, unless it was rows between neighbours, or missing children. The only place they are allowed to frequent are their own houses and the community centre.

It isn't a centre as it's at the far end of the estate. I follow the telegraph poles, keeping to the main road and eventually it's looming in front of me, an oblong block made of uncovered breezeblocks. Why make something pretty if it's somewhere as desperate as Northlands?

The steel door is half-open and I step inside. The hallway is covered with flyers for well baby clinics and smear tests. All the agencies know that this is the only place they can make contact with these forgotten women who never leave here, not even to go into the city nearby.

Northlands is built on a giant twelve-by-twelve grid, with a simple numbering system for the street names. Both those concepts are borrowed from much more successful places; Abu Dhabi is built on a grid and New York employs numbered avenues for location. I've been to both those places and nothing could be more different than Northlands.

The building is split into units around a big hall. Around fifty women sit around smoking and drinking coffee. Like feminism, the smoking ban hadn't made it this far. I feel enormously healthy next to the sea of sallow skin.

There's a notice board at the far end. I dodge a group of toddlers and navigate the baby weighing station to see if I can find Pat Haywood. Henna tattoos. Ear piercing. Vajazzle. For God's sake. Pilates. Better. Right at the bottom is Mothers for the Missing.

There's a little area of the notice board cordoned off, and pinned to it is a wreath of photographs, each with a golden pin through the corner. There must a hundred pictures, presumably of boys who have gone missing. I'm taking a risk here, I know. By placing myself in this group, I'm opening myself up to Connelly and if he has got Aiden it will look like I'm on his trail.

On the other hand, it might take a while until the news filters through and by then I'll have the information I need. I'm lifting picture after picture, changing years, changing hairstyles, mostly young boys. Just like the archives say. I feel a movement behind me. I glance round, and there's a woman standing very close to me.

'What do you want?'

I stand my ground.

'I'm Janet Margiotta. My son is missing.'

I'm figuring that the women on Northlands get most of their information about the world from Granada reports, so they won't have heard anything about Aiden apart from my appeal.

'On the telly, yeah. With your husband. Big. Bald. How old was your lad then?'

'Is. He's sixteen now. Fifteen when he went missing. That's

the thing. I want to join Mothers for the Missing. I need some help.'

She nods and her harsh face bends into a smile.

'Right. Just sign here.' She points to a slip of paper. 'You sign for you and you sign for him. 'Ave you got a photo?'

I shake my head.

'No. I can bring it next time.'

I sign the paper and she pins it to the side of the board, adding what, at first sight, looks like a lavish frill. But it's not decorative; it's a dense collection of gross sorrow and heartbreak. It's proof of life, proof that the missing boys are alive in their mother's hearts.

'Come on then.'

She marches out of the hall and along a corridor. First, second, third door on the left. It opens up into a large common room, with a table tennis table in the middle. There are two TVs, both on and showing news channels.

The Mothers of the Missing are sitting around drinking coffee and chatting. All the women in the room look pale and dour, chins resting on elbows and hair scraped back. The Northlands uniform of synthetic tracksuits and trainers prevails. Pat sits down at the top table, which is four school desks dragged together.

'OK. You can have the induction.'

She pulls out some sheets of paper and thrusts them in front of me. I look around the room, which is plastered with newspaper clippings, all in chronological order.

'Are these all the boys who've gone missing?'

She sparks up a cigarette and nods.

'Yeah. Going back to the sixties. This place has been going since then. The former Mr Connelly set it up with his money; it's ours forever. We've got a trust fund to help families who've had someone go missing.' She looks me over, acknowledging my expensive trainers and the teardrop diamond I always wear around my neck, my only jewellery. 'But I don't suppose you'll be needing that, will you? You don't live on Northlands, do you?'

I shake my head.

'No. I live in Woodhouses. But Aiden. That's my son. He had friends on Northlands.'

Pat nods. The whole audience focuses on me. It's as if I have just sworn extremely inappropriately.

'Has friends. Has. We never give up here. What do we have, ladies?'

I expect them to shout something, stand up, and be enthusiastic. But there's a few strained voices, quietly repeating what they must have repeated hundreds of times since their children disappeared.

'Hope.'

Empty hope. She rolls a ballpoint pen over to me and I fill in my name and address. I wonder how much Connelly has to do with this venture and how long it will be before the penny drops as to who I am. Pat's staring at the form with a hungry look on her face as I complete it. When I'm done she snatches it. And stands up.

'Aiden Margiotta. Aged fifteen at the time of his disappearance. Just before his sixteenth birthday.' A murmur of sadness ripples around the room and I feel the tears sting. 'Sixteen now, then. Went missing from his dad's house, Mum last seen him the day before. Police informed. Case closed after an appeal and a resulting sighting in London.'

One of the women stands up.

'Always the same. Case closed after a sighting.'

I wonder whether I should mention the CCTV and the boy, but then I would have to explain how I found all that out, and I don't want to get caught in a lie. Pat continues.

'OK, ladies. Oh and by the way, we're not just ladies, we have some fathers here as well, not today, but sometimes we get a father. And it's not just sons. Mainly, but there are a few missing daughters as well. So, Janet, what we do mainly is organise marches and the like to raise awareness of our sons and daughters and make sure that the police don't give up on us. If we hear something, no matter how small, we report it. Even if the case is closed.'

I think back to the files. None of the closed cases had any notes added. None of these peoples' reports had been filed.

'From time to time, we see a report about a body found on the news. We keep the telly on all the time to check for it, 'cause they're often hidden in regional news reports. And we keep track of all the papers. So all you need to do now is bring in a picture of your boy and we'll add it to our list. Copy it and that, and send it round the estate. Have you been in touch with Missing People?'

I nod.

'Yeah. I reported it to them and he's on their website.'

Pat nods again.

"Bout all you can do then. 'Cept keep coming here and praying.'

I feel a pain in my chest, the stress of loss, and in a way I know all these women are feeling exactly the same thing. I'm starting to feel uncomfortable about being here now under false pretences, here in what is obviously an honest spot in Connelly's hotbed of corruption. Pat sits down now, which signals the end of the induction. She places her hand over mine.

'Have a look round. Come here as often as you want, I'm here nine to five every day.' She presses a business card into my hand. 'You can call me any time.'

I smile.

'Thanks. Is all this voluntary, then?'

She shrugs.

'Nah. Mr Connelly pays me a wage to keep this place going. It's very important to him.'

'Right. Will I get to meet him, then? I've heard a lot about him.'

She laughs now.

'Huh. No. He leaves it to me. Not seen him round here for a few years. She comes in the centre now and again. His wife. Morbid cow. She hardly ever speaks, looks like she's got a poker shoved up her arse.'

I smile.

'Thanks. It's good to know there are other people like me. Not that I'd wish that . . .'

'I know what you mean, love. You're a bit posh, but in the end we all love our kids just the same. Don't we? If you need anything, yeah?'

I stand up and wander over to the news clippings. Hundreds and hundreds of browned scraps, pasted onto hardboard, detailing all the missing boys over the years, interspaced with old advertisements for kitchens. Every so often there would be a black card with a silver calligraphy date pinned over the cutting. Pat appears behind me.

'That's the date their bodies were found.'

I pull up each piece of paper and see beneath it there's a copy of the newspaper cutting from the local newspapers. Pat voices my thoughts.

'Not got much publicity, any of them. All somewhere in the back of the papers, always something else more important.'

'Like what, Pat?'

'Well, usually Mr Connelly's good causes. He's always on the front page raising them. Protesting about something or other. He does it for us as well.'

I nod and make my way around the board, like stepping

back through time four decades. Right at the beginning of the wall, every cutting has a picture of a large man with a pork pie hat, accompanying the mother in question. I look at Pat for guidance.

'Old Mr Connelly. Dead now. He set up this place and helped the mothers in the old days.'

I look at all the young women, strained smiles and puffy eyes, all wearing the same desperate expression as everyone here today. Regular rallies for missing children. Then something catches my eye. A tiny woman, half the size of old Mr Connelly, clutching her handbag. Her beady, dark eyes stared out at me accusingly. I read the caption underneath the picture.

'Bessy Swain, mother of missing boy Tommy Swain, attends a rally against the Moors Murders with John Connelly on Bonfire night.'

I stagger backward and Pat catches me.

'Sorry, Sorry. It's just all too much for me.'

I rush out of the room, through the community centre, and stand outside against the wall, breathless. I walk back through Northlands, trying to make the connection between Bessy and Connelly, and take the tram back to the station. I need to get back and read more of her story. I put up my hoodie and hurry across the grass at the back of the building, where the window is still slightly open. I climb back in and look up at the camera. The phone rings and I jump.

'Hello?'

'Hi. Jan?'

It's Mike. I sigh.

'Yep. It is. Whadaya want?'

He laughs.

'Ah, Jim Stewart said you were in the archive room, I tried before, but couldn't get you.'

'I might have been in the loo. Or had my headphones in. It's so boring, Mike, and I'm getting fucking nowhere. There aren't any links. Nothing at all.'

I can hear him tut.

'Me neither. Bloody hell, I thought I was in there. I honestly thought that those blokes would be bringing in something illegal. But there's nothing. Nothing at all. Just fucking kitchens.'

'So why does he use private contractors then?'

Mike laughs.

'Cheaper. Just cheaper. And he can just change them when he likes. He uses private contractors for everything. But honest, there just nothing dodgy about it.'

'So what next?'

'Well, Stewart said I should just finish this week to make it convincing and then I'm back on obs with you. But I'm not archiving. We'll take another bit of the operation. I'm not sitting in the fucking archive room all day. No way.'

I laugh again.

'OK. Calm down. I'm not finding anything so I expect I'll be moved on anyway. So see you Monday. Good luck.'

I put the receiver down. Like Mike says. Nothing at all. But there must be something, somewhere. The threads are coming together a little tighter and I need time to think. About Bessy and Thomas. What was Connelly doing with Bessy? What did he have to do with the Moors Murders?

CHAPTER NINE

I t's creeping me out now. I have to find out about this for once and for all. I go upstairs into the archiving lockers with the number of Thomas Swain's case file. The uniformed PC on the door waves me through and I check which way the cameras are pointing as I walk through the huge hall full of records.

We only come here if we really have to now that everything's computerised. I'm just old enough to remember when all the files were still paper; only current stuff was written down, then transferred to some kind of storage.

Microfiche, magnetic tape, we've tried them all. No doubt the information I want is stored somewhere on magnetic media, but from past experience I anticipate the flaws this carried. The archivists drafted in to transfer the paper to tape or microfiche were told to scan the police records.

That's exactly what they did. They scanned pages and pages of documents with the police logo at the top of them. Interviews, reports, all sorts of official documents, carefully signed and witnessed on every page.

What they didn't do is scan the other stuff. Every case has a central core of witnessed documents and is surrounded by scribbled phone numbers, notes, photographs that are not admissible as evidence, scraps of material, references to objects that were stored in evidence bags.

All kinds of seeming superfluous items that would never get past the Public Prosecution Service but form a vital part in understanding exactly what has gone on. They're the pieces of the jigsaw that pull the threads together ever tighter.

They didn't scan it because they didn't think it was important. They were just carrying out instructions to the letter. Scan the police documents. So that's all they did. But these items remain in the original case files, all stored here in a temperature-controlled area.

I find Thomas's file easily and flick through it. I see some handwritten pages; those won't have been scanned. Also, I see some photographs of three people. I stare at them, I feel like I know them so well. Bessy, Thomas, and Colin, the bastard, who ran off with someone else.

Bessy looks so happy in the black-and-white photograph, nothing like the hunched-over older woman in the photograph in the community centre. And there could only be maybe five years in between. Then I remember about the babies, about Pauline. Which makes me remember about the money I stole from her house. I left the woman in this picture downstairs while I stole her life savings.

My God. What am I turning into?

I press Thomas's file close to my body out of sight and move along the row to current files. They are all in bright yellow folders, and the old files are in bright red folders with 'DO NOT REMOVE' printed on the side.

Even though I know it's gross misconduct, I slide the contents of the red file into the back of the yellow one I take from the drawer. It's the file about Mike's current exploits, so I have a reason to have it if I'm asked.

I go back and push the red folder into the space I took it from and make for the doorway. The PC on reception eyes the yellow file.

'Partner's file. Wanted me to take a look. OK?'

I let the front cover flap down so that he can see Mike's name and number. He taps it into the database.

'And you are? Can I see your card, please?'

I show him my warrant card and he nods.

'Thanks. We have to check.'

I smile.

'No, no. I completely understand. I'm glad you did.'

It's true. I'm glad he did. Because now no one will ever suspect what I've done. I've been careful, but you can never be too careful. Always backtrack. I don't even know if I was missed today, how many people tried to find me in the archive room.

Usually people ring my mobile if they can't get me. Mike wouldn't have been able to as we don't ring each other's mobiles for undercover, but anyone else who saw me logged down there would have tried the landline first. Also, there's a remote possibility that someone might look for Thomas's file. Then I remember about the forensics in Bessy's house. I hadn't checked if that was in yet.

I hurry my pace to get to my car and get out of the station car park. I'm driving along, reading the sky messages. They're coming closer now, with a black scarf hung close to the telegraph pole outside the station. A lone crow sits beside it, taking an occasional peck, as I drive directly underneath.

I need time alone to think, time to just try to understand what all this means, not least my own strange behaviour. I retrace my steps in Bessy's house. Why did I take that money? Why?

Obviously, at the time, I had it in my mind that it would be for a ransom, for Aiden, and that I was convinced that I would receive a note any moment demanding a huge sum of money. They say you will do anything when your child is in danger, and it's true. I stole from a dead woman. Now it doesn't make sense.

There is no ransom note, and there is no proof he's been kidnapped or murdered. He's rapidly turning into another statistic, another piece of blue paper on the community centre notice board flapping in the breeze. I won't let him. I know that the answer is somewhere. I just know it.

I rush home and park up in the drive. I can see Sharon and Annie in the house, eating toast and nodding their heads along to what appears to be MTV. I turn my key in the door and Sharon is in the hallway before I even get in.

'I'd park your car in the garage if I were you. You've had a visitor.'

I do as she says, opening the pullover door and moving Aiden's bike and my motorbike further back. I look around. Aiden's cycling gear. Aiden's football boots, still muddy from weeks ago. Aiden's wax jacket. It's no good. I have to find him. I back the car in and lock the door. Back inside, Annie's muted the TV.

'Good job we're here. That bloody woman's a nightmare.'

I flop onto the sofa.

'Woman? What woman?'

'Blonde. A bit brassy. Maybe forty-five. Could be a bit older. Blue shell suit. Holding a hammer.'

Pat. It has to be.

'What did she say?'

'Well, she was in a car driven by a male, midforties. He stayed in the car while she got out and came running toward the house. Luckily we just caught her in time. She was just about to put your front window through. She kept shouting: 'where is she?' over and over again.'

I nod.

'It's Pat Haywood. I saw her today.'

Sharon snorts.

'Bloody hell. You didn't go up there, did you? You've more balls than we thought.'

I smile.

'Yeah. I went up there. Very interesting. Found out some stuff about lots of people going missing on Northlands over the years. Boys.'

They both nod. Annie speaks first.

'Yeah. Common knowledge. But would you want to stay there? You've got this nice place here, but if you lived on Northlands wouldn't you want to leave? Nothing stopping the youngsters, is there? Well, not the boys.'

I nod.

'Yes. I can see that. But what about the suicides? When they turn up dead?'

'Not worked out for them. Tragic, it is. Tragic. But the national suicide rate for boys is high. I expect you know that?'

I nod.

'It is. But maybe it only gets high when unexplained deaths such as these, deaths with an element of similarity, are added to the statistics. If you take that away, you're left with a load of unexplained deaths and low suicide rates.'

I think about the amphetamine and the diamorphine. The white paint and the chicken. The way all the boys had died of exposure, except the one who had been impaled on railings. About how they were all practically unreported because they all happened at the same time as other, more newsworthy, events. As if someone was waiting for something big to happen before they got rid of a body. Or took another one. Something like the Moors Murders. Annie is holding the note out.

'She gave me this to give to you.'

It's my application form for Mothers for the Missing.

Scrawled across it is 'FUCK OFF POLICE SCUM.' She's pinned the blue slip of paper with Aiden's name on it to the corner of the paper. On the back there's a note. 'You're a liar. We've never turned anyone away before, but you lied about who you are coz you knew what would happen. We hope you find your lad, but I wouldn't hold your breath. You're no different from us at the end of the day.'

Annie sighs and sips her hot chocolate.

'She was very angry. Very angry indeed. We told her that you weren't here and you were at the station. She just spat at us. Charming.'

I look around. This is looking less and less like my home. There are some new plants on the sills and some place mats with cheery scenes on them. New cups sat on the drainer, and some mince pies. They've even turned on the fake flames inside the electric fire hung in the ultra-modern fireplace.

'The thing is, she's got a right to be upset. I went to see her today and she's right, I lied. I lied to a bunch of grieving women. By omission. Didn't mention I was a DS. Just to get information.'

They nod and smile. Annie puts her cup down.

'Problem is, they've got nothing to do. If they had something to do, they wouldn't be sitting around all day.'

'But they've lost their sons. And daughters, some of them.'

Annie smiles tightly.

'Not being funny, but they should make a move to get over it. I mean, look at you.'

I pull the file closer to my chest. I want to hit her over the head with it and tell her that I'm not over it. I'm not even started.

But I don't. I'm in enough trouble already. It's only a matter of time before Connelly finds out I've been on Northlands, if he hasn't already, and passes that information on to Jim Stewart one way or another.

Anyone who's busted on Northlands gets fed to the crocodiles by Connelly's henchmen; he likes Jim to know exactly what he knows about our operations, and this will be no exception. Only it's not part of the operation, is it? It's not part of Operation Prophesy at all. It's part of my private operation.

'Yeah. I suppose. Anyway, how long you two posted here?'

I could really do with them gone.

'Well up to this morning, we were ready for the off tomorrow, but DI Stewart says we should stay.'

Oh my God. He already knows.

'You spoke to him?'

'Yep. He called about threeish, just after she'd been. We were still a bit shook up, you know, having a strong cup of tea, and he called your landline. Said he couldn't find you.'

Shit. He must have called the archive room. Maybe he'd even sent someone down there.

'What exactly did he say? Exactly?'

They look at each other, eyebrows raised.

'Just asked if you were there. Asked when we'd seen you last. Oh, and asked if anyone else had been at the house. So that's when we mentioned that woman, but I don't think he meant her. He asked if anyone apart from her had been round. And we said there hadn't. That's all really. We did try to ring you.'

I pull out my phone and there are seven missed calls. I go out the back and listen to the messages. One from Pat. Two from Jim Stewart asking me to contact him. One from Mike asking where I am. And two from Annie telling me to phone Jim Stewart. Shit shit shit. I listen to the message from Pat. She's angry.

'Message for DS Pearce. Or Janet Margiotta. Take your fuckin' pick. I don't know what I'm more fucked off about, that you came up here snoopin' or that the fuckin' coppers won't help us. Where's my son, DS fuckin' Pearce? Where's your boy? Where's all our boys? I know everything we tell you lot, everything Mothers for the Missing comes up with, gets ignored. But you need to listen very carefully to me. Something's happening on Northlands. Something's happening to our sons. Some of them. I've spoken to the mothers of them who are supposed to have topped themselves, but, without one fuckin' exception, they say it's wrong. I don't get a copper's number very often, and I can't report it openly or I'll get sacked. I can't put me finger on it. I don't know. But seriously. Look at it. Oh. And sorry about earlier, I was fuming. Don't try to call me back, cos I can't ever have owt to do with you publicly, but look at all the missing lads.'

It's the first time anyone's actually agreed with me. I suddenly feel a huge sense of relief, that it's not just me and some misdirected paranoia. I want to call her and thank her, but I can hear the landline ringing in the house and I duck around the side of the conservatory. Annie answers.

'Oh, hello, sir. No, she's not here, she was a minute ago, but she must have gone upstairs.' A pause. 'Oh. Right. Yes, of course. Coming round. OK. Righty-o.'

I see her put the phone down in the reflection of the patio doors.

'He's coming round here. Says not to let her go out until he gets here. Sounds serious. Wonder what she's done?'

Sharon crunches on a ginger nut.

'Don't know. Must be something to do with that awful woman. Or her son. What if . . . ?'

Annie's hand goes to her mouth. I run around the side of the house and into the garage. The pull-over door isn't automatic, and I haven't a chance of raising it without being noticed. So I take the bike. I roll it up the road through the familiar black spots, my heart beating fast. What if it is Aiden?

I pull the bike around the side of a wooden fence and dial Sal's number. He answers after two rings. If it was Aiden he would already know, as Jim's been looking for me all day.

'Hello?'

'Hi, Sal, it's me.'

He tuts.

'Right. Speaking to me now, are you? I did wonder after the other day, I mean, you must be able to see my point . . . Where are you, anyway?'

'Sal. Have you heard anything? About Aiden?'

'Well, there've been a couple of sightings but nothing . . . Where are you, Jan? It's very quiet. Are you outside somewhere, at this time? You want to be careful, you know.'

I end the call and push my phone into the bushes. No one would find it there. And no one would find me here. I've got a spare pay-as-you-go, just in case I need to call for help.

I ride and ride until I'm in Ney Street. I push Bessy's back gate and it opens easily. I drag my bike inside, and push the back door. It's locked, of course. It's still early evening and I can see the outlines of birds gathering on the shed rooftop, their twittering almost deafening.

Suddenly they take off in flight and I watch them swirl above the dirty Northern terraces, in and out of the telegraph poles, high above the codes laid out by men too engrossed in land to look upward and see beyond themselves. They wind around the clouds and across the setting sun before coming back to land on the rooftops opposite.

There, they sit and watch me. Nearer and nearer.

I push open the door with little effort. The house smells damp now, but not of death. Someone's been here and cleaned up the bird shit but left the black powder of forensics on the window edges. It's on the outside too, and the birds have stood in it. Bird prints instead of fingerprints.

I laugh a little at this, then go into the lounge. It's like a flashback to only a few days ago, when I stood here before Bessy's body. I wish I could turn back time, to a different path where I didn't go upstairs, and just called it in.

I've got Thomas's file, along with the other boys', and Bessy's notebook, and before I leave here I'm going to find out for once and for all what's going on here. Where all these boys are. I need to know what the connection is between Thomas and Aiden, what made them, even momentarily, sit together on the wall of a back room of a community centre at Northlands.

I open Thomas's file at the first page. Bessy's account of him, and Colin's. Black-and-white photographs of him and Bessy and Colin at the seaside. A couple out on the road. A drawing of his Billy can. A statement from his friend, and one from a former teacher. Another from his boss at the joinery where he worked.

One from a girl Thomas had dated for a short time. They say parents only ever know about 10 percent of what their children get up to. Mine certainly did. Looks like Bessy was no exception.

Then a report on the connection with the disappearance of several young men from the area from Inspector Little. It's linking the disappearances to those of some children. Their names are listed and I realize that they turn out to be the victims of the Moors Murders.

Little has pushed this, pushed for the disappearances to be investigated, but by the looks of further reports, this has been constantly vetoed. In the end, by the time the Moors Murderers have been to court, Thomas's case has been closed. He's a runaway, a boy who 'tired of his restrictive home environment.'

Following this, there are a few reports about Bessy's visits to the station and a possible reopening of the case, but this too is prevented. Then, there's a redacted section of the file. I can read enough to know that Inspector Little has been moved off the case for suggesting that a local man is involved in the disappearances. The local man's name has been crossed through with black pen all through the report.

Little has suggested that there is a connection between Thomas's case and Bessy's persistence that he's a victim of the Moors Murderers. That she's being egged on by her supporter, the same name that's been redacted. I think about the photo on the community centre wall, Bessy standing beside a huge man with a tiny hat, her half the size of him.

Founder of Mothers for the Missing. Staunch hater of the Moors Murderers and, later on, other criminals. I flick through the file and there are more pictures of them, at 'Bring Back Capital Punishment' rallies and appeals for missing boys. John Connelly.

I feel a chill run through me. This is the house Bessy lives in. Owned by the Connellys. I bet he's even been in here. I sit down below the net-curtained sash window and pick up Bessy's notebook. I've got a feeling everything I want to know is right here. Straight from the horse's mouth is always best.

BESSY

ON THE MAKE

This next part is about me on my own, and what I did, not so much to do with any gory details about *them*, I don't know if anyone's interested in that?

I had to pull myself together, quick, after the babies, and crack on nothing had happened. It was in the papers and everything. Baby found in phone box. They didn't know the bloody half of it. It doesn't matter either way now, but I sort of feel like someone should know what really happened, and why I did what I did.

By the next day I'd had a sleep and a wash and checked to see everything was all right down there. I kept going to the wardrobe and meaning to move the little mite, out of the way, till I could tell someone or bury her. But I was scared and I remembered that no one had been in the house since Colin left, so what odds was it where the poor little sod was, in the ground or in a box? No one cared about me or her.

On Thursday morning I washed my hair and had a bath, and went up to the police station just to check nothing else had happened. I'd come to my senses a bit, and I was ready to start the search for Thomas in earnest. Once I'd found him I could get my daughter back and bury the poor little mite up there.

One thing at a time, Bessy, that's what I thought. There was a big void, a gap, where I'd thought his dad had been looking for him. I'd trusted Colin to help me, but he hadn't. Thomas had been out there somewhere and no one had been looking for him.

I'd given up asking the police for help; they'd been busy with other things and not interested in a missing boy. Now all that was over, I was stuck in a prison of not knowing what to do. I'd found out that *she* was being kept in Durham Prison, and I'd thought about writing to *her*, but hadn't yet.

She was the only person who could tell me if they'd had Thomas or not. The only person. Rumour had it that *he* was a psychopath, mad as a bloody hatter. *He* must be to have done what he did to children. So there was no point asking *him*.

I'd read in the paper that *she* had a publicist, someone who dealt with it all for *her*, managed *her* affairs. I found out their name, and the prison governor's name. I put all this information in a drawer for when I felt strong enough to do something. If I ever did.

After the police station I went to see a solicitor. Colin was gone and I had no income. It turned out that the house was in both our names, and he still had to pay half the mortgage, but I would have to go to court to make him.

On top of that, he could say that he was providing for his new partner. And her children. For the first time, I realised that Lizzie had three children. Two teenage boys and a girl, about twelve. I'd inhaled sharply when I realised, as if water had gone up my nose. Colin was their dad now. Not Thomas's. I left the solicitor's and, on his advice, went to the bank.

In those days, you could still see the bank manager. I had to wait nearly two hours, but I was used to waiting. I'd been waiting since 1963. I'd never stopped hoping and expecting.

As the bank manager ushered me into his office, I wondered how I was going to survive. I'd never worked and I was forty. Harry Pearson, Manager of the North West Region, if a little plastic sign on his desk was anything to go by, shook my hand.

'What can I do for you, Mrs Swain?'

I sat up straight.

'Well, my husband's left me and I need to sort out what'll happen about the house.'

He shuffled some papers.

'Mortgaged. In both your names. Have you an income?'

I looked at my feet.

'No. My solicitor says Colin will have to pay half of it still. But I've no other way of paying the other half.'

He leaned back in his chair now.

'This is the problem with divorcing. Very sad business. I'm afraid your only choice seems to be to either get a job or sell the house.'

I stared at him. Instead of upset or pain, I actually felt fear.

'I can't sell the house; it's out of the question. You see, my son Thomas is missing. He disappeared around the time of the Moors Murders. When they found that young lad in that house, we thought it was him. But the police say he's just missing. Just missing. They don't know what's happened to him. The thing is, Mr Pearson, if he is still alive, and he comes home . . .'

Mr Pearson's features had changed. I'd noticed that. People talked a lot about the murders, gossiped and told each other the details they knew. It became like Chinese whispers; you didn't know what to believe.

But when they were confronted by people who had been involved in the investigation, those who had been next to death, they became afraid. Mr Pearson had looked horrified.

'My goodness. Well. I'm sorry to hear that. I never read that in the paper, but I suppose...'

'It wasn't in the papers. Why would it be? No one ever found his body. He's still missing. You can ask Ken Little at the station. He's been in charge of it all for us. Me.'

Mr Pearson looked paler.

'I'm very sorry for your circumstances. And in the middle of all this, your husband's left?'

I nodded.

'Yes. He's set up home with someone else. And her own kids.'

'Bastard.'

I nodded again.

'I will get a job, it's just that at the moment, I'm not feeling . . .'

He stood up, seething.

'Don't worry about it, Mrs Swain. I'll hold this in abeyance for six months, because of the circumstances. If you can pay anything, then please do, but if not, come back in six months. In the meantime, I'll see what I can do. Get you some support.'

'Support?'

'Yes. You shouldn't have to deal with this on your own. I'll get people involved. People who want to make them pay. I'll make sure that you find out what happened to your son. What's he called?'

'Thomas. Thomas Swain. He was seventeen when he went.' We both glanced at a photograph of Mr Pearson's family, three sons flanked by his wife. 'I'm sure you can imagine what I'm going through?'

This was the first time it happened. That shared knowledge that implored someone to help. Someone recognising, through their own life, how much pain is involved in my life. Mr Pearson wanted to help, and this was something I was unfamiliar with. Until now, I'd had Colin and his mam bickering at my heels, and the police not knowing if they were coming or going.

I'd left the bank a little bit more relieved, more sure that I had six months' grace. Mr Pearson told me he'd write to me when the time was up, and I was to go and see him again.

I'd walked most of the way home, but turned off at Newmarket Road. There were rows and rows of rhododendrons, and I followed it for about a mile, into my familiar childhood playground. Daisy Nook was a wood, with the River Medlock running through it.

A canal also stretched through, and me and Thomas used to come here and feed the ducks. It was the first time I'd ever seen a swan, and Thomas called it a huge snow duck.

There was no one about in the middle of the afternoon and I lay on the grass near the stream. It was completely silent, and I thought about Colin and Mr Pearson. I knew, really, that these were the least of my problems.

The gossips on the market were a fickle lot, and over the past four years they'd veered from feeling sorry for me to not really knowing what to say. In hindsight now, I could see that they must have known about Lizzie and Colin long before I did.

I'd wager they'd huddled together and made a mutual decision not to tell me. Some of them would have gone away and formed their own opinions about why all this had happened.

My son's body had not been found, therefore they concluded that he wasn't murdered. He'd left. The initial reaction of 'Little Sod!' was replaced with suspicious looks. The longer time went on, the more barbed their comments became.

'Smile, Bessy, it might never happen.'

I'd stare at them blankly, the loud voice in my head shouting that it already had. My boy wasn't safe at school or in bed. That sense of security you take for granted had gone. They'd carry on.

'Heard anything then?'

A huddle of nosey faces turned toward me, a flurry of headscarves and raised eyebrows.

'No, nothing.'

'Funny business then?'

'Yes.' But not funny for me, I think. Not funny at all.

'Wonder what made him go? You know, leave?'

I stared at the cobbled market square, then up at the clock on the market hall. I'd watch the brilliant white net curtains bellowing up from the stalls and imagine they were ship's sails pushing the days along, pushing the world round; anything to drown out the bitterness. I glanced around, ever vigilant for a glimpse of Thomas.

'We don't know he left. The police don't know what happened.'

I'd leave them to their gossip, and one or two of them would come and sit with me, budge up to me and pat my arm. But most of the time I just ignored them. What did they know?

I lay there in the sunshine, my best shoes on, and my coat still done up. If anyone had gone past they would have thought I was a mad woman, holding my hand out into the bare grass patch to my left, where Thomas used to lie.

I could only hear his laughter, not the water or the birds, just his laughter. I had been a good mother. I'd loved Thomas with all my heart. I'd had a lot of time to sit and think about it, and I came up with this: I knew that whatever had happened between me and Thomas and Colin in our little house, my intentions had been good.

My train of thought always came back to *her*. To eliminate even this tiny strand of what had happened to Thomas, *she* would know. Of all the dangers, chances, wonderings, this was the biggest, the obvious outcome. If I could only ask *her*, see *her*, and ask *her* if *they* had killed Thomas, at least I'd have an answer.

The sun was warm and I'd see the occasional bird fly overhead, I looked at the clouds for a while then I decided to go home. At least I wouldn't have to make Colin's tea. I could have some boiled potatoes and carrots I already had in, and I could stop in my nightie if I wanted to.

Colin had never really understood what I felt. I automatically thought that because he was Thomas's dad, he was the only other person who would know what I felt like. Instead, he'd been with Lizzie and her kids, playing happy family.

Six months went by quick as a flash and nothing changed, except I laid one less place at dinner and tea. I'd started cooking a lot less, mainly because I had very little money, and I'd lost weight. I took in most of my clothes and wondered what would happen next.

Each day was survival, nothing more, a wait for news, visits to the police station. Mr Pearson's letter never came so I went to the bank. He wasn't there, but I had my bank book updated and found that there was more money in my account than I expected. I wondered if Colin, who had refused to pay anything, had relented.

The next January I had a knock on the door. I opened it and a large gentleman stood on the doorstep. He'd got out of a big car, and the neighbours were out. I felt my skin pale and my legs go to jelly; was this the news I'd been dreading about Thomas? He strode in and perched on the edge of a dining chair.

'Right. I'm John Connelly. I own a lot of butchers round here. I have the meat factory down by the canal. I own shops everywhere. Up and down to Lincolnshire.'

I sighed.

'I don't understand. You must have the wrong house. I'm Bessy Swain.'

He laughed, then sobered. He looked like a nice man, all cheery.

'Sorry, serious business this. I'll cut to the chase. I'm a pal of Harry Pearson and he's told me about your little predicament. I'll tell no lie, Bessy, if I may, but I'd like to see those bastards hanged.' I knew who he was talking about; it was a view expressed by everyone. Hanging had just been abolished while they waited to go to court. 'I'm going to do everything I can to help those affected. I didn't get where I am today through having a hard heart. So. Here we are. I'd like to pay your mortgage off.'

I stare at him.

'Why?'

'Like I said, I want to help those affected. But you'd have to do something in return. You'd have to be interviewed for a paper, tell them what happened.'

My heart sunk again. As if they'd be interested in me.

'But I haven't got a story. They've never found Thomas's body, have they? The police say he could have gone missing.'

John flushed dark red.

'And they could just have easily have any number of kiddies buried up there. How do we know? We don't bloody know. And those two bastards are bloody liars, too. Bloody liars, the pair of them. I'm going to see justice. They should have been hanged.'

He pulled out an already damp handkerchief and wiped his face. I put the kettle on and sat back down, pulling my cardy round me.

'So does the bank want the house back then?'

'No. I'd buy it for you and give it you as a gift. Course, I'd still own it, but I'd swear a covenant that you can live here until you don't want to anymore. To help put your mind at rest. Harry told me you waited in every day for the lad to come home. That's a bloody tragedy, love, because chances are he's dead. Sorry. I speak the bloody truth. Course, you can understand why the police won't say this, cos there's no body. They have to say it. But I've spoken to them and they all think there's more to this than meets the bloody eye. I want you, as a mother of an abducted child, to rest easy at night. We both get something out of it. You get your house and I get some advertising.'

I wasn't sure, but I nodded.

'Problem is, it's half Colin's. That's my husband who left. So he'd get half of what's made on it.'

He laughed loudly and I could see the curtains across the road twitch.

'I've looked into it. You bought the house for £760. It's worth £2600 now. Your mortgage is for £350 and this'll go to Harry. So you'll get £2250 cash, which you'll split with this Colin. And I'll give the house to you, to live in rent-free. Just you, not this Colin bloke. He left you for someone else, so I hear.'

'Mmm.'

'What a bastard. You know, it's hard to find someone good and just in this world. Thank God for people like me and you, Bessy. Good-hearted folk with genuine good wishes.'

He seemed like a nice man, and what did I have to lose? I worked out that I'd get the house to live in and some money, as well as some security. I could sleep again.

'OK. But will I have to sign something?'

He stood.

'I'll get Jim to draw something up and you and your husband can sign. Get a divorce, too, I'll have my solicitor get in touch with you about it. All you have to do in return, love, is to talk to a few people about where you think your son is. You know, on't moor. Leave it to me, love. We'll get the bastards yet. They'll bloody hang if I have anything to do with it. Oh. And stop mithering the police. They've got enough to do and I'm sure they'll let you know if they find anything.'

The door was open now and his voice boomed out. He shook my hand and the neighbours ducked back in.

'I can see you all, you nosey buggers. Be good to this lady. She's been through hell.'

By the end of summer it was all underway. The papers had been signed, I had the money, Colin was happy because he had his money, and I just sat and waited every day, waiting for the door to open.

I'd go on the market every day, buying my dinner and tea, the occasional dress, and my Park Drives. The gossips still huddled together and called me a bad mother and wife, but it was water off a duck's back.

Not only had my son and husband gone, but I had sold my soul. I'd talked to the people from the newspaper and they'd run rings round me, making me say things I didn't want to, telling them about Thomas saying he hated Colin, the woman who interviewing me sneering when I said I'd never worked, me tying myself in knots about how I was managing to live. John Connelly put them straight, defending me at every corner—he was like my knight in shining armour.

He asked me never to mention our little arrangement, so my mouth was forced shut more than ever. So I decided I wouldn't say anything. I was empty inside, dead, just like a robot doing the same thing, day in, day out.

BESSY
DONKEY'S YEARS

That all happened in 1968. After that, one day merged into another, with no real markers as to where weekends were. My mother and father died two years apart in 1978 and 1980. I went to the funerals, but I stood at the back. I felt like they'd let me down, not really cared when Thomas went missing.

That's what the police were calling it now—going missing. They'd moved on from 'disappeared' and 'kidnapped' to 'missing.' I'd been in touch with my parents, I'd been to see them several times, but their blank stares were just like everyone else's when I mentioned it.

It was like a mist came down over their eyes, nodding and blinking, then, as soon as I finished talking, turning the subject to somat else. I couldn't work out if it was because they felt sorry and didn't know what to say, or if they were embarrassed.

Then I realised. It wasn't about them. Until I gave them somat to compare it to their own lives, they just weren't interested. My parents had never had a son, never loved me the same, couldn't wait to get me married off, so why would they care? How could they understand?

It was just like Colin, the expression of boredom. We'd all

gone through the correct procedures and come up with nothing. Because it was nothing to do with them, they just stopped there. I carried on.

I was still waiting, itching to get away from their graves to be back home, in case he came back. You probably think I'm mad, and it had been donkey's years. Donkey's years. It was something Colin would say and we never knew what it meant.

Me and Thomas used to go and look at the donkeys down Keb Lane and, for as long as we could remember, they were the same ones. I'd been there lately and they were still the same. In fact, everything was still the same, except Thomas was gone and I was no longer married to Colin.

Our divorce had come through and he'd married Lizzie three months later. It was a lovely wedding by all accounts, with her daughter as bridesmaid. I saw him after the do, playing football outside with Dennis and Jack. I caught his eyes, just standing there holding my handbag and I thought he looked guilty. Or maybe not.

It wasn't all bad, for donkey's years. I'd done a lot of paper interviews, and some for magazines, and John Connelly had raised a lot of money for me at his appeals. He was such a nice man, very polite and respectful.

Every Bonfire Night he'd have a special outing for all the people round here who had missing children, up in front of his factory. It was lovely, with Parkin and treacle toffee. All I had to do was go and be introduced as Thomas's mother, I was a bit like a sideshow attraction at the fair, a bearded lady or a strong man, the freak with something not quite right, but what choice did I have?

I'd just live on what I needed and put the rest in the bank. By 1985, I'd had quite a bit saved. I passed my driving test and John Connelly gave me what he called a 'little run-around,' so I could get to the benefits and appeals.

Oh, and I'd made a friend, a blackbird that had come to sit on my washing line. Over a couple of months, I'd left bread out in the yard. Then I left it on the outside windowsill. Then I left it on the ledge of an open window. One day, after three months, I was putting the bread out and he came to take it out of my hand.

After that, he'd come when I whistled, and I'd hold the bread out of the window. I'd called him Jack, and after a couple of years there were two of them. Jack disappeared, so I did the same process with the next one, who I called Jill, even though I know now it was a male.

They'd change every two or three years, and they were there all year long. I'd feed them twice a day, then they'd sing at dusk. That tinny light in the evenings, where everything looked golden, was my favourite time of day, where me and the blackbird would sit outside. I'd sip my tea and wonder what tomorrow would bring.

I was living a double life, and up until 1985 there was a battle going on inside me. One part of me was doing John Connelly's appeals for Thomas, appearing in public like a sad celebrity. I knew that there were other parents of missing people, there were a lot of them round here, and we used to talk at the same rallys, all about *them* and how *they* should be punished.

But John wanted me to do this for just him, and asked me not to contact the other parents. I didn't want to anyway. I'd been learning to drive and decorating my house, having an inside toilet put in, central heating. I'd had a colour TV for years and I'd watch *Corrie* in my housecoat, still waiting for that knock.

It was then, after eight o'clock, that my other self would kick in. My darkness came when the sun disappeared. I'd go outside and stare at the moon, wondering if Thomas was looking at it.

Something was certain; he couldn't be looking at another moon, just this one. Whether he liked it or not, we shared the moon.

If he was dead and buried somewhere, the moonlight would be shining on his grave, reflecting back at me. I'd unpin my hair and walk around the house, smoking and going over every detail of what had happened before he went. Had I said something wrong? Was my whole approach to mothering wrong? Had I potty trained him too early?

Even now, the women I met in the supermarket and at the veg stalls sneered as they remembered Thomas disappearing. I'd never challenged them. Why should I? They didn't know anything about how Thomas would kiss me and tell me I was the best mum in the world. He would always draw me yellow, like sunshine, he said.

I'd pace around, up and down, until I was weak with exhaustion. I'd throw myself on the bed and cry and cry, not dramatic, like, more just quiet and sad. I'd wonder what happened to that little girl and, sometimes, I'd peek in the wardrobe just to make sure everything was all right in there.

It was like I was a different person inside, living one life that was the real Bessy, sad and desperate, a life that ended with Thomas and *her*, in *her* prison cell, stopping me getting on.

The other life, my daytime life, was as normal as possible. I'd be up with the lark, no need for an alarm, and I'd feed the birds. It was entirely different in the summer than in the winter, because the days were shorter in the winter, so the nights and the crying were longer.

When May came, though, it was a relief, because I could go out in the day for longer, and pretend I was someone I wasn't. I'd smile and be polite to anyone I came across, particularly if I knew them as I wanted people to think I was getting over it.

Recovering, as they put it. I'd walk up Ney Street and around the market, never getting too friendly with anyone in case they wanted to come to my house. By now, I had stuff about Thomas everywhere. And there were the smells as well. Newspapers and cuttings, all about *them*.

No one ever came round to see me, so when I shut that door I could do whatever I wanted to, which was mostly smoke and cry.

As the number of people who had direct contact with the Moors Murders lessened, the fewer people understood why I was still waiting. All the people who lived nearby had either moved or had been convinced when Colin left that it was all my fault; I must be a bad person if both my son and my husband left me.

Ken Little had retired years ago, and when I made my weekly visit to Ashton-Under-Lyne police station, I would see a young constable who'd tell me there had been no developments, or even the desk sergeant, if they were busy.

Of course, by 1985, times had changed and there was a lot more to do. There'd been lots of children going missing round here, usually through parents splitting up and one taking them away somewhere, but more often they just disappeared. Rumour had it that most of them were boys and they'd run away, probably to London, John Connelly said. But sometimes they were murdered.

There were bodies found. Each time I heard about it on the news, I would go to the station, even though John had told me not to. Likewise, if I heard on the missing people grapevine that there was an unidentified body, I'd go to the station. I'd even begun to look at the death registers, but when I saw what a massive task it was, I put it on hold.

I'd been down to the police station one day when I saw a paper on the stand with *her* face on the front. Underneath it, there was a story about how *he* had confessed to more murders.

I went back to the police station, taking the paper with me, but they told me, there and then, that Thomas wasn't one of the children named. He was still a missing person. They told me that the Moors Murders case would be reopened. The rest I read in the papers.

I found out where *she* was, that *she'd* found God, that *she'd* been studying. Funny. My life had just stopped one day in 1964, but everything else had gone on. I'd kept Thomas's bedroom exactly how it was. Manchester United, his team, had gone on. His football, five-a-side, still played at Ashton Moss.

Colin had still gone on, married Lizzie and become her kids' dad. Ken Little had gone on, getting a long service medal and retiring to Kent; that's what his replacement told me. *She'd* gone on, even in prison. Even *he'd* been talking to the press and making a bloody drama out of it all. My life had just stopped. It might have looked like I'd carried on with my life, but inside I was dead. Stone dead.

That's when I started to drive up to Saddleworth Moor. I wasn't sure if he was up there, but it was my best chance of talking to *her*. I'd heard that *she* was going up there, to show the police where other people were buried. There was a kind of deep excitement inside my chest when I realised that there was a chance they might find him.

At first I drove to the bottom of the moor, but the police were there and they had it all cordoned off. So I drove up to the car park near a farm and walked over to a wall. I jumped over and went onto the moor for the first time. To me, it was a big graveyard.

I'd never been here before, although I'd wanted to. I wasn't even sure why. Yet when I stepped onto the grim scrub at the edge, and saw the bright purple foxgloves growing out of it, I felt like I had come home. I'd gone down to the spot where there were yellow markers, death placers, so that when they did bring *her* here they would all know where to look.

Although *she* would know where to look already, because it was *she* who had committed the crime and drawn them all here. I suddenly felt a pang of anger at *her*, a deep anxiety at all the attention *she* was getting, and wondered if it was a busman's holiday for *her,* just a way for *her* to feel the sun on *her* face as she stood on another grave.

I stood at the designated spot and looked around. It was different, but not all that unpleasant. A kind of dumbed down version of the world, all amethyst and grey, with some bright greens here and there. And birds everywhere. I looked it up later on in Thomas's encyclopaedia.

'Many of these moorland species are considered to be in danger or vulnerable. Variations in the habitat suit different species. The red grouse, merlin, short-eared owl, and hen harrier nest among the taller heather, where the plant growth provides them with cover.

In contrast, the golden plover, lapwing, and curlew are often found nesting on the recently burned open areas. Wading birds such as snipe and redshank, as well as duck, nest in the wetter areas. Moorland is also an important feeding area for the Peregrine. Many of the birds which nest on the moor winter in this country, returning to another life for half the year.'

Two lives. A bit like me. There was a covering of emerald green moss, with heather outcrops here and there. I imagined that if they had brought Thomas here, he would be resting in a warm bed underneath the blanket of moss pulled up around him, the heather duvet keeping him safe and happy in his resting place.

His pillow would be a puffball mushroom and his sleep would be undisturbed here, where it was ever so quiet. The roots would grow around him, drawing him into the ground and he'd eventually become a living part of it, turning in the peat with all the other living creatures that were down there.

What's more, I could visit him every day, sure that he was here, safe in Mother Nature's arms. I suddenly felt glad that he hadn't been disturbed, not like the other poor children. I couldn't even imagine what their families had gone through when their little kiddies had been dug from the moor and taken back into the horrors of life they had been left with.

I'd never forgotten the faces of the policemen involved in the investigation, the sorrow drawn all over their faces. I'd intentionally not contacted the families of the children who had been found there, because I was never really sure that Thomas was dead.

What if, on the day I made contact, told them what I thought, shared their grief, he walked back in? They didn't have that luxury. Their children were gone. But then again, they didn't have my torture.

The road was blocked off at both ends on the day they took *her* to the moor. I sat at the top of Pots and Pans and watched the helicopter land. I couldn't see what went on, but, like at the trial, I pleaded silently with *her* to tell me if *she* had murdered my son.

She'd confessed to the murders by now, and between them they'd named five children altogether. Three had been found, one at the house on the day, and two buried on the moor. The police started to dig again, and I stood rooted in horror to the spot when I saw the front of the paper.

They'd found Pauline Reade. The search went on for months, and every day I got as close as I could during the day, waiting for a phone call in the evening to tell me they'd found Thomas.

I'd considered getting in touch with Mrs Johnson, Keith Bennett's mother, and I'd sometimes seen her on the moor. Who was I to talk to her? Her son was officially dead, mine was officially missing. She was in the paper, on the telly; I was rolled out at John Connelly's benefits and appeals.

Not that I was complaining, I just felt sidelined, as if I wasn't good enough to go over it again and again. Her child had been named, she was on the way to knowing what happened. Mine was completely invisible still.

This might sound like all I was worried about was myself, but I was actually devastated. I'd been walking on the spot that poor girl was found just before they started digging, and it was driving me mad.

The problem was, I knew how the families felt, I knew their every emotion, I knew their torture, how every day they still thought about their child. Those children would have been in their thirties now, with families of their own. Jobs, houses, lives.

All of them gone, like Thomas. I was hysterical when the body was found, and hysterical when they didn't find the other body and closed the investigation. If there had been any hope left in me, it died that day.

I sat on the wall and watched them move the digging equipment down the path. I wanted to shout at them to take it back, find her son, find my son, but I had no voice left. I just watched with sad eyes. It was my fifty-ninth birthday, but people had forgotten about my birthday a long time ago.

CHAPTER TEN

I stare through the house and out of the back window, where, as if to reinforce Bessy's story, two blackbirds sat on the windowsill. As if to tell me that this is real. This is what you've been waiting for. I want to read more but I'm angry. I need to think it through and take action.

John Connelly. Mr Connelly Snr. Pat Haywood told me he'd organized and funded Mothers for the Missing. He was a local philanthropist and benefactor. But all the while he was making sure that all the families of the missing boys completely believed that their sons had been abducted or, like the boys last month, had committed suicide.

That their disappearance had gone almost unpublicised, pushed to the back of the local paper, runaways or young suicides.

The case notes say that Little was removed from the case. He clearly found out about John Connelly. To make things worse, John Connelly had used the Moors Murders to cover up his tracks making the mothers believe that their sons were buried on Saddleworth Moor. And who were they to question it? Like his son, John Connelly was head of a criminal hierarchy, making sure that there were enough people below him to take the blame if anything went wrong. Like Harry Pearson, who was probably on the take as well.

These influential men were using their self-made standing in the community to prey on victims from the same community. Ingratiating themselves and diverting suspicion by throwing money at it. Connelly Snr. paying Bessy and probably others, encouraging her to get involved with his campaigns, and Connelly Jnr. providing Pat and the other victims' families with facilities to meet.

It's almost unbelievable, but it fits in with everything I've suspected about Connelly. And now Connelly Snr. He'd been buying up all the houses in the area from the mothers of the missing children, then manipulating them to believe that those kids were runaways. Bessy, anyway, and probably the other poor families in the photos at the community centre.

I open the file again. John Connelly is mentioned several times in Thomas's investigation, mainly in a positive sense, as if he is some kind of mass benefactor.

For a second I question my motives and wonder if Bessy's story is true, and if Thomas really is buried on the moor with the other victims. I know that, at the time, searches were limited to digging small spots in a vast area and there is a strong possibility his body wouldn't have been found at the time. But even if he is, where are all the other boys? I turn to the back of the file and tucked into the back flap of the folder, out of sight, is a handwritten letter.

It's from Inspector Little. It's his letter of resignation. Mostly that he is disappointed that leads were not followed up, that the number of missing children and teenagers from the area has substantially increased and that there should be an urgent enquiry into Thomas Swain's case. That it should be reopened. That Bessy should be reinterviewed and Colin should be told about Connelly's meddling in Bessy's life, making her a spokeswoman for his campaign when there was never any proof that Thomas was a victim of the Moors Murders, or any other murder.

Even though she hadn't recorded it in her notebook, Bessy had talked to Inspector Little about it, urged him to dig for Thomas and when he had pointed out that there was no proof she had become confused, telling him John Connelly had made her think there was. I was beginning to see a fuller story, one where Bessy had been more desperate then even her tragic story told, not knowing who to believe and begging for help. Poor Inspector Little resigned because he knew the truth and no one would listen to him.

Pinned to his letter was a photograph. At first it looks like it was the same photograph I had seen at the community centre, of John Connelly and Bessy outside the Gables. But then I see that Bessy is standing on the other side of Connelly and there are two other women beside her. I look more closely, back through the decades, and I see it. Behind Bessy is a telegraph pole and, dangling over the heads of the women, is a row of scarves and pairs of shoes slung over. Three mothers, three scarves, three pairs of shoes.

It's dark now and I can't put the lights on. I push all the papers and the exercise book back into the folder and go outside into the yard. Bessy's yard is really a garden, complete with an army of bird feeders.

I go in her shed and find some grain. As I step outside, there's already a huge amount of birds on the telegraph wires and on the top of the shed, all twittering away. As I put the grain in they make a swoop for it, filling the yard with flapping wings and beady eyes. Bessy's friends, the blackbirds, hang back, sitting on the washing line and watching the greedy starlings.

I put the seed back and steer my bike out of the yard,

pushing the file into the storage box at the back. I'm not so concerned about getting seen now. I ride up the main roads, looking upward at the cameras, taking my time in the evening traffic.

I ride through Northlands and take a right at the end, up toward the hills and away from the city. The road out of there narrows and splits, a fork where both ways lead to tragedy.

One way leads up to the moor, several miles on. I've been up there several times, not with work, but to gawp like the other five or six rubberneckers who are there every time I go up there. I toy with the idea of riding there now, giving myself more time to think before I embark on my next move. But the other road leads to John Connelly's derelict old factory, where I'd seen Bessy standing outside on the photographs.

I sit at the crossroads and laugh. Let's face it. I'm fucked. Jim Stewart warned me that if I carried on searching for Aiden on police time I'd be suspended. Then I'd probably have to resign. I wondered how many other coppers had resigned after suspecting the truth. Even now, it seems too big to comprehend.

Why would Connelly and his father before him be abducting kids? And why would some of them turn up as apparent suicides? It doesn't make sense, except in the most horrible and grotesque of scenarios.

When Aiden went missing, and after I had recovered a little from the terrible shock, I spent an enormous amount of time wondering what he was doing, how he was eating if he hadn't touched his bank account.

I pictured him selling the Big Issue in London, eating out of bins. God knows I'm used to seeing kids living on the street in Manchester, waiting outside McDonald's and eating the half-eaten cast-offs of other people.

Like Bessy's birds, swooping in for a discarded burger or milkshake, waiting just on the eye-line of passers-by, hoping they'd decide that the sandwich they'd just bitten into was horrible and bin it. Watching people eat through fast food restaurant windows, rooting in skips after the supermarkets close.

How was he washing? How was he going to the loo? How was he cleaning his lovely teeth, brushing his hair? How, how, how? If he was alive, like they all said he was, and he'd run away, how was he doing all this?

I'd been thinking about it, a constant train of thought behind the classical conditioned reactions of driving, as I sped along the main roads early one morning. I remember it clearly; it was one of those early autumn days where the sunlight trickles through the darkened leaves.

Kicking the leaves with Aiden. Running through them and burying ourselves in the rusty piles. Picking up acorns and planting them the next year. Pressing the leaves in Aiden's books. I must look for those leaves. Leaves that he had touched, suddenly so precious.

Then, out of nowhere, it hit me. I don't know why, but the unspeakable came to me. He must have been getting money. He must have been working. What could he have been doing at fifteen? No, sixteen. Working. For money.

There was a screech and I almost hit the car in front of me. I sat there at a busy road junction, horns beeping all around me. Working. For money. For who? Doing what? No. No. No.

I sat there for a good ten minutes, until a police car arrived. Then I pretended that my car had stalled and it wouldn't start so I had no choice but to block the road. I'd caused a backlog of nearly a mile by this time, but all I could think about was Aiden, my shy little boy, being forced to do unthinkable things.

What if he was being held against his will and abused? He must be. Either that, or he was dead. Because he'd never just run. Never. I knew him. He'd never do that.

I remember snapping out of it and starting my engine.

'Thanks, officer. It's fine now. Sorry about that.'

A mile and a half tailback, apparently, but I hadn't cared. I was frozen in a frame of realization, one that I would never escape. I remember pulling over just further up the road and putting my head on the steering wheel to try to appease the physical pain I felt at my son going through that. Going through something I had fought to save him from. Protect him.

I remember clearly thinking that this must be the worst pain in the world, apart from identifying his body. What's more, other people were probably thinking it. Before I even considered any harm coming to him, people would be silently wondering if he was part of some sordid sex ring, one where young men and women were abducted and forced to submit to perverts and paedophiles, living on a basic level, like an animal. And if they objected they were punished. Or worse.

I was completely amazed and sickened that I hadn't considered this before. I was completely incensed that everyone around me had remained silent. It was so obvious now, the sad looks, the quiet nods whenever I wondered out loud where he was. They must have thought I was stupid.

Was it a mother's built in defence system? Was it a way to save a mother from the crippling pain of her child suffering? I'd broken bad news to mothers for over a decade now.

I'd stood in a pristine lounge with Mike, heads bowed, as we delivered various grades of horrendous. Your son's in custody for committing petty crime. Your daughter's been arrested for assault. Your son's been detained over a suspected rape. Your son's been arrested on suspicion of murder. Your daughter is dead.

We usually get 'It's not her. She wouldn't do that.' Or 'No. You're wrong. I know my son. He wouldn't do that.' As the case progresses and guilt becomes clear, the crumbling of the parent is visible. Sometimes it's emotional; tiny teardrops leaking out at first, followed by howling and keening. Or physical. Actual collapse.

One woman became so ill that she was admitted to the hospital. I'd had to visit her to tell her that her son had been found guilty of manslaughter. I'd asked the nurse if they had found out what was wrong with her.

'No. We can't find anything. Except that she's so weak that she can't stand. No previous medical conditions. She just keeps saying that she's in great pain.'

I'd frowned at the nurse, and shook my head.

'What do you think?'

She'd pulled me into a side corridor.

'I used to work on an old people's ward. Oldies coming in, weak as kittens. No diagnosis, no real sickness, just pain and weakness. The first thing we'd check was if they'd just lost their partner. One of them even told me that his wife had taken his soul with her when she died. I think he meant his heart.'

I'd sniggered at the time. Dying of a broken heart. Oh pleez. That's just stupid, illogical claptrap. But now it was me.

As I sit here at the crossroads, wondering what to do, I'm hurting. I've made some terrible decisions. Taking the money, taking the file, leaving the archive room, going to see Pat Haywood . . . all these things seem crazy on the face of it but each of them put snippet of duct tape over my heart, pulling it together and stopping me creasing with the ever-growing pain and realisation about what was happening to Aiden.

Like I did at the hospital, everyone around me was sniggering, wondering when I will man up and stop moping. After all, how bad can it be? He's obviously run away, hasn't he, because no one's found his body? So, Jan, what's wrong? Why are you crying? Why are you crumbling? Why are you doing everything you can to find him?

No one can feel what I'm going through, because no one else is Aiden's mum. Even Sal doesn't seem so concerned; he's taking it in stride.

I know this is a kind of madness. I know my thinking isn't rational or logical. It hasn't been for six weeks, since I realised Aiden was gone. I'm working almost entirely on instinct now, or, as some people would call it, winging it.

Like I said, a little instinct is a good thing. I'm chasing the silent messages, the invisible crime scene, the hidden world I know is around here somewhere, waiting to be discovered if only I can make sense of all the signposts, all the patterns. Gut feeling. But now I've pulled the threads together and come to a conclusion, I'm wondering if I am actually mad. Mad with grief. Mad with anxiety. Or am I saner than I've ever been?

Day to day, policing and working with people makes you used to it. Used to the horror stories, used to crime. Sometimes the determination disappears and it's all routine, bordering on the boring, and I have to get Mike to give me a metaphorical kick up the arse to remind me that this is peoples' lives that are affected.

And vice versa. If he lacks motivation I give him a push. We always work best when we're right up to the line. Working on that feeling in the pit of our stomachs, sitting in a bar afterward, with the suspect in the cells, drinking ice-cold lager. But this is more than that. I've crossed the line. My motivation is my son, the most important person in the world to me.

To make it worse, everyone else thinks I'm wrong. I've been in this situation before, with Sal. A couple of years into our marriage I was miserable. Our families were as pleased as punch that we had made a go of it. But I knew even then it would never work.

All my friends told me I was mad, that Sal was 'The One,' that I could never find someone so perfect for me. But they were all wrong. Sometimes it takes years to realize you are right, that the gut feeling you had was right all along, and in the end, when I got the divorce absolute and Sal snapped again and finally showed his true colours in front of all his family when he poured a drink over my head at a family party and called me all the names under the sun.

I just sat there, and Aiden walked out. I just sat there because it was a defining moment, something I'd made no effort at all to make happen. On the contrary, Sal had proved me right all by himself.

That's how I feel now. As if I'm on the brink of something here, something that, for some reason, no one else had seen. Then it all starts to cascade into place. Maybe other people do know about it. Other people higher up, other people who could prevent Connelly from being found out.

Operation Hurricane. It seemed like it would be so successful, but shut down because somehow Connelly had found out all the information. All the ops, all the chasing information, all wasted. And paperwork disappearing. Reports that officers had sworn they had filed, gone. Data everyone, including myself, had seen, disappeared off the system overnight.

At first Jim Stewart thought it was some kind of virus, recoverable. After all, we were the police, weren't we supposed to be secure? But it soon became obvious that it was gone, and we all began to doubt each other. If there was a small personality clash, it became a chasm of suspicion, where accusations of lies over how much work had been done and what had been reported was flying.

It had been chaos at the station for months, but when Jim announced Operation Prophesy informally, four weeks before its official launch, everyone relaxed a little. It was as if we'd get a second chance at Connelly, a chance to recover all the lost work and finally stop whatever was happening. I rationalise this with myself now. Isn't that what I'm doing too, investigating Connelly's wrongdoing?

I ride up the road to the derelict factory. The Gables. Tatters of age-old messages hang from the wires above me and my blood runs cold. It's dark now and I might as well get this over with, find out for once and for all what is going on. If anything. Like Old Mill, this could easily be used for nothing at all. In the distance, the building certainly looks like it's mostly derelict. It had never cropped up in our investigation before. Why would it? The records show that Connelly's butchers went bankrupt years ago. No activity there, so far out of town, and derelict. I find a lane reasonably far away from the gates, away from any surveillance. I push the bike into the bushes and sit down on the cold grass and phone Mike. Two rings and he's answered.

'Shit, Jan, where are you?'

I snort.

'No polite chit chat, then?'

'No. You're in the shit big time. Stewart's had me in going on about some baby in a house, you know, the one where you found that woman? He's got Sal in there right now, something about another sighting of Aiden. You know he'll be scoping him for info on your state of mind, don't you? And going into Northlands, seeing Pat Haywood without ops? He knows all about it. Fuck Jan, what the hell . . .'

'Look, Mike, just stop. I'm on to something here. I'm up at Old Mill and I'm going in. I need backup.'

There's silence. I can hear his breath. I know Mike will do this. I know he will. Despite everything, he's still there for me.

'You've got to be fucking kidding.'

'No. I'm round the side of the mill. I need assistance.'

Silence again. I expect he's trying to understand if I'm sane or not.

'Come on, don't do this. Not on your own.'

'Well, I won't be on my own when you call it in, will I?'

'No, but you'll be suspended. Straight away. No messin'. Career suicide.'

'I'll take that chance. Please, Mike. Full back up, yeah?'

'Can't you tell me a bit more? About what it is?'

I smile. Good try. He's obviously pressed the panic button on his other phone, and they'll be listening now in the operation room. Keep me on the line. Try to track me. But at the end of it, he'll phone it in.

'Sorry, Mike, have to go. I'm going in.'

I walk down the lane and, once on the main road, I duck behind a huge oak tree. I'm almost opposite the Gables, and I can see the wrought iron arch above the gates outlined on the evening sky. I look up at the moon. Like Bessy says, wherever Aiden is, we're sharing the same moon. It's a sliver of hope in the distance, a constant that connects me and my son, wherever he is.

I sit and wait, a few more minutes then, as predicted, the gates are unlocked and four black BMWs roll out. One of them is the BMW that fronted me on the lane when I was meeting Mike. Same number plate. I wasn't imagining the connection. On their way to Old Mill, no doubt. My heart sinks. So the message got to them so soon, absolute proof of an insider. Just like Operation Hurricane, Connelly's henchmen appearing out of the woodwork almost immediately when we got close to anything incriminating. But on the better side, less people here, guarding whatever is here.

CHAPTER ELEVEN

There's always a way in. Sometimes you have to smash your way in. Sometimes you have to wait. Sometimes the doors are just open, because they aren't expecting anyone to just walk in without invitation.

I know the front gates are open because I saw the guy in the last car jump out and shut them. No keys. I stand just behind the huge iron girders that form the support for the wrought iron lettering, shaped art nouveau suggesting that this place was built in the 1920s or 1930s. There's no way to tell really because most of the building is in disrepair.

I can't see any cars parked outside, so hopefully there will be minimum people left in there guarding. Even though the gates are open I press through a small gap in the wooden fence. I'm inside the grounds and I look around for a chink of light, somewhere I can gain entry. Nothing at all.

I walk around the side staying close to the perimeter, looking around all the time for cameras. There don't seem to be any. Surely it can't be unguarded, like Old Mill? Oh my God. Maybe I'm wrong again and there'll just be more fucking kitchens.

No. I see a row of strategically placed cameras pointing to the front gates. I evaluate the angles and duck below them, using my evasion training.

There are two rows of high windows, indicating two floors. No more cameras, just at the front. I stand behind them and see that the wires are networked inside, where there would be more security. I walk around the building, checking for coal chutes or grids that indicate a cellar; there are none. I arrive back at the front.

So here we are. It's like a cube, on two floors. I spot a small window at the rear on the left, probably a toilet or washroom. Or a storeroom. I walk around, looking for any gaps. Looking for any sign of life. Most of the windows are partially frosted and I peer through them, into apparent darkness.

I have to go in. I take off my jacket and wrap it around a nearby stone and push hard against the glass. It cracks but doesn't break. I push a little harder until it moves in the frame, the heavy layers of ancient paint holding it in. I wiggle a piece, like a toddler's tooth, and it becomes looser.

I drag the shard toward me and place it up against the wall. I dismantle the widow piece by piece, until it's no longer dangerous for me to climb through. As I thought, the room is a toilet.

I stick my head inside and sniff. Pine. This place is being used. For something. I heave myself up through the window and I'm standing in a small bathroom, with a toilet, wash basin, and shower. It's clean and the fittings are quite modern.

I open the door swiftly and it leads onto an unlit corridor. The whole place smells of disinfectant and I look up. False ceilings. Pristine white tiles. I make my way up the corridor to the swing doors at the other end, checking the light fittings for sensors. There are none.

Through the swing doors and into what appears to be a bar

area. Chrome and walnut, very '70s, but the sophisticated lighting gives it away. This is new technology. As I walk along the bar it lights up. Sensors here, but not for an alarm, just for the lights.

There are two double doors at the end of the room and I make for them. I hold one slightly open and peep through. There's a woman mopping the laminated flooring, and another with what appears to be a hotel cleaning trolley, standing outside a door.

I wait and wait and finally they go into one of the several doors that line each side of the corridor. I pad silently past them and open the last door on the left. It's a bedroom. Luxurious and made up with an open bar.

What is this place? Derelict on the outside, but inside a palace, complete with dance floor and bar. Maybe it's where Connelly spends his leisure time? Maybe it's where he hides away. Oh. God. Maybe that's all it is. I sit on the bed. I've got that feeling again, the one where everyone else is right and I'm mad.

Maybe this is nothing, but I still have to find out. I suddenly get a sense of something ending. The mass of blue lights would be descending on Old Mill anytime now, looking for me in the grounds with searchlights. Mike would be standing there, worried and pale, as I didn't appear. I need to get on.

I open the bedroom door and slip quickly through the double swing doors and I'm in a huge white room, not unlike the stark upper floors of Old Mill. The disinfectant smell is stronger here, and I choose the doors to the left that I know will take me deeper into the building.

The windows here are lined with a foil-like material that I haven't seen before. No one is around, so I hurry down another corridor. There's a security desk at the end of the corridor, unmanned. I scan for cameras or sensors, but there are none. I can hear voices now, and I listen at the last door to the right.

'Yeah, down at the Mill. Seems like the pigs are there en masse. Come and look on the security. Come and look, Jed.'

They're linked to cameras at Old Mill. Finally. A connection. I hear another door open further along, I duck behind the steel door at the end. Jed appears, then disappears into the room.

'Bloody hell. I hope they don't come here and find this lot.'

'Yeah. Not likely though, is it? No one knows about this, and them who do won't be telling anyone in a hurry. Anyway, them in there'll be gone soon. On Bunty Night. That's when they get rid of them, on Bunty Night, so's no one'll notice. Just the once a year.'

They're watching the furore at Old Mill, laughing loudly, and I know I don't have much time. I swing through the door and I can see the red eye of a security camera in what is otherwise a completely dark room. I know it's a camera and not a movement sensor because otherwise they would be on to me.

I move backward and feel the coldness of steel against me. It feels like a huge steel hook and I remember that this used to be a butchers. From the look of it, now my eyes were becoming accustomed, it was still in use. Enormous meat hooks, just dim shapes in the red light of the security camera, form avenues in what was obviously a refrigerated area.

I feel my way around the edges of the room, feeling for a door somewhere, but finding only another hook. I lose my balance slightly and hold onto it. It's sticky, and I expect to smell disinfectant but it's something much more earthy, much more iron-y.

Even in the darkness I know it's blood. Logic kicks in. It's a butchers warehouse. Why wouldn't there be blood? But where are the animals? Where are the carcasses? Kitchens and butchers. Just my luck.

Then I feel it. The coldness of dead flesh against my hand. Touching the firm muscle makes it swing on the hook and as it touches me again I feel something on the end of the limb, something I don't want to believe is a hand. But it is.

I feel it and feel the fingers. The fingernails. Stiff and dead, but still human. I feel the legs, the torso, the face, and the hook that pierces the solar plexus. I want to scream, but I can't make a sound. I have to hurry. I feel my way, all arms and gangly legs, short hair and skinniness. I know what it is. I know who this is.

I spin round, my eyes accustomed to the light a little now, and see another body in the far corner. I know who these boys are. I know I should go, carry on, phone it in. But instead I follow my heart and turn my phone on, lighting the room. He's an angel, hanging in midair, bathed in blue light, pale skinned and eyes shut. I hold the phone up to his face. Oh please, please don't let it be him. *Selfish, Jan. Selfish.* Let it be some other mother's son. Don't let it be Aiden.

It isn't. Neither is the other boy. I know my own son. Maybe he isn't here. I shine my phone around the room and there are lots more hooks but no more bodies.

Across from me, and in a corner, is another door. Wooden this time and set into the wall. Just over from that is another steel door. I try the handle and it's locked. I hear the far door open and Jed enters.

I duck behind one of the bodies, holding it still so it doesn't swing. He's carrying a tray and he hurries past the boys in the darkness, toward the steel door, which he unlocks.

He goes inside and my stomach lurches as the smell of fried chicken wafts past me. I move toward the door. Obviously there's someone in there. I have no choice but to find out.

I pick up a piece of chain and wait. I wait for what seems

like hour, but is only minutes. When he comes out of the room, I swing it until it makes contact with his head. It makes a deep thud and he falls over, groaning at first and then silent. He's unconscious. I drag him out of the way, over to the wooden door, which, now I open it, appears to be a cleaning cupboard. I drag him inside and take his keys. Then I secure the door the old fashioned way, with a brush stale.

I hurry over to the steel door and open it. Inside are several cells, all of them empty. I close the door behind me without locking it. It's coming together now. Hotel, cells, dead boys. My worst nightmare for Aiden.

What if he was here? What have they done with him? Maybe he's still here. I know there are more rooms beyond here, I can see doors leading off a long corridor in the distance. I rush along, unlocking the first door. It's a cell, wooden bed, toilet, washbasin, no windows. Clean and tidy, as if no one's ever been here.

I'm rushing along now, looking in any room for traces of Aiden, any small sign that he might have been here. I open the third door and it's set up like an office. Once inside, having checked for cameras and found none, it's like respite from the horror of outside.

That's what's happening to the boys. Brought here, reported missing, used for whatever depraved acts go on here, and then killed in cold blood. Oh my God. That's how Connelly is making his money. He's bringing people here to abuse these children. Charging for it. Thomas. Poor Thomas was probably here, and Aiden.

I switch on my phone again and call Mike. He answers on the first ring.

'You're in fucking trouble. Jesus Christ. Sending us there when nothing's going on? Eh? Where the fuck are you?'

'The Gables. Just get here right away.'

'You're having a laugh. Stewart won't authorise it. Not after before.'

I sigh.

'It was a decoy. To get them away from here.'

'Right. So you use the whole of Greater Manchester police as a decoy. Brilliant.' He pauses. Then his tone changes. 'Look, Jan, love, I respect you, but is everything all right? I mean, you've been doing some funny things lately...'

'Mike. I'm here, in the Gables. It used to be a meat factory.'

'Yeah, I know where it is. Old derelict building on the other side of Northlands. It's out of use. Derelict. Bloody falling down.'

'Except it's not derelict at all. It's being used to... to...'

'What? Jan? What'

I take a deep breath.

'It's being used for storing the bodies of dead boys. And keeping the ones who are alive here, but I haven't found them yet.'

'Don't tell me you're fucking inside? On your own?'

'No one would listen, Mike. You all thought I was nuts. But now I've found out what's going on. Look, just get Stewart down here.'

There's a long silence. Then he speaks.

'Are you sure?'

'I've seen them.'

'Is Aiden...?'

'I don't know. I haven't fully looked yet.'

'Leave it there Jan, leave it. Let us look. You shouldn't have to...'

'Just get here as quick as you can.'

I switch the phone off. I make a deal with myself that I'll check every door, try every lock, and then I'll get out and wait for Mike. I know he'll come. I try the window and although it's locked, I could easily smash it.

I'm on the ground floor, so this is my escape route. I open the door and move along the corridor, listening at the first door. No sounds and it's locked.

I turn the key and open it into darkness. It's the same as the last room. All clean and tidy. Pristine. I try the next room and smell it before I turn on the light. Blood. Mixed with shit.

My stomach lurches and I almost vomit at it. I turn on the light and the bed is stained with a deep, murky patch that has seeped over the whiter than white sheets. Blood splatters on the wall tell me, as if I didn't know already, what's going on here. No doubt this was the last thing one of those poor boys out there ever saw.

I go on. I open several more doors. It's an unlucky dip. Carnage or no carnage. But mostly carnage of one kind or another. Instruments of sexual torture, ropes and straps, even smaller hooks, replicas of the larger hooks outside, hanging from the walls.

I vaguely wonder if I should have waited for Mike and reinforcements, but it's too late now. This is like wandering through a nightmare, unable to wake yourself up. More rooms, some cleaned and disinfected, freshly painted, some waiting for it.

I've reached the penultimate room now and I open the door slowly. The smell is different, somehow musky, but there's no immediate movement. I flick on the light switch and at first I don't see anything.

'Is anyone there?'

No sound at all. I step in and see something scraped on the wall, the white paint peeling around the letters.

Help. Mum. Help me.

My God. Someone was here just now. The paint chippings

from the scrapings are on the pillow and the bed is warm. White paint under fingernails.

I walk over and feel the wall. It's thick with words etched into the plaster by previous occupants, covered by white paint. A whole wall of desperation. I turn round quickly and open a single wardrobe. It's dark in there, but I can make out a shape. Skinny, shaven hair, handcuffed. Hands over head to protect himself from who knows what.

'Aiden. Oh my God. Aiden.' I pull him out of the wardrobe, but he rolls up into a ball, tight with fear. I pull his arms away from his head. 'Aiden. It's me, Mum. I've come to get you. Aiden, look at me.'

The boy pulls his arms away from his face. It's not Aiden. His eyes are ringed with shadows and he looks like he's been drugged.

'I want my mum.'

My emotions finally collapse, but I can't cry yet. *Hold on, Jan.* There's one door left and I carry the boy outside and lay him in the corridor. I open the last door and see a gaunt face under the bedclothes. I'm pulling at the covers, but it's no use. This boy's unconscious and, from the looks of it, badly beaten. I lift him and pull the other boy to his feet.

'What's your name? Please, come on, lad. I'm here to help you.'

He stares at me, his thin face past the point of fear.

'Calvin. Calvin Wilson.'

'Come on, Calvin. Let's get out of here.'

We rush along the corridor to the office room and I tell him to go in there and wait for me. Then I decide I can't leave them and I smash the window and climb through, dragging the unconscious boy through behind me.

Calvin climbs through and makes a run for it, but I catch him and drag him back. We're both exhausted, but I get hold of him and hug him, I hug him as if he's my own lost son. And he hugs me back, his fingers pinching my skin. It's the first human contact I've had since I hugged Aiden just before he disappeared.

Toward the front of the factory there are three blue lights. No doubt Mike had brought just a few cars with him, just in case I'd flipped. He's running toward me as I carry the unconscious boy in my arms, and he catches hold of the other one.

'It's all right, son, I've got you. You're safe now.'

'Calvin. Calvin Wilson, Mike.'

The boy starts to cry. His skin is almost translucent in the daylight.

'I want me mam. You don't know what they did. You don't know.'

Mike looks at me.

'Aiden? Is he here? Is he here?'

A paramedic comes to take the boy from me. I shake my head.

'No. No, he's not. It looks like we're too late.'

CHAPTER TWELVE

The ambulances arrive now and I leave Mike to mark out the exit point ready for the senior officers. Jim Stewart would be here soon and I wanted to be gone by then. I run around to the front of the building, where there's still mayhem as more and more police cars arrive.

I walk through the front entrance, past two guys who have been arrested. One of them spits at me. I carry on mapping out the building in my head until I find my destination. Just off the bar area there is a door leading to a small office. I'd noticed it earlier as a potential site for guards, but now I was after something else. The paperwork.

This place was some kind of mechanism of supplying youngsters, on these premises, to clients brought here, and there had to be some record. There had to be a website, some way of communicating with the clients.

I push the door open and flick on the lone laptop. A quick look over it shows a few recent documents. It appears to have been wiped up until last week. I notice a printer with a tray.

There's a piece of paper with a photograph of a boy, around thirteen. It could be a school photograph, head and shoulders, no smiling. Underneath is his name. Calvin. It's Calvin. I feel a little light-headed, but I carry on.

I open the first filing cabinet drawer and pull out the contents. Receipts for credit cards, invoices. I need to hurry before someone comes to take all this away for investigation. I need to know the truth for myself.

Finally, I find it. The second filing cabinet is locked, and I drag up the anger from the bottom of my being and kick the drawers. Then I find a steel stapler and wedge it in between the cabinet and the drawer and it finally springs open, hitting me in the shin.

All the drawers are packed with files and finally I find a photo album. The room looks as if it's been ransacked now, but I bring out two large books and lay them on the table.

I open the first one, the least battered of them, and flick the pages back three months. Photographs of boys with their names underneath, and a number. Obviously relating to the files in the other cabinet.

I turn the pages, searching each face for my son, searching each name. I go back three, then six months. Then I recheck. And again. He's not there. Aiden isn't there. It occurs to me that he's never been here.

I flick back to the front and see a picture of Darren, and a cross next to his name. And a comment. 'Keep clean.' Random boys marked 'keep clean' every now and then. I recognise some of them from the files I read on the suicides. No recent sexual activity. My head swims, because this proves premeditation. Girls too. Teenagers, hardly grown.

I know how this stuff can go missing, like in Operation Hurricane. So I take some photographs on my phone, of the lists of client names, the boys, and the file markings.

I hear footsteps outside, people digging deeper into the building and its horrors. Shouts and gasps.

I pick up another book, a ledger, and read through a list of names, in date order. Some of the names I recognise, some only vaguely, and some I don't know at all. A list of people buying into this depravity, paying for exclusive access to underage boys and girls to do whatever they want to them.

I read through the names again, making sure I remember some of them at least, as evidence of this calibre has a habit of disappearing into the old boys' network, then close the book.

Someone else will have to deal with this. Someone else will have to weed out the abusers who visited this hellhole and made Connelly so rich. Connelly. Once again, conspicuous by his absence. Not on scrap of paper, invoice, record or address has anything to connect Connelly to this.

Although I know that he, and his father before him had initiated this crime house and kept it running through the decades as families suffered nearby and mourned their missing sons, there was no trace of him here. Or anywhere. That was the problem.

Just as I'm about to leave I spot a box in the corner. At first it looks like rags, and I recoil. Is it the boy's clothes, stored here for some reason? But then I realise what it is. Scarves. Hats. Trainers. The silent messages in an invisible world of crime.

It suddenly strikes me. The colours signal availability, and the black scarves signal unavailability—and the need to find another victim. Outside this room, nothing spoken, nothing written down, just a secret language, high above the streets.

Lisa was right. Unspeakable. I leave the books on the desk and leave the room. I'm suddenly among twenty or so police officers, standing around in the bar area. Two of them are vomiting, and the shock on everyone's faces is visible. I go over to the young uniformed police officer, who is retching, and touch his arm.

'There's a bathroom over there.'

He looks at me as I point to the edge of the dance floor, just right of the bar.

'I saw them. I saw them in there. Just hanging there. Human beings treated like animals. They're . . . they're . . .'

I put my arms around him. It's the second time I've comforted someone today. The second time I've mothered someone. But not Aiden. I hurry back outside. Mike's on his phone so I stand around, waiting for him to finish his call. I watch as the two guards I saw are led out by ashen-faced coppers who've seen almost everything. Mike turns to look at me.

'Jim Stewart's on his way. ETA five minutes. He's asking after you. Something about that house on Ney Street. You'd think he'd have other things to think about.'

I make a run for it. I run up the road and into the dip where I've hidden my bike. I start it up and drive up the lane toward the crossroads. I see Stewart's car rolling toward it, and zip past it. When I reach the crossroads I take the road to the moor. I haven't even put on my crash helmet and my hair blows in the wind as I speed through the darkness.

Oh my God. It's not Aiden. It's not my son hanging there. It's not my son in one of those rooms. I feel desperately sorry for all the mothers who are going to find out exactly what happened to their child in the next couple of hours. And for those, like Bessy, who died never knowing. But it's not me. Aiden wasn't there. But where is he?

I ride on, and down to the reservoir below Saddleworth Moor. I've probably passed Bessy on her way to the moor when I've been walking up here. I know this place like the back of my hand, but it's hard to reconcile this bleak landscape as yet another site for dead children, even though I know full well it is. The way Bessy describes it.

It's dark, but I can see the outline of the hills above the moor on the skyline, lit by the moon. There's a little shelter, built to house people who've been caught short on the moor, enveloped in the thick fog that descends quickly. There's a light and a bench and even a drinks machine. I push in a pound coin and get myself a hot chocolate.

Right. I need to think. I need to calm down and think. I pull the folder with the police files in it out of my bag, along with Bessy's notes. I open the file and pull all the pieces together. I need to get all this straight in my head before I see Stewart.

I need it not to be about Aiden, or Bessy. Connelly Snr must have started this racket years ago, somehow luring young boys into his lair. Keeping them there for the use of his clients. When he had no more use for them, killing them. He'd set up Mothers for the Missing as a way to steer those who had suspicions in other directions, like Bessy and Pat.

Hadn't Pat said that there was always something happening to keep the missing boys out of the news? Had Connelly made it that way? Had the boys been taken to coincide with other high profile crimes, like the Moors Murders, to hide them away and divert blame? Connelly Jnr had continued the family business, covering his crimes with the kitchen factory at Old Mill and lesser offences to keep us busy.

The one thing that didn't make sense was the bodies. Or lack of them. Some of the boys, like Darren, had been found in situations that could easily be interpreted as suicide. But Ted Scholes words stuck with me.

'Hiding a body is practically impossible.'

Hiding so many bodies was even more unlikely. What was he doing with them? What had Connelly done with the bodies? I pour through the files, reading every detail, rereading the cases that had been closed because no body had been found. I search through Thomas's file, all the details that are still fresh in my head from Bessy's story, all underlining the extent to which

Connelly had everyone fooled, so much that the focus was on a completely unconnected set of incomprehensible acts.

I look out onto the water and over to the moor. I'd first walked over there as a young teenager. There was nothing to mark the graves of the children, only a bunch of flowers brought by one of their mothers, of the boy who had never been found but that was definitely a victim.

When I'd taken my first step into the undergrowth, through the thigh high heather, I'd been scared that with each step I was crushing the bones of the dead children who everyone said were still on the moor. Every twig that cracked, every slip in the peat, reminders that there was an underlying fear that surfaced in the minds of those who chose to walk here.

But like Scholes said, it's practically impossible to hide a body. True, some of the children have never been found, and there really is no way of knowing how many there were. The ones who were named were the ones whose parents entered a new nightmare of knowing what happened to their dead child. Out of limbo and into hell.

But where were the bodies? I go back over the notes, then pick out the pile of news cuttings and photographs. Bessy and Colin, holding baby Thomas. A generation before Sal and I, but the same scenario. All smiles. Bessy and Colin with Thomas riding his first bike. Ditto. They feel like family now, like a long lost uncle and aunt, someone I know so well.

Fast forward, Bessy in the local paper appealing for the whereabouts of her son. A policeman standing beside her, probably Inspector Little. Next, Bessy standing beside John Connelly at a rally to bring back capital punishment. She looks tiny beside his huge bulk, and he's smiling widely. Bessy's clutching her handbag tight. There's a platform and several people gathered to the right.

To the left, just at the edge of the photograph, I catch sight of something familiar. The trees on the skyline are poplars, and just in front of them I can make out the wrought iron work of the Gables. The rally is being held round the side of the Gables, outside the walls, on what is now a huge car park.

There's a Guy Fawkes in a barrow and, to the right of the wall, a bonfire. A huge spiked gate, that has been bricked up now, gives me a clear view of the back of the building. I hold the photograph under the dim light in the shelter and look into the background. No additional structures. It's exactly the same as when I saw it an hour ago.

Except for one thing. To the right of the back of the building a huge plume of smoke bellows from the ground. There's a man standing to the side of it wearing what appears to be a rubber mask, hauling up a storm drain cover.

'No smoke without fire. No smoke. Without fire.'

That's what the pregnant Connelly girl had said, just before she went away. It's almost too horrible to comprehend again. A human waste disposal unit. And hadn't I just heard one of the guards tell his colleague that they would get rid of 'them in there' on Bunty Night? This the Connellys' MO, using significant events to cover their tracks. Bunty Night. Bonfire Night. Guy Fawkes Night. A regular annual celebration of justice, of all things. Fires lit throughout the land. In this case, from the photographs, huge fires outside the Gables, for the community. Families. Children. All while other children burned in the distance, the huge fire and the sulphurous smell of fireworks covering the smell of death.

I can see the sun beginning to peep over the hills now, and morning is approaching. I desperately need to get back to the station, to get back home, to file this last piece of the puzzle. Then, whatever the outcome with Jim Stewart, I can start looking for Aiden again.

He's after me for something about Ney Street and the baby.

He must have the forensic report back by now and it's linked me with a little wardrobe in a tiny terraced house where there's been nothing but tragedy over the years.

It could all have been so different if someone would have listened to Inspector Little all those years ago. But, like Scholes said, without a body there is no murder. It's slightly different these days with forensics, but even now, there needs to be a body for closure.

Then it strikes me. That's why some of the boys turned up as suicides. If no bodies were ever found, this would draw attention to the missing boys. The fact that teenage boys with problems were sometimes turning up having committed suicide kept the spotlight off the missing boys and onto the boys' own problems. Making it look like the boys had just given up, taken to a life of drugs and finally overdosed, with verdicts of suicide or accidental death would prevent them being linked, except by their social deprivation. The girls had simply disappeared. Looked into, but again marked as teenage runaways.

All lumped into a statistic, so anonymous that no one noticed the white paint or the chicken or the fact that they had all taken the same drugs. Run away and/or committed suicide. This was the first assumption made about Aiden's disappearance, but I wouldn't believe it. Just like Bessy wouldn't believe it about Thomas. Just like the Mothers of the Missing wouldn't believe it, but they were intercepted by something evil and manipulative, all so that high-profile perverts could get their kicks.

I curl up in the corner of the bench in the shelter and open Bessy's notebook. Chances are that if Stewart has found out why I was really at Ney Street and what I found before I called it in I'll have to give up the notes.

It might be a good idea anyway, just to show him how I knew so much about John Connelly. It's not just me who pulls stories together, their ever-tightening threads pulling at the skin and bones of the truth.

Jim Stewart got where he was today by going the extra mile, a little bit further than was required by the operation. No doubt he's been thinking, too, thinking about what I'm up to, thinking about Connelly, Operation Prophesy, hating me and loving me at the same time.

Now, with little left to solve, he won't revel in the glory of solved crime, he'll be waiting to snip off the loose ends of the tight threads, make sure nothing can come unravelled. That's why he wants me. He knows full well I must have had help with this. I couldn't have solved it without anyone's help, and he's got an inkling it's to do with Ney Street and the baby.

He knows all right. But I'm not just driven by the same things he is. I've got extra. I've got my son to find. I want to march into ops and tell them all about the baby and the notes, drop the money on the desk, hands on hips and tell them it was all necessary, what did they expect me to do? When they asked what I was doing at Ney Street, look at them for longer than I should and tell them I was searching for my son, who by the way, is still missing.

Like everything, it's complicated. Complex. It's easy to make a plan, one-dimensional and flat, with all the arrows pointing to home. But life's just not like that. I'd tried to tell Jim and Mike about the messages, all excited about Connelly's sky messages, trying to explain them in terms of secret codes and silent words—but before I'd even embarked on it, they were bored, tapping keys, checking text messages, yawning at my explanations of how complex a case is.

Jim knows I'm right. He knows. But he's invested in his stakeholders, his budgets, his simplistic Venn diagrams, and evermore computerised flowcharting of operations. No room for something being found outside what we think we are going to find. For someone to turn over something new. Like he says, there's no I in team.

No. It doesn't work like that. There are no heroes, no one officer who gets away with something just because they've solved a case. We have to stick to the plan. I'm in a catch-22, I've dug myself into a real corner, one where on one hand, I've solved a crime, laid bare Connelly's real, sordid, murderous business, but on the other, I've stolen evidence from a crime scene in order to do it.

I stare at the notebook. I need Bessy for just a little while longer, just until I know, deep down, that I can hand myself in, that I've exhausted every avenue in my search for Aiden. So I'll stay here for a while, at least until the initial horror of the Gables has subsided, and let them do their job.

The sun is shining now and there's dew on the heather, making a low mist. I can hear bird song and a tapping on the wooden roof of the shelter. A moment later a huge black crow flaps down in front of me, making me jump. It hops around and calls out, and soon a few more drop out of the sky and onto the scrub land.

A car backfires in the distance up on the Huddersfield Road and they startle and fly up onto the telegraph wire just above the shelter, weighing it down so that I can see them clearly, and they can see me. Nearer and nearer. I start to read Bessy's story.

BESSY
GIVING UP

After the case was closed it got worse. Every week there was something else in the papers. Something about *him* and *her*, or about the families. I was still going down to the police station every week, but sometimes I didn't go in, I'd just sit on a bench outside, knowing what they'd say.

I liked the routine. Same as breakfast, dinner, tea, and a drive out, the police station was what held my life together. The house where it all happened had been demolished long ago, but I'd sometimes go and stand where it was, like I did all those years ago, and try to get a sense of what happened.

John Connelly had passed away. They said it was a heart attack. He'd left me a large sum of money in his will, it seemed too much, but I didn't argue. After all, he was very rich. He'd been very good to me, that man, and I won't have a word said against him.

Because of his kindness I'd never done a day's work all my life, always been looked after by him. I put the money in the bank, with the rest of the money he'd given me. I was getting state pension now, and that paid for my little car and my food and gas and electric. I put the money I had saved in a high interest savings account, and if I wanted something urgent, I would draw some of the interest out.

John was dead now, so there would be no more income. I knew I had to look after what I had so I pulled my belt in tighter. I didn't go to his funeral, it wouldn't have been right; but I'd always remember him. Instead, I sat in the house, cutting out all the news reports about *them.*

He'd gone on hunger strike. It riled me that *he* still got attention in the papers. I wrote to the prison and told them to make *him* eat. *He* should be kept alive to remember what *he* did, all the harm *he* caused.

As I'd been following *his* life since 1964, I'd seen how *he* liked to live it up in the papers, say stupid things then say *he* hadn't. Make confessions, then go back on it. When John had died, I'd sent for information on the murders and bought all the books that had been written, which were a lot. There was even one published by *him,* but I didn't buy that one.

I sat and read them all through, and one thing stood out to me: in 1987 *he'd* told a reporter that *he'd* killed five more people. *She'd* said that *she* knew nothing about it, but *he'd* said *he'd* killed more people.

I thought about it a lot, wondered if I should go and tell the police. The reports said that they had looked at all the other reports of people missing near the time, and nothing had matched up. What about Thomas? Had they forgotten about him? Had everyone, except me?

It was in the papers that the mothers of the children they had murdered had all either gone mad, had to be sedated, or went on Valium. I wasn't surprised. Some of them had got divorced. I knew, firsthand, that their lives could never be the same.

They'd had to sit through the trial, and all the reports in the papers about those two, they were like celebrities now, with that Lord saying she was innocent and him making out he's insane, then him trying to get it proved he was sane.

All the time, there was a set of people living in the North West of England whose lives had been ruined. Those poor families would never forget about what happened, and worst of all, there were probably more bodies up there. Maybe Thomas?

All those reports were all for attention. Losing a child was terrible, especially in those circumstances. It's the worst thing that can happen to you. One minute they're there, joking and arguing, even being a nuisance, but they're there. Next minute they're gone. I was starting to think that something was wrong with me, too.

It wasn't so much how I felt, because I was always in the most amount of pain I could be, and everything else was just an echo. It was more how people were looking at me. I'd stopped having my hair cut at the hairdressers, and begun to trim it myself. It had gone completely grey now, and I shouldn't wonder why with all my worry.

I didn't wear makeup anymore, and I always wore practical shoes and clothes. I was clean and tidy, and I didn't think it was my appearance. I'd noticed that sometimes when people were speaking to me, I'd be able to listen for a minute, then I was distracted by my thoughts, my wanting to get home in case Thomas was there.

Some people had asked me outright if I was OK, and told me I seemed 'off with the fairies.' I suppose I was really. I was somewhere in an imaginary world where my son was safe and alive and here, beside me, carrying my shopping bags.

As for *her*, *she* made a documentary that was shown on the TV. *She* said that *she* wished *she'd* been hanged. I know that was what John Connelly wanted. He'd campaigned to bring back capital punishment, wheeling me out as an example of the suffering caused by 'those bastards' as he called them.

Beside the campaign stand there were always advertisements for his shops, and for other peoples' businesses, but on the whole he was kind. In the years before he died, he started to call it a road show and had music blaring out. I didn't hold with this, but who was I to say anything? He knew what he was doing, did John. How would I live otherwise?

The TV documentary said that *she'd* written hundreds of letters to someone describing what had happened. With John gone, I had nothing to stop me contacting people, so I phoned the papers. *They* were in the papers, so why shouldn't I be? I spoke to some stuck-up teenager who asked me if my son had been murdered. When I said I didn't know, she said she'd get back to me. She never did.

I looked some organisations up in the phone book and told them what had happened. It turned out that there were lots of missing people, thousands of them. There was a new organisation that matched up missing people with unidentified bodies, and lots that searched for your missing person and sent them a letter. The Salvation Army did that as well, so I wrote some letters to Thomas and sent them off. I wrote them in the best way I could, emphasising that he wouldn't be in trouble if he came back now, that I'd understand.

Dear Thomas,

I'm writing this because you've been missing now for a long time, and some people have offered to help me to try to get in touch with you. I've been looking everywhere for you, and think about you every day. I still live in our house on Ney Street, and you can come round any time you like. The past is the past, love, and I won't even mention it if you don't want to. I'd just like to see you again.

I do love you very much, Thomas, happen a bit more than I should, because it seems other people recover from this. I haven't met anyone yet who has, but that's what they say.

If you do want to get in touch, let these people know. If you don't for whatever reason, please remember that your mum loves you and I've kept your bedroom just as it was. There are birthday cards and Christmas presents, all in the sideboard, for when you do come back.

I'll sign off now, love, and I hope I will see you soon.

All my love, Mum

I practised writing it over and over again. It didn't seem enough when I read it back. How could anything be enough, though? There weren't really any words that could tell him how I felt, how I had fretted over this for the best part of my life. If I put about the crying and his dad, it would sound like I was blaming him. I worried over it for days, then left it at that.

There were three things I could pin my hopes on here: Thomas writing back and his letter being passed to me, Thomas getting the letter and deciding he didn't want to write back but letting the agency know, and no response. The problem was, they couldn't tell you where the missing person was, only the result.

Someone from London came to meet me in Manchester and took my details. She took my letter and read it to see if there was anything inappropriate in it, then she said that she would see if he had an address and didn't really want to be found, and if he did, she would send it and see what happened.

She told me they searched the electoral registers and benefits agencies for missing people, just in case. She told me she'd make enquiries and find out if Thomas had been mentioned in *her* letters. She'd also mentioned that she thought for crimes like this, people should be hanged. The poor girl had a blank look I recognised—the glazed look of someone that no matter how much the sun shone, there was always horror and pain at the back of your mind. I was glad that *she* wasn't hanged. *She* was the only way I could find out if Thomas was murdered. My only chance. I tried to find out how to contact her, but there didn't seem to be a way.

Months later, the woman phoned me and told me that *her* letters didn't contain anything different from *her* statements, as *she* didn't want to incriminate *herself* more. *She'd* got herself a spiritual counsellor, someone who *she* could confess to, unburden *herself*. By all accounts, *she* was trying to say that *she* was under *his* control, *his* spell, and it was because *she* was in love with *him* that *she* did those things. That *she'd* been a woman who had been led astray. And because of this *she* was appealing for release.

In all the time since Thomas had gone missing and then the babies, I'd never lost my sanity fully. I'd cried, and I'd talked to myself, and to the blackbirds. I'd lain on the grass at Daisy Nook and not spoken to another human being for weeks, but, on the surface, I was reasonably sane.

The thought of *her* out of prison, free to walk around, near kiddies, free, made me ill. Thoughts of my daughter growing up with someone else being her mum, and the dead baby in the wardrobe. I didn't eat for a while and I became very upset. Not depressed, because I was still doing my routine to a point, but I was very upset and angry.

I looked at a picture of *her*, posed writing. I knew *she'd* been trying to get parole for a long time, and I knew it had been blocked. The developments recently, seeing *her* on the TV, in the papers, with people supporting *her*, telling us that it was *his* fault *she* did it, it didn't wash with me. It did unsettle me, because it meant people were taking it seriously. *She'd* been able to do a degree, *she'd* become a Christian. *She* looked old.

I looked in the mirror, and I looked a lot older than *her*, but I didn't look my age. I don't know if it was the routine or the slow pace of my life, but I'd aged well. I was still walking the moor every day, in the morning at dawn, going to see Thomas, paying my respect to a part of my life where I was imprisoned. After that first day, when I'd been so taken by the heather, I bought a little bit and planted it and looked up its meaning.

Heath heather: A low evergreen shrub or small tree, native to Europe, Asia, N Africa

and especially S Africa. (Genus: Erica, c.500 species. Family: Ericaceae.) Heather: A small, bushy, evergreen shrub (Calluna vulgaris), native to Europe, especially N and W; in Scotland it forms the major food source of endemic red grouse. A rare form with white flowers is considered lucky. (Family: Ericaceae.)

Heathen: This word for non-Christian or pagan is common in all the Germanic languages. It appears in Old English as hâþen in the year 826. It clearly arose after Christianity, but had to be quite early for it to appear in all the Germanic tongues, sometime in the 4th century or earlier. Most words of this age have unclear etymologies, but this is not the case with heathen. It is believed to have originated in Gothic and spread to the other Germanic tribes. In the 4th century, Ulfilas, bishop of the Goths, translated the Bible into Gothic. In Mark 7:26, which reads "Now the woman was a Greek, a Syrophoenician by birth . . ." Ulfilas used the word haiþnô in place of Greek, or as it appears in the Vulgate gentilis, or gentile. Haiþnô literally means dweller on the heath. The heath is associated with the regeneration of life, and the Triple Goddess symbols of the maiden, the mother and the crone, where birth, life and death are symbolised in the life force. So the original sense is remarkably the same as the modern sense, someone living beyond the bounds of civilization and who has not received the word of God.'

Sounds about right to me. Heathen. *She* was 58 and I was 74. Both of us had been allowed to age, yet both of us were still focused back in 1964, when children, who would now be middle-aged, suffered and died. They didn't get any older. They were children forever. I still thought of Thomas as a teenager, because I had no other point of reference. I still looked for him everywhere I went, my eyes searching out young boys about his height, who look familiar. He wouldn't look like that now, but in my mind he was still waving goodbye to his mam and he cycled to work. *She* was looking back down the years and trying to find a way to escape, to be free. Over my dead body, I thought. I still wanted answers from *her*. I needed to know exactly where *she* was.

Just as I thought it, there was a knock at the door. I tied my hair back and sprayed air freshener round the room. I'd been smoking sixty a day again, and my visits to the moor had made me perspire. I suddenly realised that the room smelled like sweaty cheese, so I opened the back door to let some air in. If this was Thomas now, he'd wonder what the bloody hell had got into me.

It wasn't Thomas. It was Lizzie.

'Bessy, love. I've just come to tell you that Colin had a heart attack. He's up at Ashton General and he's asking for you.'

I got my coat and followed her. Her son was driving her in his car, so we went up there. She didn't speak to me all the way there. When we got out, she turned round and looked at me, right in the eye.

'I'm sorry, Bessy.'

I smiled.

'Never mind that now, love. Let's just see to Colin, eh?'

I started to walk in, but she grabbed my arm.

'I just wanted to tell you, he never forgot about Thomas. He spoke about him every day. And you. I should never have . . .'

'Don't worry yourself, Lizzie. It's all water under the bridge now.'

'But you never remarried. You never met anyone. I thought you might be still holding a flame for Col.'

I snort.

'Col? No. My life stopped when Thomas went. There was no room in my life for a man.' I glanced at her son, leaning against a wall, smoking a cigarette. 'Put it this way. Can you imagine if you came out if this hospital and he was gone? You never saw him again and no one ever knew what happened to him?'

She paled.

'I never thought of it like that. I just thought he'd run away.'

I smiled.

'Well, he might have. He might have had his reason to go, and all. Or he might have been murdered, by them two, or by someone else. It's the not knowing, Lizzie.'

'Did no one help you, Bessy? What about the police? Colin didn't say much.'

We're walking along the hospital corridors now, hurrying toward the intensive care unit.

'They did, but what could they do? They never found any clues, or a body, or him alive, so what could they do?'

We reached the ICU and the curtains were drawn round his bed. Lizzie pulled them open and went to the side of the bed. There was a steady blip, blip, blip of a machine and I flashed back to our wedding day, all those years before. The man lying on the bed now was a faded version of Colin, someone grey and ever so slightly blue.

'Bessy's here, love. Look, it's Bessy.'

He turned his head slowly and our eyes met.

'Bess. Bess.' His hand reached weakly across the bed, and Lizzie took his other hand. 'Have you found him, love?'

I felt dizzy. I thought he'd forgot about us. After all these years, he remembered. Me and Thomas.

'No, love, not yet, but I will.'

'He was a good boy. You've done well by him.'

Lizzie was sobbing on the other side of the bed.

'So did you, Col. You were a good dad.'

Lizzie looked panicked and I realised I had said 'were.' But we both knew.

The blips got slightly faster and he turned his head toward Lizzie. I turned to leave and there was just a constant beep. The nursing staff ran in and Lizzie cried out, but he was gone. I sat in the waiting room, waiting for her to come out, to make sure she was all right. I wasn't sure that it was any of my business, but I couldn't leave her in here alone. At first I was upset, I cried a little, but then I realised that this was what would happen to me.

I felt a little spark of excitement in my stomach, a feeling I hadn't had since before Thomas had gone. It made me laugh out loud. I put it down to shock, but as I walked out of the hospital and left Lizzie in her son's arms, I heard a strange, but familiar sound. I could hear birds singing.

I looked around the hospital grounds, and a song thrush was calling out. I'd heard the blackbirds singing, Jack and Jill and all their ancestors, singing in my yard, but outside my little circle of safety, the world had become flat and joyless. Dangerous. Suddenly, it was alive with birdsong. I hadn't heard that bloody birdsong for donkey's years.

I walked back through Ashton and over to Daisy Nook. I could smell the grass and hear the trickle of the steam, and of course, the birds. They were everywhere, and a big goose came to see what I had in my bag. I giggled like a schoolgirl and gave it a polo mint.

There was a spring in my step when I walked up Ney Street, a sense of excitement for the future, because now I realised there might not be so much of it for me. Less suffering, less torture, less madness, less worrying. The end was in sight and I was delighted.

BESSY

SHE'S GONE

I'm getting to the end of it now and funnily enough, this is the bit I can't remember as well. I can remember forty years ago like it was yesterday, but the past few years, well?

Anyway, Colin was dead and I made friends with Lizzie. She'd come round sometimes and we'd have a cup of tea. She'd always look around the house, like she was imagining Colin there, and at the same time I was imagining I wasn't there.

Don't get me wrong, I wasn't suicidal or anything like that, I was just weary of it all. I did the same thing every single day. I'd got up at dawn for years, first light. This was different in winter and summer, because of the length of the days. I didn't wear a watch or have a clock in the house. Why would I need one?

Like I said, I did the same thing every day. The rhythmic tick-tock of life kept my feet moving through the daylight, stopping me from stopping, the ever-present moon spurring me on, the knowledge that a person can't just disappear completely and somewhere, even if it was in his mossy bed, with the heather duvet, Thomas was bathed in the same moonlight as I was.

I'd go up to the moor and do what I had to do there, then I'd go home and in the afternoon I'd walk up to Daisy Nook. I might call on the market or go to a supermarket, but usually I got enough food for the week in one go.

Over a long time I realised that my visit to Wardle Street when all this first happened might have turned out to be wrong, as all the reports released by *them* said that the first kiddies had been murdered somewhere else, in a house *they* had lived in at Bannock Street. I went there quite often and sat outside, wondering if Thomas had been here. There was a kind of yearning in me, a calling out to whatever was left behind of someone.

I was sure that there was a trace of him somewhere, a kind of thread between mother and son that I was holding one end of and Thomas the other. He was lost and if I shouted loud enough, and pulled the thread as hard as I could, he'd find me again.

Occasionally I'd be walking somewhere and I'd remember me and Thomas being there together. A different feeling would flood me, a sort of happiness and love, tinged with desperate sadness. I suppose a lot of the reason I kept going back to those places was because of that feeling. It was like being with him again, his smile and the way he stood, his voice, I could see it all clearly, then it was gone again.

I'd also met up with a group of people, mostly mothers, but some fathers and friends, whose children friends had gone missing. Mothers for the Missing. Some of them had disappeared in the sixties, around the same time as Thomas, but there were lots of people who had missing relatives over the decades. Turned out to be run by John Connelly's son, Sean. Never met him, but they're a good family, that. They even carried on giving us a party on Bonfire night, in the same place. John's factory went to the dogs a long time ago, but Sean kept his memory alive every year with a big bonfire just outside the gates.

A woman called Pat organises them these days. Her boy went missing at the same time as that Harold Shipman business. Poor bugger. Never found him, and it's made her hard. She always reserves a special place for me at the meetings, because she told me that Thomas was the first case she ever knew about. She told me that load of people had gone missing on the estate over the years, more than we think. Loads. Some of them came back.

But she seemed to think that if it were a young lad who went missing, that would be the last we'd see of him alive. Funny really, she always looked like she was trying to work something out, always troubled, always asking questions. Happen she thought she knew something, but if she did, she never let on.

We'd sit around and talk about things our kids used to do. Pat's wonderful; she organises charity walks and all sorts. She even gets speakers from down South to come and tell us about dredging rivers and forensics. I went to meetings and helped to post out posters and flyers for them.

You could always tell when someone was new. They'd be crying and wondering what would happen. Then you'd see the shell build up around them, just like it had with me, and they'd become quieter and more reserved about it.

Some of them stopped coming to the groups, but others came every week. I'd get a phone call from time to time asking me to come to the community centre where we'd all crowd around a TV, watching the news. It was usually Sky news, as they have all the coverage. A presenter would talk over a scene of a body being removed from a shallow grave, and we'd all be half praying it was our loved one, so we'd know what had happened.

It was one of those times when I found out. There'd been a rumour that a decomposed body had been found in a railway yard, so I made my way to the community centre, and we made a pot of tea and sat down, all in our individual little cells of sadness, fixed on the screen and sat. About halfway through the report a picture of *her* flashed on the screen and I moved my hand unexpectedly, spilling tea on my skirt.

'Moors Murderer has died in hospital from a serious chest infection following a suspected heart attack two weeks ago.'

A slow hand clap began, but I was listening to the report. *She'd* been given last rites by a Catholic priest. *She* had a mother. I'm not sure why that surprised me. I wondered what sort of terrible life *her* mother had, knowing what *she* had done? And *her* family?

I didn't feel sorry for *her*. I started to cry, but it wasn't for *her*, it was for me, and Thomas, and Colin, I suppose. It horrified me that *she* might be in the same place as Colin and Thomas now, and I was still here.

I'd gone home and sat crying for hours. What hope was there now? *She'd* been my only hope. I needed to ask *her* if *she'd* picked Thomas up that day, if *they'd* thrown his Billy can over the wall, if *they'd* done heaven knows what to him and then killed him and buried him on Saddleworth Moor.

I vomited twice in the kitchen sink and then sat on the back doorstep to get some air. My latest blackbird, who I called Kylie, even though he's a male, hopped along to see me and I threw him some bread. He'd fly up and sit on my hand to eat it, fluttering about.

It was November 16th and soon there'd be a gap until spring. Blackbirds don't really migrate; they sometimes just go where it's warmer. Kylie might come back, or it might be another one, but the blackbirds, and many other kinds of birds, focused on my tiny back yard for goodies such and bacon rind and seeds.

When I was buying them specially in the market I'd imagine they were for my grandchildren, like sweets or little trinkets. I think that's why I named them all, they were my adoptive grandchildren, sent by Thomas so I wouldn't be alone.

I'd bought some little plants for the backyard, some heather and some mosses, especially from the garden centre. I'd brought a few little plants back from the moor as well, just to keep the new ones company.

I had them in some half barrels that Colin had brewed some Poitine in all those years ago. If I saw old paint cans dumped in the ginnel, I'd grab them and wash them out and plant sunflowers and all kinds of plants.

Over the years it had become a bit of a sanctuary and I'd made a trellis for each of the three yard walls and grown clematis up it. It made it all a bit more private. I could sit out there in my pyjamas or in my slip, smoking cigarette after cigarette and throwing bits to my little bird children.

I tried to find out where *her* funeral was, so I could go and ask *her* mother if *she* had said anything about Thomas. I'd realised by now that the police wouldn't tell me anything. I'd written letters but they were always returned unread by the prison. They were also wise to the missing people group and wouldn't tell them anything.

By this time there was a quarter of a million people going missing every year. Quarter of a million! A woman from the agency told me this, and she said that most of them turn up sooner or later, but it could be years.

I met her in a café one day, trying to find out what was happening now *she* was dead. It was the same woman I'd met years before, she looked heavier now and she told me she'd had a baby.

'Aw, that's lovely, pet. Now you look after it. Is it a girl or a boy?'

She smiled.

'A little girl. Emily.'

'Oh, lovely, how wonderful.' I sipped my tea. 'Where is she now?'

She was shuffling paper and I suppose I looked quite relaxed.

'Oh, in childcare. We both work full time. We have to.'

I snorted.

'Well you look after her. You don't know what might happen to her.'

She stared at me and tapped her pen on the table.

'You know, Mrs Swain, this isn't an evil world. There are lots of people just going about their daily business and enjoying their lives.'

I nodded.

'I know. Sorry, it's just that one bad person can ruin a lot of peoples' lives.'

'Mmm. But people recover, don't they? And I'm here to help.'

My face was red now, and I could feel the heat.

'Recover? From losing your son? Can you imagine if Emily just disappeared when you got home? If you never found her again? How would you recover from that?'

Her eyes misted a little.

'But she's in trusted childcare. And, if I might say, Bessy, your life's gone on, hasn't it? Since all this happened.'

I could see my reflection in a sugar dispenser. I looked a lot younger than my years and I had a round, smiley face. I didn't look mad or diseased, or even odd. I just looked like a normal person.

'Not by choice. Because it had to. It just does, doesn't it, day after day? At first it was because Thomas needed something to come back to. Now it's just because I wake up each day. I expect that will end soon and I can't say I'll be sorry. Not that I'll bloody know about it.'

She wrote a note down, no doubt some rubbish about me being depressed or suicidal. There must be a whole forest of notes about me somewhere, all about what I'm like, but I bet none of them say heartbroken, or dead inside.

'I'm sorry you feel like that, Bessy. I am.'

She was, I could tell. It didn't help though. I got to the point.

'The thing is, with her dead, I've got no one to ask about Thomas. I wondered if I could have a copy of the police files about him, and the files you have, you know, the letter I wrote and all that? I'd like to just go through them and see if I can spot anything.'

Her expression was blank.

'Erm, not really, they're private.'

'But I can have them. I've looked into it. The data protection act. I can have anything to do with me. You have to let me.'

'But they're not to do with you, Bessy, are they? They're to do with Thomas.'

'What do you mean? I've written letters and given statements. That's to do with me and my son.'

'And you can have anything back that you've contributed. But you can't see Thomas's files.'

A niggle of irritation was wriggling inside me now and I knew she was going to say something I didn't like.

'Why not?'

'Well, in some cases, and I'm not saying this is the case with Thomas, when we contact the missing person, they indicate that they don't want any contact with the person who makes the enquiry. It's their right as an adult to do this. And we have to respect their rights. Going missing isn't a crime. They haven't done anything wrong.'

My mind wandered back to Colin's mother and Colin, both

dead now, and their mocking, telling me he'd run away because I was a bad mother. The market gossips, headscarves tight under their nasty little chins, picking at the sore of my desperation, pointing me out as the woman whose son and husband both left.

'So there's a chance that the police, and your people, have known all along where he was and because he said he didn't want contact, I've never been told?'

She looked at her notes. Now she couldn't even look me in the eye.

'A possibility. But I don't know if this is the case here. I can't say.'

'But the police have told me that it's a missing person enquiry until they find a body and they haven't been able to find Thomas. That's as far as they've told me. Could there be more?'

'They work on the premise that it's so difficult to hide a body that someone would have found him by now, if he was dead. And I know that there's the Moors connection, which sort of makes a mockery of it. But if they had found him alive, and he'd asked not to be identified, then they won't tell you. Try to look at it from Thomas's point of view. He's entitled to that privacy, isn't he? They're his human rights.' Of course, she was right. I'd just thought it would be simple, they'd find him and tell me. I'd never thought seriously that he might not want me or his dad. 'Of course, that might not be what's happened here.'

I stared at her for a too long time.

'What do you think? Do you think he's dead? Off the record, as a mother?'

'That's not fair, Bessy. You shouldn't ask me that.'

'Well, I am asking. What do you think?'

'OK. Off the record, but I'll deny it if you repeat it. I'd press the police to search the moor again. I'd never give up. Not unless he turns up.'

It was cryptic, and I couldn't work out if they really knew

where he was or not. I spent a long time after that weighing up if I had done anything to make him leave. Was it the arguments with Colin? Did he really hate me like he had said?

That led to torturing myself with what had happened if he had run away. Had another woman took him in and fed him? Did he call her mum now? Did he still look up at the moon, our moon, and tell his children, even grandchildren now, about how he had another mum somewhere once?

I'd started smoking even more and I was on sixty-odd a day by now. I'd rub lemons on my hands and teeth to try to get rid of the brown stains, and use an air freshener spray on my clothes before I went out.

The walls in the house were brown, and when Lizzie came round we'd fill ashtray after ashtray wondering about the world. We never broached the subject of our children, the children Colin had brought up. Except Thomas. We talked about Thomas and what had happened. But not the other children. Hers were still around, producing grandchildren for her to love and spoil. I had my birds and a dead daughter upstairs.

The more we reasoned, the more desperate I became. With *her* dead and *him* mad, the police saying nothing and not letting me see my own son's files, I let my mind run over the is he dead/is he alive more than I probably should have.

Lizzie was talking to me one day and she told me about her friend whose husband had run off, and how she'd been to see a psychic. I told her that I didn't believe in that sort of thing, but in the back of my mind it kept reappearing. It was as if I had a head full of sticky notes, yellow Post-its that kept jostling to the front of my thoughts. I couldn't forget about the psychic, and I ran through every possible scenario.

What if I could get in touch with my dead son? What if I could? Or at least someone who knew? And that's how I met Sarah Edwards.

BESSY
THE DAY OF RECKONING

I'd never really been what you would call religious. Me and Colin had got married in church and I suppose I had some beliefs, but matters had been confused for me when Thomas went missing, mainly because it made me wonder why God would do this to me. But I hedged my bets both ways, because I wanted to think of Thomas in heaven if he was dead. And *her* in hell.

The idea of going to see a psychic had grown inside me and eventually it burst out at the missing group. As we all sat round looking sad, clasping our teacups, and talking about the next campaign, as they now called their searches, I broached the subject.

'I was wondering if any of you had been to see a psychic? You know, someone who gets in touch with the other side.'

There was nodding and it seemed most people had, at some time. Jenny Coombes, whose fifteen-year-old son had gone missing four years ago, spoke up.

'I have. I went to see a reader and she read my cards, then did a session. She told me he was buried in Gloucestershire.'

I gulped.

'Really? Did you believe her?'

'Well, it's a possibility. But I don't know. It was all a bit weird, but she did seem to know a lot about me and my family.'

I thought for a bit, then the conversation moved on to decomposed bodies. We'd booked a speaker who would tell us at what stages in time bodies decompose. Many of the people in the group felt that they needed to know this so that they would know, if their loved one was dead, what state their bodies would be in at any given time.

I wasn't really interested in that, and decided to use that time to go and see a psychic instead. At the end of the session, Billy Moore, whose sixteen-year-old son had been missing for twelve years now (Billy always wore a T-shirt with his sixteen-year-old face peering out) handed me a business card. It was neat, white and gold, and tasteful, which reassured me. I didn't want any funny business.

'Psychic and Clairvoyant. Let me help you. Sarah Edwards, MSc.'

The card looked authentic and when I looked at the address, on the A635, I realised that I'd driven past her home many times.

'Have you been, Billy?'

He nodded enthusiastically.

'Yeah. She was very good. Told me a lot about what I was going through and about where to look and that. Very good. I went to see her twice. She charges fifty quid an hour, and you book half a day. Might be even better for you because of where she is, you know, with her being up there and all that.'

I went home clutching the card, driving with it on the dashboard, I kept looking at it. This could be where I found my answers. I rang her as soon as I got home and booked a half-day session with her for a week on Tuesday.

As usual, life stood still apart from routine, a strange

calmness that gathered around major events, and on that Tuesday morning I actually felt a little excitement. I gathered up all the reports I had, just in case she wanted to see the background, although if she was psychic, wouldn't she know?

I had no idea how it worked, except that she would be a go-between for me and people who were dead. I smiled a little and wondered what would happen if I got Colin? He'd be pleased, and I'd be able to tell him me and Lizzie had made friends. He'd like that. Not my mam and dad. Didn't want them. Or Colin's mother. Or *her*. Not *her*. I'd have to tell the psychic that.

I drove up there and parked up on some spare ground opposite. It was the other side of the moor to where I was used to, and it looked different from here, a sea of purple heather sloping down, then upward.

Now and again, I'd realise how desperate I was, and this was one of those times. I went through all the things I'd done, all the places I had been over the years to try to find Thomas, but this beat the lot. Everything else had been in the real, solid world, even the pining and the walking over the moor. I'd been to those places because I was not sure and I wanted answers, I wasn't sure if he was dead or alive and I was waiting for some confirmation.

Even on the moor, I sat and waited for an assurance, a feeling that he was there, something that had not arrived so far. Now, this seems like I'm admitting he's dead. How would this psychic woman get in touch with him otherwise? I was a bit shocked at this at first, and I stood and checked myself in case I definitely had come to this conclusion, without realising. I hadn't.

There was no surety, no definite decision. I was still as numb and cold as I had been for the past however many years it had been. My shell was intact, and nothing had punctured it, giving me a little piece of mind.

I stood at the wall for ages, leaning against the brambles and wondering how *they* could have done it. The house across the way was empty and I thought about buying it, just to be near. It was too big for me; I'd be rattling in it. Eventually I went over and knocked on the door. I'd been expecting something out of *Arabian Nights*, and her to be a bit exotic, but she wasn't. And you know, she was quite plain, but pleasant.

She asked me in and the house was done out in reds and creams and it was very nice. Her carpet was like a doormat all the way though, sort of woven and rough.

I looked around to see if there was any evidence of a family, but there wasn't one photograph. She had a lot of plants inside and out, and there seemed to be a lot of bees.

Little birds chirped away and hovered near the open windows and I felt a little bit more at home when I saw them. There was a huge red sofa in the lounge and she waved for me to sit on it. It looked like she was very successful at what she did, and it made me feel a bit more confident about what I was doing.

We sat down and she took my hand straight away.

'Right, Bessy, you don't mind if I call you Bessy? You know how I asked you to bring something of Thomas's?'

I handed her his Manchester United pendant, the one handed to him by one of the players in 1960. His prized possession.

'That was his. From his room. I've kept it all the same.'

She was looking at me and nodding. She actually looked interested, not like the people who I usually talked to, waiting to get to another client or just not interested because it isn't them. A sense of relief came over me, something I hadn't felt for a while. I wouldn't have to watch what I said to her, she understood.

'Really? Tell me a little bit more about Thomas and what happened to him?'

I told her what I'd told you here and she never took her eyes off me. She'd squeeze my hand at the hard parts, and she nodded sadly when I told her Colin was dead. I didn't tell her about the babies. I'm not sure why, except I thought she might call the police. Her expression changed only once, when I told her that I didn't want any contact from *her*.

After an hour of talking, she led me to a large oak table in the dining room. I went to the loo, and when I came down she'd made tea and there was a cloth over the table, dark blue.

She shuffled some cards and did a tarot reading, which I didn't understand. She was hell bent on telling me what would happen in my future and it struck me than that if she were genuine, she would know the plans that were beginning to crystallise in my mind.

I let her carry on until she had told me about my house and my friends and my car, then she stopped. Her face went funny and she put her hands face down on the table.

'I'm getting something, Bessy, I'm feeling something.'

There was more nodding and frowning and exaggerated hand movements, then she went rigid. It made me jump a bit.

'I've got Colin here for you. Colin, what do you want to tell Bessy. Mmm. Mmm. You're happy where you are. It's warm and nice.'

I sat up straight.

'Can you tell him that me and Lizzie are friends now?'

She told him and she appeared to be listening to something else.

'He says, that's good, love. That's good. Look after each other.' I couldn't really see Colin saying that, he wasn't that sort, but he might have changed.

'Can you ask him if he's seen our Thomas?'

She didn't flinch, and she asked him.

'He says he's here, love. He's here with him.'

I was crying and saying, 'Is he really, is he? Colin, is he all right? How do I know? How can I find out?'

She pulled out a big drawing pad.

'Thomas is asking me to draw it for him. He says he's safe now, Mum, and it's all over. He's been seeing how you were going on and loves you. And thanks for looking for him. But he's been here all the time.'

'Where? Where is he?'

'I'm here with my dad, Mum. But I'll show you where I am on the earthly plane, by getting Sarah to draw it.'

I sobbed.

'I'm sorry, love, I'm sorry for not looking after you better. I've done everything I could to make things right.'

She scribbled on the paper with pencils, drawing a map.

'It's all right, Mum. I'm fine, it's nice here and I'm happy. Now you be happy as well. I've got to go now, but I'll be with you all the time. Love you, Mum.'

Sarah sat at the table with the map in front of her.

'Well. How was that, Bessy? Thomas and Colin both there for you?'

She beamed brightly. I didn't really expect her to understand how this would affect me, but I was totally elated. The joy and upset at the same time flowed through my tears and it took me an hour to calm down. I'd been there five hours by the time she handed me a marked-up ordnance survey map of the moor, with a red dot where Thomas's body was.

'So what do I do with this now? Take it to the police?'

'You can do. But they don't usually do anything. Really, it's just so that you know for sure. You do believe Thomas and Colin, don't you? It's for your peace of mind.' She put her arm around me and walked me to the door. Her head tilted to one side and her mouth pursed. 'You can rest easy now. Bessy, dear. Come back any time. Any time.'

I handed her a cheque for three hundred pounds and went back to my car, clutching the map. I tossed my papers in the back, but rested the precious maps on the front seat.

When I got home, I looked in some reference books I had for the coordinates, and some public reports about where the bodies were found, and the spot on the map was just around a rock outcrop from where the bodies had been found. My stomach lurched and I was sick again.

I sat there all night, planning how I would go there tomorrow, and walk to the spot where Thomas was buried, finding out the exact position before I went to the police station. It all made sense now; I'd been right all along. I was pleased and kept telling myself it was the best three hundred pounds I had ever spent.

I'd sat on the back step until it was dusk and the birds had stopped singing. I got changed and lay in bed until I couldn't stand it anymore. I went to the outhouse, where the old toilet used to be, and I rummaged through Colin's tools that he'd left.

His small shovel was there, still strong, and I took it into the house, along with my walking boots. I pulled them on over my fleecy pyjama bottoms and put a waterproof coat on over my nightie. I went round and got the car from the side of the terrace and put the shovel and the map on the backseat.

The drive up to the moor was busy, with people out and about in the towns, until I got onto the A635. I decided to go the other way to the moor, over the reservoir, because I knew that path better.

I left my car and stepped into the darkness, carrying the shovel and the map. It was a fairly long walk, but I knew every step. The ground was squelchy and I knew that, in daylight, there was cow and sheep muck everywhere.

It didn't matter, because for once I had a purpose. Most of the time I was wandering around aimlessly, from one nightmare to another, but today had been a treat. I hadn't felt so strong for ages, carrying the shovel and my bag.

I knew my way, all right, it was almost second nature. Until I got to the gate. It was quite dark but the moon was almost full and lit the moor brightly. There was no light pollution here and I could see the stars twinkling. I looked up as I walked and I could see the swirls of the Milky Way.

My feet caught on the jagged rocks and I could feel the bruises through my wellies. I knew there was a path somewhere, and when the heather started to brush my knees, I bore left until it was shorter and more trodden down.

Now and again I'd hear a rustle in the scrub, an animal startled, or a grouse making a dash for it, and usually I'd stop to look, to see if I could get a good view. Not tonight—I had a mission. I was quite cold by now, but in a frenzy to get there. Soon, I came to the rock outcrop and the spot on the map.

I switched my torch on and circled the ground, wondering what to do next. It was in this second that I realised that I didn't have a plan. Almost everything else in my life so far had been carefully planned.

I'd taken my eye off things once before and look what had happened. Now, there was no room for chance, everything was preplanned, a prearranged routine. For a second I wondered what I would do if I found Thomas's body here? Call the police? Or did I just want to know for myself?

I stood there, imagining the glory of being right after all those years, of holding up Thomas's remains like some morbid proof of my sanity. I'd be recognised, and counted in as one of the other mothers, part of the club that had formed, through no fault of their own. People would start to care, and believe me.

They'd finally start to listen to what I'd gone through, my pain and heartbreak.

I flashed the torch around and rested it on a mound. Then picked it up and rested it on a high rock and started digging. The spade cut through the moss and heather and into the dark peat. There was an earthy smell, and I dug a little bit more. I was too warm now so I sat down, but immediately felt cold. It was just peat.

So I turned round and dug in a spot opposite. I dug quite deep, until my back hurt, then started to dig sideways. The dirt was everywhere and I was covered from head to toe. I knew what peat looked like, but I had no idea it was so wet and dirty. There were a lot of roots and bits of wood, and eventually my spade hit something hard.

The shock went through my body and I scrambled into the hole and bent to touch the object. It was a glass bottle, an old style glass bottle with a stopper. I sat in the hole and wondered how it had got there.

I felt a little bit sleepy and my mind wandered to a programme I'd seen on the telly last week, about some engineers who had been digging hundreds of feet under the ground to build a new tube line under Istanbul.

They'd drilled and dug and done lots of work, and the deeper they got, the more things they found. Eventually, they found thirty-six ships, preserved in the ground since the 1800s. I didn't believe it at first, but it was online as well, and the people who discovered them reckoned they'd been in a port that had been destroyed by an earthquake or a landslide, and the port had fallen into the sea.

Someone else thought that it was to do with rising or falling sea levels. I don't think any of them knew, and it didn't really matter, but it did make me think. As I lay there in that hole, I wondered if the earth was getting bigger, closer to the moon, because of all the rubbish we're covering it with. If those ships were hundreds of feet down, how deep would this moor be buried in another two hundred years?

Happen someone dropped this bottle a hundred years ago and then there was a bad storm, and since then it's been churned up in the earth, until I dug deep enough. Thirty-six ships! I remember laughing and falling asleep, but waking up a bit later on and feeling a bit woozy. I got up and walked up and down, but I felt a pain behind my eyes and a bit bilious. I carried on digging to keep me warm, but I was slower now.

After about half an hour I sat down again. I was tired now and I decided to see if I could feel Thomas here, feel his presence, like I had tried to at the houses and at Daisy Nook, and in the market. I tried to focus, but I was so tired I couldn't. I was falling asleep and I remember thinking it wouldn't matter if I had a little kip.

I also remember thinking that Thomas wasn't here. I couldn't feel him. As I drifted off I remember wondering what Sarah Edwards really was? Who would be cruel enough to send me on this journey?

CHAPTER THIRTEEN

I snap the book shut. Unbelievable. That poor woman, digging up the moor in the middle of the night. And that Sarah woman. How could that be allowed, making money out of other peoples' misery?

Bessy was braver than me. All her commitment, all her heartbreak. But she never gave up. I feel physical pain when I think of Aiden as a child now, of winter days and my pulling on his hat, of his squealing with delight as I chased him. Our regular visits to the passport photograph booth—I kept all the photos.

They were once a treasure, the start of something big; a relationship that would last for life. But now they're just more painful reminders. Yet I can't put them away. I have to leave everything as it is.

I gather all my belongings. It's chilly and my feet are numb. I want to carry on reading but I can't stay here any longer, I have to go home and deal with things. The first thing I'll do is send the WPCs on their way. Their forced encampment has made the house change, whether it wanted to or not. I wonder if they'll take the cushions?

My next thought is about the Gables and my urgent need to tell someone about the photograph and how he disposed of his victims. The net closes tight around Connelly and his vile doings, while another one unravels around me, the story I've guarded so closely, so silently, the one that started with Bessy, pokes through the holes and struggles to get out.

I'll have to tell Stewart where I got the photograph. And why. I know I'll have to. So I'll go home and make sure the house is locked up tight, just in case I'm arrested straightaway. I think about Bessy again, and how she left the back door open for Thomas, which was how I got in there in the first place.

I consider doing that, just in case Aiden comes home one night, cold and wet looking for his mum. Ironic, isn't it, that I was only trying to find him, only trying to do the right thing, but somehow it's twisted my thinking and I ended up stealing from a dead woman?

It's over now, and although there's always another Connelly to step into his shoes, that's if they've even found him to arrest him, I expect his cronies will lie low for a while now. Besides, I might not be around long enough to need anyone to guard me. As I start up my bike, I think about the possibility of admitting everything, and the possible sentence I will get. Thrown out of the force, probably prison.

As I speed home my ears are ringing with the sounds of last night, the retching of grown men and the horror in Mike's eyes. Then my elation, my joy at not seeing Aiden's face. Pictures of Bessy, digging in her nightclothes, finally falling asleep on the moor, and Sarah counting her money.

It's sunny now, and crisp and when I zoom past the crossroads I see the road's been cordoned off with yellow tape and two uniformed officers are standing drinking brews. I barely register with them. Why would I? They've got bigger fish to fry now.

I want to know if Connelly is in custody, if Mike and Jim found anything else. I picture the mothers of the boys, each one collapsing with grief. Pat. Her face crumbling as she realizes it's all been a setup, she's lost her son and her life and all the time people nearby knew. Mothers and fathers of boys missing years ago, nodding sadly, as if they knew all along, but dying inside as they hear the details. I want to go in and help with the operation debrief, do my job.

I desperately want to stand there while they are told that their children are dead, and tell them that I know what they are going through, this time I do. Not the empty words I've used before, the platitudes my job requires of me. I know how they feel. But instead I drive home.

I know something's wrong even before I park up. The garage door is slightly open. There's faint glow from under it that means the kitchen light is on, and the side door is open. I turn to check that the police car is still there, and it is. I park up the bike and pull off my crash helmet.

A sliver of orange light tells me that the front door is slightly open and I push it a little. Is it Aiden? Has he come home and not found me here, so looked in the garage for me? My heart jumps a little at the thought of going inside and up to his room.

Is he there, lying on his bed with is headphones on, tapping his foot, smiling at me? Do I flick on the kettle and make him a hot chocolate, just the way he likes it? I blink into reality and the image disappears. It's replaced by what appears to be a dark stain on my carpet. Hot chocolate? No too red. Blood. But how can it be?

My line of vision widens to the sofa. The coffee table is knocked over. The TV is on and it's the end of a drama. *The Notebook*. The bit at the end where Noah and Allie are by the piano. The bit that always makes me cry.

I can feel the tears in my throat now and this time there's no holding them back. I walk around the sofa and see the pink bunny rabbit slipper, one of the ears is twisted underneath in an awkward position, just above a snapped ankle. Her foot caught underneath the television stand as she fell backward. Fell. Fell. Did she? Would a fall be enough to crack open her skull?

Sheila's eyes are closed and her mouth is twisted in pain. She's bunched up, her foot straining enough for the bone to rip the skin, and I want to release it but I can't. Did she fall? If she has, why would the coffee table be over? Why would the drawers be open in the sideboard?

I go through to the kitchen and see Sharon sprawled out on the tiles. She's facedown, but from the side of her cheek, I can see, she has heavy bruising. She's clutching a small butter knife and there's an unbuttered piece of toast on the kitchen side. I feel her neck for a pulse, but there is none.

Looking closer, I can see a blade sticking through the blue winceyette of her dressing gown, making a small puncture. No blood. As I turn to check the garage, I remember that you should never try to remove a knife from a body, never open a wound.

Another body lies in the kitchen doorway. A young woman I don't know, someone in their early twenties, in a police uniform. I can hear the credits roll on the film now, as I step over her and go upstairs.

It's completely ransacked. The bathroom is smashed, all the bath panels have been removed and the shower screens ripped apart. I go to my room and it's a mountain of jumbled clothes and MDF. Everything has been piled high on my bed, and I automatically look upward, then feel guilty.

Three dead bodies and I'm worried about the money. Who the fuck have I become?

The ceiling tiles are intact and I stand on my dressing table, which has been pulled out, to see if it's still there. It is. Exactly where I left it. Of course it fucking is. No one else knows about it. Only Bessy.

I panic. I haven't got to the end of her story yet. For all I know, the next bit of her notes could say that she informed the police or told a relative or even a friend, or Mothers for the fucking Missing. Jesus. *Come on, Jan. Come on.* I've got so used to looking up, reading the skies, that my heads in the clouds.

Still standing on the table, I assess the room. It's hard to tell how it used to be, but I crouch down and think about what whoever did this could be after. What did I have that someone would need? I don't have any money of my own.

I don't have any police business kept here. Nothing at all. Obviously someone thinks I am hiding something. Is it Connelly, a payback for finding him out? What am I hiding? The money, but it's not that. Unless they've killed three people and left empty-handed. What else? What else have I got here that someone else would want?

My eyes scan the room and finally rest on the remains of the small fitted cupboard in the corner of my bedroom. I jump down and pull away the debris, waiting for Aiden's passport and bank card to drop out from behind the hardboard. But it's gone. It was that.

Oh my God. Maybe I was wrong? Maybe Connelly does have Aiden, as a special case, holding him to get at me. Somewhere, else, away from the Gables. Keeping him prisoner, a bargaining tip for when it all comes on top.

Now he's going to take him away for good. But why would he do that? Why would he do any of this, now it's over? Revenge? Or just because he can.

Just because he can, because it makes him powerful. Like the terrible signs in the sky, holding everyone's fear high above them, reminding them that all he has to do is drop it and . . .

I rush downstairs. The money can wait. What Stewart

doesn't know will keep for the time being. This is more important. I pick up the house phone and dial the ops room. It's engaged, and I phone Mike. He's engaged too. Of course he will be. They'll all be at the Gables, sorting their way through the carnage.

I dial the ops room again, pressing redial every time I hear the engaged tone. Come on, come on. I notice that there's a terrible smell for the first time, shit and blood, not unlike the rooms where the boys were kept. Death. That horrible sense that someone has suffered. Someone's life has ebbed away.

My mind races away from death and onto the passport. What would they want with Aiden's passport if they didn't have him? Aiden must be leaving the country. There's no other reason for it. But why would Connelly take Aiden abroad? To sell him?

The thought repulses me, and I force back vomit. It wouldn't be outside what Connelly was capable of, after all. And he did seem to have singled me out for some reason. *Come on. Come on.*

Then I see it. In the middle of all the fucked-up murder and the topsy-turvy furniture, I see it. Beside the torn ligaments and the bunny rabbit. I see it. Or, rather, I don't see it.

I replace the receiver and scan the floor. I pull the coffee table away and reach around the floor for any sign of it. The small bronze statue of an eagle I bought in a junk shop in Italy in what seems like a lifetime ago. I researched it and found out it was a maquette. A scale model of the real thing, which, by some serendipitous occurrence, stood in a museum in Sal's Italian hometown. It turned out that the area Sal's family came from, Catania in Sicily, was very close to a raptor sanctuary. Famous for birds and famous for mafia connections.

We'd joked about it, but now it seemed eerily real. Sal

denied it, dismissed it as conspiracy theory and ridiculous, but now I wonder if cruelty and violence is somehow genetic.

He'd coveted the eagle, his eyes glazing over and a vein in his forehead thumping every time I picked it up. I say maquette, he says plastico. We couldn't even agree on that. I had it valued and it turned out to be worth in excess of ten thousand pounds, so I kept it locked in a reinforced glass-fronted cupboard in the lounge where I could both see it and keep it safe.

Sal loved it as soon as he set eyes on it. It was as if he already knew what it was, a little piece of his hometown, a little piece of him. When we divorced, he listed it as his, but I produced a receipt to say I had paid for it and I kept it. Because I knew how much it would get to him.

I bend down and see that the glass is not broken. It has been carefully opened with a key that only Sal and I know the whereabouts of, and locked again after the tiny bird has been taken out. I reach up above the curtain rail and the key is gone.

I perch on the edge of the sofa, not really wanting to believe what seems to be happening. Sal? Sal? Why would he do this? What would he want with Aiden's passport? I suddenly remember the packed bag with the bank card and passport in the side of it. I run upstairs, through the debris and the bodies, and I stand on my dressing table again to reach the money.

No one will know I've been here. I rush back downstairs and try to leave the house, but I can't. I can't just leave them here like this. But I have to go right now. I try the ops room one more time, but it's still engaged.

So I jump on my bike and speed down the road helmet-less, the money dangling from my arm in a carrier bag. Stopping at the place where I dropped my phone last night, I retrieve it and drop the money there instead. This is a black spot, no surveillance, no phone signal. So it should be safe from prying eyes. Prying eyes.

How could I have missed it? My head is filled with Sal's stock sayings, one of the things that had endeared him to me. 'Keep your friends close and your enemies closer.' Sal in the station, wandering around the ops room, preparing for our appeal. So angry when I took him to the interview room. Sal in Jim Stewart's office. Sal, when we were still together, going for a pint with Mike. Sal. Waiting for me in the cloakrooms after work like a dutiful husband. Sal with my phone. Sal with my work notes. Why had I never seen it before? Why?

Had I been too caught up in my domestics with him to realise that he hated me so much that he would use me to get information?

Then it hits me. He must be working for Connelly. He must be. Otherwise, why would he need to run now? I backtrack, Sal in the background of everything. My phone call to him yesterday, he asked where I was. Was I outside?

Sal's face when I'd found the passport, his anger. Sal, earlier on, in Jim Stewart's office, probably while he took the call from Mike. Sal could have alerted Connelly. He was the one who cleared the Gables, fed Connelly the false information I had given Mike. Further back, to Operation Hurricane.

Sal offering to keep Aiden for weekends while I worked long hours, then bringing him back just before I arrived home and making me coffee. Talking to me. Asking me about what had gone on. I hadn't told him any of the details, but I probably had said enough to hint at what the operation was about. He'd always shown an interest, even when it became clear that he resented my job.

I'm outside his flat now. I remember the security camera. I pull around in the background and go behind the post that holds it and throw and old rag I find on the steps over the lens. First time. I must be getting better, in my desperation.

Then I park under the balcony, just to be sure. Two steps at a time I reach the front door, pressing all the buzzers over and over until someone buzzed me in. I push my ear against the moulded plastic and hear nothing. So I feel for the key and it's still there.

I turn it and push open the door quietly, but I already know it's too late. Sal's coats no longer hang by the front door. The hallway is empty, and as I walk through to the lounge, it's like the first time I visited the flat with him before he moved in, to make sure Aiden would be OK here.

Empty. Except for a note on the kitchen side, alongside a stack of blank notepaper. I pick up the paper and feel it. It's the same paper as all the other notes were written on. All the notes I thought were from Connelly.

The note tells me to check my phone. I turn on my mobile, fumbling with the buttons and will it to operate after a night outside in the damp. It does, and immediately beeps loudly into the echoing emptiness.

Lots of texts and messages from Mike, but only one from Sal. It's a picture message. It's him holding the eagle and two plane tickets, with his thumb over the destination. He's too far away for me to see the time of the flight, but the backdrop is a thick plastic barrier and the flash from the phone has reflected in it.

I peer at the picture, looking hard, and I can make out the outline of someone in the reflected light, the shape of a body I gave birth to, that I am so familiar with. The way he stands, slightly to one side, a piece of hair that tufts out in every photograph he has ever had taken. It's so obviously Aiden.

There's some text underneath the photograph. It says 'I Win.' And he's right, he does win. I sob at this now, because it's true. In between all the chaos and death, all the mothers who have lost sons, all the frightened little boys who have been murdered, through all Bessy's suffering, Sal's right, he does win.

He's taken my son away from me. Aiden's not dead. No. He's gone with his father, probably to a new life, without me. He was alive all this time, God only knows where, him and Sal planning this whole thing.

Sal and I were drifting apart, and Sal needed information. A way to get close to me. A way to get close to ops, to find out what was going on. It crosses my mind that he might have kept Aiden prisoner, but this falls away quickly when I look at the photograph.

They were standing in Manchester Airport, for God's sake. He's smiling, and Aiden's taking a photo. Sal. The man I lived with for all those years, is standing in Manchester Airport, smiling, just after murdering three policewomen. He knew about Connelly and what was going on at the Gables. Why else would he run now? The man I had lived with. Slept with.

I feel the vomit rising and rush out of the flat. I can't risk being sick in here, having my DNA all over the place. So I shut the door, wipe it and replace the key. Then I rush down the stairs and vomit in a litter bin around the side.

CHAPTER FOURTEEN

I n ten more minutes I'm back at my house and calling Mike.
It's engaged twice, then it rings.

'Jan. Thank God. We thought something had happened to
you. Are you OK?'

I feel a lump in my throat and tear run down my cheeks as I
look at Sheila, blue around the mouth now.

'No. No. Get round here quick. I've been trying to call for
over an hour.'

'Yeah. All the lines have been busy. What is it? Where are
you?'

I look around. I'm at home. Except it isn't home anymore.
And it never will be again. Not without Aiden.

'My house. Get here quick, Mike. Something terrible's
happened. Bring backup. And some ambulances.'

Mike's silent for a while.

'Is it Aiden?'

'No. It's the policewomen who've been here. They've
been . . .'

'On my way. I'll get everyone who isn't up at the Gables up
there. We'll be there in a minute.'

The line goes dead and I find myself walking upstairs and going into Aiden's bedroom. None of this seems real, and I check my phone again, just to make sure I'm not mistaken. I'm not. The picture is still the same.

I look out of the window and over Northlands. In the distance I can see that the nearest main telegraph wires have been cut. The black dots that punctuated the sky were gone now, probably bits of tat lying in the street, all their meaning diffused as soon as they hit the ground.

The messages are gone, and nowhere to hang any more black flags. Further up, I see a plane jetting through the midday sky. It could be any flight, but it could be the one carrying Sal and Aiden to who knows where. I can't believe it. And that's why I'm here.

When it first dawned on me that Aiden had disappeared, had gone missing, and everyone suggested that he might have 'gone off' to 'be with his friends,' I couldn't believe it. I wouldn't. And part of the reason for this is that he hadn't taken anything.

Of course, the obvious items he would have taken were his bank card, passport, any kind of ID. But it wasn't even this that convinced me. I knew that if Aiden had planned to leave there was one thing that he would never leave behind.

He was a small child when Ruby came to stay. She was a Jack Russell, with a lively personality to match. She was adorable. When we bought Ruby and brought her home. She had a double link chain around her neck that hung like a necklace, weighed down by a tiny piece of jet that Sal had found on the beach at Whitby and made into a pendant. Ruby was Aiden's best friend from the age of four until he was eleven.

When she passed away he didn't speak for a week, then after returned to normal. Until one day, two years later, when I was cleaning his room. I opened his drawer and came across

Ruby's collar and the pendant, hidden away in one of my jewellery boxes. I hadn't noticed Aiden standing behind me.

'Put it down.'

His face had been approaching evil, the same look as Sal had when he was angry and ready to flip.

'Aiden, don't speak to me like that. And who said you could have this box? It's mine.'

His face relaxed.

'Is it? Is it yours? Dad says that all this will be mine when you die, so why not cut out the middle man?' He snatched the box away from me and grabbed the chain and pendant, holding it up in front of me. 'Have your box. Have it. But don't ever touch this again. OK?'

The moment broke and I threw down my duster.

'You cheeky little sod, Aiden. After I die? Is that what you want?'

It was back to Mother and son after a moment when I wasn't really sure who Aiden was.

'No. I didn't say it. It was Dad who said it.'

I nodded.

'I bet he did. Well, you'll have to wait a long time because I'm not going anywhere yet.'

He'd laughed and swung the chain around in his hand.

'But that's not true is it? You're going to work. You're always going to work or coming home. So you're always going somewhere.'

Although we'd never talked about Sal's hate of my job in front of Aiden, those words could have been straight out of Sal's mouth. And wishing me dead. Just the sort of thing he would say. Cut out the middle man. It was the first, but not the last time that I had wondered exactly what he had been filling Aiden's head with. But we were close, weren't we? Nothing Sal said could ever come between me and Aiden, could it?

I open the drawer. Of course, it's gone. The chain and the pendant, along with a small collection of football cards, the ones that were quite valuable. I check the rest of the room and nothing else seems to be missing, except Aiden's teddy, Jezzer. I go back to the drawer, remembering that Aiden had an old photograph of me and him playing with Ruby in the park, one that he treasures almost as much as the chain.

I feel around the back of the drawer, finding bits and pieces that evoke memories. Finally, my fingers touch the smooth paper and I realize that he hasn't taken it. But as I pull it out I see that I'm wrong. In fact, he has taken half of it. He's ripped the photograph right down the middle and left the piece with my laughing face. Without Aiden and Ruby to put me in context, I look crazed. And I was a little crazed. With love. I console myself with the fact that maybe only Sal had been here.

Then it strikes me. Had Aiden been here and seen the carnage? Had he seen death? If he was, he was implicated. I'd never wanted a moment of pain for him and even now, knowing what he had done to me, I still feel faint knowing that he could have been a part of this. No. It would have been Sal. In any case, it's too late now. I can hear Mike's car outside and I'm downstairs, frozen to the spot, as he walks in and sees Sheila first.

'Jan. Jan, are you OK?'

He rushes over and puts his arms around me, looking all the time at the mess and the bodies.

'I've been here ages, Mike, trying to get through. What the hell's going on?'

'Fucking Connelly. When he got word that we'd busted the Gables, he made a run for it. Ordered all the CCTV and the phone networks to be disabled as a last hurrah. Bastard.'

I draw away from him.

'So you haven't got him? He's still on the loose?'

Mike shakes his head.

'Yeah. We've had a few sightings at the airport. Put out an All Ports call. Probably gone by now. But he won't be back.' He moves into the kitchen and I follow him. The airport. Oh my God. Not with Sal and Aiden. Keep your enemies closer. Mike feels Sharon's pulse in exactly the same place I did. 'Poor buggers. They didn't stand a chance. Whoever did this is an animal.'

The rest of the team arrives and a couple of paramedics check the bodies over. I stay crouched onto the bottom stair, watching as my house is dismantled. There's a sense of anger, and unspoken air of camaraderie, after all, these girls were coppers, and this is a copper's house. We're all in it together. Like Sheila has said, they were like my sisters. Whoever did this is an animal.

Of course, I had the chance to tell Mike who did this when he said it. I could have told him all about Sal and Connelly, but somehow it didn't seem like the right time. He's leaning on the back door now, checking his phone. I go over and try to find out what happened last night.

'So. What went on after I left?'

He nods and smiles.

'Ah. After you left. Where did you go, by the way? Not here, obviously.'

'No. I went up to the reservoir. I needed to get my head together.'

He sniggers.

'Story, more like. Stewart's looking for you.'

'Oh yeah. Why?'

He puts the phone away.

'How did you know? About the Gables. How did you get that information? And don't give me no shit. How did you find out?'

I think about Bessy. No. That would be a betrayal.

'I just had a hunch. I was looking at some old cases and I don't know, I found out John Connelly was a butchers and . . .'

'So it was Mr Connelly in the butchers with a knife. Fuck off, Jan. You've been a wild card lately. Everything around you turns to shit, doesn't it? There's something more. Something I can't put my finger on.'

The threads, Mike, draw the threads together. Do me a favour and realise it was Sal. But he doesn't.

'Yeah, well, I've had a lot on my mind. You know, Mike, most of it fitted together. You know, about Aiden and the other missing kids. I don't know, maybe it was the extra motivation. Do you know I've spent every waking hour since Aiden went missing, wondering if some criminal has got hold of him? You've got a son. How would you feel if you had no fucking idea where he was. Eh? Now ask me again what more there is. He's my son, Aiden, and those boys are all sons. That's the something more.'

He's gone very pale now and he backs away from me.

'But they don't happen that often, these kind of cases, do they? Life's just not that dangerous you know. For kids, like.'

'Isn't it? Few and far between? Eh, Mike? It's more dangerous than we think, because it's unthinkable. That's what someone said to me many years ago, and I believed them. But if I had my time again, I'd never let Aiden out of my sight.'

I think about Ted and his wise words. Mike shakes his head.

'Yeah, the unthinkable, carried out by crazies. Psychopaths. Only you're right, there seems to be a lot more of it these days. A lot more.'

A paramedic comes in to examine Sharon's body and we move over to the window. I can feel the tears welling up as I realise the women who only this morning called me sister were prepared for the mortuary.

'Is there? Is there really a lot more, or do we just hear about it more. John Connelly has been prolific in this area from around 1960, and his son after him. Selling young boys and girls to clients visiting the Gables, then, when they're finished with, killing them and disposing of their bodies, one way or another. Yes, I've said it. That's what he was doing, using those kids to placate the criminal acts of those prepared to pay large sums for it. Looking back in the files, back to the sixties, it was suggested then that he was involved in the disappearances, around the times of the Moors Murders. But he used that as a cover for his own criminal activity, portraying himself as an upright member of the community. When all the time he was doing this. Not that we've got any solid proof.' No. Only Bessy's notebooks, which I can't submit as evidence as then they'll know I took them.

Mike sighs.

'But what more could we have done? It's like, no body, no murder. What more could we have done?'

I stare through the window as Sharon's body is covered, ready for a body bag.

'We could have listened. To people like me. To mothers and fathers. To good coppers with a hunch.'

He nods.

'Yeah. You're right. But where do you draw the line? If we do that, we'll be taking statements off psychics next.'

Psychics. As if on cue, Jim Stewart appears at the door and I remember that I have no idea if Bessy has told anyone about the money. But he bypasses me completely and looks around the room.

'Bloody hell. Who'd do this?'

Mike and I look at each other. He beats me to it.

'Some kind of psychopath. Some kind of twisted fucking psychopath.'

Jim shakes his head. He looks very tired and drawn. I can't

tell him about Sal. I can't. Because then I might be telling him about Aiden. Jim continues.

'Psychopath season round here at the moment. What with all that business up the road.' He turns to me. 'Unorthodox methods, but well done for calling it. You shouldn't have gone in there on your own, though.'

I look at the bloodstained tiles.

'Am I suspended, then?'

He laughs and it somehow sounds inappropriately loudly.

'No. No. Not for now. But take a couple of days off, just to settle yourself down. You've been through a lot. I had a word with your husband the other day . . .'

'Ex-husband. Ex. Husband. Sir. Please. Ex.'

'Ex-husband. He was saying that you are a bit, well, how can I put this, more highly strung than usual.'

I snort.

'How the fuck would he know? With respect.'

'Well, he does spend a lot of time with you, and he's been supporting you through your problems with your son. Who, I'm pleased to say, doesn't appear to have been involved in the terrible business at the Gables.'

It's difficult, but I control my temper. Watch what I say. It's not the time.

'As far as you know. Who's to say they haven't got rid of him, like some of the others?'

Jim nods.

'Well, he wasn't in any of the records. I personally supervised a search of those records for him as we were afraid that . . .'

'Yeah, well, that's one less dead boy to worry about isn't it? For you, anyway. Was there anything else? I need to find somewhere to stay.'

Mike intervenes.

'Won't Sal put you up for a bit? Till all this is sorted out.'

I stare at Jim, to see if he flinches, to see if he knows anything. He doesn't bat an eyelid.

'I can't contact him. I've been trying to phone him.'

Instead, he fixes me with his gaze. He touches his head and points at me.

'Oh yes. There was one more thing. That woman, the one in Ney Street who you found, did you know there'd been a baby's corpse found in the house? The forensics came through and said it'd been moved recently, probably the same day. And there was something about some forensics being there. Did you search the house? It's just that there's also been some neighbour claiming that she was loaded. Claims she saw the old woman with a bundle of notes in her shopping bag but we looked at her bank account and we didn't find much. Any ideas?'

'Mmm. Jack told me about the human remains. Anyone could have got in, though, the back door was wide open when I tried it.'

Mike interrupts.

'But wouldn't anyone who went in call us?'

I nod.

'Yeah, unless they were after . . . something. You know, a thief.'

Jim shakes his head.

'Sad business, this day and age, old people lying dead in their homes for who knows how long. Bloody hell.'

'Good job I found her then, isn't it?' More than they know. Without Bessy, I'd never have been able find out about the Gables. 'And before you ask, I got the info on the Gables from the archives. Put two and two together. And when I was up at the reservoir last night, I remembered something else I'd seen, when I was up at the community centre, a picture of old Connelly outside the Gables gates, with what appeared to be a grid with a furnace underneath it. Could that be how, you know . . .'

Mike nods.

'Yeah. Yeah. There is a huge brick crater, set quite far back, leading to some corrugated iron doors, looked like a strange area but . . .' I see the horror spread across his face. 'You don't think . . . ?'

I nod.

'Yes, I do think. I also think that they only burned the bodies every bonfire night, so as to not attract attention at a derelict building. That's what I heard one of the guards say.'

Mike shakes his head.

'This is fucking unbelievable. Too horrible for words. It's something you would never think would happen.'

I nod again.

'Exactly. And that's how they got away with it. They relied on us being good people. On us, hardened police, even us not believing that someone could be so evil.'

They both stare at me. Jim scratches his head.

'Are you sure you got this from research? Just from reading the archives?'

Yes. Yes. I did. But not the police archives. The archives of someone's life, someone who needed to let another person know their reasons. They passed it on.

'Yes. I got it all from reading the archives. You know, it's like old time detective work, before computers. Now we're just sitting at desks watching CCTV. Reading peoples' phone messages, checking bank accounts. Obviously you need the backup and the evidence, but it doesn't hurt to think about it and do a bit of background.'

Mike nods, but neither of them agree. Mike looks around. The forensics team is here and it's obviously time to go.

'Look, just try Sal again and if he doesn't reply, come back to the station and we'll sort something out.'

I go upstairs with a forensics guy, who marks down exactly what I take from my room.

'Anything missing that you have noticed? Not that it'd be so easy to see. But anything valuable gone?'

Yes. Yes. Something valuable has gone. My son.

'Not that I can see. But I'll try to think once, you know . . .'

'Yes, of course, Mrs Margiotta.'

'It's DS Janet Pearce, for the record.'

He pulls his hood down.

'Oh. Right. Sorry, only Jim Stewart said . . .'

'OK. My name is not Margiotta. It's DS Pearce. Got it?' I pick up a letter from my dressing table and show him. 'See? DS Janet Pearce.'

He holds his hands up in mock dismay.

'Right. That's fine. No need to get upset.'

I walk downstairs with my overnight bag. I slip out the side door and grab the archived cases and Bessy's notes out of my bike box before Jim and Mike leave the house. No. No need to get upset is there? Dead bodies everywhere and my son taken away by his father.

As we walk toward Jim Stewart's car, I try to resist it but I can't. I try to resist fighting against the inevitable, that Aiden has chosen to go. And not even taken a photograph. It's still not right. Aiden would never go voluntarily. He would never leave like this. And that's why I almost forget my instinct to duck when the first bullet is fired.

It glances my cheek, but I manage to push Jim to the ground as the second one hits the garage door. Mike is lying beside me and for a moment I think he's hit, but he rolls over and speed dials tactical. I hear him speaking gently but clearly.

'Two gunmen in a car. Opposite Jan's house, where the others were killed earlier on.'

CHAPTER FIFTEEN

I put my hand on Jim's arm and he moves it to one side, just to show me he's OK. Mike's still got his phone to his ear, waiting for the next move. He rolls back toward me slowly.

'Jan. Can you crawl to the edge of the car and see if those four who were over there are OK? And get Jim's phone. Mine keeps going dead. All the phone masts are out. You need to keep a line open with tactical if you can. Apparently it's getting a bit rough out there, some comms are out, probably to let Connelly escape undetected. Oh, and intelligence says there's a contract out on us. That's what they're here for.'

I nod. Then I roll. I can just see under the car, over to the other side of the road. One of the uniformed is trying to get my attention. He's making the sign for one man down, and I give him a thumbs-up. I roll back and Jim hands me his phone. I open the address book and scroll down past all Jim's relatives and friends, scrolling to reach T. But I stop at S. Salvador Margiotta. Why has he got Sal's number? I didn't realize they were such good pals.

Time and a place, Jan, time and a place. I scroll down and call tactical, and the line's no better on Jim's phone. Minutes pass without anything happening at all and then I hear a car door open and the crunch of gravel, closer and closer, up my drive, stopping for a second. I can see his feet. Vans. White socks. Thick ankles. I can feel Mike staring at me, his eyes wet with fear. He takes my hand and whispers quietly.

'If this is it, I want you to know I always believed you. I get it. I always did. I was just worried about you.'

Closer and closer, until he's nearly on top of us. He's at the other end of the car, opposite us. I hear him take the safety catch of the weapon and I think I hear him take aim. Then I hear a shot. We all tense. Ready for the impact, and I wonder which one of us it will be.

I see the starlings on the roof beyond the trees scatter and reform in a swirl, and then I hear a crash as the gunman crumbles to the ground. More footsteps, turning into a run, this time getting quieter then, further away, a single shot and they stop.

We all lay quietly for a moment, until a black figure lowers his gun.

'Get up. Up. Go, go, go. Into the van.'

We all somehow get up and make a run for it, over the dead gunman, away from his dead friend. I see three policemen carrying their injured colleague into their car and speed off. I didn't wait to see if they avoid the body in the road, but I suspect they don't by the dull thump of tyres hitting tarmac. We make it to the van and the doors are slammed shut. There are two armed policemen inside, and one of them takes off his helmet.

'Is everyone all right? Sir?'

Jim nods.

'Yes. Yes. Just take us to ops. And I want an armed guard to pick up my family and take them to Point C. Mike?'

Mike shakes his head.

'I suppose I'll have to. Yes. Can I phone my wife and let her know?'

Jim nods.

'Yeah. You can if you can get a signal. It's like the wild fucking west out there. Jan? What about you?'

I stare at him. Has he suddenly forgotten that my son is missing and my ex-husband is a bastard?

'Just me, sir. Just me.'

He frowns.

'What about Sal?'

In some ways I'm glad he's saying it. It kind of proves that he's not in league with him, not unless he's very clever and bluffing. But I doubt it.

'Why would Sal have anything to do with this? Sal is nothing to do with me.'

He nods now.

'Yeah. I know. I do know. But he's got your best interests at heart. Me and Sal, we've become kind of close, you know. He does care about you.'

Again, this would have been an ideal opportunity to tell him that Sal had killed three of his officers and skipped the country. But again, I don't. I can't. So I don't say anything. I reason with myself that there'll be plenty of time later on to put all the pieces together, when I know what really happened.

We sit in silence until we get to the station. I guard my bag as if it was my life, and as we make a dash from the van to the door, and finally behind the bulletproof glass we can breathe again, I still wonder where they are now. Where they have gone?

We are rushed through to ops, armed guards on every door, and finally we meet with the rest of the team who have rigged up a huge TV screen. Naturally, there are already news crews around. They've been there since yesterday, since the first police car arrived at Old Mill, and would have followed to the Gables.

No doubt they would be outside my house right now, and at key points on the estate, which in a way, we're all glad of, because it gives us some idea of what's going on. Jim's telling ops that he won't risk the lives of any more men. He's telling everyone that we need to keep calm and wait until nightfall when it should all quieten down.

Jim's telling everyone that we've prepared for this and that we'll have it under control within twenty-four hours. I tune back into Jim's briefing.

'So, as we can see, word's got out about the Gables and the goings-on there. Connelly's not the most popular bloke around here right now. But, like us, he's got a plan B and him and the top tier of his organization are long gone. Even so, we've put an All Ports out and also notified other forces of his potential involvement. Our long-term goals are to find them and bring them to justice. He'll still be surrounded by people he trusts, maybe abroad, but he's obviously left a legacy here, part of it being to assassinate several members of this team. So, as a result, we've temporarily moved their families to Point C.'

I'm sitting at the back of the room, holding my bag between my legs. I glance at the computer in front of me, which is alternating between the blacked-out CCTV cameras in the area, occasionally finding one that Connelly's thugs have missed.

Now and then there's a glimpse of a road on the estate or a park, or a road junction. I watch the serial numbers of the individual cameras as they trip over, making a mental map of exactly where they are, and what Connelly's escape route would be.

I jot it down on some scrap paper for later, confirmation that he headed for the airport. Jim's still talking about what will happen next, and I zone out and press 'Escape' on the computer. I reset it to a certain time and a certain route.

There's a camera outside Sal's flat, and one just around the corner. There's a great one at the traffic lights on the high street, then one on the roundabout. Then they turn onto the motorway, and there are cameras on every bridge until the turnoff for the airport. Naturally, the airport is full of cameras. So I plot the route and scan the first camera, frame by frame, for any sign of Aiden and Sal. I start at 3.30 and fast forward, scanning every frame.

Nothing for a while, then at exactly four o'clock, two grainy figures emerge from Sal's flat and walk toward a BMW that pulls up as the door opens. I slow the frames down, and I see Aiden's face clearly for the first time in months. He looks the same. Except he's smiling. He's carrying the travel bag and he's smiling at the driver, who high fives him.

He and Sal nudge each other, like a father and son who are excited about going to a football match, not skipping the country like criminals. No. Not *like* criminals. They *are* criminals. They get in the back of the car, like celebrities, and I wonder what they are to Connelly. Like Jim said, Connelly's top tier would be removed, sent far away to regroup.

I track them to the traffic lights and freeze the frame as they pass, the camera on Aiden's side. He's smiling widely, looking out of the window. No one has captured him. No one is leading him away against his will. My sixteen-year-old son is going on a criminal adventure with a man who, it turns out, I hardly know.

I follow the car through the various cameras as it speeds down the M60 and turns off at the airport. Then at the entrance to the airport, they get out of the car and take their travel bags. I watch their backs as they approach the double doors, and then Aiden turns around and looks back at Manchester.

Is this the bit where he momentarily thinks about me, about

his mother? About his room, and where he lived? About Ruby and the bedtime stories? He stands there for a while, then, as if to prove me wrong one last time, he spits on the ground and follows Sal.

I persevere. Through the airport, over to departures, harder to track now. But eventually I find them at the American Airlines desk. Sal takes out his phone and hands it to Aiden, who takes a photo of him. I silently will Aiden to turn around, come back, come back to me. There's not even an All Ports call on them because only I know they have gone.

Even now I hold a hope that he won't go through to the gate, that he won't leave. But he does. As they check in and immediately go through to catch their flight, to Cuba, it seems, Sal puts a protective arm around Aiden's shoulder. Then they've gone.

I roll back the footage until they're there again. This will probably the last time I ever see my son. I save the whole of the footage into one file, then open the desk drawer and rustle around for a blank disk. It draws Jim's attention, but I'm ready for him.

'Everything OK, Jan? This is really important, so I hope you're taking it in.'

All eyes on me.

'Yes, sir. Sorry, I was just trying to find out what route that bastard used to escape. Tracking the CCTV to find where he was off to. Predictably, all the blacked-out cameras lead to the airport.'

There's a reverent silence. Then Jim points at me.

'Thanks. Can you save that as evidence?' He points around the room. 'Are you lot taking this in? Lateral thinking. She's practically solved this case single-handed, using her head. Thinking outside the box. Now I'm not saying you should use any unorthodox methods, but you can learn from her. Don't go into buildings on your own, always get backup, but do follow up leads. You're detectives, for God's sake.' He rubs his head, then says what I expect everyone in the room has been thinking since the Gables was busted. 'How the fuck have we managed to miss this one? It's been going on for forty years, to one extent or another. But we've managed to let it slip through our fingers.'

Obviously, I can't resist. I breathe in and as I breathe out, the words escape.

'You could have listened to me. About Aiden. And wondered why all these teenage boys were going missing.'

He shakes his head and perpetuates exactly what he has been doing wrong.

'But teenage boys run away all the time. We can't possibly investigate all of them, can we? You must see that.'

I nod.

'Yes. I do see that. But the first thing I want you to do when this is all over is to compare all the missing boys files with those poor lads up at the Gables and see exactly how many have actually run away. And how many kids have been murdered.'

His eyes betray him. They say that I should think myself lucky that Aiden wasn't up there. But he doesn't say that.

'Anyway. Good work, Jan. We now need to focus on containing the aftermath.'

I stare at the screen, one last look, then I close down the CCTV program and take the flash drive, slipping it into my bag. I press 'Delete' and wipe any trace of Aiden and Sal from the machine.

Even now, I don't want anyone rushing to the airport and arresting Aiden. Guilty, maybe by association, but I can't do it. I can't. It's a catch-22. If I get Aiden back, he's implicated and I'll lose him all over again. At least this way he'll have his freedom, of a sort. No one knows I know, and it's going to stay that way. The downside is that I can't send them after Sal, but it's becoming clear he's involved and it's only a matter of time until they go after him.

Mike and I are led through to the back of the station, into the yard. Jim appears and smiles at us.

'I've got you two to thank for saving my life back there. I won't forget it. Mike, you'll go onward to Point C until this is over. Jan, we've secured a property in Saddleworth, out on the Huddersfield Road, where you can stay. I'll need to talk to you about your sources. There's also some unanswered question on the case of that woman, you know, the one you found in that house in Ney Street. Something wrong on the forensics. If you've got anything to say about it, tell me now. Jack's calling for an investigation into why you were in there, but in the light of what's happened since, I doubt it'll go anywhere. But I want the full story. So . . . ?'

I shake my head.

'Not sure what you mean? What's wrong with the forensics?'

He smiles.

'If I told you that I'd have to kill you.'

I get into the car. Jim thinks he's so clever, his cryptic little threats are supposed to keep me in line, yet he was so fully taken in by Sal. His head's tilted to one side and I can see that he still thinks I'm slightly unhinged. Sal would have told him that I'd always been like that. A bit unpredictable. Quirky. Any inference he could muster that I was a little bit mad, without actually saying it.

The man driving the car is someone I have met before, someone familiar to me, and I relax. My guard is a special ops guy, Piers, I know from training, and they take the scenic route across the city, avoiding Northlands, and upward to the crossroads.

They take a right, up past the moor and farther on, out of

the country and on to a remote cottage at the end of a long track. Piers checks it all out, then we go inside. Someone's been here and the heating's been on. There's a TV and I flick it on and watch Sky News as the car pulls away. Piers goes upstairs and comes back down minutes later.

'All seems OK. I'm going to be staying here with you. I checked it all out earlier, and there are three bedrooms, I've left the en suite for you.'

Could be worse, I suppose.

'Great.'

'I don't know how long we'll be here. Until it's safe, I suppose. But there are some great walks. I'll have to come with you, of course, but we'll need to get some exercise.'

'OK. I'm just watching what's happening. Kind of makes me wish I was still involved. Is there a computer?'

He smiles.

'No. No broadband up here. Not even sure that there's a phone signal. Which is good. No one can find you. Why? Were you hoping to work from here?'

I nod.

'Yeah. I've got some loose ends to tie up.'

'You've done enough. You're a legend in your own lifetime. How did you do it?'

'Good old detective work. Looking everywhere, and eventually something comes up. You follow the lead, and sometimes it leads to nothing. Mostly. But you have to persevere. You have to carry on. Never give up.'

He nods.

'Never give up. Yeah.'

I sigh and look out of the window into the dusk. There are no telegraph poles here, or trees near to the house. Yet starlings have grouped together on the high wooden fence around the back of the cottage. Nearer and nearer.

At one point today I thought I was going to die. I felt my heart thumping when I heard the gravel footsteps. But it's not my time yet. I've got more to face. I remember now what Jim said about Bessy and the forensics, and wonder how I'm going to explain it. Particularly as someone has appeared now to state that she was loaded and there may have been money in the house.

I guess I have a lot to explain really. All about Sal, Aiden, how I knew about the Gables. So inevitably, I will have to tell about Bessy. Still, at what seems like a conclusion to all this for me, Aiden gone, Connelly gone, Sal gone, I still feel like there's more. I think about the money and the notebook and what I need to do. Maybe Bessy has something to say about it. Maybe the notebook is, in the end, a living will?

I go up to my room and fall into the warm, clean bed. I have the notebook, where I left Bessy unconscious on the moor, and I open it again, prepared to lose someone who has become an informant and more than a friend.

BESSY

FORTY BIRTHDAY CARDS

I woke up in hospital the next day with a banging headache. It turned out I'd passed out and nearly died of exposure. My knee was bandaged up and I felt my legs, just to make sure they were still there. After dinner the doctor came round to see me.

'Mrs Swain, I'm Dr Hussein. I've come to ask you about last night. Is that OK?'

Dr Hussein was a tiny girl wearing a white coat.

'Are you qualified? I don't mean to be rude, but you don't look old enough.'

She smiled.

'Yes, I am. And I'd just like to chat about last night. I'm the hospital geriatric specialist and I'd just like to assess you.'

'Geriatric. Bloody hell, I'm only seventy-nine. There's nothing wrong with me.'

'So why were you on Saddleworth Moor digging in the middle of the night?'

I suddenly realised that I hadn't been to the doctor's for years and I hadn't been in hospital since Thomas was born. Thomas. I'd been awake more than five minutes and I hadn't thought about him.

'I was looking for my son. He's been missing for over forty years. A psychic told me to dig there.'

She'd sighed.

'What psychic? And I still have your husband as next of kin. Is that right?'

'No. He's dead. And Thomas is missing. So there's just me.'

She looked at me and tilted her head sideways and it reminded me of Sarah.

'So there's no one to look after you? Have you been managing on your own?'

'Yes. For forty odd years. On my own.'

'You can get help, you know. A cleaner, or meals on wheels.'

'I don't need a cleaner. I can do it myself. Thank you. Sarah Edwards. That's the psychic. She was lying, wasn't she?'

Dr Hussein sighed.

'I'll get the police to come and see you. I think they have your car. Is it a blue Micra? You can tell them all about Sarah Edwards. Did you pay her much?'

'Three hundred pounds. She said she had Colin and Thomas there with her.'

I thought back to only yesterday and wondered what I had really expected to get out of it. It wasn't as if she had tricked me, really. I knew she was a psychic and she knew I had a missing son. If you add it all up, she was obviously doing to tell me she was in touch with them. Otherwise, why would I go?

In the brilliant light of the hospital ward, it sounded ridiculous. Dr Hussein probably thought I was cracked, all this about a bloody psychic and then digging up the moor. She told me a man walking his dog had found me.

'Was it an Alsatian?'

She frowned.

'I've no idea. Why?'

'Well, I go up there every day. Every day for a walk and to

have a look round. It's a beautiful place. I know it's not very nice, with the bodies and all that, but it's very picturesque.'

'So you're seventy-nine, you're still driving and you're up on Saddleworth Moor every day? What's your secret, Mrs Swain?'

I laughed.

'A stress-free life, I reckon. No, I like to keep busy.'

She talked to the nurses and came back.

'You can go home later if you like. I'll see you again in a month and we'll do a test for dementia. Age-related of course, just to be on the safe side.'

I sunk into my pillows and sighed.

'I don't think you understand, Dr Hussein. I haven't got dementia, or Alzheimer's. I'm dying of a broken heart. You see, nobody ever cared about me. I've been wondering what's happening to my son for more than forty years. I haven't known if he is alive or dead. I think that would send anyone a little bit crazy at times. I was just looking for my baby.'

I could see her glancing at her watch as I was speaking. Probably late to pick her own kiddies up, or thinking about what to make for tea. Just like everybody else, it was nothing to do with her.

'There are special people you can talk to about that, Mrs Swain. Would you like to make an appointment with one of our counsellors?'

I scratched my head and a piece of heather fell out of my hair.

'Why do we need special people? Why don't people care?'

Dr Hussein was writing something in her notes and she didn't answer me. I suppose I already knew the answer. These days especially, with all the missing people and the child abuse.

It's always in the papers, how there are lots of people murdered all the time, and kiddies going through all sorts. I'm sure it didn't used to be like that. Only for me and my son. Oh, and the poor children who were murdered. You hardly ever heard of it.

Now it's happening all the time. I wondered if people were getting more evil, or if it was just because we hear about it more through being online and all that? I expect there were always bad people, but where were all the good ones? The ones who claimed to be looking after us, like Dr Hussein.

I looked at her, she had a little smile and she was humming as she wrote. Probably thinking about her own life, trying to pin my madness on some medical cause, Alzheimer's, dementia, or my age. Not giving a bugger about what I've told her, just offloading me into some bloody cause of a disease that she can fit me nicely into.

'As I said, I'll make an appointment for you. You will come, won't you?'

I nodded, but I never went back. I went home and the police called round, asked me if I wanted to make a complaint against Sarah. But what was the point? By now I'd worked out that she just wanted to help me. How was she to know I would go up on the moor in the middle of the night?

She probably just thought I'd pin the map on the wall and look at it, or show the police and they'd do nothing. Of course, I asked them if they would take a soil sample from the place I'd been digging, and they agreed.

They told me it would take a month to analyse and, after three months, I received a letter saying that the sample did not contain human remains. I put the letter into a suitcase packed with forty years' worth of letters just like that one.

Life settled back into normal and years went by in a flash. Nothing changed, no news of Thomas or *him*. A couple of books had come out and I'd read them from cover to cover, looking for details I might have missed. And I'd found out about the Internet. I was online. I was part of a group online that looked for missing people.

You could post up a picture, and they would meet up and run marathons and raise money. They were a bit like modern day John Connelly events, with bunting and crying mothers. I got in touch with them and taught myself how to send an e-mail, soon I was sending them all over the place.

It all came to a head in 2007 when that little girl went missing in Portugal. At first I was sure she'd be found, but when I saw her mother, with her empty eyes and her sadness, I recognised it straight away. That woman was like me, living a life, holding her husband's hand, but the story running through her mind was a rerun of that day, wondering what she could have done better.

They say she left the kiddies in a room while she went across the road for dinner. Well, I can tell you, I left Thomas in his cot while I nipped next door for a brew, but it didn't mean I loved him any less. It just means that I'd underestimated the dangers. Dangers like child killers. We all knew they were there somewhere, but we don't talk about it. No one did before, and no one does now.

Just after that there was another case where the mother had faked an abduction. It started me thinking about how cruel people can be, how life is hard enough without these things happening. We never talk about them, those dubious situations where a little girl can be hidden in her uncle's bed. What kind of woman would be party to that?

The aspersions cast on the other little girl's mother, the papers saying that her parents killed her. Life is so cruel, and the world is so beautiful. My mind goes full circle to *her,* an excuse for a woman, someone who could do those horrific things to who knows how many kiddies then blames love?

I know better than anyone what the moor is like, its terrible beauty. After all, I nearly died there myself. How could *she* go there time after time and see the crushing beauty, yet know there was such horror? I guess that's how *she* got her thrills.

Somehow it seems more appropriate, more expected to say that about a man, but a woman? Hadn't *she* been up there with her dog, something *she* loved, while they buried the bodies? Hadn't *she*, a woman who could have been a mother herself in time, listened to a little girl scream for her own mother? People had still defended *her*, saying *she* was swayed by *him*, that *he* overpowered *her*, and maybe there was some truth in that.

Later in life, though, when *she* found God and said *she* carried a burden of guilt and wanted to be forgiven, then, couldn't *she* have just told the truth?

It struck me, as I watched that poor woman whose little girl had been taken in Portugal get thinner and thinner and more drawn, suffering peoples' comments about her parenting when her little girl was gone, and I realised that I had never told anyone the whole story of how I felt.

I'd never had the opportunity, in forty years, to tell people I was shrivelled inside. That I still thought about Thomas all the time. No one's attention span could stand it, because it wasn't to do with them. It wasn't their child. From time to time at the missing people groups, I'd still recognise the chilly shell around someone and we'd nod our recognition, but it was too hard to put it into words, and it sounded stupid no matter how you said it.

There was no getting away from it, like so many others, I was just a body, going on day by day, with no hope for the future. I looked in the drawer of the dressing table and there were forty birthday cards and forty Christmas cards. I'd stopped washing Thomas's sheets now, but I still laid the table for him.

I still looked at young boys, only the other week I saw someone in Manchester who looked like Thomas and followed him up Piccadilly. Of course, it couldn't be him. Because Thomas would be sixty-odd now. I was losing my grip and things were slipping. On the outside, I was the same old Bessy, but inside I was an old woman, confused and upset.

I'd had to stop going to missing person meetings because I was falling asleep. The hospital had written to me and told me that I needed to contact the DVLA to have my licence retested, or I might not be driving legally.

One sunny morning, after I'd been up the moor, I set off for the solicitor's and gave him my instructions. I knew it wouldn't be long now, I'd been online researching my options and how long people live, and I'd made all the decisions I needed to make about my future.

All I could do now was carry on with my routine until the time came. Like I mentioned before, I've never been able to tell anyone all this before, that Sarah woman was the closest I came and she didn't give a toss, she just wanted my money. It's not such a bad world on the face of it, but if you scratch the surface you'll find that human life is very shallow, and the best pleasures are in the depths of nature.

BESSY

WE'LL SHARE THE MOON

So, I'm popping this in the box upstairs on my way to the airport, past the park where Thomas used to play, past Daisy Nook. Past the Market, and I can just see all those nosy buggers pointing and saying 'There she goes, that Bessy, shirking her responsibilities.' I can see them now, Macs and headscarves all over the place, pecking at peoples' misery like a kit of pigeons at dawn.

Actually, they're nearly all dead now, and so are some of their children. I keep a look out in the obituaries of the Ashton Reporter and they're dropping like flies.

I was never one for funerals so I never went to any of theirs. Why should I? They made my life a bloody misery, pointing and calling me and making out I was a bad woman because Colin left me. A bad mother because my son disappeared.

If I could go back and have that time again, just after he went, I'd stand in the middle of the market and tell them how much I cared about him, about the clouds and the geese and the birds, and how I made his butties every day with more love than I knew I had.

They wouldn't have listened, though. They just wanted

something to talk about, something to rip apart, before the days when we got all that from *Eastenders* and *Corrie*. I can remember the days when we had no telly at all, nothing to stare at all day, and you could count the people you knew and things you'd been told on two hands.

Now, with the telly and that Internet, you can find out anything. Those women, they were a fickle lot. Some of them even called me mad, crazy, and said I should have been locked up. Happen they were right, because that's what happened to most of the other parents with missing children.

I've suppose you're wondering why I've decided to go? Well, it's partly because I got a letter the other day from the DVLC asking me to surrender my driving licence. It turns out I've got cataracts, and I had noticed that I couldn't see as well at nights.

They can't operate because of my age, and Ben Hartley down the road had his done and he can't see at all now. I'd been for my hospital appointment, sitting waiting in a room full of families. All the other old people had someone with them, their family or friends, someone sitting looking worried about the misty-eyed blurriness of old age.

I suppose they were all standing on the edge of an abyss, wondering when their moment would be. Donkey's years ago, just after Colin died, it seemed almost impossible that the day would come when I would too.

In that hospital waiting room I could almost taste the moment. I had a bit of a laugh to myself, betting that none of these folk had football season tickets or holidays booked; most of them looked like they were falling to bits.

They'd called me in and messed about with my eyes for a bit, and told me they couldn't do anything with them. They'd stared at me for a long moment, expecting me to burst into tears or at least hold my hand across my mouth. I knew what I should do; I'd seen it on the TV on *Casualty*. A bit of hysteria, or some tight question would have fitted nicely, but as I'm already dead inside, I couldn't make the effort.

They asked me to sit in the waiting room, and as I walked through I wondered if anyone had popped off while I was in there. Half an hour later, they called me back in and that nice little Dr Hussein was sitting there. She'd taken my hand and shouted at me like young people do to old people.

'Now, Bessy, are you all right? I'm glad I've got you here. You didn't come back for your appointment.'

I just shook my head and looked in my handbag for my car keys. But she carried on.

'So. I'm going to send a social worker round to your house. You can't carry on living alone, Bessy, not now your eyes are going. Do you understand?'

I'd sighed heavily and looked at the door.

'Can I go now?'

'Yes. But we'll send someone round as soon as we can. I'm afraid you'll have to stop driving as well, Bessy. And we'll find you a place in sheltered accommodation, with lots of company.'

I got up and went, and I could see them, exasperated looks on their faces, silently agreeing with each other that I was losing my mind. I knew that what was actually happening was that I wasn't agreeing with them. I suppose I could have sat in all day, staring at the television, just like a lot of other old people do, but it wouldn't be the same. I'd made my life for myself, set it up a certain way, and at my age you don't want any change.

Anyway, I've put my car keys in with my house keys. I've sold the car to a nice young man at the end of the road, number 32, he's agreed I can keep it 'til I go; I told him I was going to live with my son, and I suppose in a way I am. If whoever could take it over to him I'd be ever so grateful. And the house. I've instructed my solicitor to make sure Mr Connelly knows after I've gone.

There's a bit of money put away and that'll go to Mothers for the Missing. Hopefully they'll use it to buy a bigger television for the community centre, and some proper coffee. They've gone global, now, you know, our little group. They've got a website and a Twitter and a Facey book. They can put pictures up what everyone in the world can see, so that wherever they are there's a better chance of them seeing it and coming back.

We can see other people too and it told us that there are still a lot of people missing, but most of them turn up. It's just the people like me, and a small group of other mothers, who drop under life's radar, suffering an unbearable torture inside while we try to act normally in our outside lives.

Everything else can go to charity. I've packed up what I can from the bedrooms up and boxed them, they're on the floor in the front room, and I've put address labels on them. Except Thomas's room. I've left that as it is, just in case. I expect that if you've found the letters, you've found that poor little mite. But I hope you can see that there was no malice, I just didn't know what to do. No. Not at all. I hope everyone understands that, I really do.

The thing I'm most worried about is the birds. The little blackbirds in the back garden. I can't bear the thought that they'll be sitting outside my kitchen window, hungry and waiting for food. It makes me feel like when Thomas first went, and the other one in the phone box, as if I was abandoning someone.

I can't stop them coming, either. They know where the food is, where to look. I like to think that from the first one I made friends with, Jack, then Jill, these are all their family. Over the years they've come back, and I've helped to bring them up, like I could have with my own if it hadn't have been cut short.

One year I found a baby bird, it'd fallen out of the nesting box, and I took it inside. It was so small that it was all heart, a visible beating in its chest while it lay still, occasionally opening its mouth for a bite to eat.

I fed it with a little dropper and wrapped it up in some tissue paper in a box. It grew and grew into a bigger chick, then I'd let it out on the kitchen table and it walk about, chirping and eating bits of bread. It was tiny and at first I thought it was a wren, but then it grew a red patch on its chest and I knew it was a robin.

One day, when I was feeding it some birdseed I'd bought from Schofield's hardware specially, it hopped up to the sink. I thought it was after a drink from the water I left there for the blackbirds, but it flapped and fluttered and flew up to the open window.

It sat there for a minute, then glided onto the holly bush, making a perfect Christmas picture in May. Then it flew away. It never came back, and somewhere inside I felt a little bit better because I knew it could survive without me. And I suppose Jack and Jill's kiddies will. I've left a note with the estate agent to tell anyone he shows round about them, but I don't expect he will, because I could tell by his face that the ravings of a mad old woman would put the buyers off.

You know, I like to think of someone as doing what Thomas would do when I'm gone. It's one of the things that's made me put this off, the thought that everything would just be left. I found out about it last year, when it was on the telly.

I'd thought about it lots of times, especially since that day at the hospital, when I realised that one day I wouldn't have to wake up to this. I'd heard a story that someone who did it went to hell, and although I'm not a believer, I'm backing my odds both ways—how do I know that Colin and Thomas aren't up there waiting for me? Knowing my luck, it'd go wrong anyway, and it'd just be another thing to weigh on my mind, another thing I'd failed at.

So I'd rung them up, and it took me a while because it was a foreign number and I had to get the dialling code through BT. When I did get through, I made an appointment in Manchester for the next week. The man was very nice, and he explained to me what I would have to do, the aeroplane and all that, did I have a passport, where I would go and how much it would cost.

I met him five times over the next couple of months, and by then I was convinced. So I went home and filled the forms in, wrote a cheque for £9,247 and pressed the envelope closed, but the next day when I went up on the moor I got a funny feeling that it was going to happen anyway soon. After all, I'm in my eighties, and I can't go on forever. I'd decided against it while I was up there, as if it was wrong, because although it was so bleak and dull, it was alive in another way, and I was a part of it. I was walking through it every day and without me there it just wouldn't be the same, would it?

I'd come off the moor that day and driven home thinking that I wouldn't do it, I'd stay as I was and just wait for something to happen. I knew that some people lived until they were a hundred, and I just couldn't bear another ten years or more living like this. On the other hand, I'd still have my blackbirds.

When I got home that day, I let myself in and there were two women sitting in my living room. It'd been a shock at first, and my stomach lurched at the thought that someone had died, but then I realised that there was only me left. They'd come to get me.

'It's all right, Bessy. We let ourselves in through the back door. Did you know you'd left it open, love? Of course not. Let me make you a cuppa.'

They were in the kitchen, touching my things. One of them snapped the window shut and I could see the birds outside on the sill, shut out of my world now, as the women moved my pots around.

'We've had a bit of a tidy up, Bessy. We've ordered a home help for you, twice a week, until we find you something else.'

I sat down heavily. If I was weary before, I was desperately tired now.

'I don't need anyone here. I'm all right. Can you just go, please?'

They ignored me, tutting at the brown rings on my white kitchen surfaces, the smell of bleach cutting through the ciggie mist. I took one out of the packet and lit it up. One of the women turned.

'Could I ask you not to do that, Bessy? This is our workplace and we reserve the right to be respected in our workplace.'

She turned back to her scrubbing, the other one pulling a mop out of a bucket, breaking the cobwebs and scattering dust everywhere. Respect. That was a good word. Where was my respect?

All I wanted to do was live here quietly until the day I didn't wake up in the morning. I just wanted to carry on with the deep groove I'd driven into the world, my routine, my time.

I'd managed to keep out of sight mostly for the biggest part of my life, hiding in my home, visiting the usual places, no variation because it always ended like this. The normal people, those who were charged with the care of us slightly imperfect human beings, taking over and shovelling hardcore into the groove we have ordered our lives with, smoothing over the crack with whatever means they can.

I know they mean well, and I know it's their job. I know that they do deserve respect in their workplace, as they're now calling my home, so I stub out the cigarette.

'You shouldn't leave that door open, Bessy, someone might come in and steal your things.'

I snigger at the thought of someone stealing piles of old newspapers and Thomas's clothes from the sixties, and they look knowingly at each other. I could almost see them ticking the dementia boxes on their sheets, neither of them having asked me anything at all about my life, what I'd been through, or anything.

'We've had a bit of a tidy up and we've brought some forms with us, applications for sheltered accommodation, where you'll be with other people your own age. They have bingo and even karaoke.' She makes a swaying movement with her body and they both laugh. 'They'll make your meals and you'll have some limited cooking facilities, a shared laundry, and suchlike. Is that OK, Bessy? Do you know what karaoke is, love?'

I nodded and sipped the tea they've made. One of them is telling a story about how her sister is good at karaoke, and I was dying for a ciggie. I open the window again and one of the birds flew in and sat on the sink. I broke up a cracker and sprinkled it on the side. The woman in blue stood behind me.

'Shoo. Out, go on, out. Bessy, that's not very hygienic. Birds in your house. And all those crumbs.' Her hands were on her hips and she turned to her friend. 'We're going to have to action this sooner rather than later. I'm gonna have to ring social services.'

They got their coats on and the other one smiled at me.

'It'll probably take a couple of months to set you up, Bessy, and sort this place out, but in the long run it'll be better for you.' I just looked at the floor as they opened the front door. She turned back quickly. 'Oh, and that letter on the mantelpiece, behind the clock, I've run up the road posted it for you.'

The door slammed shut behind them and I thought, 'Well, that's that, then.'

Someone else had made the decision for me. I was glad in a way, because if she hadn't posted the letter I'd be in the old people's home by now, or the bottom block if they had their way.

I got a lot of letters from them, about the sheltered accommodation and hospital appointments, but I just went out all the time, on the moor, to the market, even into Manchester. I went to Daisy Nook, lying on the grass, looking at mine and Thomas's clouds, seeing faces and flowers and even a giraffe. All the colours seemed brighter now it was all settled. I'd sometimes lie there until dusk, and wait for the moon, so that I could be sure that Thomas, wherever he was, would have looked at the same thing as me recently. It was my favourite time, but twice people walking dogs had called the police, thinking I was ill, and I had to hurry up home.

I'd sit on the forms on Ashton Market, newly built again after a fire that left only a shell. I knew how it felt. I'd look into the crowds but I didn't know who I was looking for now. The seventeen-year-old boy had grown into a man and I had no real idea what he looked like.

I'd met with people I'd gone to school with, and not recognised them from my memory of them as a teenager. Now, anyone could be Thomas. The middle-aged man with his wife, the grey-haired loner, the alcoholic sitting in the bus shelter in his dirty mac with a bottle of cheap wine—all these people could be him, in any part of the world. I still kept waiting for the postman, waiting for a letter from Thomas and I still didn't lock the back door, just in case. Because you never know.

I carried on and avoided social services and my only sadness was that I had never told anyone all this. Then when I knew I was going, and that someone would find her upstairs, about the moor and *them*, I thought it was a good chance to get it all out before I set off. It took me some sleepless nights to write it all down, I tried to write it as if I were there and it took me right back, tears an' all, but I hope it explains that upstairs and, well, things in general. I've enjoyed meeting all those people who live by the moor, who I see every day. That bloody Sarah, be careful of her, not all she's cracked up to be.

Listen to me, telling people what to do! So I'm off now to catch my flight. I've heard it's nice, they take you to this flat and play music while you're on a machine that does it all for you.

They give you a drink to have. I'll just drift off and not wake up, and all the pain will be gone. I'm ready for whatever's on the other side. I'm not scared for myself, I'm bloody glad, but I'm sad for the birds, and for the moor—I think I'll be missed.

That's why I'm asking you to arrange for someone to stay at the house for a couple of days, to see to the birds. I've arranged for them to send me back, arriving a week on Tuesday, and by then everything should be taken care of.

So, Cheerio, and don't worry, it's what I want. Anyhow, whoever you are, thanks for your help and I hope you can do this little thing for me. Even if you don't I expect the world will turn like it always has without me. I'm just going to have a little sit down and a piece of toast, say my goodbyes to Thomas and this house, then I'll be off.

CHAPTER SIXTEEN

I never did tell Jim about Aiden and Sal. Even though I know Aiden's alive, I still need to protect him. I don't know if he was with Sal when he murdered my colleagues, no one does, so the way I figure it is innocent until proven guilty. They'll find Sal soon enough, but I'm not taking any chances.

I know he's complicit in all this, that no one's forcing him to go with his father, but I can't completely know he's guilty. Or believe it. That he's taken part knowingly. Another maternal defence, maybe? I don't know, but I need to keep him safe still, in case one day he remembers me and comes back into my life. So I didn't tell.

I got together with Mike and we went through the papers that were confiscated from the Gables. I felt sick to the stomach, looking into the faces of those poor young people, tying them into my notes and building the background to a case. I turned the pages, willing Thomas not to be there. But I carried on. Turning back time until 1963. August. Don't be there, Thomas, be alive somewhere, with a family. Don't be there, or buried on the moor. Don't fulfil your mother's worst nightmare. Don't be there.

But he was there. Right at the back of the book. The first boy. 30th August, 1963. Thomas Swain. A black-and-white picture of him, surly and smiling slightly. Thomas Swain. Aged seventeen. Bessy's instincts were wrong, but somehow right.

She knew exactly what had happened to her son, but not the who. She was egged on by her fear and John Connelly. Preyed on. I turned the pages, back through the years to the present day, all those boys, and their mother and fathers trapped in a perpetual wondering about what had happened to their child.

After I finished Bessy's notebook and realised what had happened to her, I had a good long think about things. I went out walking on the moor, just like she did every day, with Piers stumbling along behind me. He might be a crack shot with big muscles, but he's not very good at fell walking.

One day we were walking along and I recognised the skyline. I knew where we were, right at the point where all the pictures were posed in the sixties. As soon as we stepped into the heather I felt a fear.

It's like those icebreakers you do at college, where you fall backward and trust someone to catch you. I never really knew what to expect, even though there were only two choices. My fear of doing it was disproportionate to the outcomes.

This was the same. I would either find a good, clear foothold and confidently make good progress, or feel something nasty, something furry or slimy against my leg. Or worse, the crunching of bone.

My legs are already sore from days and days of walking, and this is a real test. I tried to see through the dense plants, past the brightness of the tiny purple flowers, past the pale wooden trunks of the bonsai trees, onto the dry ground. Suddenly, right in front of me, a flock of small birds erupt from the heather; all around them is a halo of pollen, clouds of it billowing into the atmosphere.

It scared me so much that I started to cry. Huge sobs for Aiden, and for Thomas. For Bessy, who never even got to make her own decisions, even at the end. It was the first time I'd cried since I'd found my police colleagues murdered, and I just stood there and bawled my eyes out.

Then I went back to the cottage and packed up all my belongings and booked a ticket to Cuba. Even after all this, I can't let Aiden go. I just can't let my boy go. If I send people after him, bring him back, he's in trouble. All I can do is go to him.

I go home, but don't go in. I merely take my bike out of the garage and load it with the same bag I brought with me. I stop at the travel agent's to pick up my ticket, and my excitement builds. Of course, I have no idea where they are in Cuba, but I can go to the Embassy and try to find out. I just need to see him, make sure he's all right.

I drive along the M60 and take the correct turn off, held in traffic for what seems the longest time. I'm scanning the skies as usual, force of habit, but this far out there is only the occasional hanging signal, looking almost accidental.

I feel a little bit more optimistic; I'm doing something, taking action. To find my son. It feels like the right thing, a pull inside me that I can't ignore. The traffic starts up again and we drive along at snail's pace, sun shining and the light dancing on the chrome handlebars of my bike.

I see a small boy peering at me through the back window of the car in front and he pulls out his tongue. I pull a face and he waves at me. I wave back and we're at a roundabout approaching Terminal 1. The car pulls onto the roundabout and I've got a clear view ahead, clear enough to see a low wire with a sign that tells me that no vehicle over a certain height can enter.

Suspended from the wire is a small brown shape, two arms, two legs and a head, with a noose around its neck. Even from a distance I can see that it's Jezzer, Aiden's teddy. As I pull the bike off the road underneath the wire, an image of Aiden, asleep in his bed with Jezzer, flickers into my consciousness and I wonder how we got from there to here. How did that happen?

There is no way on a busy airport road to scale the pole, skim across and release it, but I stand and stare for a while. It hasn't stopped. The messages are still there and this one is clearly for me. This is the only road into Terminal 1. I'd have to come this way to follow them. I look at the airport buildings, so near, and wonder what I should do.

I so desperately want to follow Aiden, reason with him, find him, bring him home, but this is a definite sign that I should not be doing that. A warning. My heart is breaking, and, as I turn the bike around and ride away, I can't see the road for my tears. I will find him one day, I will follow him, when all this is done and Connelly is brought to justice, I will. It's not over.

So I went home. It had been almost a month since my house was turned into a crime scene, and when I had turned the key in the lock I hadn't really known what to expect.

At first glance it was as if nothing had ever happened there. Some things were different, like the new carpet, light blue, and the new sofa, almost the same as the old one. Some of the furniture had been replaced, but the insurance had taken care of it all.

I'd been advised not to go back there, to sell the house and move somewhere else, but I couldn't. Things on Northlands had returned to normal now, in fact, better than normal. Without Connelly dictating, the whole place was more relaxed.

Crime figures had fallen and Jim had put liaison officers on the estate to try to help people understand what had happened. So today is my first day back at work and I feel a little bit nervous. I knew I'd have to face the music sometime, but I've already made my decisions about how much I'm going to tell. After all, it's my prerogative.

I pull out of the drive and watch the neighbour's curtains move. I expect they're not best pleased to see me back, what with their quiet little avenue being shot up only a month ago.

I drive down the road and park up at the corner shop, the Tesco Metro that has two doors, one on the front and one on the side, grabbing a carrier bag from the self-service terminal on the way.

I nip through to the side, and out into a blackspot. I rush across the road and down a narrow overgrown alleyway and reach under a thick privet bush. It's still there. I pull out the money and push the damp package into the carrier bag. Then I hurry back by the same route and get into my car.

Once at the station, there's a small silence as I enter the ops room. I'm unsure as to whether it's dismay or reverence, until someone starts clapping. There's more clapping and smiling, and I nod and smile back as I tap on Jim Stewart's door. He waves me in and I sit down.

'Back to work, is it?'

I nod.

'Yes, sir. Glad to get back.'

He's got his hands clasped in front of him.

'Just a few things before you do. I wanted to ask you how you found out about the Gables? And if it's got any connection with that deceased woman from Ney Street? Only we've found out that her son was one of the boys who . . .'

'No, sir. I told you already. I saw a picture in Mothers for the Missing at the community centre, you know, with Pat and the others. It matched up with some in the files I looked at, older files.'

'And was Mrs Swain's file one of the files you might have looked at?'

I shrug.

'Could be, they were files about missing boys. So if her son was missing, then it's a probability.'

He sighs.

'How can I put this? You see, I have to wonder if you were looking for the missing boys at all. Because, back engineering it, we didn't know about the missing boys until we found them, did we?'

I nod.

'Actually, we did. They were all on the files. All I did was pull them all together.'

'But how did you know where to look?'

I laugh.

'I'm a detective. I covered all bases and I got lucky.'

He considers this. He knows full well he isn't going to get any more out of me. We both know how this looks, but he'd have to prove it. As I suspected, he tries another route. He's good.

'And then there's the forensics. When they came back, you were all over a box that had been in an upstairs cupboard in Mrs Swain's house. How do you explain that?'

My heart's beating fast now, but I keep my cool. I lean forward.

'My DNA will be all over that house. I went upstairs to get a blanket to cover her up with. As you know, her body was damaged and I was trying to show her some respect. I touched the bed, the curtains, maybe even the cupboard. I certainly touched things in the kitchen, and probably leaned on stuff in the lounge. So maybe the forensics person transferred my trace onto whatever it was found on? I didn't pick any box up.'

It was true. I didn't pick up a box. Just half of the contents. Jim nods.

'Yes, that is a possibility. But all this seems to be bound up with Mrs Swain, she seems involved somehow. Funny how . . .'

'She is involved. The reason I was in the area was because I was looking for Aiden on Connelly's patch. I had an inkling it was some kind of revenge kidnapping, so I was looking for him. Then I hear the woman talking about the smell and . . .'

He laughs.

'You can drop that now. We all know you went for Connelly. All I want to know is who told you? Who made you think it was him?'

'Made me think? No one. Like I said, I thought he had kidnapped Aiden as some kind of revenge for Operation Hurricane, and I was looking for him.'

Jim stands up.

'So your husband didn't mention it?'

I freeze.

'Ex-husband.'

He sighs.

'OK. Ex-husband. Sal. Did he tell you?'

'No. Why? What's Sal got to do with this?'

As if I didn't know. But I have a feeling I'm going to hear something I don't like.

'We've got intelligence that Sal was involved with the Gables. He was the fixer. Arranging for clients to visit. Carrying around a catalogue. That sort of thing.'

I stare at him.

'Sal?'

He nods.

'Yes. For years, it seems. We've got pictures of him with Connelly as he left yesterday. Apparently, he's high up in the hierarchy. Which means that we still can't do Connelly for anything. We've still got nothing solid on him, nothing that would stand up in court. Nothing to connect him to the crimes or the crime scene. But plenty to connect Sal. And now he's disappeared. Have you had any contact with him lately?'

I stand up now and spin to face him.

'Hang on. What are you accusing me of? I want representation . . .'

'I'm not accusing you of anything. You see, people like Sal, they plant a seed, get information out of people like you, without you knowing. I just wondered if you'd . . .'

'If I'd told him any police business? Is that what you mean?' He doesn't say anything but his eyebrows rise. 'Really? Me? What about you, and the cosy little chats you've had with him in here? Nodding and smiling while he tells you how mad I am, how I've lost the plot? Sound familiar, does it? With respect, sir, I think it's you who's been had here.'

He's bright red now and I fold my arms and wait.

'Well, he did have a point. I mean all that stuff . . .'

'Over Aiden?' I move closer to him and lower my voice. 'Remember that day when we nearly died and you sent your family to Point C? Well, just imagine what you would do if one of them didn't arrive. How far you would go to get your child back?'

He bends a little closer to me.

'Why? How far have you gone? What have you been telling your husband? Enough for him to pass onto Connelly? Enough to ruin Operation Hurricane, eh?'

I take my phone out of my pocket.

'Ex-husband. Ex-fucking-husband. And look. I don't have his number on my phone. I don't need it. I'm divorced from him and we don't talk. I don't even know where he is. How about you, sir? Have you got Sal's number on your phone?' His hand goes to his pocket and he covers his phone. I see him count back to the only time I ever had his phone, and my scrolling through the address book. 'Let's have a look then. Why would you have Sal's number on your phone?'

He falls into his seat.

'It's not what you think.'

I nod.

'But you don't know what I'm thinking. All I know is that you told me that Sal's a good man, has my best interests at heart, and he's a friend of yours. Oh, and now I know he's been selling kids to strangers, letting them use a building he has connections with to abuse children, and you seem to have his direct dial.' I sit back down opposite him. 'I'm pretty good at putting two and two together. Gathering all the information and forming it into a crime shaped theory, then investigating it. So before you start throwing accusations about, have a look at yourself. Sir.'

We sit there for a moment longer, staring at each other.

'Is that all? Only I was going to go to organise Mrs Swain's funeral, seeing as she died alone. Is that all right?'

He nods.

'Do what you want. You will anyway. I just want to say that I didn't . . .'

'You don't have to say anything. I was just pointing out that some things aren't what they seem to be. But if I were you, just to be on the safe side, I'd delete that fucking bastard off your phone. Just in case anyone ever questions your motives.'

He's already doing it. I leave and go to my desk and watch him through the glass of his office door. I don't think for one minute that he was involved with Sal or Connelly. He was a pawn in Sal's game. But he's right. All the threads of the case were woven together with Bessy's story.

I see Mike and he waves at me. It's his first day back too, and he looks tanned and fit. He sits down beside me.

'How's tricks?'

I laugh. Mike's made tea. Everyone else is out at a people-skills seminar, and there's a lapse in work in the wake of the storm. He's stirring his tea carefully.

'I'm thinking of leaving.'

He says it simply, not as a provocative statement, and somehow that's worse.

'Why? What's happened?'

We look at each other, and the shared vision of the past two months flickers between us. I nod.

'It's just that I never thought I'd ever have to see something like that. Accidents, yeah, bad enough, and especially those with kids, but they are what it says on the tin. Accidents. No one meant it. It was. An. Accident.'

I draw him.

'Like what though? You've seen loads of dead people. Hundreds, probably.'

His eyes are glazed over.

'In there. Those kids. Not just the dead ones. Calvin. I've got a son. I just feel like I need to spend more time protecting him. And my daughter. It's just that the world's suddenly such a fucking dangerous place.'

I pour another sachet of sugar into my tea. I can't look at him.

'It always was, but I read somewhere that we're programmed toward optimism. It's the only way we can survive. Anyway, aren't you doing that here? Protecting them?'

He nods.

'Mmm. But so were the parents of those kids. And other kids who've been murdered. No parent wakes up one morning and thinks that today they won't protect their child. It's inbuilt. The problem is how dangerous the world is. Full of nutters.'

We sip in synchronization.

'Yeah. And in this case, they were organised.'

Mike snorts.

'Exactly. Like-minded psychopaths. Must have been over fifty people involved. High profile too, by the looks of the evidence. Two or three boys taken a year, a young girl every now and then, all those men coming to . . . It's horrible. Unthinkable, what them kids went through. And not just the people who went there, either. They're just the people who operated the whole thing over time. There's a whole shadow land of shady fucking characters who visited there too. Well. We all know what happened there. I just can't imagine what made them do it. With young boys and girls. Children. They must have known what the score is, what happens to them? It's just too horrible for words. I know I have to do my job, but this, it's shocked me to the core. It must have you too.'

I know he means the scenes at the Gables, but I know he means Sal too.

'I had no idea, you know. About Sal.'

He touches my arm.

'God, Jan, I know, how could you have? But how can you bear it, on top of everything else?'

I stir my tea again.

'I don't know. I just don't know.'

'Anything else on Aiden? At least he wasn't there, you know . . .'

'Yes. He wasn't. And no, nothing else. Nothing at all.

I tidy a few papers on my desk.

'So are you really leaving, Mike?'

He sighs.

'I don't know what to do. This has changed everything. I used to think that people were basically good.'

'We've all got our flaws, Mike.'

Too true. Mine's sitting in the boot of my car right now. A big bag of stolen money.

'Yeah, yeah. I know. But it's almost as if the bogeyman's around every corner. There's always another weirdo wanting to have sex with kids, or to kill and rape women, or to shoot or stab someone for no reason.'

'But we're the police, Mike. We already knew that.'

He's holding his hands out now, pleading.

'But it used to be the exception. Didn't it? The odd case. Now it's fucking everywhere. All the stuff with young girls lately, now this, with young boys. Then the ticking time bomb with the old cases and the children's homes. Same old story. All over the news, victims coming forward but can't pin it on anyone because they've buried their tracks. People asking why we've not done anything about all this. But when it's run by big-time fuckers like Connelly, they get other people to do their dirty work and hide behind them, living the high life. We've still got to work our way through the client list from the Gables yet, and someone on that might talk but I doubt it. I really doubt it. And Connelly's still out there, with no charge sheet.'

I tap my teaspoon on the desk. I don't even want to think about Connelly and his freedom. It makes me think about Aiden and Sal.

'Few and far between. No murder without a body. Problem with that is, what if you're clever enough to hide the body. Or bodies? What do we have then?'

Mike nods.

'A few solved crimes and a shedload of unsolved. Lulls us into a false sense of security.'

'And the evidence was there all the time. All someone had to do was take an interest. Pull it together.' I look at him. He's sullen and disheartened, the way I had been when my old boss had explained it to me, and I suddenly realise the reality. I need Mike. I need him as my partner. 'The plus side is us, mate. For every one of them, you know, big time, boys at the top, there's someone like you and me who will do anything to help stop them. All we can do is keep on keeping on. Yeah?'

He nods and waits a while, then he swings around to face me.

'So do you think Aiden's dead, even though they haven't found a body? Because that's the test, isn't it? Will you carry on looking for him? When nobody knows for sure, it's the hope that keeps them alive.'

I answer him quickly.

'No, Mike. I don't think Aiden's dead. No.' *Dead to me, though. Dead to me.* 'And I'll never stop looking for him.' It isn't over.

CHAPTER SEVENTEEN

I t's quiet at the station so I go home early. I need some time to find out where everything is in my house, to see what's missing and what's been added. As I drive back, alongside Northlands, I look to the skies.

Even after the airport, it's a habit. Looking for CCTV, mentally mapping the cameras and their ranges. They're all shiny and new, part of a vamped-up system, replacing the spray-painted lenses and twisted metal that failed us previously. Looking for the messages along the telegraph wires and on the phone masts.

They're back. Not so many, but a couple of hats slung over the newly strung wires. We're going digital now, aren't we? Going back underground. What will the birds do then, when there are no wires? I wonder how people managed to pull down the cameras and some of the wires in the first place. It must have taken a lot of effort.

Someone must have wanted to make a clear path out of Northlands for Connelly. Someone who's still here.

Bonfire night's been and gone, this year without bodies

burned up at the Gables, and at least I'm thankful for that. I'm looking for the birds, the various kinds that haven't flown away for winter, but are still sitting here on the high wires, watching. Ever watching.

They're here and there, and every now and then I see a crow or a baby magpie. One for sorrow. As I drive away from the city and into the suburbs the numbers of birds increase, as if they somehow want to live where we are, scavenge in our yards and gardens, ready to swoop at any minute.

Bessy loved them, her birds. But look what love does to you. Look what love did to Bessy. The same birds she loved pecked her eyes out, probably before she was cold.

I park up and slam the car door. Fucking neighbours. They're all at the windows, seeing that DS Pearce is doing today. Is she being tailed by some gun-toting crazy today?

Their disgusted faces somehow blame me for the behaviour of someone who was trying to kill me. But I'm quickly learning that this is what this fucked-up world is like. Don't turn your back or someone will peck your eyes out.

I go into the house, still lit by the orange glow bulbs Sheila had bought. I wonder if they are the same ones as I look around. I move some CDs to their old home. They're all sorted into alphabetical order, so I shuffle them and move them around. Same with the books. It's as if someone has come into my home and filed my life.

The kitchen is well stocked with food that I don't eat, but I leave it in the cupboards and in the fridge. The floor has been cleaned and, by the look of it, regrouted. Not a trace of blood anywhere. But you can tell. There are little signs. A chip out of the lounge doorframe, where the blunt instrument that killed Sheila was swung. I run my fingers across it slowly.

I go upstairs. My room has been practically rebuilt, all the cupboards match now. My clothes have been hung in some kind of colour-coordinated system, and I pull out a white dress and push it in the middle of the black jackets and trousers. My bed has been screwed to the wall, something Sal never got round to when we bought it.

There's a box in the corner of the bedroom with 'odds and ends' written on the top of it, and it contains some old wedding photographs that, it turned out, had been trodden on until the glass in the frames shattered onto the carpet. My toiletries are in a newly fitted corner unit, taller than the other one. I peer behind it and run my finger against the new plaster.

Aiden's room. I stop at the door. This is the only recognisable place in the house. I'll never know if he was here that day. I'll never know if he witnessed the carnage. Everything points to the fact that he was.

Unless he told Sal exactly where Ruby's chain was. I go over it again for the millionth time, the photograph, the CCTV high five. The smiles and the larking about. I open the drawer and pull out a black snapback cap, Aiden has worn this. My beautiful son, the boy I loved so much and he loved me back, had worn this cap.

I look at it closely. How can it still be here and he's gone? Not so long ago he was lying on this bed and I was reading him a bedtime story. Now he's missing from my life. From this room. I sit on his bed. Had I missed it somehow? Had I been totally blind to one side of his personality, one where he could disregard me completely? How had this happened? How had the beautiful child who said that I was the best mum in the world, how could he forget about me?

I don't cry, because there's no point. And anyway, the pain's so deep inside me that it hurts to breathe. Crying won't help, it'll just stop me getting through another day, ground me with my red eyes and my blocked nose. Fuzzy head.

That's what my time away has taught me. Whatever happens, you are going to wake up tomorrow and you have to carry on. You can either cry yourself to sleep and be useless in the morning, or you can hold it inside.

So I'm holding it in now as I put the cap back in the drawer now, and shut it. I think about Sal and how he quickly came to the conclusion that Aiden had run away. Too quickly. He knew where he was all the time, but he played along with it. All to get information. It was obviously him who had ruined Operation Hurricane.

I think back and wonder when all this could have started. He'd always resented me working, and when we split up he told me that he had changed jobs and that Aiden could no longer stay during the week, but he could stay all weekend if he wanted to.

He bought the flat and decked it out with fancy furniture. I had assumed that he had used the money from my buying him out of the house. It probably goes right back to when Ruby died. He'd sat with Aiden while I took her to the vets. When I came back, Aiden was sobbing in his room and Sal was smirking at me.

'He hates you now.'

I'd tutted.

'Fucking hell, Sal. What've you told him?'

Sal was laughing.

'The truth, Janet. The truth. That you've murdered his dog.'

I'd gone to Aiden and he'd refused to speak to me or look at me. Tears turned to cold anger, then to brooding, and eventually, when I tried to talk to him about it he just shook his head at me.

I'd given Sal the benefit of the doubt, that, so soon after the divorce, he wasn't using the 'child as a pawn' classic response. I ignored him. But he'd planted a seed then and God only knows what lies he'd fed Aiden since then.

Over the past month I've picked my phone up twenty-seven times with the intention of telling Jim Stewart all about where Sal had gone and that he had Aiden with him. About what they had done. But each time stopped myself. Because this way, there was a chance that I would see Aiden again. At least this way he would be free to come back when the time was right. If it ever was.

I go back downstairs and switch on the TV. It's almost as if I'm living in a hotel, except for Aiden's room. Of course, I'll keep it like it is for a while. Until I feel a little bit stronger. I'll keep his Manchester United bedspread and what was left of his collection of football cards. All his board games, although all of them require more than one player. All his school books.

Because, when he comes back, he might want them, and somehow it's proof that I'm a good mum. I am. A good mum. At the bottom of my soul I know how this has happened. It takes a long time to unravel itself every time I think about it, as if it needs to be coaxed out.

Because once it is through and revealed, it can never be hidden again. Not completely. As soon as I saw the note in Sal's flat I knew exactly what this was about. 'I Win.' And he did win. In fact, he said he would. The day I asked him to leave, he told me he would. He promised me that he would take my son.

'Our son, Sal. He's our son.'

'Right. Our son? Not that you'd notice. Anyone would think that you just recruited me as a sperm donor, while you worked and played Mummy on your days off, I provide you with a little plaything.'

It was one of the only times I lost my shit with him and I didn't come worst off.

'But I love him. I love our son.'

He nodded and brought his face close to mine, very close.

'My son now. Because I'm going to make it my life's work to take him away from you.'

He'd turned and walked away and I'd gone upstairs to look at my sleeping boy. It seemed ridiculous at the time, divorce talk. I reasoned with myself that every acrimonious divorce was full of threats like this, and I was just glad to see the back of Sal.

Even when Aiden started to stay with him most weekends, I just imagined boy's days out at football and KFC. I never pried into what they did together. I simply upped my weekend work hours, not wanting to be in the house alone. I won't let my imagination go there. Not to where Sal had introduced Aiden to Connelly. Probably been to the Gables.

But I had worked one thing out. Sal knew the score, he knew exactly what was going on. So he was simply doing what he said he would. Keep your friends close and your enemies closer. By keeping Aiden by his side, he was keeping him safe. Nothing would happen to him in the bosom of Connelly's underworld, not with Sal heavily involved. Nothing except my little boy gradually becoming used to crime until it seems normal, enjoying the privilege that comes with towing the line Connelly's empire directed.

He's not coming back. A pool of terror wells up inside me as I hear myself thinking that I'll never see Aiden again. I could die without ever seeing my son again. He was alive all the time, hiding somewhere until Sal said it was time to go. I probably spoiled it by finding the passport. They would have been gone by the time we found out what was going on at the Gables if I hadn't found it.

I haven't quite spun round to 'how could he do this to me' or what I could have prevented because my mobile rings and then my house phone starts to ring. I answer the mobile first. It's Mike.

'Jan. Mike. Can you meet me at Bicester Ave at ten? Pat Haywood's been found suspended from her loft ladder. Still alive but in a bad way. A neighbour says someone saw a man exiting the property at the back.'

Mopping up, we call it. Clearing the debris after a horrendous crime has been committed. Because there are more people affected than the criminal and the victim. It's like a wave effect, touching the lives of everyone around them.

'Yep. I'm on it.'

I click off the phone and answer the still-ringing landline.

'Jan Pearce.'

'Jan, it's Jim. We've got a situation on Northlands. Pat Haywood. Can you get there as soon as you can? I'll send backup. I've already called Mike.'

'Yes, sir. I'm on my way.'

So. It's all back to normal. We all know where we are, and we've all got a job to do. Mike's still here, for now, and what Jim doesn't know he won't miss. I've got something to do before I attend, though.

I've been carrying around the £44,000 with me everywhere and now it's time. I push it into the same shoulder bag that I had with me that day at Bessy's and hurry out to my car. I drive up to Mossley and stop outside Pauline Green's house. I get out and look through the window.

A woman who I expect is Pauline is sitting at the table with a small girl. Her husband is reading the paper and looks up as I pass the window. I knock on the door. The little girl pulls it open.

'Nana. There's a lady here.'

Bessy's great-granddaughter. Pauline's behind her now.

'Come away, Elizabeth. Yes, love, can I help you?'

I don't miss a beat.

'Yes. I'm with greater Manchester Police.' Her hand goes to her mouth. 'It's OK, nothing is wrong. It's just that there have been a lot of burglaries around this area and we're just advising residents how to keep safe.' I show her my warrant card, with my finger over my name.

'Come in then, love. Come in.'

I stand awkwardly in the tiny lounge. Her husband holds his hand out.

'John Lewes. This is Pauline, my wife. And Elizabeth, our granddaughter.'

I nod and breathe out deeply. I look around their tiny home, warm and welcoming, smelling slightly of rice pudding. Finally. Something that isn't broken. I'd like to sit down in the easy chair and rest, just for a moment. It's making me smile when I know I should look like I'm on serious police business.

It's obvious that this family love each other. John has a protective arm around Pauline's shoulder. She's small, like Bessy, and Elizabeth is standing slightly behind her. They're protecting each other. They're all relaxed and a way that I realised I haven't seen for the longest time; they're happy. I can just feel it and it's seeping into my soul and warming me.

'Lovely to meet you. I'm just here to advise you to keep all your windows and doors locked. And if you want to register your valuables with the police, make a list and phone the station.'

John stares at me.

'Is that it?'

I nod.

'Yes.'

He sighs.

'Well, with all the goings on around here, you'd think the police had better things to do.'

I nod again.

'Yes, we have. I'll get on now then.'

They stand and stare at me until I back out of the room. Pauline smiles and shuts the door behind me. I get in the car and drive round the back. I count the houses in the back alleyway until I get the right one, and pull the gate open.

I take the shoulder bag with Bessy's money in it and leave it on the back doorstep. I stand there for a second with Bessy's notebook in my hand, almost unable to part with it, but it's not mine, it never was. So I push it into the side pocket of the bag and half hope it's overlooked in favour of the money.

Maybe Pauline will get it and know that she is the abandoned twin. I leave the yard and pull the gate to. Then I bang it and I hear the door open.

'Ey, John love, come here. Someone's left a bag on the back step.' The door shuts again. I hurry down the alleyway and get back into the car. I sit for a moment, finding myself wondering if I could ever have what Pauline has, if I could dare to hope for it?

One thing's for sure, I can't do anything about the random acts of unkindness, the lack of care some people show for the lives of others. Not directly. But I can turn it around a little by doing this. Be kind. Be good. Be on my best behaviour. And, if I do enough, one day I might get to see my son again.

I drive back home and change into my night work clothes. Black pumps, black jeans, and a black T-shirt. I turn off all the lights and wonder if Pauline will hand the money in. I wonder if she will hand in the notebook. Probably not. The sofa is slightly out of its usual position and I stumble over it.

I've moved it to fit in a tiny cat bed and some milk and cat food. A little grey-barred kitten stretches and yawns and sparks a little hope that I won't be completely alone; a little joy. Percy

Number Two. I backtrack and go back through the house in darkness, into the kitchen and turn the key in the back door.

I open it and throw out a handful of grain. I hear the flapping of wings, then silence. I close the door. Best leave it unlocked. Just in case. Because it's not over.

THE END

AKNOWLEDGEMENTS

The idea for this novel was formed many years ago when my life was very different. I'd just read *Beyond Belief: The Moors Murderers* and it affected me deeply. Since then I have spoken to hundreds of people about how it affected them, and this novel is my fictionalised attempt to convey the depth of feeling around these terrible crimes and how the experiences of families of missing people in general.

It took a long time for Bessy's and Jan's voices to get onto the page, but they finally made it. I'd like to thank everyone I've ever spoken to about a missing loved one, including Missing People and Greater Manchester Police. Thank you to the families of missing people I met along the way, I hope every single one of you finds an answer.

Thank you to everyone who has had editorial input into this novel. Many of my writing friends have helped me to get this far with it, I want to name you all but the list would be enormous. I want to thank all the members and former members of WriteWords for cheering me on and my various writing groups for allowing me a forum. I'm also grateful to those in the publishing industry who believed in this novel – I may have gone the 'scenic route', but I got there in the end.

Thank you to Bloodhound Books for publishing this book and to Betsy Reavley and Abbie Rutherford.

Thanks to Anstey Spraggan for her constant encouragement and to listening almost daily to my Bessy and Jan dilemmas. Thanks to Clodagh Murphy, Michele Brouder, Paula Daly,

Fionualla Kearney, Keris Stainton, Sarah Painter, Belinda Whitehead, Zoe Lea, Claire Allan, Luisa Plaja and Trina Rea for their encouragement and for reading my work.

Thanks also to Lindsey Bowes for her constant support. To Bridget Davison, Deb Kevens, Amanda Saint, Louise Cole, Phil Murphy, Kathy Calderwood, Neil Tonepohl, Elinor Davies, Jill Playfair, Beth McCann, Lisa Roberts, Deborah Power.. If I've missed anyone, thank you too, I've met some incredibly generous people on this journey.

Big love to my children Michelle, Victoria and Toby, who are so precious to me and have been patient when I've launched into book talk and spread the word about my writing, and to my grandchildren Evan, Leah, Phi and Lincoln who I love very much. My parents raised me in the area the book is set in and I'm grateful to my mother for her reminiscence of the Moors Murders. Also, my brothers Stuart and Gary for believing in me and helping me to finally be who I really am. I wish my grandparents were here to read this book as they would have recognised Bessy's world.

Finally, I'm eternally grateful to Eric Bourdiec for his patience and love and cups of tea and for encouraging me to never give up.

ABOUT THE AUTHOR

Jacqueline Ward is a writer from the North West of England. She is a Chartered Psychologist and Scientist and her debut psychological thriller, *Perfect Ten*, was published by Corvus Atlantic Books in 2018. Her second psychological thriller, HOW TO PLAY DEAD, was published in November 2019.

Jacqueline is the author of the DS Jan Pearce crime fiction series and a speculative fiction novel *Smartyellow* and enjoys writing short stories and screenplays.

Her psychological thriller *The Replacement* was published by Bloodhound Books in April 2023.

She holds a PhD in narrative and storytelling which produced a new model in identity construction. Jacqueline has worked with victims of domestic violence and families of missing people as well as heading a charity that deals with the safety and reliability of major hazards. She received an MBE for services to vulnerable people in 2013.

A NOTE FROM THE PUBLISHER

Thank you for reading this book. If you enjoyed it please do consider leaving a review on Amazon to help others find it too.

We hate typos. All of our books have been rigorously edited and proofread, but sometimes mistakes do slip through. If you have spotted a typo, please do let us know and we can get it amended within hours.

info@bloodhoundbooks.com